Beyond #3

Praise for *Beyond The Red*

"Ava Jae's *Beyond the Red* is a sand-swept fantasy of court politics, rebel attacks, and forbidden romance. While reading, I had flashes of *Star Wars*–a new planet, a fascinating culture, a fresh look on a ruler struggling to keep her power–and I had to know what happened next. Dangerous, exciting, and fast-paced, *Beyond the Red* is a story not to be missed."

–Francesca Zappia, author of *Made You Up*

"Packed with political intrigue and smoldering romance, *Beyond the Red* left me craving more of Kora's and Eros's story and the unique, fascinating universe that Ava Jae has created."

–Sarah Harian, author of *The Wicked We Have Done*

"*Beyond the Red* is a sweeping, compelling romance in a complicated and gritty world. Intrigue and heart on every page–I couldn't put it down. I'll be following Ava Jae to see what comes next!"

–Kate Brauning, author of *How We Fall*

"I loved this book! I couldn't put it down! What a fantastic debut, perfect for fans of *Firefly* and *Star Wars*. Ava Jae's *Beyond the Red* packs a punch, a total thrill ride that will keep readers turning the pages. I stayed up all night reading it. From page one, I was sucked in. Jae's writing style is a perfect mix of stop and go, and her world comes to life within the first few pages. The action was power-packed, and the star-crossed romance had me begging for more by the end."

–Lindsay Cummings, author of The Murder Complex series

"Ava Jae has built such an interesting world in *Beyond the Red*. With forbidden romance, gritty action, and thrilling danger, this debut is one to watch. And here's hoping for a sequel!"

–S. E. Green, award-winning author of the Killer Instinct series

"I loved *Beyond the Red*! Ava Jae's science fiction world-building is a perfect blend of a fantastic, foreign alien civilization and achingly human desires all packed into an explosive mix. I couldn't help but root for crafty Kora as she navigated court politics, revolutions, and dangerous secrets. And Eros! His determination balanced with a sense of humor about his fate made him such a swoon-worthy love interest. The action started swiftly and didn't let up. I can't wait to read more from Jae!"

–Lindsay Smith, author of *Sekret* and *Dreamstrider*

"A thrilling blend of science fiction and fantasy, *Beyond the Red* sketches out an exciting new world full of romance and intrigue. I can't wait for future installments!"

–Kat Zhang, author of the Hybrid Chronicles series

Book 3 of the Beyond the Red Trilogy

THE RISING GOLD

AVA JAE

Sky Pony Press
NEW YORK

Visit our website at www.skyponypress.com.

10 9 8 7 6 5 4 3 2 1

Library of Congress Cataloging-in-Publication Data is available on file.

Cover design by Kate Gartner
Map design by Kerri Frail
Interior design by Joshua Barnaby

Print ISBN: 978-1-5107-2238-5
Ebook ISBN: 978-1-5107-2239-2

Printed in the United States of America

To the outcasts.

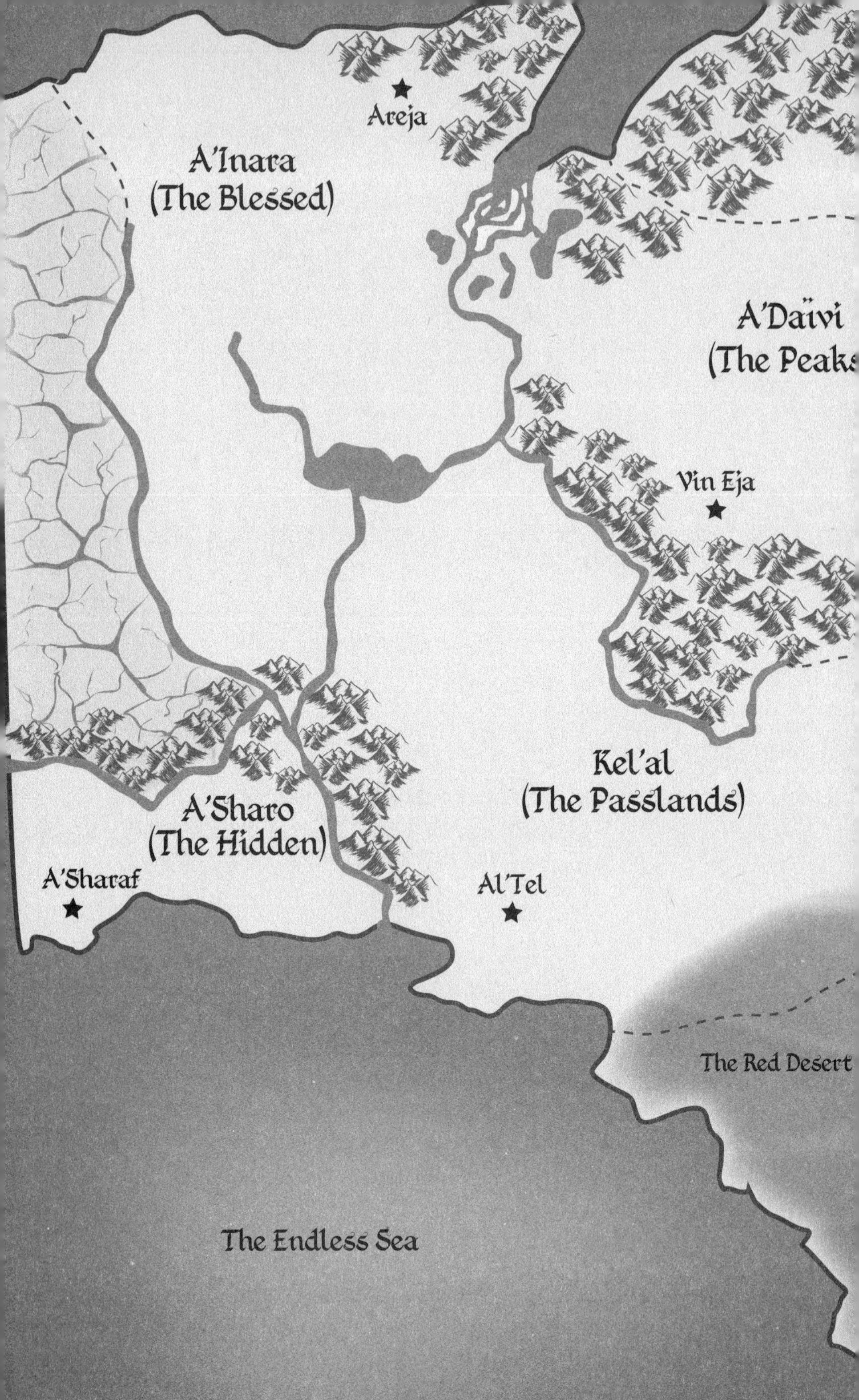

Areja
A'Inara
(The Blessed)
A'Daïvi
(The Peaks
Vin Eja
Kel'al
(The Passlands)
A'Sharo
(The Hidden)
A'Sharaf
Al'Tel
The Red Desert
The Endless Sea

Al'Invino
(Divine Lands)
Dura Kol
Kaza D'In
Sekka'l
(The Scorchlands)
Niro d'Tol
Shura Kan
Asheron
Denae D'Aravel
Al si Ona
(Land of Riches)
The White Sands
Al si Elja
(Land of Suns)
a's Throne
Vejla
Enjos
The Endless Sea

PART I

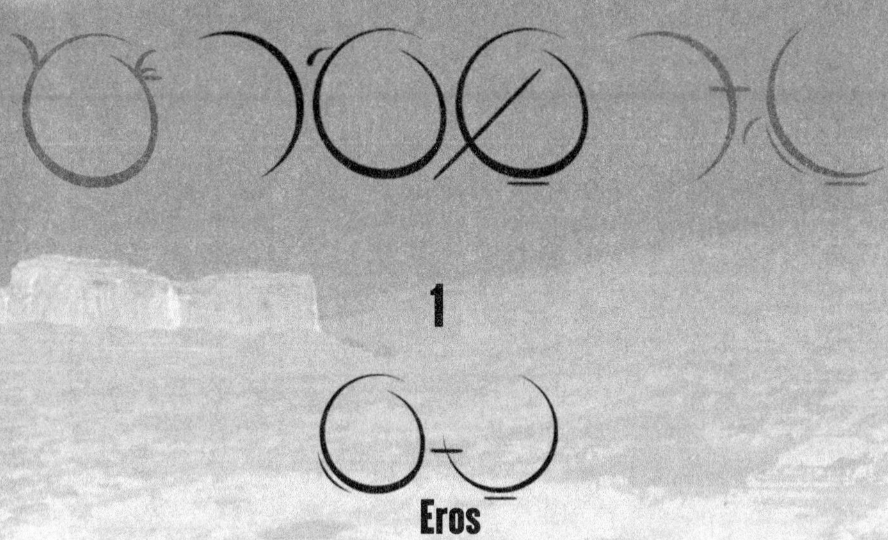

1

Eros

Deimos bet me his bike I would toss up. It's not just any bike, either—it's a top-of-the-line model, barely a couple terms old, sleek black and red with aerodynamic angles and a low purr that Day would've completely flipped sand over.

His betting something he knows I want—bad—I think was his way of giving me extra motivation *not* to toss up. As if tasting my food twice with an acid aftertaste the second time wasn't enough of motivation to try to keep my morning meal down.

It'd almost be a sweet gesture if I wasn't on my knees on the cool tile, sweating over the waste basin, breathing through my nose and praying to every star and spirit out there that I can pull it together before I have to go out there and become ruler of the world.

"Fuck," I whisper. Then, louder, "I can't do this. Fuck. Deimos, I—"

"You can," Deimos says, rubbing my back. He sounds sure. How can he be so sure? "You have to."

Well. That part's true at least.

"If you're going to toss up, just get it over with already," Mal says somewhere behind me. "At least you'll feel better after and won't have to worry about tossing up on the priest or something."

Stars and sands alive.

What if I lose my meal on the priest in front of the whole fucking world?

"See, but if he does that, then he doesn't get my bike. And *Kala* knows he wants my bike." I'm staring into the black hole at the bottom of the stone basin, but I can hear Deimos's grin in his words. Smug bastard.

"Not like your bike is going anywhere anyway," Mal says. "Seeing how you two are boyfriends or whatever now."

Despite my churning stomach and the hot bile threatening to climb up my throat, a wisp of a smile tugs at my lips and I glance up at Deimos just to see–yup, he's blushing. The purple flush creeps up his neck and colors his face, but he smiles back at me.

I'm not sure that we are. Boyfriends, I mean. Mostly because we haven't actually done anything besides, like, that hug or whatever after the match, but Mal's around us enough to hear Deimos's endless flirting so I'm not surprised he thinks that.

He's not completely wrong, anyway.

Someone knocks on the door. Probably the designer trying to make me look good for the–

Oh.

My stomach swoops.

The coronation.

"*Shae*, we'll be right out," Deimos says. He loops his arm beneath mine and hauls me to my feet. "You're fine. Wash your face with cold water. You'll be fine."

My stomach sinks lower at the thought. Splashing my face with cold water is pretty much guaranteed to tilt me over from almost panic to on-the-floor-can't-breathe-full-fledged panic. Not that Deimos knows that. Or anyone knows that.

"Pretty sure Mija out there will kill me if I do that after she spent so much time making my face look good."

It's a good excuse. Deimos laughs. "That's probably true. Just breathe through your nose, *shae*? I promise, everything will be fine. Coronations are easy—just walk to the front, do what Arodin says, and accept the mark of *Sirae*."

"Also the dinner formal," Mal says. "With all the food. Don't forget that part."

"How could we forget with you reminding us every couple breaths?" Deimos snickers. "And the formal, *shae*, but that's not until tonight. Eros will get a break before then."

My head feels thick. Full of sand. The room feels strange around me, like I drank too much, except I'm sober. Sweat drips down my temples. Mija will probably tut over that, too.

Deimos steps in front of me and grips my shoulders hard. The pressure feels good—grounding. "Focus on me," he says, as if it's ever possible to focus on anything else when he's in the room. "I know you're nervous, and that's normal. This *whole* reaction is normal, I promise you. My father told us every year the story of how he tossed up on the priestess when he was coronated."

My eyes widen. "Are you kidding me right now? Deimos, you seriously think that's going to make me feel any—"

"My *point* is what you're feeling is normal and even if the worst happens, you'll be fine. My father was still coronated. The priestess shrugged it off. It didn't matter. You're only Sepharon, Eros—you're young and have emotions and people understand that." I arch an eyebrow at him. He pauses, then smiles apologetically. "Well, not *only* Sepharon. Human, too, but it's a saying. I just mean you're not *Kala* and people don't expect perfection. *Shae*?"

I'm not really feeling okay, but I guess that doesn't really matter anymore. I just have to get this over with. "*Shae*," I answer.

Deimos smiles and releases my shoulders. My skin buzzes in the absence of his hands. "Good. Let's get you cleaned up and get out there before you miss your own coronation."

"Wouldn't that be nice?" I murmur.

Mal snickers.

Mija groans the mo I step out of the washroom. "What have you done to your face?" She crosses the distance between us in two long strides and frowns down at me, lifting my chin with her finger. "You look pale and sickly."

"Thanks," I say.

"Boys," she murmurs, turning back to her tray full of paints and powders and liners and whatever else. "I thank *Kala* every day I was born in an age where I could realize my life as a girl from a young age without dispute. Our ancestors in the Southern regions weren't so lucky."

Mija is *lijara*–specifically, her assigned gender at birth didn't match her real gender. I'm not sure exactly how that works when Sepharon men are supposed to be able to control the sex of the kid at conception or whatever, but Deimos says it happens.

Mija hums as she looks over the tray, then picks up a jar and a brush, turns back to me, and stares. "Why are you still standing?" She points to the hovering pillow-seat-thing she brought with her. "Sit so I can finish my work."

I do. I close my eyes as she brushes some powder on my face, then traces over the faint marks on my face with a wet brush, then lines my eyes with stars-knows-what.

"Okay," she says at last. "Open your eyes."

When I've done that, she taps her chin and looks at Deimos. "What do you think? At least he doesn't look ill."

The warmth of Deimos's smile radiates into my chest like heat from the suns. The way he looks at me—his eyes slightly lidded as his gaze swoops over me from head to toe and back again—sends a thrill through me. "*Naï.* He looks perfect."

The warmth tingles over my heart and prickles my cheeks. Mija hands me a mirror. My skin looks smooth and even, and my eyes are lined in black, which makes my gold eyes look—brighter, I guess. Impossible to ignore. I guess that's the idea.

Anyway, Mija's right. You can't tell I was breaths from tossing up just a few mos ago.

"Are we finally ready?" Mal asks from my bed. "I'm bored."

Deimos looks at me. "What do you think, Eros?"

I take a deep, shivering breath and pull my shoulders back. My heart thrums in my chest and my stomach still tingles with heat and my palms are getting cold and sweaty already but this—this is as good as it's going to get.

I'll never be ready, not really.

But it's time.

It's finally time.

As soon as I walk into the throne room, the people start reciting.

The throne room is enormous—at least twice the size of Kora's throne room back in Elja—and large enough to fit several small buildings in the space. It's easily the largest room

I've ever been in, and I never really understood why it needed to be so blazing big until now.

The room is packed with people. Wall to wall, standing room only, all the way down to the space in front of the throne itself, where the High Priest, Arodin, stands with a long line of guards dressed in their formal black and gold uniforms. Only an aisle for people to walk through–for me to walk through–has been left open.

There must be more than a thousand people in here–and that's not counting the orb guides whipping through the air, streaming everything to glasses worldwide. And yet, the people are reciting so perfectly it sounds like one low, booming voice.

I walk slowly down the aisle like Deimos showed me. He and Mal walk behind me–they'll follow me down the aisle and stand in the front with the *Avrae* of the other nations, and the Emergency Council. I think Deimos said the people are reciting a poem written about the coronation of the very first *Sira*, Jol d'Asheron. Something about how he was chosen by *Kala*, and how *Kala*'s chosen will always be marked with gold eyes or whatever. I can't really focus on the words. There are too many gazes on me–they buzz on my skin and dance down my spine. I try to keep my stare forward. At Arodin, who is smiling at me almost encouragingly, which . . . I didn't expect. But I guess that's good.

At least the High Priest doesn't hate me.

A quarter of the way down the aisle and the people's voices hum in my ears with my heartbeat. Their words blend together and weave into my blood. The tile is warm under my feet and the air is hot–thick–glistening on my skin.

Halfway down the aisle and somehow—somehow—this is really happening. I'm in the throne room in the highest palace on the planet. From the statues of the stacked letters of *Kala*'s name to the gold of the mosaicked walls and the impossibly tall, arched ceilings. Black banners with gold lettering and an intricate maze-like gold design along the borders line the walls—and with a start I recognize the crescent and circle with the carefully placed lines that Deimos taught me is my name in Sephari.

Somehow, this is real.

I'm nearly down the aisle. The reciting words carry me like a wave, drowning out the pounding in my ears, the rattle of my breaths, the panicked hum in the back of my skull. The weight of a thousand gazes clings to every inch of me; I want nothing more than to disappear, but this, this is my new life. This is my new reality. And it's the only one that didn't end with Mal and me dead.

I reach the end of the aisle. Step up to Arodin, nod, and face the people, like Deimos said I should. Mal and Deimos have taken their places beside the other *Avrae*, but I'm pretty sure some are missing. There are eight *Avra* total, but only six are here. I'm not sure what that means. Probably something insulting. I'm not really surprised.

Kora's here, though.

She's standing next to Deimos, smiling at me as the room finishes reciting the poem. I'm not sure if it's okay for me to smile back—I think I'm supposed to be stoic, or whatever—but I do meet her eye and nod at her.

Then the room is deathly silent. Not a whisper or a cough. The silence is almost a living thing, spreading into every crevice of the room, until all I hear is my own thrumming pulse and terrified breaths.

My hands are shaking at my sides. I pull my sweaty fingers into my fists and resist the urge to wipe my palms on my pants.

"*Ora'jeve*," Arodin says, "to the honored citizens here today, both inside these walls and out; to the blessed citizens watching from the city squares and their homes all around the world. To all of you joining us on this fated set to usher in the next *Sira*, the eldest and only son of *Sira* Asha, Eros. May *Kala* guide you in all that you do, Eros, and grant you the wisdom and strength of your father and his father before him."

The wisdom and strength of your father and his father before him seems a calculated way to avoid talking about Roma. A way to say they don't want a repeat of the *Sira* who ordered genocide.

It's as much of an acknowledgment that what Roma did was fucked up as I'm going to get from them, I guess.

I'm not sure if I'm supposed to say anything. Arodin is looking at me, so I just nod.

"You've come a long way, Eros," Arodin says. "I'm certain your father would be very proud of you."

It's an innocent enough thing to say, but my dad's words from the recording that landed me here still play in my head: *Eros, you are the true* Sira, *and you are the only one I want to inherit my throne*. The way he looked at the camera, the way I could almost imagine he was looking at me, he was here–

It shouldn't hurt. I didn't even know him. But somehow hearing the high priest say he thinks Asha would be proud of me makes the back of my throat hurt and my eyes sting. Just a little. Not enough for it to be obvious, but it's there.

I'd never wished that I'd grown up anywhere but camp, anywhere but the Kits' cluster of tents. But standing in front of Arodin, with Asha's words fresh in my mind, I can almost picture myself here. Younger, since it wouldn't have taken so long if Asha hadn't died, and with my dad, the *Sira*, standing by my side and smiling at me.

I can't wait to meet you, son. I love you already.

Would I still have been just as terrified?

Would I still have wondered if this was a mistake?

I close my eyes and force the thoughts away. It doesn't matter what may or may not have been. That other world will never be my reality.

This is.

"Thank you," I say. The words come out tight–a little more strangled than I wanted to let on.

But Arodin just smiles and gestures to the ground. "Please kneel."

I do, taking deep breaths as I lower myself. In and out, the air shivers on my lips. My hands are still shaking and the tile is cooler than the sweltering room but still warm on my knees and toes. I rest my hands on my knees and my insides are vibrating so quickly it'll be a miracle if I don't shake apart.

This is–this is really happening.

Two other priests–a man and a woman–walk over to Arodin's side. They're both holding stone bowls, one black, one white. Arodin dips two fingers on his left hand in the white bowl first, then the black. His fingers come away clear, but glistening, as he turns to me.

"Close your eyes." Arodin's cold, slimy fingers start above my right brow and drag down over my eyelid and onto my cheek. I have no idea what that stuff is, but it smells kinduv like flowery herbs and it tingles on my skin.

"May *Kala* see through your eyes, vessel of the Almighty One." Arodin runs his fingers down my left eye too. There's a pause, then his fingers touch my left cheek and–oh no–run over my lips to my other cheek.

"May *Kala* speak through your mouth, vessel of the Blessed One."

I keep my lips as closed as I can without grimacing. The wet streaks on my face buzz more intensely. I don't remember Deimos saying anything about this. This is–I'm not sure I like this.

Another pause, then Arodin's hands press against my chest and back, over my heart. Both hands are drenched in the stuff and it drips down my chest and back in thick, humming lines.

"May *Kala* fill you with their essence and guide you through every challenge, every high, every low."

Arodin lets go of my chest–a pause–then his thumbs press against my cheekbones, under my eyes, as his fingers wrap around my head. "Open your eyes," he whispers.

When I do, Arodin smiles and nods. "May you guide us all, Eros, *Sira* da Safara."

Then he steps back and bows.

And so does the rest of the room.

And just like that, it's over.

I'm *Sira*.

And I won Deimos's bet, after all.

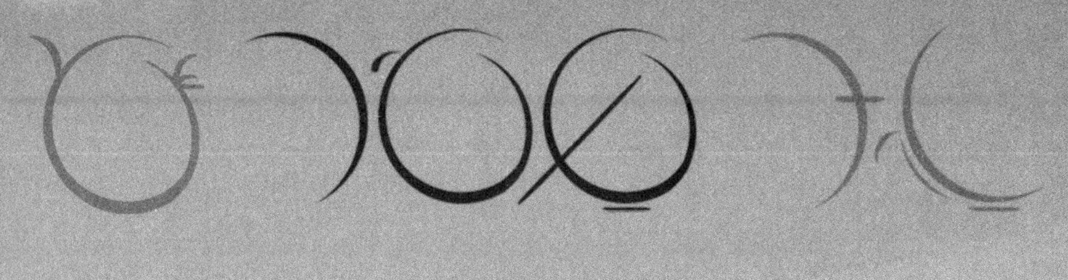

2

Kora

"Truly, your face looks ready to split in two, you're smiling so wide." Uljen smirks at me, but he's smiling, too.

"I'm so relieved," I answer. "And *Kala, sha*, happy too. Eros deserves this. He's going to be a great *Sira*, I'm sure of it."

Uljen nods and faces the courtyard fountain, circulating gold-tinted water into the dark basin. There are fewer people standing back here—most are congregated nearer the entrance to the courtyard, waiting for Eros to arrive. His hands are clasped behind his back and he holds himself like a soldier: shoulders back, head high even as he looks into the water below. His confidence is magnetic—I wish I had a fraction of it.

I step next to him and look at my reflection, jolting a little at the pink, scarred skin of my arm mirrored back at me. Though I've recently stopped covering my scarred arm, seeing it still sends a hot spike through me—a breath where I want nothing more to hide it again, to forget my bloody, terrifying coronation.

But I take a deep breath of the hot, dry air and bury those feelings deep. I have nothing to hide.

"You don't seem so convinced," I say to Uljen. "About Eros."

Uljen shrugs. "*Ken Sira* is a stranger to me. You know him better than I do, so if you think he'll do well in his new position, then I trust you."

"Hmm." I crouch in front of the fountain and dip my fingers into the warm water. "I sense there's more you want to say."

"You're rather perceptive this set."

I glance up at him with a smirk.

"I don't like it," he says. But then he laughs a little and runs a hand over his neatly tied back hair. "You're right. I just worry how someone without any political experience whatsoever will handle being the most powerful ruler on the planet . . . but it's not right of me to question that considering my lack of experience for my own position."

"It *is* a little hypocritical, *sha*." I stand. "But it's a fair enough question. If Eros were trying to rule alone, I'd worry, but he's not. He'll certainly establish *Avra-kaï* Deimos d'A'Sharo as his official advisor if he hasn't already, and I'm sure Deimos will create a strong, experienced Council to help guide him. Eros may not have the experience yet, but he'll be surrounded by people who do."

Uljen nods. "That's good to hear."

"This is a good thing," I say. "You'll see."

"I sincerely hope you're right." Uljen pauses and glances across the courtyard, full of royals and upper-class citizens alike, speaking quietly over cups of *azuka*. "You said Eros knows he's meeting you here?"

I hesitate. "Well, Deimos knows, so I assume Eros knows. But even if he didn't know, this is where he'd be headed after receiving the mark of *Sirae,* anyway."

"Short a few royals, I see."

I grimace. I'd noticed that too—the *Avra* da Sekka'l and Invino weren't at the coronation, which is incredibly disrespectful and not exactly a promising sign. I'd mostly expected that behavior from Sekka'l—or even Ona, given that's where Lejv is from—but Invino's absence is worrisome. Invino holds the religious capital of Safara—and much of the rest of the religious bodies around the world follow their example. But oddly Arodin was there to officiate the coronation, so it seems the Temple itself supports Eros even while our most religious territory doesn't, which . . .

Well. I'm not sure what to make of it, to be true, but it can't possibly be a good thing.

"I did notice that, *sha*."

"Do you think Eros cares?"

"Probably not. But Deimos and his Council members certainly will. They understand the potential implication and impact that Eros doesn't right now." I purse my lips. "But that's a discussion for another set. Today we should focus on celebrating. Eros has earned it."

"Speaking of which." Uljen nods as Eros, Deimos, and Mal enter the courtyard, all dressed in Ona's finest. Even Deimos, who always wore A'Sharo's colors before, wears black and gold.

When they enter, Mal sticks close to Eros, likely using him to navigate through the crowd with his limited vision. Deimos's hand is on the small of Eros's back just for a moment before he drops it and they lean toward each other. Deimos says something and Eros nods as he rubs his left hand where—oh.

Interesting.

Arodin chose to put Eros's mark of *Sirae* on his hand. It follows the light, sharp lines and curves of his faint *Kala*'s mark, from his wrist to the first knuckles of each of his fingers. The mark of *Sirae* is often placed somewhere readily visible–like an arm, chest, or neck–but this is impossible to miss no matter what Eros is wearing, which I suppose was probably the point.

There's no disputing Eros is *Sira.* Not anymore.

From across the courtyard, Eros looks at me as people approach him. He nods politely at the bows and greetings as I move forward through the crowd. A pale stick of a man rams into my shoulder. I stumble half a step back and scowl at him. He bows, mumbles an apology, and melts back into the crowd.

I don't have time to be irritated over the interaction, however, because when I look up Eros is standing in front of me.

The bruises from the fight–and the attack the night before the fight–are still visible on his chest, but faint on his face. It's been only a couple sets since the match, though, so I suspect the faintness on his face has more to do with coverup than healing. Still, even with the visible bruises, even with the uncertainty in the way he drifts through the crowd, Eros looks right here.

He may not feel it yet, but I've never been more sure that this is exactly where he was supposed to be. Respected, and in a position of power in Sepharon court.

I bow to my *Sira*, and to my friend.

"Kora, you don't have to–" Eros starts, but I straighten and shake my head.

"I do. I'm your friend, Eros, but I'm also an *Avra* and if I don't show you the respect you deserve as one of your greatest supporters, then no one else will either."

Eros opens his mouth—to protest, probably—but Deimos nudges him. "She's right. Get used to it, *Sira*." His eyes twinkle with that last word as he flashes a bright grin.

Eros's face reddens slightly, but he smiles and runs a hand through his hair. "This all just feels . . . surreal."

"I'm sure. You'll become accustomed to it, but regardless, it's good to see you, Eros. And you as well, Mal and Deimos." Deimos nods and Mal waves. I smile, then remember Uljen standing awkwardly at my side. "Oh, excuse me, how rude—Eros, this is my advisor, Uljen. Uljen, *Sira* Eros."

Uljen bows for a second time. "It's an honor to meet you, el *Sira*."

"It's good to meet you, too. I heard about your appointment." Eros's gaze drifts to me. "I think it's a good thing what you're doing, Kora. I'm proud of you."

I smile. "Thank you."

"Will you be staying in Asheron long?" Deimos asks.

"Unfortunately not; Uljen and I have a lot to take care of in Elja. But we'll see you at Daven and Zek's wedding, right? That's just seven sets away."

Eros blinks and glances at Deimos, but Deimos smiles warmly. "We'll definitely be there. I can't wait."

Eros smiles. "I didn't realize the wedding was so close."

"*Sha*, well I suppose you've had a lot of other things to worry about as of late."

Eros nods and Deimos turns to him and lightly touches his arm. "It'll be a good way to solidify Daïvi's support. Plus I'm sure you'll want the mental break in seven sets."

"Will there be good food?" Mal asks. "I wanna come if there's gonna be something decent. Like *kelo*, that stuff is really good."

Eros smirks. "I'm sure there will be, and you can come if you want."

"Cool."

"We should probably talk to other people, too." Deimos glances around the courtyard. "We have a lot of people to greet and my brother is giving me that look–but don't worry, you'll like Nikos. He's much more reasonable than Sulten, thanks to *Kala*."

"Great," Eros mumbles, looking distinctly unpleased. "More people to talk to."

I snicker. "*Or'jiva* to the life of a royal."

The stick-thin man who bumped into me earlier steps behind Eros, glancing at him with distaste. I arch an eyebrow at him. A flash of silver–

"Eros!" I gasp.

Eros spins and catches the man's wrist just as he strikes with a knife. For a breath the world is suspended, Eros and the man shaking with strain as Eros grips his wrist, keeping the knife suspended mid-strike.

Then Eros slams the heel of his free hand into the man's nose just as Deimos wraps his arm around the man's throat and yanks him back, holding him tightly. Guards are on the three of them in a blink as someone–Uljen–steps in front of me.

"Are you all right?" he asks urgently.

"What? I wasn't the one attacked! Is Eros–"

"We're fine." Eros steps beside Uljen with Deimos, not even winded. The attacker somewhere behind them is screaming something about half-bloods as guards wrestle him away. More guards try to usher both Eros and Deimos out but Eros waves them off. "Excitement's over," he says loudly to the staring crowd as the man's screams fade. "Back to . . . whatever we're doing."

"Whatever we're doing," Deimos repeats with a smirk. "*Shae*, very regal of you."

Eros laughs, breaking the tension. "Quiet."

"You don't actually want that."

"*Naï*, I don't." Eros shakes his head and smiles at me. "Thanks for the warning."

"Of course, I'm just . . ." My heart still beats uncertainly in my chest. "Relieved you're both unharmed."

Eros smirks. "They'll have a try a lot harder than that to get rid of me."

And I wish it weren't the case, but I can't bring myself to smile.

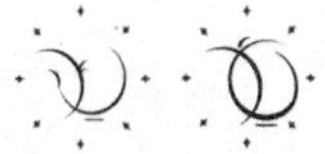

When we arrive in Elja, the suns have set and the four moons paint the scarlet sands with silvery light. I take a moment to let the night warmth paint my closed eyes and fill my chest.

Uljen waits quietly at my side until I open my eyes and turn to him. "Ready?" He gestures to the palace entrance.

"*Naï*," I answer honestly. "But that hardly matters."

He smiles thinly and follows me inside. An orb guide races up to me the moment my feet hit the tile. I try not to look displeased—not that the guide would know the difference—as it whirls in the air in front of me. "Message from Torven Emani d'Elja for *Avra* Kora Mikale Nel d'Elja," it chirps.

I pull the ties out of my hair and let it hang over my shoulders as I comb my fingers through it. Uljen stares at me and

I raise both eyebrows at him. He clears his throat and averts his gaze, his face just barely purpled.

Hm.

"Go on," I say to the guide as I move down the hall.

The guide keeps a pace ahead of me as it projects Council member Torven's face in the air. "Kora." Torven smiles. "I hope your travels went smoothly and your time in Asheron has gone well. The Council need to speak with you before you complete the set–we have a couple important matters to discuss that can't wait until the morning. Do let us know when you've returned so we can set up a quick discussion. Oh, and bring Uljen. He is your advisor, after all. We'll see you shortly."

The projection disappears. I sigh and nod at the guide. "Let the Council members know I've arrived and will meet them in the library shortly."

The guide spins in the air then shoots off down the hall. I glance at Uljen. "Congratulations. You're officially invited to Council functions."

"Thrilling." He smirks.

"Oh please, we both know you're thrilled. It means the Council has officially accepted you, and you know it."

Uljen's smirk stretches into a smile. "Guilty."

"Mhm." I shake my head and turn toward the library. "Well, at least I won't have to suffer alone."

Uljen laughs. "That bad?"

"In all likelihood–*sha*."

"Well, in that case I'm honored to suffer at your side, Kora."

"You should be. It's quite an honor."

"It is," Uljen says seriously. He hesitates, then his fingers brush my scarred shoulder, sending a jolt directly to my heart. I stifle a gasp as I stop walking and face him. "I apologize," he says quickly, pulling his hand away. "I didn't mean to startle you—I just, I want to say something before we face the Council."

I gently press my hand over the buzzing spot on my skin where he touched me.

No one is supposed to touch me without asking.

Does he know that? *Doesn't* he know that?

I'm not sure if it bothers me because he didn't ask or if it bothers me because the last person aside from servants to touch me was Eros, too many sets ago, before I became *Avra* again. When our touches were kisses and our kisses were good-byes.

But still, I didn't—*dislike* it. My skin is still humming and a part of me *almost* wants him to do it again. But of course, that's not permitted. At least, not out in the open like this.

"You're not supposed to touch me without asking," I say. "Now that I'm *Avra*. I'm not angry, but I want you to be aware. If the guards had seen they may have . . . reacted badly."

Uljen blinks. "Oh, of course, I apologize. I knew that, I-I wasn't thinking."

"Apology accepted. You were saying?"

Uljen pushes some long strands of hair out of his eyes. "Right. I wanted you to know though I wasn't initially sure working with you would actually be fruitful, I appreciate the way you've taken my perspective into account, and I truly believe you were meant for this role. I'm honored to be at your side."

I have to admit, the honesty is unexpected. There's so much falsity in politics—from overblown flattery to half-truths concealed behind smiles. Lying is dishonorable and most avoid it to an extent, but that doesn't mean honesty. It just means everyone knows how to twist words until they barely resemble their original meaning anymore.

As they say, the most dangerous lies are buried in truth.

"Thank you," I say. "I . . . that's not what I was expecting."

Uljen laughs slightly. "*Nai*? What were you expecting?"

I lift my unscarred shoulder. "Truly, I couldn't say."

"Do you know what to expect with this meeting?"

I grimace and ignore the twisting of my stomach. "Nothing pleasant. It never is."

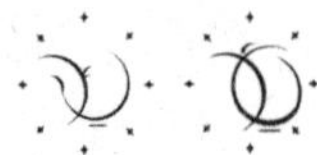

Uljen and I are the first to enter the library's meeting room, but it doesn't take long for Roek, Torven, Izra, and Barra—my four Council members—to enter. They immediately kneel on the cushions across the table from Uljen and me.

"It's good to see you, Kora," Torven says kindly. "And you must be Uljen. *Kala* smiles on our meeting, *eran*."

Uljen nods. "Thank you. I'm honored to be here."

"I'm sure you are," Roek says flatly. I imagine it must take him quite a bit of self-control to resist the eyeroll undoubtedly itching behind his bored gaze.

Uljen purses his lips. I ignore Roek's obvious attempt to belittle us and Barra's smirk. Barra reminds me of Jarek—too much muscle than any one person should have, even in his graying age, but with half of Jarek's reasonable nature. Which is saying something.

"At any rate." I turn to Torven. "You summoned us, and I presume it wasn't just to meet Uljen."

"It wasn't." Torven nods. "We're sure you're aware the people are awaiting news on Dima's trial, and we wanted to emphasize the importance of beginning his trial as soon as possible."

My heart sinks to my toes.

Dima's trial.

I hadn't forgotten, of course–how could I even begin to forget that my brother will finally atone for his crimes? How could I forget for even a breath that the atonement may cost him his life?

I'd never before wished I was the *Avra* d'Invino, where execution as punishment was outlawed ten cycles ago. But right now, with the prospect of watching my brother kneel before an executioner's blade an all-too-real possibility–oh, how I wish it.

"I'm aware," I say. My voice comes out tight. I take a steadying breath and press my palms against the floating table. "I know it's important, and Dima must face his crimes. I swore before I'd get it done, and I won't break that oath."

Even as the words slip from my lips, they hook into my heart and pull and rip. The truth is, I'm not sure how to feel about Dima's trial, not really. There isn't any question in my mind that he should be punished in some way–for trying to kill me, for nearly killing Serek, for giving Roma the excuse to slaughter redbloods, for executing citizens who dared protest him and imprisoning those who dared protest the execution. Dima's crimes are a pit digging into Safara's core–they're a mountain threatening to topple over and bury us both beneath it. And it should feel good knowing my brother will atone for what he's done but–

What if?

What if the atonement is my nightmare scenario?

What if he's sentenced to death?

Though we hadn't seen eye to eye in cycles, though he tried to kill me and sabotaged my rule, though our relationship once cooled to something hard and deadly sharp, I've never spent a set on this planet without knowing he was here too. We've shared our lives, intertwined in a way only twins ever experience.

Losing him would be a deep, agonizing pain I don't want to face. It would rip a hole into me I don't think I could repair.

I want Dima punished, *sha*. But I don't want him to die.

"Good," Roek says. "It's incredibly important you don't let this go, Kora. The people are waiting to see whether you'll allow him to face the justice he deserves or whether you'll allow your womanly weakness to cloud your judgment."

My mouth opens and closes.

Womanly what?

What did he just to say to me?

"What did you just say to me?" The words are out of my mouth before I can stop them. Izra and Torven are both staring at Roek while Barra is smirking–again–and Roek just–

Womanly *weakness*?

"Please, Kora, there's no need for false outrage. You know exactly to what I refer."

I laugh. My blood is boiling and I'm laughing and there's a crack in Roek's stony composure; his brows crease, just slightly, and it's all I need.

I'll show him womanly weakness.

"Oh, let me assure you, Roek, my outrage is *incredibly* genuine. Evidently I must remind you I am your *Avra*, and you will address me as your *Avra* and only as your *Avra*." I lean forward, pouring the heat of my outrage into my gaze as I drill into his eyes. Roek glances at Izra and Torven on either side as he clasps his hands on the table and this–*Kala* knows this feels good.

I dig deeper.

"Perhaps we should practice, just to be sure you understand. When I speak to you, you will address me as . . .?"

Roek presses his lips into a flat line. A vein throbs in his temple. But his voice is even when he says, "*El Avra*."

"That's right. Now as for my *womanly weakness*, perhaps you'd like to explain *exactly* what you mean, while keeping in mind I am your *Avra*."

He hesitates. Choosing his words carefully. Good.

He better be nervous.

"I simply meant it's important not to allow your . . . attachment to your brother and heightened emotions to get in the way of Dima's deserved punishment."

"So attachments and emotions are a woman's weaknesses, are they?"

Roek licks his lips. "*Weakness* was perhaps not the wisest choice of words. But I'm certain you are aware women experience these things more intensely than their male counterparts. It's only natural for women to have strong attachments and emotional experiences–"

"Are you truly attempting to convince me men don't have familial attachments or emotions?" I return my flattest, coldest stare. "Do you not feel an attachment to your mother? Your wife? Your son?"

"Of course I do. But–"

"And if something were to happen to them, if they were to die, for example, would you not weep?"

Roek stiffens. "Of course I would. But I wouldn't let those attachments or emotions get in the way of doing my duty."

"And neither will I." I stand, pulling my shoulders back as I tower over the kneeling men. "I'm well aware, Roek, that you, and Barra, and certainly others, are convinced I'm at a disadvantage simply because I am a woman. There's little I can do to change that misguided opinion, but nothing could be farther from the truth. My *compassion* and *empathy* allow me to understand the people in a way my predecessors never bothered to attempt. And I understand full well they want Dima to go to trial, and he will, as he should. Now if that's all"–I look at Uljen. He stands–"then I will be retiring for the night."

I don't give them the chance to respond. I walk right out the door with my head held high and my heart racing. I walk down the quiet aisles and I–I can't believe I just did that.

I just told off Roek in front of the Council.

I just *disciplined* a Council member.

And *Kala*, it felt amazing.

"Well," Uljen says, hurrying to keep my pace. "That was certainly something."

"*Or'jiva* to the ugly underbelly of Eljan court." I smirk. "*Kala*, that was satisfying."

"You were incredible in there. Even I was intimidated." He laughs a little, and I grin.

"Good." We exit the library and walk into the hallway, our footsteps patting softly.

"There is, um, something I meant to say that I didn't get a chance to mention at the meeting."

I frown. "Oh. I apologize, you should have said."

"*Naï, naï,* I didn't want to lessen the impact of the excellent way you ended that meeting." He chuckles, but the smile slips quickly off his lips. "Unfortunately I did hear some rumors at the coronation that I wanted to discuss with you."

I glance at him. He's worrying his lip and his eyes are uncertain as he meets my gaze. Whatever he's about to say, it's not good.

"Go ahead," I say with a sigh.

"There were . . ." Uljen hesitates, then lowers his voice. "These are just rumors of course–nothing concrete. But there were whispers at the coronation that the reason Sekka'l and Invino hadn't sent their *Avrae* to represent their nations was because they intend to secede."

I stop. Stare at him. Repeat his words again, just to make sure I heard correctly. "Secede? You mean–become independent nations again? Not under the *Sira*?"

"Those are the rumors, *sha*." Uljen grimaces. "But again, they were just whispers and could very well be conjecture. I don't think we should panic just yet but I wanted you to be aware of the possibility."

I bite my lip. "Thank you, Uljen. I hadn't heard that so I appreciate the disclosure."

Uljen just nods. We walk until we go our separate ways–to his rooms and mine–but even as his steps disappear far behind me, his words pound in my mind, again, and again.

The nations can't just *leave* because they don't like Eros. They can't risk centuries of peace and dissolve the unity that has made us a stronger people because they don't like Eros's heritage.

Can they?

3

Eros

Can't breathe. Can't see. Blackness smothers my nose, my mouth, presses against my eyes with a hot, engulfing grip.

I try to scream but the darkness rushes into my mouth—thick, dry, like an expanding, foul-tasting cloth. It crawls down my throat as the back of my head bursts with pain and my knees hit the sand.

The pain explodes around my body like bursting stars. My mouth tastes like rust—sticky warmth drips down my face and paints my lips and the pain comes again, and again, and again until—

The suns are up and the white sand is gritty under my knees. Lejv is beneath me. Lejv is beneath me and the thick, pointed shard of his staff is in my hand. I'm pressing into his neck as he stares at me, wide eyed. The bump in his throat bobs and he says—

He whispers—

Make it quick.

The scream rips from my throat and I shove the shard into his neck. And the blood, oh, the blood, deep purple and hot, slickening my grip on the shard, painting my hand and climbing up my arm.

Lejv is dead, but he's not dead, and he smirks at me and says one more word: *Animal*.

Something rough wraps around my neck–tight–and yanks me back. I claw at the cord digging into my throat as sand scrapes my back and Lejv's blood climbs over my shoulder and onto my chest. I gasp for air but nothing comes. The blood climbs up my neck and over my lips and onto my tongue–

On my knees in front of a huge black rock. Grooves scarred into the surface where the blade has crashed down again and again and again. The suns beat my back and my heart pounds against my chest and I want to live, I want to live–all I've done to deserve this is survive in a world that wanted me dead.

Someone shoves my head onto the chopping block. The rock is hard against my skin.

Mal is staring at me, standing just a few paces away, his hands tied behind his back. His eyes are wide. I brought him here. This is my fault.

My vision blurs up with stinging tears. "Mal, don't look," I say. "Close your eyes. I'm sorry. I'm so sorry. I love you. Don't look, Mal, please, please, please–"

"You're okay, you're okay, you're okay. Eros, please wake up, you're scaring Mal. You're scaring *me*, *eran*, wake up. You're okay. You're safe. I promise, Eros, I promise . . ."

The noise caught in my throat twists into a choked sob–but I can't, I can't, Mal is here.

So is Deimos.

When did Deimos get here?

"I–fuck." I wipe my face. My hands are shaking so bad. So is everything–the bed, the walls, the air–me. It must be me. I can't stop.

Deimos helps me sit up. Mal sits silently to my left, hugging his knees. He has his own room now, and obviously so does Deimos, so if they're both in here while it's still bitter-night-dark, then I must have been screaming again.

Fuck.

"I'm sorry," I say quickly. "I woke you guys up again. I'm sorry, you can go back to sleep, I'm fine. Really. Just ignore me next time."

Mal snorts. "Yeah, right."

"I mean it–"

"You're the *Sira*, Eros," Deimos says seriously. "Anything short of screams of pleasure coming from this room is going to attract immediate attention from the guards."

"Screams of pleasure?" Mal says. "Did you really have to go there?"

Deimos flashes a crooked grin. "Didn't I?"

I didn't notice the guards, not at first–too dark. But Deimos is right–my bedroom is full of them now. Lined up at the edge of my bed, watching me with unreadable gazes.

Some first night as *Sira*.

"Sorry." I wave my hand at them and my heart jerks at the black ink tracing the marks on my skin. Still not used to my new *Sirae* mark. "You can go back to your posts. I'm fine. I'm not in danger."

They file out with a nod. I sigh and run my hand over my face.

No fucken way I'm getting any more sleep now.

"C'mon, let's get you back to bed," I say to Mal. "I'm sorry for waking you, little man."

"I'm not little," Mal mutters. And, I mean, he's right. He'll be fourteen in a couple months. He's already getting taller and it won't be long before his voice drops and all that—that stuff.

Which is weird to think about but uh. "Not little," I say. "Right, you're right. Still, you need to get some rest."

"Pants?" Deimos suggests, and it takes me a mo to register what he means. Since Mal has his own bedroom now, I'd been sleeping naked, and I'm definitely not walking the halls with my ass for all to see.

"*Shae*, on the floor," I say. "Thanks."

"Not that I have any objection to getting a good look," Deimos says. "Just for the record."

The half-laugh tumbles out of my mouth. Feels good. "I'm sure. Give me my pants."

Deimos hands them over with a smirk, and I slide them on before getting up. Mal navigates expertly around my bed and holds his hand out until he reaches the wall, then slips out the door first.

I glance at Deimos. "*Ej,* remember when you said after I became *Sira* we could get Mal a tutor to teach him how to use a . . . stick thing?"

"Walking stick, *shae*. I'll look into it."

I nod and we follow Mal into the hallway. The guards clear space for Mal to move along the wall, nodding at him as he moves, not that I think he sees it. But maybe they're doing it for me. To show they'll respect him, even in these small ways.

Mal will never inherit the throne, but he *is* kinduv a *Sira-kaï* now. At the very least, he's royal or noble or whatever. Maybe when he gets older he'll play a more political role. Maybe he'll be the first human representative in Sepharon politics.

I don't really know if that's possible or if he'd even want to, but just that he's here and treated with respect is more than I ever thought possible.

"So what's considered tall for a human?" Deimos whispers. "Is Mal considered average for his age?"

"A little taller than average, but for the most part, *shae*," I say.

Deimos arches an eyebrow. "A little *taller* than average?" He furrows his brows. "Really?"

"I was the tallest at my camp. And the tallest when I was at the Remnant, too."

Deimos stares at me. He's not *that* much taller than me—we line up pretty well, actually—but he *is* taller and still definitely not considered the tallest of Sepharon guys. "Your people are small," he finally says.

I smirk. "They think *your* people are giants."

"Well, I like to think we're *built* like giants, if you understand my meaning."

I groan and Deimos laughs.

"Fuck," Mal says loudly ahead of us. "Get a tent and pillow, won't you?"

"Tent and pillow?" Deimos grins. "Now that sounds intriguing. I understand the function of the tent, but why a pillow?"

"We're definitely not having this conversation," I say. "Also, watch your language, Mal."

"Why? You swear all the time."

"Yeah, but I'm also–"

"Only six cycles older than me." Mal stops walking, turns around, and crosses his arms. "I know you're taking care of me, but you're really not that much older than me. And you're not my dad. I'll swear if I want to."

I open my mouth to argue, but Deimos puts his hand on my shoulder. "Is this really worth the argument?" he says softly.

I bite my lip. Mal's bedroom door is right there. The endless sleep deprivation brainblaze is already chiseling behind my eyes and every mo spent here arguing pointlessly over swearing I don't really care about is a moment I could be– well. Not doing that.

"Whatever," I say. "Just go to bed, okay? I'll see you in the morning, Mal."

Mal huffs but enters his room.

"Could be worse," Deimos says. "He could be having sex. Have you talked to him about sex yet?"

"I'm not talking to him about sex."

"Why not? *Someone* has to."

I sigh heavily and lean against the wall, pressing my palms against my eyes. "Can we talk about something else?"

"Of course. I'm sorry." Deimos gently touches my hands and pulls them away from my face. "Your hands are still shaking."

The echo of the scream tingles in the back of my throat. I can still taste the blood in my mouth. Like a mouthful of rust and salt, only slippery and thick.

Make it quick.

"I don't remember the last time I slept through the night," I say. "I'm *Sira* and I don't know what the fuck I'm doing. And my thirteen-cycle-old nephew is getting sick of me. And he's right, I'm *not* his dad, and I don't know what I'm doing with him either, and I'm–" My voice cracks.

What the fuck am I doing? Why did I ever think I could do this?

"This was a mistake," I whisper. "I'm not supposed to be here."

Deimos places his hands on either side of my head and looks me square in the eye. "Look at me," he says, as if I could look at anything else. As if, this close, his breath painting my lips and his skin on mine, I could look at anything other than his mismatched eyes and the asymmetrical markings on his face.

As if I'd want to look at anything else.

"It's overwhelming," Deimos says. "Even for someone prepared their entire life, being a ruler–let alone *Sira*–is always overwhelming. What you're feeling is expected and normal. And to be clear, it's *good* that you're nervous and scared because it means you're taking your position seriously. You understand the implications and responsibility."

I'm not sure about that. More like the taste of responsibility is freaking me the fuck out and I'm pretty blazing sure I haven't even *begun* to understand the full responsibility and implications, which scares the stars out of me because if I'm unravelling at just this taste, how will I ever manage the full extent of the job?

But I don't say that.

"But you're forgetting something," Deimos says. "You're not doing this job alone. No ruler does–there are advisors and Councils for a reason. I'm here to stay, Eros, and I'll be at your side every step of the way. I've set up your first Council–it's mostly made up of men who served under your father, with some newer people with perspectives I think you'll appreciate.

We're going to tackle this together and you're going to be just fine." He smiles softly. "I know it doesn't feel like it, but I promise you're going to be okay. And in the moments you're not, I'm here for you. Just say the word, *shae*?"

I can't manage a smile back, but the buzzing in my chest and the weight in my blood eases, just a bit. I can breathe a little more deeply. The world isn't going to topple over on my head, not yet.

"*Shae*," I say at last. "Thank you."

"It's never a worry, Eros. I'm honored to be at your side." Deimos lowers his hands to my shoulders. My skin hums under his, sparking hot with every movement.

"I'm really grateful you're here," I say softly. "More than I can describe."

Deimos smiles and slips his arm around my shoulder as we turn back to my room.

"So . . . since you're here," I say, "there is something I wanted to talk to you about."

"Oh, Eros, that's very kind of you, but you don't have to tell me how irresistible I am. I'm well aware, I assure you." I pinch his side and he laughs. "Ah! That hurt."

"You're fine."

"I know I am, but thank you for noticing." I roll my eyes, but he's done it–I'm smiling, which I think was probably the point because he grins back at me. "*There* we are. Okay, what was it you wanted to talk to me about?"

I take a deep breath and rub the mark that starts at my wrist. "I'm *Sira* now, so I make law, right?"

Deimos hesitates and nods. "You do, *sha*. And you have advisors to help you do that, who you'll meet at the Council meeting later this set."

"Okay." I take another steadying breath, ignoring the vibrating hum gathering in my chest. "I know the first thing I want to do." I glance at Deimos, who's just looking at me expectantly. So. I guess I'll just say it then. "I want to abolish slavery in all territories. No one should be owned like a . . . like a thing. And it shouldn't be illegal to be free, like it is for humans now."

"Hm," Deimos says. "That's true."

I run my hand through my hair. "I'm thinking enslaved people should be given the option to either continue their work for a living wage, or otherwise we should set up assistance shelters to house them and help place them in new homes and find jobs."

"You've thought this through." Deimos smiles softly.

I nod. "I want it done."

"Well, I'm glad you have some direction," Deimos says. "Slavery has actually already been completely abolished in Invino, Daïvi, Kel'al, and Ona for a generation or so—the servants in the palace here are all paid a living wage. It's also partially outlawed in A'Sharo, and I can tell you it wouldn't be difficult to convince my brother to go all the way and completely abolish the practice, both for moral reasons and because it'd better ingratiate A'Sharo with the other territories. I imagine it won't be difficult to convince Kora of the same. But you're still left with Sekka'l, who, judging by their refusal to attend your coronation, aren't especially fond of you."

I hesitate. "So making a global law against it would really only affect A'Sharo, Elja, and Sekka'l."

"Right, and I suspect only Sekka'l would care about it, as slavery creates a much more significant portion of their economy, so they'd have the largest financial ramifications. That was the excuse they'd used a generation ago when the first wave of anti-slavery sentiment began, and I don't have any reason to believe that's changed. But as they already seem to dislike you to begin with . . ." Deimos shrugs. "If I'm being honest, I don't see you ever having a particularly positive relationship with Sekka'l. If this is important to you–and I believe it is–I wouldn't compromise just to appease them."

"I don't plan to."

"Good." Deimos pauses. He runs his thumb over the stubble on his chin. "You *will* anger some with this decision, particularly the wealthy–there are always ripple effects–but enslaved people are exclusively used as personal assistants these sets, except in Sekka'l. Not that it makes it any better–enslavement is enslavement regardless of the type of work they're forced to do, and I don't want to excuse that, but I don't think it should be overly difficult to implement and I believe overall it will be received positively. We can talk about this with the Council."

I nod. "So what's the process for making a new law after talking it over with the Council?"

"Nothing complicated. You make the announcement and, as *ken Sira*'s word is law, it becomes law."

I arch an eyebrow. "That's it?"

Deimos snickers. "That's it. As for now, I'm guessing you won't be sleeping for the rest of the night, so how does some *ljnte* and a review of the duties you'll be expected to perform as *Sira* sound?"

"The *ljnte* sounded good until the review part." Deimos laughs and I smile and shrug. "But I guess it won't be so bad since you're sure to make it entertaining."

Deimos's eyes sparkle with unspoken mischief. "Always."

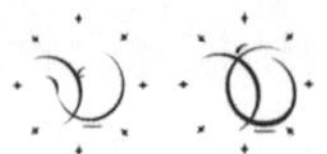

Unlike the Emergency Council with one representative for each territory that still has a living former *Avra* plus the former *Sira*, the regular Council has eight members. Deimos says most Councils across Safara just have four, but the number is doubled for the *Sira* since the job is so big, and also eight is a sacred number or something. Unlike humans, they have eight sets a week and eight terms a cycle, so I probably should've guessed that.

Ordinarily I'd be skeptical of a room full of Sepharon who are supposed to give me the benefit of the doubt and treat me like any other new *Sira*, but Deimos picked these people himself, so maybe it won't be so bad.

Maybe.

The meeting room where the Council gathers is small compared the monstrous size of the other palace rooms, but it's still large enough to fit, like, fifty tents easy with space between them. The white sandstone walls are scattered with black and gold mosaics. There's a long crescent table in the center, and the Council members all stand as I enter, lined up on the closer side of the table, leaving an entire table side for Deimos and me. Or maybe just me. I'm not really sure where Deimos is supposed to sit.

The Council members bow as I walk to the far side of the table, in the center, at the top of the curve, and face them.

They're not what I expected. I'm not sure what I expected. A room full of old men, I guess. But this . . . is not that.

The Council is half women, to start with, and one person whose gender isn't obvious. Of the remaining three guys, one is older, one is middle-aged, and the other doesn't look more than ten cycles older than Deimos and me. He's the youngest Council member save for maybe the androgynous person–the women are all middle-aged or older.

I honestly hadn't expected this much diversity in the room. It's kinduv nice.

"Um, welcome," I say. "I'm honored you've all chosen to join me s–thank you."

"It's an honor to serve you," the ungendered Council member says lightly. The others nod.

They're still standing. I'm not sure if I'm supposed to sit first, or if I'm allowed to sit first. Deimos didn't mention this detail. I'm pretty sure I'm overthinking it, but what if I'm not? If I've learned anything in my time in Asheron it's that every tiny thing means something.

I glance at Deimos. He looks back at me, then looks at the cushion I'm supposed to kneel on, then back to me, his eyebrows slightly lifted.

Okay, I guess I'm supposed to sit first. So I do, and the others follow suit.

Everyone is looking at me. They each have Sephari letters projected over the table in front of them–I'm assuming their names, but I'm still trying to learn how to read Sephari. I know it reads right to left instead of left to right, like English. And the big, swoopy letters are the vowels. But a person's name isn't just the vowels, so even though I recognize a couple Es and Os–which I've learned from my own name–that doesn't really help.

Do they know I can't read?

Has there ever been a *Sira* who couldn't read? I'm guessing no.

"Why don't we start with introductions?" Deimos says. "Just to get everyone acquainted, and so Eros can understand your unique perspectives."

They go through their names and where they come from and their experiences. There's too much information for me to remember it all–I'm sure Deimos has it all memorized anyway, so I'm not too worried.

One of the middle-aged guys–the one who sits directly across from me, Rion–was Asha's personal advisor, like Deimos is for me. He smiles a lot more than I'd ordinarily expect from a middle-aged Sepharon guy, and he's got the general Ona look–slightly lighter skin than Eljans, but the same short dark hair and multi-toned eyes. He has a trim beard, though. That's a little different.

He's also the first to speak. "I understand Deimos has been teaching you the expectations and role of *Sira* to the best of his ability."

I nod. "Deimos has been a huge help."

"I'm certain that's true. There are, however, important differences between the way one raises an *Avra* and the way a *Sira* is prepared." He looks at Deimos. "Not to offend, of course, I'm sure your guidance has been more than adequate for Eros thus far."

"*Naï*, it's fine." Deimos waves his hand. "I'm aware I'm not fully equipped to teach Eros the ins and outs of being a *Sira*. That's why I felt it was important to appoint someone who *has* worked with a *Sira* before."

"I'm glad." Rion smiles. "And I'd be honored to help you prepare, alongside Deimos, Eros. Just to supplement what Deimos doesn't know to teach you."

"That's fine," I say. "Thank you."

Rion bows his head.

"Now onto more pressing matters," Kenna says. "I'm sure you know we have a lot of immediate issues to tackle, *el Sira*."

I nod. "I know the nanites are a top priority. What can we do to get that fixed as soon as possible?"

"Ah, that's my area of expertise," the Council person says. Their name was Tol. I think. I'm pretty sure. "I'm your Scientific Advisor. I'll be working with the technological team and updating you with their progress and ideas."

"Tol is very skilled at their work," Deimos says. "They worked with Serek to help write the code that allowed nanites to create physical objects–like Serek's sand bike. It was groundbreaking work."

Tol grins. "It was fascinating work. I look forward to returning to it, once the nanites are fully restored."

"How long do you think that'll take?" I ask. "I'm aware the lack of nanites is a pretty serious problem."

"I can't say for sure," Tol says. "But if you establish it as a priority–"

"I'm making it a priority," I say. "I don't think anyone will object to that." I pause and glance around the room, but no one does. "Good. It's a priority."

Tol nods. "Then I'll direct all of our scientific resources to that aim. But even then, I imagine it'll take many terms at best to restore even our most basic functions planet-wide. And likely a cycle or more to move on from basic functions to secondary luxuries the nanites provided us. Assuming the blackout didn't heavily damage the machine that creates the nanites, of course."

I frown. "Is that likely?"

"It's not unlikely."

Great. I sigh. "Just make it a top priority."

Tol nods.

"I was thinking," Deimos says. "It might be a good idea for *el Sira* to meet the scientists and see the research facility. Just to become better acquainted with the way things run and meet the people who will be in charge of such a monumental task."

It feels weird for Deimos to refer to me not by my name, but as his *Sira*. The *Sira* part still feels like a coat too big for me to wear, but the part before it—*el*, my—I don't mind that part.

Even though everyone else says it, too, I kinduv like that part coming from him.

"That's not a bad idea," Tol says. "I'm certain the team will be honored to meet you, *el Sira*."

"Sure," I say. "That's fine with me."

"Good," Kenna says. "With that settled, we need to talk about Elja."

I frown. "What about Elja?"

"I'm sure you're aware it was Dima who pushed Roma to order the nanite attack that killed so many redbloods," she says. "He lied to manipulate the former *Sira* so that Roma would lash out. Such an act can't be left unpunished."

I hesitate. Dima *did* play a part in the attack, they're right. But it kinduv sounds like they're trying to pin the whole thing on him, which is giving him way too much credit.

"I don't disagree," I say. "But Dima didn't come up with the plan himself, as far as we know. Roma was already looking for an excuse to lash out at the humans. Dima's lie gave him the excuse he wanted, but even if he hadn't, I'm sure Roma would've come up with some other excuse anyway. He was determined to kill off the human population."

"We don't know that for sure," Kenna says.

I shrug. "Maybe not, but while I think Dima should be punished, I won't blame him entirely for the nanite attack. He didn't force Roma to send out the order. Roma made that decision on his own."

"That's true," Rion says. "But Roma isn't here to suffer the consequences of his actions, and the people need to see some retribution. We must try him here in Asheron, in front of Safara's highest court."

"I'm not convinced punishing Dima is the answer," the oldest Council member, Menos, says. Everyone looks at him skeptically, but he seems undeterred. "Roma isn't dead–he could be woken from his comatose state and put on trial himself. And to make a statement about Elja's unacceptable role in inciting a war crime, Elja as a nation should be punished."

My stomach twists. Punish a whole nation because Dima is a murderous asshole? "*Naï*," I say firmly. "We're not punishing all of Elja for one man's actions."

"He wasn't just a man." Menos shakes his head. "He was their *Avra*. He represents their nation."

"But what he does isn't dictated by the people," I answer. "The Eljans had nothing to do with Dima's decisions. They don't deserve that." The first part of what he said sinks in, too. "Wait, waking Roma up? Absolutely not."

"*Shae*, I don't think that's a good idea either." Deimos frowns. "Not to mention it seems disrespectful, given Serek's final act was to put the former *Sira* into a comatose state, rather than using the nanites to save his own life. Waking him up would make Serek's sacrifice pointless."

"I agree," Rion says. "I don't believe we should wake Roma. His punishment is wasting the rest of his life away in a heavily armed cell, unable to experience anything. It's a terrible punishment I wouldn't wish on anyone."

I nod, though I don't say what I'm thinking. That even if most of the Council members wanted to wake Roma up, there isn't a chance in the blazing Void I'd agree, not because it'd be a waste of Serek's last act–though it would–but because I sure as the suns wouldn't trust them not to try something with another legitimate *Sira* alive.

Fuck that. I didn't spend the last fourteen sets fighting for my life just to bring that asshole back to life and jeopardize everything all over again.

"We'll try Dima here," I say. "I won't punish all of Elja for his actions, but trying Dima here in Asheron will send the message that we aren't going to just let go what he did, either."

"I agree," Deimos says. "I think that's the most effective way to move forward. Let Roma continue his punishment in silence, out of the view of the people. He'd hate that, if he were conscious enough to acknowledge it."

The rest of the Council nods. And just like that I guess I've made my first decisions as *Sira*.

Even though it's not the kinduv decision I wish I had to make, it kinduv feels good. I'm doing this.

At least I'm not falling apart on my first set.

"There's one more thing." I glance at Deimos, and he nods. I face the Council again. "The Remnant are fighting for human rights, and we may not agree on methods, but I want to fight for humans, too. I want to abolish slavery throughout all of the territories as soon as possible. The sooner the better."

Menos arches an eyebrow, but Rion is the first to speak. "You know, your father was speaking of doing the same before he was killed."

A lightness scatters over my skin. "I didn't know that."

Rion smiles. "I suspect the two of you have a direction much more similar than you might think."

Before I can answer, the doors whoosh open across the room and four guards enter, dragging someone in–I can't see who, though, because the Council members and the table are in the way. I'm pretty sure people aren't supposed to just stroll into these meetings, but I'm not sure if guards have some kinduv clearance the rest of the staff doesn't, which would make this okay.

I glance at Deimos, trying to ask without asking. Deimos scowls and stands, so I guess the answer is no, this isn't okay.

"What's the meaning of this?" Deimos asks. "How dare you interrupt a Council meeting unsolicited?"

"My deepest apologies," says one of the guards. "We debated waiting until the meeting was over, but *el Sira* must be notified immediately of this breach."

Breach? Breach of what? I stand and the two Council members across the table from me move aside so I can face the guards and their–

Oh, fuck.

"Hey there, nephew." Shaw grins up at me from his kneeled position on the floor. "Or should I say King of the Stars-Damned Universe?"

4

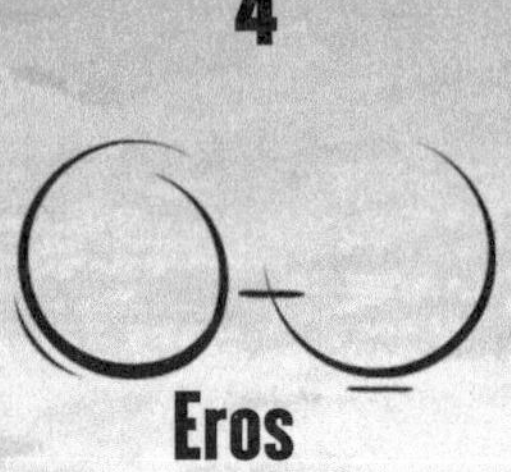

Eros

"Everyone out."

I can't believe Shaw had the balls to just walk in here like nothing. I haven't even been *Sira* for a full fucking set yet. The Remnant can't possibly have expected me to have already started making moves for them, can they?

The Council members bow and file out without hesitation, except for Deimos, who glances at Shaw, then glances at me with a furrowed brow. "Do you want me to . . .?"

"*Naï*, you stay," I say. I look at the guards. "You four can wait outside. He isn't a danger to me."

The guards nod and follow the Council members out. The door hisses shut behind them.

"What are you blazing doing here?" I ask. "Couldn't wait for me to have a full set as *Sira* before walking in like you own the place?"

Shaw snorts. "I was dragged over the mo I stepped through that security perimeter at the front of the complex. That's *hardly* walking in like I own the place." He stands and brushes sand off his legs. "Scraped my knees up pretty good, too."

"What do you want, Shaw?"

"What? No, *how are you, Uncle Shaw?* No *how's mom been doing*? Nothing?"

I keep my face flat. "I'm not calling you my uncle, and you're not here for small talk. Spit it out."

Shaw sighs dramatically and looks at Deimos. "Tough crowd, this kid, huh?"

Deimos just stares at him with his *decidedly unimpressed* face; he doesn't speak English, so I doubt he understood anyway.

"Fine, fine." Shaw stretches his arms over his head. "Obviously I'm here with a message, namely to remind you that you made us a promise. The Remnant expects you to advocate for–and establish–human rights and representation in the government. That means freeing enslaved people, throwing out this outdated monarchy for an equal system with humans in high places–you know what we want. If you break your promise, we'll have to make good on our end of the deal, consequences, blah, blah, blah, you know how it goes. Should I be translating for your boyfriend?"

"I'm not sure why you bothered coming out here," I say, ignoring that last bit. "I obviously haven't had enough time to do much yet and you're just repeating what we already agreed out in the desert."

"Think of it more as a reminder." Shaw smiles. "Both that we expect you to hold up your end of the deal and that we're willing and ready to make good on what we promised, too. We're watching."

I bite my tongue. Do my best to keep my face expressionless. "I'm aware. Look, I haven't forgotten our deal and I haven't forgotten about trying to make life better for humans, either. You know I'm just as invested in that as you and the rest of the Remnant are. But I can't just do it overnight. I'm not forgetting about our agreement–I'm even moving to end slavery–but I need some time."

"How much time?"

I run my hand over the back of my head, touching the buzzed hair at the nape of my neck. "I'm not sure. I'm still learning how everything works and I'm already making some big changes but I can't do everything all at once. I'll probably need at least a cycle just to stabilize before I keep expanding the laws. And I obviously can't touch government structures before I even learn how they work."

Shaw snorts. "Well you better learn the robes fast because we're not giving you a cycle. Even if you don't *do* anything right away, we need to see you talking about reworking the government publicly and clearly making moves toward that goal."

Heat creeps up my neck. "I can't restructure the whole government right away–they've barely accepted having me as *Sira*. They'll toss me out if I try to completely revolutionize their government the way you want on set one. C'mon, Shaw, I have to be smart about this–"

"Listen, kid." Shaw crosses his arms over his chest. "How you manage it politically isn't my problem. We don't *want* your time as *Sira* to be a nightmare, but while you're *learning how to do things*, humans are dying."

He's right. It'd be so easy to dismiss him, to brush him off like sand on shoulders if he was just being an ass for the sake of it, but he's right. This world has been shit to humans for so long, and I'm finally in a place where I can do something about it.

But I barely know where to even start. Or how.

Shaw shrugs, as if reading my mind. "Figure it out. This visit is just a courtesy call–our terms aren't up for negotiation. Not anymore."

I snort. "You were never interested in a negotiation to begin with."

"Nope." Shaw smirks. "So what do you say?"

I shake my head. "I'll do my best, like I said I would, and I *will* fight for humans, but I can't promise you immediate changes."

"Shame. And I was just starting to like you."

I scowl. "Guards!"

The door slips open and the four who dragged Shaw in enter, eyeing him suspiciously.

"Escort him out," I say. "And make sure he leaves Asheron. For good."

5

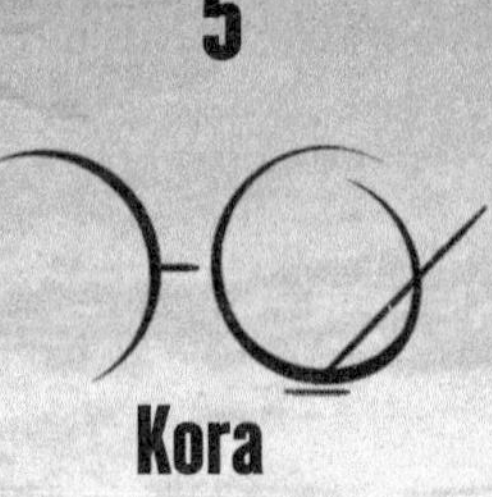

Kora

The suns are high overhead when Uljen finds me in the garden, gently running my thumb over sands-soft flower petals. I close my eyes and smell their sweet scent, letting the memories the scent brings unfurl in my mind.

Like our seventh birthday, when Dima and I flash-froze fallen petals and made each other bracelets and headscarves.

Like collecting petals with Mamae to tint a bath.

Like hiding in flower bushes to jump out at Dima when playing *Amari Hari* when we were twelve.

"Did you ever collect fallen petals?" I turn to Uljen and smile at him.

He blinks and scratches his temple. "I don't think so? Not that I remember, at least." He pauses. "My sister does, though. For garnishing plates and sweetening desserts."

"Oh, you have a sister? How sweet." I smile. "Do you two get along?"

"I like to think so." He offers me the glass he's holding. "I apologize for abruptly changing the subject, but Eros is trying to contact you. I thought you might want to see before the communication request expires."

It takes me a breath to process his words. Eros is trying to contact me? I don't mind—of course I don't, I'm always happy to hear from Eros—but given that I was *just* in Asheron the other set, I hadn't expected to hear from him in some time, if at all.

I hope everything is all right.

"Thank you." I take the glass. "I can handle this alone."

Uljen hesitates. "While I'm sure you're more than capable of taking care of the situation without aid, I'd like to remind you I *am* your advisor and should be included in political matters."

Heat prickles my cheeks. He's right. Of course he's right. I'm just . . . still not quite used to having to share these meetings and decisions with someone else. Dima was my second before Uljen, but he rarely demanded an audience to my meetings or stood by my side. He was too busy with Jarek, and, apparently, plotting to take my throne.

But I have to trust Uljen. I can't use him as my advisor if I don't fully trust him to do his job. And part of that job is being at my side when I speak to other leaders—especially when that leader is the *Sira*.

Even if that *Sira* is Eros.

"Of course," I finally say. "I apologize, you're right. Come join me." I slide aside on the bench I'm sitting on to make room for him then balance the glass in the air ahead of us. I gently place my palm on the glass then pull my hand away as Eros's projection appears over the glass.

"Kora," he says, "good to see you again."

"Likewise," I answer as Uljen sits next to me. "I hope everything is all right; I wasn't expecting to hear from you so soon."

"It's . . ." Eros shrugs. "It'll be fine. I do have to talk to you about something that I suspect you're not going to like, though."

I purse my lips. I suppose a conversation like this was bound to happen eventually. "Go on."

Eros sighs and runs a hand through his hair. "It's about Dima. I need him brought to Asheron so he can be tried for inciting a war crime or whatever they're calling it."

My stomach swoops. Dima tried in Asheron? "What?" Why would they want him tried in Asheron? That doesn't make sense, unless–unless they want to make an example of him. "This is an Eljan matter," I say quickly. "He'll be tried here in Elja, through the Eljan court system, where he will answer to the Eljan people."

"It's not just the Eljans he hurt, though," Eros says. "By pushing Roma to order the extermination of humans, he created an inter-territory incident that killed people around the planet. This is bigger than Elja."

I shake my head. "I'm well aware of the scope of Dima's actions, but he *also* committed crimes against the Eljan people specifically during his short time as *Avra* here. It's my territory's responsibility to try him–not yours."

"Like I said, I knew you weren't going to like this, but this is how I have to handle it. I'm doing you a favor–if Dima isn't tried in Asheron, the Council wants *all* of Elja punished instead–"

"Punished for *what*?" The outburst is louder–more incredulous–than I intended, but I can't believe he just–is he *threatening* me? "Are you even listening to what you're saying? The Eljan people had *nothing* to do with Dima's actions–in fact, their *protesting* his actions resulted in some of them getting *executed*, which is another reason Dima must be tried here in Vejla."

"I can't just do nothing. The Council–and the people, not to mention the humans I promised to protect–expect me to make an undeniable statement about how Dima's actions will not be tolerated–"

"Dima didn't order the genocide, Eros. That was Roma. Who, I'll remind you, you have in your custody."

"Dima pushed Roma to make that decision by *lying* to him–"

"I can't believe you." I stand and the glass shifts up to keep me in view. Dima can't be tried in Asheron–there isn't a chance he'd get a fair ruling there, especially given the way they can't try Roma. And yet, that's likely exactly why they want to try Dima–as a stand-in for Roma. So it appears they're taking action. So it appears *Eros* is taking action. "I'm aware of the difficulties of ruling and trying to appease your people, but you will *not* use my brother as a sacrifice to–to save your reputation!"

"Are you kidding me?" Eros scowls and his background shifts as he stands, too. "This isn't for my fucken reputation, Kora! Your brother incited a war crime!"

"And I *told* you, he'll be tried. Here. In Vejla. Not in Asheron to use as some kind of example. *Kala*, since when are you so weak willed?"

"*Weak willed?*"

"*Sha!*" Heat builds in my skull. "Only a weak ruler would cave so quickly to their Council for the sake of looking good, knowing full well it would cost someone their life."

"Sands and stars above." Eros runs his hands over his face and takes a deep breath. "I'm not trying to *look good*, I'm trying to make the right decision. Dima's actions affected way more than just Eljans, and this is the only option that doesn't involve unnecessarily hurting your people."

My eyes narrow. "*Unnecessarily hurting my people?*"

"I'm just telling you how it is, Kora. If we don't get Dima tried here in Asheron, the Council wants–"

"I don't care what the council wants!" The words explode out of me. "It doesn't matter what the Council wants, Eros, *you are* ken Sira. You overrule the Council, you overrule everyone, and you can tell them *naï* to punishing my nation for no good reason just as easily as you can tell them *naï* to trying my brother in Asheron when he should clearly be tried in Vejla."

"The only clear thing to me right now is you're *clearly* too biased to make sure your brother–who *tortured* me and wanted you dead–is tried fairly."

I can't handle this–him–anymore. And I have never been happier that our romantic relationship didn't work out, because if he's *this* infuriating to try to work with on a political level, I can only imagine how nightmarish it must be to try to work with him as a lover.

Naï, I'm done with this conversation. And with him.

"Goodbye, *el Sira*," I say stiffly. "And good luck to you when Invino and Sekka'l secede."

I end the connection before he can answer and throw the glass on the bench beside me. My skin is burning with the words I wanted to say building up behind my lips and trickling back down my throat.

"*Kafra*," I swear, my heart vibrating in my chest. "He's going to take Dima."

Uljen grimaces. "You have a solid argument for keeping Dima in Elja. He may reconsider once you've both . . . calmed down."

I press my hands to my face and take a long, steadying breath before looking at Uljen again. "He's *Sira* now, Uljen. You know as well I do that he can and will do whatever he wants."

6

Eros

"What did she just say?" My heart is a fist punching its way out of my chest. My voice is strangled, tight with the vice of her words still gripping my mind.

Did she just?

"Something about . . . secession?" Deimos frowns. "I hadn't heard anything about that. Although Sekka'l and Invino didn't send representatives to the coronation, which was incredibly disrespectful, but I didn't think . . ."

"Can they do that?"

Deimos sighs. "I don't know. But I don't think that's a priority right now—we don't know that she has any real indication they intend to secede. She was angry and probably just saying whatever felt good."

"Like she has the right to be angry." I scowl and stand, pacing across the warm tile. "What in the Void am I going to do if she doesn't cooperate? I thought she was just—aren't they *supposed* to listen?"

"Well, *shae*, actually." Deimos leans back on his arms and sighs. "To be true, Kora's refusal could cause a war if neither of you wavered, and it sets a bad precedent. She's an *Avra*, and the *Avrae* are supposed to obey you. Not to mention she's supposed to be your closest ally–if not even she listens, it doesn't really set an encouraging example for the rest of the territories who don't have such a good relationship with you."

"I wouldn't call our relationship good right now." I run my hands through my hair and grip it tight. Why does she have to make this so blazing hard? "*Kafra*. I don't want to start a war over this. Or over anything right now. It's literally the last thing we need."

"I wouldn't recommend that either, but on the other hand, her refusal makes you look bad if it goes public."

I pace and pace and my heart pounds harder–harder. The tightness in my throat spreads to my chest, builds in my face. I grip Aren's bracelet and run my thumb over my ink. This room is a fucken sun and I can't–I can't–

How am I supposed to rule if my own allies don't even work with me?

If my supposedly *closest* ally doesn't work with me?

How can I expect anyone to take me seriously as *Sira* if Kora goes and fucken ignores me when I try to make a move? She's supposed to be my friend, my ally, and I've barely started and she's already sabotaging me.

Can't breathe. My head hurts and everything is tight and my ears are roaring and I can't–

I can't breathe.

"*Ej,* Eros, Eros, look at me." Deimos is in front of me. Close. He was across the room before. When did he get so close? Deimos grabs my hand and pulls it against his chest. "Breathe in." He inhales. "Out." He exhales. "With me. Come on. Breathe in."

I do. His heart beats against my palm, steady, smooth, strong. His eyes bore into me and his skin is warm and we breathe together. In. We're so close. Out. Together.

"Whatever happens, I'm with you." Deimos smiles weakly. "We'll handle this together, *shae*?"

"I don't know if I can do this," I whisper.

"That's okay."

I arch an eyebrow. "It is?"

"Sure. Because I know you can, and I know it strong enough for the both of us." He says it so genuinely, it's hard not to believe him. Deimos lowers my hand but laces his fingers with mine and pulls me back to the bed. My hand prickles where my skin touches his as he flops back on the bed and pulls me down with him.

We lie on our backs and stare up at the ceiling. Slowly, the tight, can't-breathe heat drips out of me as I mirror my breaths with Deimos's. We lie on the bed, looking up at the tiled ceiling, Deimos's thumb softly running back and forth over the back of my hand.

That's it. That's all we do and it's–it's nice.

I can breathe again.

"You know," Deimos says after a while, breaking the quiet. "I never noticed this before, but the pattern of the gold tile on your ceiling looks like a giant penis."

A laugh bursts from my lips before I fully register what he just said. "What? *Naï* it doesn't."

"*Sha* it does, look." Deimos grins and points with his free hand. "That there is the tip, *shae*? And then it thins out there, and down there it becomes a circle . . ."

"A penis with one ball, maybe."

"Well I never said it was perfect, but you shouldn't judge someone for only having a single–"

I roll over on top of him and cover his mouth. His eyes light up and crinkle with the laugh bubbling out of me, then my face is in the crook of Deimos's neck and we're laughing so hard my stomach hurts.

Until the laugh dies away, and, well.

If I'm being honest, shutting him up was really only an excuse to do this. Get close to him. And it seemed like a good idea at the time, like something I could completely get away with in a not-obvious way, except now that the laughter has faded and Deimos is looking at me and his hard body is pressed against mine and my one leg is between his and my fingers are breaths away from slipping into his thick hair–

I kinduv can't breathe again. Not in a panic-y way like before, but in a *what am I fucken doing?* way. Because look, I've *thought* about messing around with guys before, but like, in an abstract, this'll-get-me-off-even-though-it'll-never-happen way.

But this is different, and real, and here. I'd hardly call myself experienced with girls because no one ever wanted anything to do with me. I'm definitely not experienced with guys. But Deimos probably is. Deimos is magnetic, and unfairly attractive with a personality that makes him doubly impossible to ignore. There's no way he hasn't messed around with guys before–there's no way he's half as inexperienced as I am.

So what I am doing?

"You're thinking too much," Deimos says softly. He touches my cheek and my face is instantly on fire. "Which is understandable. I know this is all overwhelming, especially alongside the *Sira* stuff, so there's no pressure, *shae*?"

I want to smile back at him. I want to be ready and I don't want to be thinking–I want to press him against this bed and kiss him like I've been itching to kiss him for what feels like forever. I want to kiss him the way I think about kissing him when I'm alone in bed. And I've never worried about whether I sucked at kissing or how to move and where to touch, and I've never worried about how experienced the other person was or wasn't and it never mattered before but right now, even with everything else going on, it's the only thing I can think about.

What if I kiss him and it doesn't do anything for him? Or worse, what if I kiss him and it's so bad he laughs at me?

"Where's Mal?" I hate myself for saying the words as soon as they're out of my mouth. But if Deimos is disappointed, he doesn't show it.

"Exploring the grounds," he says casually. Even though I'm still on top of him. And our faces are really blazing close. And I'm a fucken coward. "I've assigned a guard to shadow him, just in case. But he's in the most secure palace complex in the safest city on the planet, so I wouldn't worry."

I just nod.

"Look . . ." Deimos sighs and gently pushes me off and rolls on his side so he's facing me. "Let's take the rest of the set off, *shae*? You desperately need to relax and de-stress before you have a breakdown. Maybe try to get some extra sleep. I know the nights haven't been the easiest for you."

My face burns again, but this time not because of our closeness. I look away. "It's not a big deal."

"You wake up screaming, Eros." Deimos hesitates. "You know you can talk to me about it, right? Or anything. If you need someone to talk to, or want to vent, or—or whatever you need. I'll never judge you."

I sit up and sigh. "I don't really want to talk about it. Or think about it. Bad enough that it already takes up my nights—I don't need it invading my sets, too."

"Okay." Deimos pauses. "But if you change your mind . . ."

"I know, I—thank you." I run my thumb over Aren's bracelet—it's getting kinduv worn and soft from my constant rubbing. What would Nol think of me being here? Or Esta? Or Day?

Maybe not Day. I don't think Day would've liked me being here.

But what do people back at camp think? Gray wanted to use me, but I can't even begin to say what everyone else would have wanted. I don't even know what the Sepharon people want from me, beyond getting everything back to normal.

"How am I supposed to know what everyone wants?" The question is out of my mouth before I've fully processed it.

Deimos blinks. "I'm sorry, you've lost me. What are we talking about?"

"It's just—I'm *everyone*'s ruler, right? And I've got all sorts of advisors to help me make the best decisions and that's fine, but how do I know what the people want?"

Deimos looks genuinely thrown by the question. "The people . . . want what's best for Safara."

"I don't know about that. I think a lot of people want what's best for themselves, or for people they care about." I pause. "I want to establish a way for people to be able to make their wishes known. Human and Sepharon alike. Maybe . . .

somehow through the glass or something. So the people feel heard, you know?"

"Hmm. That's a good idea. I'll talk to Tol about it—they'll probably be able to get a team to put something together relatively quickly."

A knock at the door interrupts us. I get up and the door slides open as I near it. My four always-there guards are there with a woman I don't recognize, wearing a super-long uniform I haven't seen before. It's like a black cape that swirls around her body and reaches all the way down to her ankles.

"Apologies for interrupting, *el Sira*," Kosim, my personal bodyguard, says. "Medic Zarana is requesting an audience with you. She says it's urgent."

The woman—Zarana, I guess—nods and bows. "I assure you I would have sent a message through Deimos if it wasn't absolutely essential I spoke to you immediately."

Deimos comes to my side and frowns. "Sounds serious. What's wrong?"

Zarana hesitates. "It'd be better if I showed you both. If it's not too much trouble, I'd like to show you what I'm seeing in the infirmary."

I nod, keeping my face steady even as my stomach twists into knots. Whatever this is, it's sounding worse by the mo. "Lead the way."

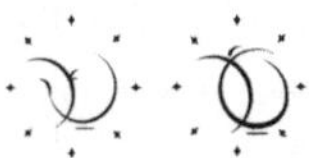

I didn't really appreciate how huge—and organized—the medical center is the first time I was here. Granted, the first time I was here it was the dead pre-rising hours of the morning and I was badly concussed and everything hurt. Deimos had to help me walk over and all I could focus on was trying not to choke on the blood pouring out of my nose and down my throat and not passing out from the agony pulsing through me.

This time around, my body still aches from that attack—and from the fight afterward—but it's dull, easy-to-ignore background noise.

To call it a room isn't really accurate—the medical center has its own separate building in the palace complex and this "room" takes up a third of the second floor. Unlike the rest of the complex, the room is more ground-toned—white, silver, blue, and gray are the main colors. Most unusually, the floor isn't stone, but thick strips of gray—wood, I guess? It's just as smooth as stone, but not as hard under my feet. I kinduv like it.

We follow Zarana down a long, main aisle, passing—rooms, I guess, but the rooms don't have walls, just curtains. Back in Elja, the infirmary had nanite screens to separate one room from another with blurry, partially transparent "walls," and I'm guessing that was the case here, too, but they probably have to make do with curtains until the nanites are back up and running.

When we reach the end of the aisle, Zarana takes us down a side corridor, past actual rooms with actual walls and doors. They're all labeled, but we're walking too fast for me to try to remember enough letters to read anything.

Finally, we reach a door with two guards at the end of the hall. I glance at Deimos. It's weird that there are guards here, right? What is there to guard in a hospital? And are they keeping us out, or keeping someone in?

Zarana presses her palm against the door, and it whooshes aside. The guards barely look at us as we enter a tiny room, big enough for maybe five or six people, tops. There are shelves and sinks and a glass door with another small room behind it.

"You'll need to decontaminate," Zarana says. "Both as you enter and when you leave. After the decontamination, I'll give you gloves and filter masks in the final prep room."

I raise my eyebrows. "Why do we need to decontaminate and use gloves and filter masks?"

Deimos eyes her warily. "I'd also like that question answered."

"Right, of course, I apologize." She sighs and tucks a strand of black hair behind her ear. "It's all a precaution. You won't actually be in contact with any of the patients I'm going to show you–nor will you be in the same room as any of them–but we're entering a quarantine zone and–"

"*Quarantine*?" Deimos's jaw slackens. "You mean for *illness*?"

Zarana purses her lips. "Unfortunately, *sha*."

I glance at Deimos. "I thought the Sepharon didn't get sick."

"We didn't," Zarana says, "but not because we aren't capable of getting sick–because we eradicated all illnesses through nanite technology, everything from minor, inconvenient viruses to deadly strains. But now without the nanites, it seems . . ." She frowns. "Well, as I said earlier, I think it'd be best for me to show you."

My stomach churns. I've seen illness kill people back at camp–strains that spiked fevers, made them bleed out, or had them emptying their stomachs until they dehydrated or starved. Whenever anyone at camp got sick, we put them in quarantine, too–granted, with less technology and more avoidance than anything else. Even minor illnesses meant no contact with people outside of the family until you got better—more because it was too easy to spread disease, have it mutate, and permanently fuck up a small population than anything else.

But I can't imagine the Sepharon would go through the trouble of quarantining someone this thoroughly unless it was something serious.

The room behind the glass door is the decontamination room, not completely unlike the decontamination I went through when I first entered the Eljan palace complex. The room fills with some kinduv blue smoke that smells—like really clean air, I guess. It's not bad.

That's followed up by a purple smoke that smells ridiculously sweet but kinduv makes my eyes water and skin tingle. Then the glass door ahead of me opens and I enter the last prep room where Zarana, Kosim, Fejn, and Deimos are already waiting.

"Good." Zarana hands me what looks like a stiff-fabric shell, about the size of my hand. It's made of the same hard, woven stuff their water bottles are made of, but this is black with blue edging. Zarana points to a bump at the top. "Put this part on your nose and the rest over your mouth. It'll seal to your face and provide air filtering."

Deimos presses his on, waits a mo, then lowers his hand. I can't see his mouth, but I don't need to to spot the smile crinkling around his eyes. "How do I look? Fashionable, *shae*?" I'd expected his voice to be muffled under the shell-like mask, but it sounds the same. Must have some built-in mic thing. Or maybe the fabric somehow doesn't mess with sound? I'm not sure.

Zarana puts hers on with one hand as she hands Kosim and Fejn theirs. I carefully slot the bump over my nose and push the rest over the lower half of my face. It curves over the bridge of my nose, around my mouth, and partway over my chin. I press gently and the edges touching my face go cold for a mo until it goes back to a normal temp and I let go. It stays, stuck on my face like a sticker plant.

Weird.

"Kinduv smells strange," I say. "Like that blue smoke."

"It's the sanitation," Zarana says. "You'll become accustomed to it." She pulls open a drawer and inside is a thick, shiny, white-ish liquid. She dips her hands in to partway up her forearms then pulls them back out. The liquid slides seamlessly off her hands, leaving behind a thin white layer that dries almost immediately.

"Gloves," she says to me. "They peel off easily, so don't worry, but again, precaution."

After we've all got the weird gloves and mask, Zarana takes us through one more door into another hall with glass walls looking into individual rooms. I'm not sure how many rooms there are–the hall goes on for a while–but at the very end is a room with a woman and teen boy, maybe a cycle or two older than Mal. It's kinduv hard to say because he's sitting in the corner, knees pulled up to his chest, face in his knees.

The woman is pacing back and forth across the room, talking to–the kid, I guess, since no one else is in the room and the walls are soundproof, not that he seems to be listening. Her lips are cracked and the veins in her neck are dark and bulging.

"So what exactly are they ill with?" Deimos asks.

"That's the problem–we have no idea. We've gone through a full archive of all of our known diseases, even the *really* old historical ones, and nothing matches their symptoms."

I frown and step toward the glass. The woman doesn't seem to have noticed us–she's still pacing and talking and throwing her hands in the air while the kid just sits perfectly still. "Symptoms like what?"

"Fever, the bulging, dark veins, delusions, queasiness, and their eyes seem to be . . . darkening."

"Darkening?" Deimos frowns and peers into the room.

"They're getting a gray tinge, even the white part. But what concerns me is how quickly the symptoms are taking hold. She and her son are merchants in the complex. When she came in with her son this morning, they just had fevers and felt ill. The protruding veins, darkening eyes, and delusions started not a segment later. And the medications I've given them aren't doing anything for the fever."

I frown and glance at Zarana. "Do you think it's fatal?"

"If I can't get their fevers down, it will be."

My stomach sinks. "Great."

"Do we know if anyone else is ill?" Deimos asks. "If they're complex merchants, that means they're exposed to loads of people in the palace marketplace–and likely outside of the complex, too, as they come in and out all the time."

Zarana sighs. "*Sha*, well, that's just it. These two were my first with the symptoms, but in the four segments they've been here, eleven more have come in with similar symptoms. They're still being processed and examined as we speak, but they'll be brought here, too."

Thirteen sick people in half a day. On a planet where the Sepharon haven't had illnesses in generations. On my first fucking set as *Sira*. Great.

"Keep us updated," I say.

Deimos nods. "A report at the end of the set would be helpful."

"Of course." Zarana hesitates. "If I may, I'd like to suggest you don't leave the palace today. And keep those masks with you–just in case. I'll have them distributed for the rest of the palace staff, and you can take an extra for your nephew. But if this strain is in the complex marketplace, you may want to consider decontaminating the full complex and staying indoors until we can locate the source of the outbreak–if this is an outbreak."

"*Is* this an outbreak?" Deimos asks.

Zarana bites her lip. "I don't want to start a panic. But I wouldn't have called you so urgently if I wasn't greatly concerned."

"We need to find Mal," I say to Deimos. "I don't want him wandering around if there's a chance he might get sick."

"I can call Varo and have him return Mal to his room, if you'd like, *el Sira*," Kosim says.

"Thank you." I glance back at the room and my heart jolts. The kid who was across the room is just on the other side of the glass now, staring at us.

And his eyes, end to end, are a solid sheet of shiny gray.

7

Kora

"Have you heard the news?"

Uljen strides quickly into the dining hall as I sip my morning tea. It's been two sets since Eros's coronation, and to say there's been a lot going on is an understatement, so I'm not entirely sure which news he's referring to.

"Which news?" I ask. "The part about the *Sira* not changing his mind about wanting Dima dead? Or the part about Sekka'l and Invino refusing to answer why they didn't attend his coronation? Or maybe the part about Eljans wanting a date for Dima's trial and my not having an answer for them yet isn't going to be acceptable for much longer?"

"All of that." Uljen kneels across from me but doesn't reach for food. "And none of that." He slides his glass across the table. On it is a report about–

I choke on my tea. "Disease?"

Uljen nods. "Sixty-two reported ill on the first set, most outside the complex, but a few were merchants on the palace grounds. The palace complex physicians have stopped accepting patients from outside the complex, they shut down the marketplace until further notice while they decontaminate the complex, and the central Asheron hospitals are all setting up strict quarantines."

"*Kala alejha*," I whisper. "Sixty-two in a single set. This is serious."

Uljen nods. "The symptoms seems to take hold very quickly, too. People feeling slightly ill in the morning were inconsolably sick by the end of the set. Some of the patients even became violent."

"But it's isolated to Asheron?" I ask.

Uljen nods. "For now, *sha*. I imagine it won't be long before it spreads to greater Ona if they don't do something more than quarantines."

"Good." I sigh and brush hair out of my face. "I hope Eros, Deimos, and Mal don't get sick."

"As far as I know, the *Sirae* family and Deimos aren't affected."

I nod and glance at my deep blue, clear tea. I was already a little queasy over the conversation I'm going to have to have with Dima and Jarek. Now with this news it'll be a miracle if I manage to eat anything at all.

"Preventative steps." I look up at Uljen. "We should talk to the medics about distributing some sort of immune-system booster, or something of the sort, to fortify our people against it. Just in case."

"That's a good idea." Uljen drums his fingers on the table. "We may want to consider shutting down our borders from Onans, as well, until the disease is managed. Or at least from Asheron citizens."

I frown. "We do a lot of trade with Ona."

"*Sha*, that's my concern."

I shake my head. "I'm not sure we have the resources to do that. We're getting about a quarter of our emergency food supplies to cover the famine from Ona. I don't think Daïvi and Kel'al could make up the loss if we stopped accepting from Ona."

"But if the food is contaminated . . ."

My stomach twists and chest tightens. Contaminated food is a concern to be sure, but on the other hand . . . "The food doesn't come from Asheron—it's largely from the Northern part of the territory, in the farming region. As long as the disease remains localized in Asheron, I don't want to cut Eljans off from their food supply just yet."

"Fine." Uljen sighs. "But if it spreads outside of the city—"

"Then we'll discuss this topic again. But the first priority is talking to the medics about immune-system boosters."

"I agree."

I nod and try to sip my tea. The sweet, fruity taste is—too sweet on my stomach. Too substantial. Which doesn't bode well for the rest of my meal given it's just hot, flavored water.

Uljen hesitates. "You seem distracted."

"I have to talk to Dima and Jarek. About . . ." I glance at him.

He must catch my meaning because he grimaces and nods. "Not an easy conversation, I imagine."

"*Naï*," I mutter. "I don't imagine it will be."

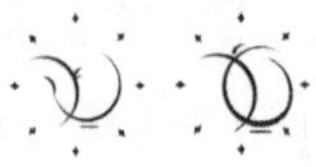

"Kora, *or'jiva*." Dima smiles as he steps further into the room, out of the doorway—he's not permitted to leave his room. "Come in, please. It's good to see you."

I force a thin smile as I step past my brother and into his bedroom. Jarek nods at me from his spot on the floor, huddled on the far side of a projected circle with a line horizontally across the center and small, evenly spaced circles mirrored on both halves of the larger boundary circle. Individually decorated glass marbles are scattered across the board—they're playing *Si-So*. My smile warms. I used to play *Si-So* with Dima all the time when we were children.

"Would you like to join us?" Dima asks, sitting across from Jarek. "We've only just started, so it's not a problem to start a new game."

Jarek snorts. "You're only saying that because you're already losing."

"I am not!" Dima laughs. "It's only been one round!"

"Exactly."

I smirk and sit to the side of the board, between them. "It's fine. I won't bother you long anyway."

"Naï, c'mon, join us, Kora." Dima smiles. "When's the last time we've played *Si-So*, hmm?"

"Cycles. If I recall correctly, you stopped playing with me because you didn't like me beating you all the time."

"That sounds like Dima." Jarek snickers.

Dima's face colors, just slightly, and he scratches the back of his head. "I—*sha*—well. I don't remember the precise reason but . . ." He shakes his head then grins again. "The point is, it's been too long! So join us, please. For me."

"Losing that badly already, hm?" I laugh as Dima groans. "I suppose I could stay for a game, if Jarek doesn't mind starting over."

Jarek lifts a shoulder. "It doesn't bother me. I'll just beat him again anyway."

"*Sha, sha,* we'll see." Dima waves his hand over the game, resetting the board. The marbles rush back to their prospective sides as Dima fiddles with the projected controls on the board, splitting it three ways.

A short time later, Dima has lost and Jarek and I tied for victory. Ordinarily we'd play another game with just Jarek and me to determine a winner, but I can't push off this conversation any longer–and besides, Uljen is still waiting for me so we can speak with the medics.

I've put this off long enough.

"I'm afraid I didn't visit just to play *Si-So* with you both," I say as Dima and Jarek put the game away.

"*Naï*, I didn't imagine that was the case," Dima says. "Although you're more than welcome to stop by for such a purpose. I'm rather starved for entertainment in this room."

Jarek arches an eyebrow, and I smirk. "I'm sure the two of you come up with plenty of ways to entertain yourselves."

"Well, *sha*, but Jarek can't spend all his time with me. He's still in the guard, as you well know."

"I'm aware." I sigh. "At any rate, I'm actually here to speak with you both about . . . the trial."

Dima's smile fades, but he nods as he rolls a marble over his palm with his thumb. Jarek's eyes widen. "A trial? So soon? I didn't imagine that would happen for at least a term, given everything going on."

"I imagine everything will be decided by the end of Okona."

"But–that's not–"

"I wasn't going to push it so quickly," I say. "I thought we had time. But unfortunately, Er–*ken Sira* has motivation to try Dima in Asheron. And I think we all know if that were to happen, there's little chance it would end well for Dima."

Dima keeps rolling the marble silently in his hand. Jarek stands and paces. "Please tell me you haven't agreed. I know Eros is your friend, but–"

"I told him *naï*." I pause. "But as you both know, *ken Sira*'s word is law. If he pushes this . . . Elja can't afford a war with Asheron and Ona, and certainly not over protecting Dima, who the people recognize as a criminal."

"He's not *just* a–"

"It's all right, Jarek," Dima says softly. "She's right, and so are the people. I am a criminal. I deserve to be tried fairly."

I nod. "The important part there is *fairly*, and I truly don't believe you'd get a fair trial in Asheron. They'd blame you for Roma's crimes as well as your own and likely . . ." The sentence dies on my lips. I can't say it. I don't want to think it.

Does my brother deserve to be executed? He tried to kill me. He almost killed Serek. He ordered the murder of innocents just for protesting. He tortured Eros for sets on end and gave Roma the excuse he needed to order genocide. He has blood on his hands.

Does that warrant a public execution?

I'm afraid of the answer the Vejlan court may come to.

I know the answer the Asheron court would order.

"Execute me," Dima says. "It's okay, Kora. You're not telling me anything I don't know."

"It's *not* okay," Jarek snaps. "We can't just hand him over to Asheron for slaughter."

"I agree," I say, but my voice is tight–on the edge of breaking. "I agree," I try again. "Which is why I'm accelerating the trial here in Velja. My hope is if we start it here quickly enough, *ken Sira* will let it go, because we're already taking care of it. And now that he's distracted with this plague, we should get it done."

Jarek pinches the bridge of his nose and sits next to Dima. My brother puts his arm around Jarek's shoulders. "Thank you," he says. "Sincerely, Kora. You've shown me much more grace than I deserve."

I sigh. "You're my brother, Dima. I wasn't going to turn away from you."

"And that's what makes you better than me." He says it so simply, so confidently. Like no one would ever question it.

I suppose they wouldn't.

"No matter what happens, I won't let them kill you," I say. My heart pounds with the words. It's not a promise I'm sure I can keep, but the words ring true in my ears nevertheless.

I won't let them kill my brother.

I won't.

"Thank you," Dima whispers. But the glisten in his eyes, the pain in his smile, the shaking of his fingers–clenched tight in Jarek's hand–

He doesn't believe me. And I'm not sure he should.

8

Eros

It's been twenty-four segs—a full set—since we learned there's a fucken plague racing through the capital of the world, and 142 people have gotten sick.

And two—the mother and son we saw yesterday, who came in first with those haunting, darkening eyes and black veins—have already died.

"It acts quickly," Deimos says, sighing as he looks over the report Zarana sent us during the midday meal. "I suppose in a way that's a mercy. Seems like those last segments aren't pleasant."

"Except for the part where it doesn't exactly give us a lot of time to save people." I pick apart the *kata* wrap, my stomach twisting in nauseating ways way too intense for me to even consider eating. And that's without the dull, pounding brainblaze sitting behind my eyes and the full-bodied exhaustion weighing on every muscle.

I didn't really sleep last night.

At all. Again. Too busy thinking about everything going wrong, everything I'm supposed to fix. Everything I can't even begin to tackle. Every passing set is a reminder the Remnant could make everything worse at any time. And it's not even like I don't *want* to make things better for humans—of course I do—but I can't shake the feeling that the stuff I'm trying to do won't be enough for them.

They don't just want human rights—they want a complete revolution. Even if that means making me a casuality.

Mija tutted over me in the morning as she painted away the shadows under my eyes, muttering how lucky I am to have her. She's not wrong. After she's done, I almost look rested.

"Well, *shae*. But the good news is it also makes it much easier to identify who is carrying the disease and who isn't. Zarana says the incubation period seems to be around six segs. It likely won't be long before they're able to develop some sort of detection test so we can loosen the border shutdown by testing those who come in and out."

"Mostly out, if we're being honest," I say.

Deimos grimaces. "*Shae*. Mostly out."

"At least you won't have to keep everyone *totally* trapped in the city for too much longer," Mal says. "Otherwise they'd start to lose it of boredom. Like me."

Deimos smirks. "You know, Mal, if you're that bored I'm sure Eros and I can find something for you to do. Study, for example. I'm already arranging for an accommodations tutor to teach you how to use a walking stick, but I could likely find you one to teach you our history and politics as well."

"That actually sounds like a good idea," I say. "Why aren't we doing that?"

"Never mind," Mal says. "I'm not bored. I'm the opposite of bored. I'm really busy actually. Busiest I've ever been, really."

Deimos snickers and even I manage a smirk.

"That's a shame," Deimos says. "If you're so busy, I suppose you won't have time to come with us to Daven and Zek's wedding. I hear the food will be *incredible*, with multiple courses and some of the best desserts you'll find on Safara—but never mind that. You're clearly too busy."

Mal hesitates. "I'm sure I could take a few sets off. You know. For politics. Since it's important for us to go and everything."

"Uh-huh."

"Are we actually still going to that?" I ask. "Not that I don't want to—I think it'd be great—but with the outbreak and everything . . . is that a good idea?"

"I'm not sure if it's a *good* idea, but a worse idea would be skipping it." Deimos plucks my *kata* off my plate and places it on his. At my look, he just shrugs. "Well *you're* clearly not eating it."

I shake my head. "Why would skipping it be a worse idea?"

"Well, we're not just going for fun. The Daïvi are our strongest supporters—especially now that you're having a bit of an argument with Kora."

I don't correct him on the understatement. Kora's called twice since our argument—both calls that I ignored. I know her. She's not calling to apologize. She's calling to try to change my mind. And it's not fucken happening.

"You have to remember, interterritory relationships are incredibly important, especially given Invino and Sekka'l are . . . being difficult. It'd be considered incredibly rude if you backed out now, and you'd risk angering one of your few supporters. As long as none of us get sick before then, we have to go."

I nod. "I guess that makes sense."

"Damn," Mal says. "That's too bad, I guess we'll just *have* to go then, ugh, what a bummer, I don't know how we'll survive it."

I smirk and ruffle his hair. Deimos snickers as Mal grins and eats his food.

"Okay," I say. "So we're going. When do we leave?"

"Four sets, so we still have time to prepare and try to get things settled here first."

I don't mention that it seems unlikely anything will be "settled" in four sets. I'll be lucky if things aren't four times as bad as they are now.

Deimos rests his hand on mine and squeezes lightly. It's a small thing—just a reassuring touch with a worried, thin smile—but it calms the buzz prickling around my stomach, just for a mo.

I don't know how in the stars things will settle down, but I have to try to believe they will. And for everyone else's sakes, I have to act like I know they will.

I don't know that they will. But I squeeze his hand back anyway.

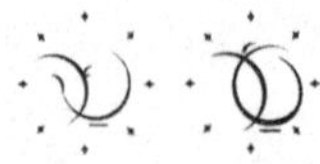

After the morning meal, Deimos and I go back to the Council to finish talking about the communication network for the people to make themselves known and the law abolishing slavery. Most everyone is on board with the communication thing, but they also agree some people will be pissed off by the new law—especially the wealthy, and doubly so in Sekka'l—but

I don't care, and neither does most of my Council. Owning people is wrong. That's all there is to it.

I make my first announcement in the throne room, feeling too small on the intricately carved glass throne even as I hold my head high and shoulders back and look into the orb guide broadcasting me for the world to see. And then, when it's all said and done, I spend segments talking to *Avrae* across the territories about how to best implement transitional resources for now-freed servants who need homes and ways to support themselves.

By the time it's over, I feel like I've had the longest set of my life—and it isn't even mid-set.

Afterward, Deimos, Mal, Kosim, Fejn—Deimos's personal guard—and Varo—Mal's personal guard—and I all put on our filter masks and leave the palace out the back, where we're less likely to run into people. The complex marketplace has been shut down until further notice, so the grounds are way emptier than usual to begin with, but I guess it's an extra precaution.

Kosim is leading the parade, and I don't really question him. He seems to know what he's doing and cares about doing his job right. Or at least, that's the impression I've gotten from working with him for a couple sets.

We walk to the far northern end of the complex, where a gleaming glass bubble woven with blue metal—like the glass was shattered then put back together again with molten blue metal—shimmers under the heat of the suns. It's blistering out here—the hottest time of the cycle is coming fast—and the reflected heat ripples in the air in dancing waves as we near the weird building.

"This is the science lab," Deimos says as we stand in front of the dome. "Or rather, this is the museum portion. The laboratory itself is actually underground–I'm not sure how deep it goes, but my understanding is it's pretty enormous."

"Cool." Mal grins.

"Underground like the Remnant?" I ask.

"Well, *shae*, you didn't think the Remnant built those tunnels themselves, did you?" Deimos smirks. "We've had underground systems in place for centuries. They're especially popular in less hospitable regions–deserts, mountains, that sort of thing. Many of our oldest ruins even have complex tunnel systems in place."

Interesting. "So the Remnant repurposed what was already in Enjos."

"Most likely." Deimos pauses. "I do believe there's a tunnel system in place from the palace to buildings all around the complex, isn't there, Kosim?"

Kosim arches an eyebrow. "How do you know about that?"

Deimos smirks. "I dated an Asheron guard once. It didn't last long, but he told me some very interesting stories."

Kosim purses his lips. "That's true, *sha*."

"Then *why* did we go the burn-into-a-flaming-crisp way?" Mal asks.

"You three need to get registered before we can take the tunnels anywhere." Kosim shrugs. "As registration happens in the science building anyway, this was the most practical route."

Mal grumbles and crosses his arms.

I smirk. "It's almost like you didn't grow up in a desert even hotter than here."

"It's not just the heat," Mal says with a pout. "I just really hate the light reflection on this sand. It makes it even harder to see than usual."

"Maybe the techies can make you darkening glasses," Deimos says. "Talk to them about it while we're there. I'm sure they won't mind."

Mal frowns. "They probably have more important things to work on than glasses for me."

Deimos shakes his head. "There are *loads* of techies. I'm sure one of them will be able to make the time–they may even have some on hand already. You're not the only one who doesn't love the suns' glare, you know." Deimos pats his shoulder. "We'll ask."

Kosim walks up to a glass panel framed in gold–it slides up like an opening mouth and Kosim gestures us inside. We all enter and I grimace. I mean, the place is amazing–sleek white floors, cool metal statues that look like poured molten metal frozen in time, and projections all over the place showing one scientific process after another. Above us is a glass floor so clear it looks like the people standing up there and shelves and statues on that floor are all floating in the air.

It's incredible in here–but it's also like walking into the suns. It's even hotter than it is outside.

Kosim clears his throat. "Ordinarily this building is nanite-cooled, but you know . . ."

Yeah. We know.

"It'll be cooler underground," Deimos says. "But we have to get registered, *shae*? Let's get that over with so we can get out of this *kafran* heat."

Registration, thankfully, doesn't take long. One of the building staff sets us up on a glass, taking our handprints, scanning our faces, and taking a voice clip from each of us. Once that's done, she leads us to a huge glass box sitting on the far side of the room. Two doors slide open on the box as we approach, and our bodyguards and Deimos waltz right into the box like it's no big deal.

Mal leans toward me. "What are we walking into?" he whispers. "Is there something special on the floor?"

"It's a . . . don't worry about it. Just stick with everyone." I guide him forward until the doors close behind us.

It's kinduv hard to breathe in the box–the heat is so thick it feels like inhaling soup. And the tight fit in the box is kinduv making me itchy. My heart stutters in my chest as sweat slips down my temples and back, glistening all over me like a second skin.

We're all facing the doors and I have no fucken clue why.

"What is this?" I finally ask. "Why are we standing in here?"

"It's an elevator." Deimos gently knocks my shoulder with his. "Don't worry. It'll take us down to the lab."

What the fuck is an elevator?

And how is a fucken box supposed to take us anywhere?

"Are you–"

The floor shifts and–sinks.

It's sinking into the ground.

Stars and suns alive we're sinking into the fucken ground.

My pulse hammers in my ears as packed white sand walls replace the room we were just in and we sink lower and lower. I don't think I'm breathing. All I hear is drumming. I grip Aren's bracelet on my wrist and grit my teeth. It's really fucken hot and the air is too thick and there are too many of us in this tiny box and the glass floor below us just shows–black.

We're descending into a hole in the planet that goes on for stars know how deep.

"*Ej*, Eros. Are you okay?" Deimos is frowning at me. "You look a little pale."

"This is the coolest thing ever," Mal says. "We're like flying into the planet."

Flying isn't the word I'd use. More like falling. We're falling into the planet.

Oh, fuck.

"Hey." Deimos stands in front of me and holds my shoulders. "This is fine. We're fine, see?" He grins. "It's a controlled descent. These elevators are very safe, and we'll be opening up into the floor levels soon, which I think you'll like. Just relax, *shae*? We're fine."

Kosim glances at me. "Is he having a panic attack?"

"*Naï, naï.*" Deimos waves his hand. "He's okay, he's just not used to this. Right, Eros?"

I gulp. "Uh. Sure."

"Good. Oh, *ej*, look." He moves aside, sliding his arm around my shoulders so I can see–oh.

"Wow," Mal whispers.

The endless packed white sand is gone–instead, we're lowering into the largest room I've ever seen; it goes so deep I can't even see the end of it from here. The room is split into different sections with projections creating divisions, and hundreds of people–maybe over a thousand?–in black and gold uniforms walk around from division to division. The walls are lined with enormous glass screens that seamlessly cover floor to ceiling.

This must be it. The lab.

"Impressive, *shae*?" Deimos says. "And this is just one floor. Like I said earlier, I'm not even sure how many floors there are. More than ten, because that's the lowest I've ever been."

Kosim groans. "How in the world did you get clearance to go ten floors deep? You weren't even registered!"

Deimos snickers. "I may have dated an Asheron techie at one time, too."

"*Kala alejha*." Kosim rolls his eyes.

I bite my lip and focus on the room as we slowly lower to the ground. It shouldn't bother me that Deimos has dated so many guys–I mean, I'd expected as much, given his personality and general attractiveness–but it just confirms what I suspected: that he's way more experienced than I am. Which isn't hard to do given my serious lack of experience in general, and especially with guys, but the divide may be even wider than I thought.

So that's great. Because I wasn't out of my depth enough as it is, I guess.

The glass doors slide open and we step out of the terrible broiling box–into the coolest air I've felt in ages. I close my eyes and take a deep, slow breath as my sweat chills on my skin. Stars, it feels good.

"Told you it'd be cooler down here." Deimos pats my shoulder. "Are you okay now?"

I swallow and nod. "*Shae*. I'm okay. Thank you."

"It's nothing." He smiles and lowers his arm off my shoulders as a woman approaches us. She wears her hair short, like Eljan military-cut short. She also wears what I'm pretty sure is the same uniform all the guys wear here, which is interesting. And she's tall–like, taller than me.

"Deimos, it's wonderful to see you again." She smiles a bright smile that's almost–flirtatious? Which is weird because I didn't think Deimos liked women. Then again, he never actually said that, and I never actually asked. Maybe she doesn't know? But she knows Deimos, which means she probably knew him before I knew him, so that seems unlikely. Maybe I'm just reading too much into this. It's just a smile. She's allowed to smile without it meaning anything.

Fuck. This is ridiculous. Stop being jealous.

"Dara, it's wonderful to see you." Deimos smiles back. "And might I add, you look fantastic–and happy. I'm glad to see you doing so well."

It takes everything in me not to narrow my eyes at him. *Am* I reading too much into this?

Maybe they're friends?

Her smile widens. "Thank you, I appreciate it, truly. I really am very happy. And *Sira* Eros, it's an honor, truly, to meet you." She bows. "My name is Dara, as Deimos said. And you must be Mal."

"*Shae*," Mal says casually. "Um. Good to meet you."

"I'm glad you've all come down." Dara looks at me. "We certainly have a lot to discuss. But before I begin, I'd like to introduce you to my team."

"Sounds good to me," I say, and Dara nods, turns around, and starts down the long aisle running down the center of the giant room.

"Wait, *she's* the techie you dated?" Kosim hisses to Deimos.

Deimos grins. "Close, but not quite. I dated her twin brother, who also worked here for a time until he transferred to a facility in A'Sharo."

Kosim sighs. "Of course you did."

Someone Deimos dated transferred to A'Sharo. Where Deimos lived. That sounds like a serious relationship thing—unless it was a coincidence. Was it a coincidence?

I glance at Deimos. Somehow I doubt it was a coincidence.

Fucken—stop. I need to stop.

Deimos smirks and we follow her a decent way down the room, through a projection wall with text I can't read scrolling endlessly into the steel floor. The partitioned area has a bunch of different—stations, I guess—each with more glasses than one person could ever need and all sorts of different tools I don't recognize. They look complicated. Like something you might expect to see in a hospital or some kinduv engineering room.

Dara's team has, like, twenty people, and I definitely don't remember most of their names, though they all introduce themselves and say how great it is to meet me. It's weird, being in a room of Sepharon who genuinely seem not to hate me. But then again, they could all just be good actors. They know they're stuck with me, so in their place, I'd pretend to be nice and happy about my appointment, too.

Still. Even if it's all fake, it's a nicer introduction than I'm used to getting.

"So where are we with the nanites?" I ask when all the intros are over.

"Excellent question," Dara says. "We're now at a point of convergence where we have to make a decision as to which direction to go in—something I was going to brief you on anyway, so it's really rather convenient you came to us." She smiles.

"Um. Okay. So what's the decision you have to make?"

"In terms of reestablishing the planetary nanite system, we have to decide what to prioritize. We can either focus on trying to revive the damaged and dead nanites–which is faster, but could cause problems if the damage is too severe and they malfunction, but unfortunately, we won't really know the extent of the damage until we attempt to bring them back online. Alternatively, we could prioritize making and coding new nanites, but doing so will take much longer, as will distributing them worldwide."

I hesitate. Speed is obviously pretty blazing important here, especially given the disease and the imminent famine in the Southern regions–Ona included. But then again, trying to rush this could cause its own problems. "What kinduv glitches are we talking?"

Dara purses her lips. "It's difficult to say and would vary depending on the coding. For something less consequential, patchy sand screens, for example. For something more important . . . " She lifts a shoulder. "Partial healing jobs at best for the medical nanites–worsening damage at worst. Or crop assistance nanites that malfunction and kill the crops or leave them diseased. Or rotten or poisonous flash-grown food."

I grimace. "And the time difference between the two options?"

"If all goes well, we could have the first wave of revived nanites working by the start of the next term. If we have to start from the beginning, I don't imagine we'll have anything ready for public consumption before the end of the cycle. At best, *maybe* we'll have something ready by . . . Hana? Djelo?"

I scratch the back of my head and glance at Deimos. Hana and Djelo are half a cycle away. I'm not sure we can wait that long, but then again, the possible glitches sound . . . not great.

"Would it be possible to test revived nanites here first before attempting to distribute anything?" Deimos asks.

"Absolutely," Dara says. "It'll delay the process some but I'd certainly recommend that."

"Okay," I say. "Can we split the team? Half the team works on reviving the crop assistance and medical nanites, and we'll see how that goes in the lab, while the rest works on getting new nanites up and running. I get it'll probably take longer that way, but at least if one process fails, we'll have a backup."

Dara nods. "My team isn't the only one working on it, so that's definitely possible. I'll speak to the other team leaders and we'll split up and do that immediately."

"Thank you."

Dara bows and turns to address her team while Deimos, Mal, our bodyguards, and I slip through the projected partition and back into the main room. My chest aches with the weight of the decision I've made and the possible consequences—but I've made a decision.

I'm actually doing this.

Deimos's fingers graze my lower back, sending a wave of tingling heat up my spine. "You did great," he says with a smile. "I'm proud of you."

I smile back. It feels good being here—surrounded by people treating me as their leader, and I couldn't have anyone better at my side, helping me through it.

Maybe I can actually do this.

"*Shae*," Mal yawns. "You did great, congratulations. Now do you think you could use those impressive *Sira* powers to get us something to eat? I'm starving."

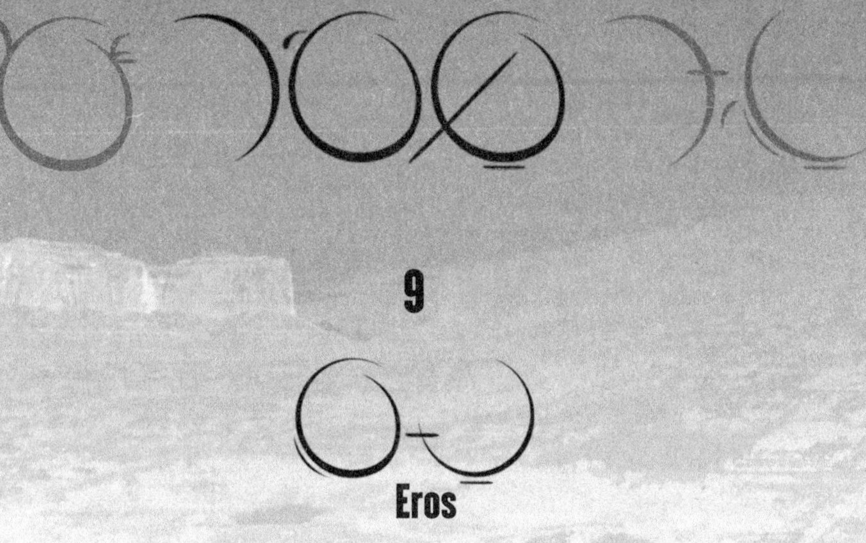

9

Eros

Immune boosters, it turns out, aren't like the prickly gel-patch things they've slapped on me before. Instead they're little, fist-length metal canisters with awkward mouthpieces sticking out of them and Sepharon writing on them I can't read.

"What am I supposed to do with this?" I turn the canister over in my fingers.

"You breathe it in," Zarana says. "Put the entire mouthpiece is your mouth, bite down on it, close your lips around it, then breathe in through the mouthpiece until it clicks and the medicine stops releasing."

"Uh-huh."

"It's easy." Deimos grabs one, puts it in his mouth, and demonstrates. He only breathes in for less than half a mo before the canister clicks and he pulls it out of his mouth. "See? Done."

The mouthpiece feels awkward behind my lips but I do as instructed, and yeah, it's easy, but it also makes the room smell like soap and my mouth taste like . . . something bitter and gross.

"That's disgusting." Mal wrinkles his nose.

I grimace and Deimos laughs. "Shae, it doesn't taste the best."

"But now you're all hopefully protected," Zarana says. "Or at the very least you're less likely to fall ill."

"These are getting distributed throughout Asheron, right?" I ask.

Zarana nods. "We're working with the guard to get it done. The apprentices will all be spending the set in the city with guards to make sure everyone gets inoculated, and they'll also be distributing face masks to anyone who hasn't already received one." She picks up a canister and points to the mouthpiece. "These are also designed to work with the face masks–it clips in and releases the medicine into the mask, so no one will have to take off their mask and risk contamination in the city."

I nod. "Good. And the quarantines?"

"Established in all eight of Asheron's hospitals, in addition to the twenty centers we've set up throughout the city. So far people seem to be reporting quickly. They trust us to do our best to help them."

I nod. "Have we been able to help them?"

"Well, the masks have helped and the immune boosters will as well."

"*Naï*, I mean . . ." I sigh and run a hand through my hair. "Has anyone been able to survive this yet?"

"Ah." Zarana grimaces. "Well, we have about twenty fatalities, but we have a pretty sizable group who've been sick for over thirty-six hours and haven't succumbed to the disease yet. It seems some are more equipped to fight it than others. We're doing the best we can to give them all the best conditions possible to fight this while the research team continues to try to develop a cure."

I nod and Deimos touches my shoulder. "You should record a message to send out to the capital citizens. They're hearing updates from the feeds, of course, but it'd help them to see you're invested and paying attention to what's happening and you care and are involved."

I frown. "A message saying what?"

"You could talk about the importance of voluntary quarantine," Zarana says. "Reminding everyone how essential it is to keep each other healthy and report people acting strangely or who you suspect might be ill to the hospitals to get them help. We're also setting up decontamination centers throughout the city today and tomorrow, so you could encourage them to use those when they've been out of their homes for extended periods of time, or if they suspect they've been exposed to someone ill."

"A lot of it is common sense," Deimos says. "But the point is to make it clear you're not ignoring what's happening and you care about making things better for them."

This still terrifies me—the whole *talk and the world will listen* thing. Going from permanently ignored to permanently watched isn't something that's just gonna feel fine overnight, I know that. But every step like this still turns my insides to goo.

Still. This is my life now. "All right." I take a deep breath. "Let's do it."

We record in a random hallway, which Deimos suggests because recording from the throne room might serve as a less than positive reminder that I'm safely tucked away in the palace while everyone else is stuck at the outbreak site. I do my thing, covering all the points Zarana and Deimos suggested, while Mal sits across the hallway looking bored as fuck and Deimos watches me with a gaze that makes the air dance on my skin.

I'm like two mos away from blushing when the recording ends and Deimos smiles at me.

"And *that*," he says as the guide flies away, "was the undeniable first address of a *Sira*. Well done, Eros." He slips his arm around my shoulders and my heart thrums in my chest as he brings his lips so close to my ear his breath warms my skin. "I knew you'd be a great *Sira*."

10

Kora

On the sixth set since Eros's coronation, Uljen and I stand in the center of Vejla, handing out immune boosters to the endless swell of people crowding as close as the guards will allow them to to grab their own preventative. And see us, too, I suppose.

It was Uljen's idea for us to help hand them out in person–something I never would have considered without his suggestion. But it's a good idea; it shows the people we don't consider ourselves too removed from them to be directly involved. It says we care and shows Eljans I'm keeping my promise of trying to do things differently than my first attempt at ruling.

And I think it's working. Even though these circumstances are far from ideal, the people approach us with smiles and leave with thankful bows and nods.

It's a relief to be out here without people screaming for my head.

Vejla's center isn't what it used to be–though the buildings here are tall and covered in detailed engravings and mosaics, layered with history, they're also some of the oldest buildings in Vejla and the age shows. I hadn't prioritized the maintenance of the city as I should have, and though I attempted to change that shortly before the disaster of my lifecycle celebration, the city will need a serious infrastructure project to really bring it back to what it was. And though that may not be a top priority right now–not while our crops our dying and I have to focus on keeping my people fed and healthy–it *is* something I want to get done. Even if just for morale.

This is Vejla, and I won't let it crumble.

"Thank you, *el Avra*," a woman says with a smile and a bow as I hand her a booster. I smile back and reach into the tub of boosters–my fingers glance against Uljen's and a spark shoots into my elbow. I gasp and yank my hand back, my face warming as Uljen grins.

"Don't worry, *el Avra*," Uljen says. "I don't bite unless you want me to."

My lips part and my face is baking in the suns and he just . . . he really just said that. To me.

Uljen laughs. "I apologize, that was forward. I don't mean to make you uncomfortable."

I snap my mouth closed, grab a booster, and mutter, "I'm not uncomfortable," even as the imagine of him nipping my shoulder sets my face on fire.

"*Naï*? Are you sure?" he teases.

I ignore him and smile at the next people who approach–two teen girls around my age, holding hands. As I hand them boosters, the taller of the two bounces on her toes. "Can I just say–I'm so glad you're back. It's amazing seeing someone like us ruling."

Their words aren't ones I ever expected to hear, but I'd certainly hoped and dreamed and prayed I would, especially when I was young. And hearing them now, after everything—it's a cool drink under the inferno of the twin suns. And it spreads a smile so wide across my face my cheeks hurt.

"I'm glad to hear it," I say. "I hope I'll make you both proud."

"I'm sure you will," the shorter girl says. Both bow and they quickly leave, boosters in hand.

The line of people waiting for their boosters snakes side to side across the main street and far beyond what I can see, even with more than thirty of us handing out boosters together. It's going to be a long set, but this—this is what I became *Avra* for. To help my people. To earn their respect and loyalty.

To become better than I was.

11

Eros

It's been a long four sets—and an even longer six sets since my coronation. Quarantines, boosters, masks, people sick and dying, the complex shut down to everyone who isn't essential to keep the capitol running, multiple decontaminations a set, and the ever-present terrifying question of what will happen if one of us gets sick . . .

I don't want to even consider the possibility of Mal or Deimos ill. I need them healthy and happy like I need food, like I need water, like I need air. I can't lose anyone else. I can't.

I won't survive it again.

But so far, at least, everyone seems fine. Or at least, everyone seems healthy—and Mal's started getting lessons on using a walking stick, which he carries around everywhere now. Though he's also made a point of telling me he's in grave danger of dying of boredom, but you know. I'll take that over risking him getting sick any mo.

Even better, Tol says they have a team almost done putting together the communication network. They think they'll have it ready to unveil to the public after we get back from the wedding.

Which means, just for now at least, on a hovercraft on the way to Daïvi, I can relax. Or try to, anyway.

"So this thing flies?" Mal peers out the window of the hovercraft skeptically, pushing his darkening glasses higher on the bridge of his nose. "Like a bird? Does it have flapping wings or something?"

"It has wings, but they don't flap," Deimos says. "It works more like the beds and tables. They float, *shae*? It's similar technology but much, much stronger."

"Hm." Mal flops back in his seat. "At least the chairs are comfy."

He's not wrong. I don't know if all hovercraft are like this, but this one is the definition of luxury. The seats are large and so cushioned it's how I'd imagine sitting on a cloud would be like. The windows are large and so clear it almost looks like there are missing sections of wall. And between each group of four chairs–two on each side, facing each other–is a floating circular table-like surface. Then there are the glasses in the hidden pockets on each chair's arm, plus the glass embedded in the table. And there are so many rows that even though there are ten of us total–Deimos, Mal and me, each of our personal guards, plus Mija and three extra guards–we all have room to spread out and then some.

And that's before we get to the food selection–there's a menu I can't read on each glass, but it has pictures and everything looks amazing. And there are drinks–mostly really strong-smelling *ufrike*. And herbs. And Deimos said we won't need to use them, but there are apparently bedrooms somewhere, too.

Somehow I don't think all hovercrafts are like this but you never know.

My glass hums—Kora again. I wave my hand over it, rejecting the call. I'm not going to listen to her justification for why I should let her murderous brother slide. Or why fucken Dima is more important than supporting me.

Deimos slides his hand over mine and stars dance on my chest. He pushes the glass away and smiles at me. "You look like you're thinking too much."

I run my free hand through my hair. "Probably. How long will it take to get to Daïvi?"

"Not too long, four segments or so. Which means you have four segments to relax and try to breathe."

A low hum fills the hovercraft and the walls and seats and floor *vibrate.* Is it supposed to do that? Is that normal?

"I know what you're thinking," Deimos says. "And *shae*, this is all normal, don't panic." He grins.

"You're enjoying this, aren't you?"

"Enjoying what? Flying?" He leans close—so close his lips nearly brush my ear as his hot breath washes over my cheek. "Or do you mean seeing you slightly ill at ease? Because you *are* irresistibly cute when you're a touch nervous."

His words hum against my ear and trickle down my spine and settle—hot—between my legs. I try to brush it off with a laugh and nudge him away with my shoulder but I sortuv doubt he's going to fall for that.

"Hey," Mal says, propping his glasses onto the top of his head. "If you two are going to flirt for four segs, I'm going to sit in another row."

I open my mouth to tell him we'll behave and he can stay, but Deimos puts his hand over my mouth and grins at Mal. "You may want to move then."

My whole body warms and prickles. Mal groans, but he's smirking when he slides off his seat and moves down the aisle, feeling his way past a couple rows with his stick before he plops down next to Mija, who grins at him and ruffles his hair.

Well. Okay then.

Deimos moves his hand and grins at me. "Well, that's adorable. Your face turns more red than purple when you blush."

"Shut up." I run my hands down my face and sigh with a smile. My smile fades, though, as I glance at Mal several rows ahead of us. "You don't think he's actually upset about moving, do you?"

Deimos snorts. "*Naï.* Even if we weren't flirting, he doesn't want to be stuck at your side at all times anyway. He'll enjoy having a row's luxuries to himself, trust me."

I hesitate, but Deimos touches my shoulder. "You should know, *shae*? When your brother began dating his future wife, did *you* want to be stuck with them all hours of the set?"

Stars and suns alive. It feels like so long ago when Day and Jessa started seeing each other, but Deimos has a point. Day was unbearable in those early sets, pining over Jessa when they were apart and swooning over her when they were together. Granted, I was a lot younger than Mal is when that happened, but I definitely remember hating it.

"You . . . have a point."

"I know." Deimos smirks. "I've lost count how many times I ended up stuck with one of my mooning brothers for long, unwanted segments. Besides." He threads his fingers between mine–his unmarked fingers slipping over and next to my inked ones–and rests his head on my shoulder. "I'm tired of holding back and being *professional* in front of everyone. We finally have some time away from the public or political eye and I'm going to take advantage."

I smile and lightly squeeze his hand. He squeezes back. And this–this slow, careful thing unfolding between us–it feels good. It's in the pressure of his weight against my arm and the warmth of his cheek on my shoulder. It's in the light touch of his fingers between mine, the circles he's tracing on the back of my hand with his thumb.

It's quiet, and soft, and feels like breathing–really breathing freely–for the first time.

I don't know where this thing between us going, but I want more than anything to find out. And I'm going to enjoy every breath of it along the way.

12

Kora

Daïvi's palace is nothing like Elja's or Asheron's, which share a somewhat common architectural aesthetic of mosaics, detailed engravings, and sandstone walls. But Daïvi doesn't have a desert, and its capital, Vin Eja, looks little like Vejla and Asheron. It has its own unique beauty.

The palace itself is made to look like a mountain, a nod to the mountainous region of Daïvi's north, which is considered a blessed region. The walls and floors are made of huge, polished slabs the size of a grown man of *sennak*, a light blue rock webbed with white and silver. Columns too thick for me to wrap my arms around and engraved with writings from the *Jorva* from top to bottom are spaced out down every hall, towering over me.

And the ceilings here–so high it almost feels as though the palace has its own artificial sky.

"This is amazing," Uljen says softly, craning his neck to peer at the ceiling. "Is the ceiling engraved, as well?"

I squint at the shiny rock above us and hesitate. "Possibly? It's hard to tell from down here."

Uljen nods.

We move out of the dining hall's entrance as others crowd in behind us. The room, as enormous as it is, is already filling quickly with royals and upper-class citizens and likely Zek's relatives. Long, rectangular tables full of snack-like small dishes and drinks reach from one side of the room to the other. Enormous glowing geodes hang from the ceiling, filtering multicolored light into the room. Musicians at the far end of the room fill the dining hall with rhythmic drumming as dancers perform in front of them.

It's all incredible and uniquely Daïvi in a way that warms me; Mamae always loved the culture of her home. We didn't get to visit Daïvi as much as we would've liked, but I'll never forget the stories she told me about her childhood and the way her eyes lit up the few times we *could* visit.

Daïvi may not be my home, but it is a part of my history.

And yet, even with that history, even with the part of me that wants to relax and just enjoy this, a sinking part of me knows Eros is going to walk through those giant doors at some point and I'll have to face him.

Eros, whose home I destroyed.

Who saved my life.

Who I kissed and turned away from.

Who I apologized too late to, and who I lost.

Who wants to execute my brother in his territory. Because *sha*, there'd be a trial, but we both know Dima would be saddled with both his own crimes and Roma's in an Asheron court—and that could only end with my brother on his knees before an executioner.

Maybe I bear some responsibility for Eros's apathy regarding Dima's well-being—after all, it was in saving my life that Dima captured Eros and tortured him for sets on end.

But I wasn't expecting Eros to agree to my request for Dima's sake–I'd hoped he would've respected my wishes for mine. But apparently not.

And now, if I'm being honest, I don't really want to see him at all.

I grab a glass of spiced *azuka*–a Daïvi special. Unlike the stone flutes in Elja, the cups here are made of glass, probably at least in part to show off the beautiful drinks. In the glass, the spiced *azuka* looks like a deep blue sky–if skies were blue–scattered with silver stars that swirl around when I move the cup or sip the drink.

I close my eyes and take a deep breath as I take a gulp. The warmth trickles into my chest as the spicy sweetness lingers on my tongue. I'm not going to drink too much–wedding or not, I have to keep my wits and represent Elja the best I can–but maybe the drink will dull the anxious edges of my breaths.

"Kora."

I open my eyes. Uljen is smiling at me and has his hand extended. I'm not sure why he's extending his hand. Unless . . .

"Dance with me?" Uljen nods to the space in front of the drummers, where people are dancing in long rows, arms intertwined over each other's shoulders.

"You know how to dance *balaika*?" I ask with a raised eyebrow.

"Not really," he admits with a shrug. "But they look like they're having fun, and I'm sure you'll teach me."

I smile and take his hand. "I'd be happy to."

We join the last row, with my left arm over the shoulder of a blushing girl around my age, laughing as she dances, and my right over Uljen's. Uljen slides his arm over mine and grins as we move side to side–right for eight steps, left for eight, right for seven, left for seven–faster and faster until we start over at eight again. The steps are easy enough and Uljen catches on quickly, whooping with the others, his face lit up with the biggest smile I've ever seen from him.

It's contagious. Soon, I'm smiling and laughing and whooping, too, as my feet move faster and my breaths grow hot and the drumbeat pounds in my chest like an extra heartbeat, but stronger, making my bones shake and head vibrate, until the song ends and we break apart with cheers and whistles.

I'd forgotten how loud, carefree, and full of energy the Daïvi are. It reminds me of mamae, with her endless smiles and the way she'd tease father's stern demeanor. It reminds me of the night she taught Dima and me how to dance *balaika* when we were eight or so, arm in arm, dancing until we were a breathless, giggling heap on the floor. I love it.

"Are you all right?" Uljen frowns and hesitantly reaches toward me, then stops. "You're crying."

I wipe my thumbs under my eyes to clear away the tears hopefully without ruining my liner. "I'm fine," I say with a smile. "Just remembering. I'm happy."

"Okay." He smiles and glances around as a new drumbeat begins and the crowd pairs up. "I don't know this dance either." He grins.

I laugh and take his hands. And we dance song to song, in pairs, in groups of four, in lines, moving with the thunder of drums echoing in our lungs and laughter in the air.

I can't remember the last time I've been able to unwind like this. Even at my lifecycle celebration, I was tight with nerves while anticipating the announcement of an engagement that never happened. But today isn't for me. Today is to celebrate someone else's happiness. And it feels so, so good to soak in the collective joy and celebrate together.

Long strands of Uljen's dark hair slip from his tie as he dances and sweat glistens on his bronze skin. His movements are occasionally slightly stiff, slightly careful–while he seems to have mastered walking without pause, I imagine dancing with a prosthetic leg takes some practice–but his smile is easy and free. I suspect I'm not the only one who hadn't been able to really let go like this in a long time–the relief and ecstasy is in his glistening eyes and the way he tosses his head back when he laughs and shouts with the crowd.

Kala, his happiness is radiant.

Then we do a turn and I catch a glimpse over Uljen's shoulder. To the entrance of the hall, where three familiar faces smother the laughter in my chest.

Eros, Deimos, and Mal are here.

And Eros is looking right at me.

13

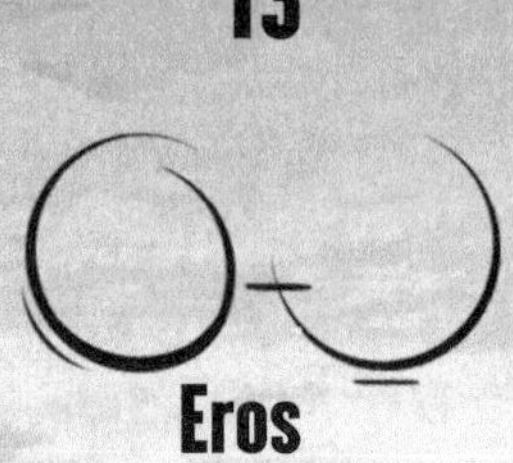

Eros

The last thing I want to be thinking about right now is Kora, so naturally she's the first one I see as we enter the hall. Miraculously, it looks like she's actually having fun–I was starting to think *fun* wasn't a language she'd learned–and even more surprisingly she's dancing with a guy. He has burn scars on his face, chest, and arm, so I'm pretty sure he's her new advisor or whatever.

Which–even though I'm irritated as fuck about this ridiculous Dima shit she's pulling–good. I'm glad she's moving on. I sure Voiding have.

Deimos's hand touches the small of my back, skipping warm sparks over my skin. I glance at him and he smiles, and then I'm smiling because it's impossible to see him smile and not smile back.

"This will be fun," Deimos says. "The Daïvi are my second favorite people to party with."

I smirk. "Second favorite?"

"Well, I'm partial to my own, of course." He grins and laughs a little. "But the Daïvi make a close second."

"I'll pretend I didn't hear that," a woman says, nearing us with a smirk. Her long brown hair is braided back and her eyes are just two colors–purple and blue. I haven't met her yet in person, but Deimos showed me *Avra* Riza's photo on the trip over.

"Heard what, *ol Avra*?" Deimos grins and bows, and so do Mal and I, although actually I'm not sure if I'm supposed to bow since I'm *Sira*, but uh, oh well. I'd rather be too polite than accidentally blaze someone off.

Riza bows to me and smiles. "It's an honor to have you in my home, *Sira* Eros. On behalf of my people, we welcome you with open arms to our illustrious territory."

It's still bizarre getting treated so well by other Sepharon. I keep waiting to get used to it, to hear *Sira* before my name like it isn't a tacked-on, mismatched piece. But so far, at least, the whole thing still feels artificial. Like some out-there fever dream, or some elaborate joke that'll end with me on my knees in the Arena and a crowd full of Sepharon laughing that I ever thought any of this was real, even for a mo.

But even though the disconnect is still there, I push it away and say what I'm supposed to. "Thank you."

Riza nods and her gaze catches on Deimos's hand still on my back. Her lips quirk into a smile as she extends her arm, gesturing to the huge hall in front of us. "Please enjoy the welcoming festivities as our final guests arrive. The ceremony will begin shortly."

"We intend to. Thank you." Deimos gently nudges me forward and I take Mal's shoulder as we move into the crowd.

I make a point not to look at the dance area where I last spotted Kora.

I don't want to see her.

Deimos, Mal, and I mingle. We kinduv don't have a choice—or at least, I don't, but Deimos and Mal choose to suffer through it with me, Deimos because he's Deimos and Mal I suspect mostly because he doesn't know the layout of the room and also we get cornered next to the table full of hand food, which is probably all the motivation Mal needs to put up with the political talk. He also "accidentally" nudges people with his stick when they get too close or crowd him, which I pretend not to notice. Just means he's fending for himself. Good.

I'm hungry, too, but eating and talking at the same time without being disgusting has never been a skill I mastered, so I ignore my stomach and focus on the warmth of Deimos's hand on my back instead. It's a little thing, a light pressure, but his determination to touch me however he can, whenever he can, is a constant reminder he's here. I don't have to face any of this alone. And it's enough to keep my breaths even and raging energy inside me calm.

We talk to more people than I could ever bother trying to remember the names of. Or rather, they talk to me, and I nod and comment when I can and mostly try to focus on just looking interested in between while the conversations drone from one to the other. Person to person, the topics are mostly the same: my new position, the nanites, the disease situation in Asheron, and my least favorite topic: my background.

"So it's true you grew up in the desert with the redblood rebels?" one girl asks, eyes wide and hand over her mouth like I just admitted something horrifying.

"With the human nomads, *sha*," I say. "Not the kinduv rebels you're likely thinking of, though. Mine are a peaceful people who try to keep to themselves."

She leans uncomfortably close and touches my arm, her voice dripping with false sincerity. "That must have been so hard." She doesn't care what my life was like. I'm just some sideshow to her.

To most of them, probably.

The truth is, it was hard, but not for any of the reasons she's thinking. It wasn't living off the desert (though I'll admit some cycles were better than others) or not having much in terms of technology, luxuries, or possessions that made things hard.

It was being seen as less than. Being treated like a freak at best and an enemy at worst. It was the hopelessness of knowing bone-deep I wouldn't get a happy ending, of knowing my best-case scenario was dying alone in my old age.

It wasn't until recently that I started to believe that last part might change. But just a cycle ago, I didn't just think those things, I was sure of them. The world wouldn't let me believe anything else.

I settle with, "It was a quiet life." I don't say *until Kora blazed everything up*, even though that's the truth.

"Your story is so inspiring, though," she says, and she's still touching my arm, and I don't know how to move away without seeming rude, and she's smiling at me and it's kinduv weird and making me prickly. And not in a good way.

When she finally leaves, Deimos is scowling. He runs his hand over my arm, where she was touching, like brushing away the residue of her fingers. Which I don't mind–that whole interaction felt gross–but even though Deimos didn't say a thing it seems to have instantly soured his mood.

"You okay?" I ask.

"She shouldn't have touched you," he mutters, running his hand over my arm one last time.

Before I can answer–or process–Riza interrupts with a smile and brings us to the table at the front of the room, the only horizontal table and the last one before the section of dancers and drummers. Riza has us sit next to her off the center of the table and Mal bobs his head to the music as Deimos and I talk to Riza and her husband, whose name I forget.

I'm not sure how long we talk and pick at food, but the whole time Deimos has his leg pressed against mine, and sometimes he rests his hand on mine and twines our fingers together for anyone to see. And it's a relief to be able to let him casually announce our–whatever we have–with quiet touches and glances and smiles. Everything with Kora was so hidden, so much denying and resisting and hating myself for wanting her despite all the shit she put me through.

But this feels so much better. This feels like breathing easy, as inevitable as falling asleep under the stars once was. And a part of me thrills at knowing Deimos *wants* our thing to be obvious to everyone, at seeing him unafraid to hold my hand or touch my back or stand and sit closer than friends ever would.

I honestly never thought I would get this. Someone like him wanting to be with someone like me. It always seemed like a fantasy for someone else, someone Sepharon or human but not both. But I'm here. This is real. He's real. And stars, it feels so good to be wanted.

After a bit, someone whispers something to Riza and she nods, stands, gestures for the drummers to quiet, and announces it's time for the ceremony to begin.

Time to watch two Sepharon men get married.

Fuck. Even the thought of it makes me smile.

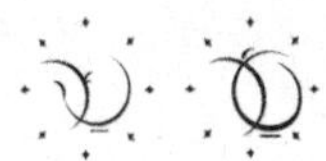

Weddings with nomads were always a modest thing. I mean, we didn't have a whole lot to begin with, so that was a big reason why, but we'd also break out the few luxuries we did have: our oldest, most carefully aged brews, an extra helping of meat for everyone–sometimes, if we were really lucky, someone would get their hands on some candy sold in the nearby cities through trade.

Before Day's wedding, he went out with a bunch of his soldiers and they hunted down a *kazim*–or sandcat, as we called them. He didn't tell anyone besides the people going with him–because if anyone had known, we obviously would've talked him out of it since it was dangerous as fuck–but he went out with a hunting party before the suns came up and came back midday dragging two adult cats behind them. I don't know how they did it without losing anyone, but somehow they returned with only a couple scrapes and bruises. Nol was horrified and told him off and Jessa cried because, let's be honest, he could have died pulling a stunt like that, but the next set at the wedding, no one cared about the danger because damn.

We ate really fucken well at his wedding.

But the ceremony itself was a simple thing. The couple would walk hand-in-hand around a fire seven times while vowing their love and devotion to each other. Then four people closest to them–two chosen by each person–would bless them in some way, with gifts, or a promise, or reassurance. At the end, the four people would form a circle around the couple while the couple kissed, making it official.

The whole thing never took long–I guess we were always pretty eager to get to the fun part after of eating and dancing and getting seriously drunk. It was simple, and sweet, and quick, and then we'd party all night as the couple disappeared together to spend their first night together.

Nomad weddings, apparently, are nothing like Sepharon weddings.

The dining hall, I guess, isn't elaborate enough of a venue, so we all go outside to a section behind the palace that's basically the biggest garden I've ever seen in my life–and that's saying something since Elja and Asheron's royal gardens are nothing to smirk at. The garden is about the size of the dining hall we were just in, and there are rows of cushions set out on the carved stones set up as a floor. The suns are setting, and glowing white flowers light a path down the center as everyone files in and sits in a row. Riza leads Deimos, Mal, and me to the front row, and I start to sit on my knees but Deimos nudges me and nods to Riza–she's sitting cross-legged on the cushion.

Thank the stars. I fucken hate sitting on my knees.

The trees surrounding the garden are tall, with dark purple, blue, and bright red trunks. Their leaves are white, gold, and orange, and they're weird shaped, kinda like a palm with star-like edges. Mountains paint the horizon ahead of us, bright white and blue against the deepening purple, blue, and pink sky. And though the suns haven't set yet, the moons are bright tonight, three out of four visible.

It's a nice spot. I get why they wanted to have the ceremony out here rather than in the palace. It's freer out here—and undeniably Daïvi.

Mal shivers next to me. "It's kinduv cold out here," he whispers.

I nod. I hadn't noticed it much when we arrived initially since it was still pretty warm, but now that the suns are setting, the temperature is definitely dropping with them. I can't imagine it gets *too* cold here this time of cycle, but it's not the southern heat we're used to, either.

"Do you want me to get something?" I whisper back.

Mal snorts. "No, I was just saying. I can handle it—it's not *that* bad."

I smirk, even as he crosses his arms over his chest and rubs his arms, just a little. But he's right. He'll be fine.

Two men walk down the center aisle—not Daven and Zek, but Riza's husband and another guy I'd guess might be Zek's dad. They step to the cleared section ahead of us, surrounded by elaborately set up flowers of all sizes and colors, then turn around and face us.

"Thank you so much for joining us, everyone," Riza's husband says. "Uma and I are delighted—and honored—to present to you our sons, who will be declaring their love and promising themselves to each other in front of their friends, family, honored guests, and of course, *Kala*."

Whoops and cheers break out in the crowd and I can't help but grin. The Daïvi are so energized and alive—I love it.

"I always joked with Zek he should marry up to increase his station," Uma says. "But when Zek told us he'd begun courting *Avra-kaï* Daven, his mother and I didn't believe him."

Snickers and laughter fills the air as Uma grins. "In fact, his mother and I were *so* sure it was just a fantasy, we teased him mercilessly about his *Avra-kaï* boyfriend until Zek arrived unannounced with Daven at his side. His mother was so shocked she fainted when she opened the door–fortunately I was there to catch her." He laughs with the crowd as Riza's husband–whose name I really need to learn–snickers next to him.

"Zek has always been a very respectable and hardworking young man, in the time that I've known him," Riza's husband says. "Riza and I are honored–and ecstatic–to welcome such an upstanding and genuine man to our family. We're also relieved the politics haven't scared him away yet–and after tonight, he'll be stuck with us." He winks as the crowd laughs louder. I smirk. In a way, I can kinduv relate to Zek–I may not have gotten pulled into the politics through a wedding, but the whole royalty thing is foreign to me, too. I don't know that I'll get a chance to talk to him today, but I might like to.

"In any case"–Riza's husband waves his hand, gesturing for Zek and Daven to come forward–"Let's get started, shall we? Come on over, my sons."

Zek and Daven walk down the center aisle hand-in-hand, grinning as people sitting along the aisle throw flower petals and leaves at them. They look so fucken happy together, faces flushed, laughter in their eyes as petals catch on their clothes and cover the aisle. It's sweet, seeing them like this, like nothing in the world could steal the light from their smiles.

I've never felt that kinduv happiness.

When they finish walking down the aisle, they step in front of their dads and face us. *Avra* Riza and another woman–Zek's mom, probably–walk up to the guys and kiss both of their cheeks.

Then Riza holds her hand out and Zek's mom gives her a–

Whoa, wait, is that a knife?

It's a knife.

I glance at Deimos, but he's watching calmly, like this is no big deal, and like knives at weddings are totally normal so I guess in Sepharon culture they are. Mal taps my arm and I lean close to him.

"I don't think I'm seeing right," he whispers. "What is she holding?"

I hesitate, then whisper back, "A knife."

Mal arches an eyebrow, then mutters "never mind" and leans away again.

Both guys turn up their left hands, palms up, and Riza slices each of their hands. They barely even flinch. Then Zek and Daven clasp their left arms together–Daven holding his arm on top, to the crook of Zek's elbow, Zek holding his arm firmly against Daven's, gripping Daven's elbow with his bloody hand. Almost like they're going to shake, except they don't–instead, Riza pulls two long silky strips of fabric, one blue, one white–Daïvi's colors–and wraps their arms together.

Oh wait. This is familiar.

This is kinduv like what Kora did when I took a blood oath to protect her.

"I, Daven Rin Sejo da Daïvi, take you, Zek Amar da Daïvi, as my chosen husband. I swear on our blood I will care for you and love you on our best sets and our worst sets, on the sets we're at our happiest and sets we can't find anything to agree on. I swear to be by your side and lift you up for all the segments of my life, and to be the best version of myself possible. I swear this in front of *Kala*, in front of our family, in front of our friends, as I declare you, Zek, the love of my life and partner of my soul. I love you and I will always love you."

Someone sniffles next to me. Deimos flushes when I glance at him, and he rubs his teary eyes. "Quiet," he whispers with another sniffle. "That was beautiful."

I smile and slide my arm around his waist, pulling him closer. He leans against me, ever so slightly.

"I, Zek Amar da Daïvi, take you, Daven Rin Sejo da Daïvi, as my chosen husband. I swear on our blood to make you laugh, to make you smile, to do everything in my power to make you feel as loved, wanted, and happy as you make me. I swear to be your ear when you need to vent, to be your mouth when you can't say what you need to say, to be your eyes when you need someone to look out for you. I swear this in front of *Kala*, in front of our family, in front of our friends, as I–" Zek's voice cracks. He pauses and presses his fist to his smiling mouth as he takes a deep breath and blinks his glinting eyes. "As I declare you, Daven, the love of my life and partner of my soul. I love you and I will always love you."

Deimos isn't the only one sniffling anymore–along with teary-eyed people in the crowd, Zek's mom is outright sobbing in front of everyone as she hugs her husband, but she's smiling, too.

A guy walks over to Zek and Daven, holding one of those tattoo ring things. He unwraps the cloth around Zek and Daven's arms, but the about-to-be-husbands don't unclasp their arms. Instead, the guy clasps the ring around both of their arms and holds it in place as the edges light up and it starts marking them.

I guess it makes sense the Sepharon would get markings for this, too. I wonder what it'll look like when they pull apart.

After a few mos, the ring stops glowing and the guy pulls it off. Daven and Zek slide their hands down each other's arms until they're holding hands and have a bloody, purple streak over their skin, then they hold their clasped hands over their heads and everyone bursts into cheers and applause.

And just like that, Daven and Zek are married.

Deimos slips his hand into mine again, squeezes tight, and traces my mark with his thumb. And with Daven and Zek holding their bleeding hands together and grinning, Zek laughing through his tears, with Deimos holding my hand tight and sitting so close I can smell the sweet spice of his skin, something deep inside me aches.

I never let myself want this before. I never let myself imagine what it might be like to swear myself to someone and promise to spend our lives together. I never let that be even a fantasy, not for me, because I never believed it could be. It was impossible, so there wasn't any point in wanting it.

But now I do. I want it more than I've ever wanted anything.

And it's terrifying.

14

Kora

Though Uljen and I sit with the other royalty at the evening meal—as is expected, because I'm *Avra* again and Uljen is my lead advisor—I make a point to sit nowhere near Eros. Partially because the center of the table is reserved for those close to *Avra* Riza and partially because I want to enjoy my food before I confront him in private.

Because I have to confront him. Unfortunately.

Still, knowing what I have to do makes it hard to pay attention to the conversation and laughter and smiles. This is a happy event—as it should be, and I *am* happy for Daven and Zek, truly—but Eros still wants to execute my brother in Asheron and I can't let this opportunity in person to try to make him see reason slide. He can refuse to take my glass calls however much he wants—and so far he's ignored my calls twice—but he can't ignore a confrontation in person. And I won't let something as vital as my brother's life go without a fight.

"You seem tense," Uljen whispers to me. "People are noticing. Try to smile a little, *sha*?"

I glare at him. "Did you really just tell me to smile?"

"I . . ." He sighs and runs a hand through his hair, jostling some strands out of his tie. "I didn't mean it like that. Just that you look ready to murder someone at a celebratory dinner party."

I take a deep breath and relax my shoulders. I glance at Uljen and I'm still not smiling, but it must be at least a little better because he laughs quietly and shakes his head.

Come to think of it, that probably means I look worse. But his exasperated laugh is contagious and tugs the corners of my lips into a small–very small–smile. Better than nothing.

Eventually, the meal ends, and Daven and Zek thank everyone for celebrating with them and welcome everyone to stay or go as they please as the festivities continue for the rest of the night. Most people go back to dancing or chatting or partaking in more drinks and herbs–or all three. Eros gets up with Deimos and Mal and they walk somewhat aimlessly around the room, talking as Mal bobs his head to the drums and Deimos gestures animatedly.

I suppose that's as good as it's going to get. It's loud enough in this room that few will be able to overhear what we're speaking about, anyway.

My stomach is a fist when I approach him. My lungs are stone and my hands are brittle leaves ready to break. I'm not sure how to even begin to convince him to change his mind, but I need to figure it out, and I need to figure it out now.

I can't let him take Dima.

"Eros," I say by way of greeting. "Deimos, Mal, good to see you."

"Hi, Kora." Mal smiles.

Deimos and Eros look distinctly less pleased to see me, but Deimos at least fakes the smile well. "Evening, *el Avra*."

His use of *el Avra*, rather than my name, is deliberate. It's a step back into formality, a reminder that our relationship is no longer something as simple and carefree as friendship.

That's not new information, but it still plucks a twinge of sadness inside me nevertheless.

"I'm going to skip the formalities, as I suspect they won't be heard or appreciated anyway," I say. "I need to talk to you about Dima, Eros. I know you believe your trying my brother in Asheron is the best thing for everyone, but my people–"

"I'm not doing this," Eros cuts in. "If you want to talk business, you can wait until I get back to the capital."

I scowl. "*Naï*, I can't. This isn't something we can just push off, Eros. My brother's life isn't a bargaining chip for us to dangle whenever it suits us best. He *must* be tried in Vejla, where he will get a *fair* hearing and *Eljans* will decide what to–where are you going?"

Eros has turned his back to me and is headed for the door, his hand on Mal's shoulder.

Heat burns like a fire licking at my heart. He's ignoring me. That *kafran* bastard is actually just walking away like I'm not speaking to him. I step forward. "Where are you going? We're not done discussing–"

"Kora." Deimos steps toward me and Uljen moves forward, arms crossed over his chest, almost like he's trying to protect me. Which is unnecessary because Deimos would never hurt me, but also–is Uljen getting protective of me? He's my advisor, not my bodyguard, so that's not his job and yet . . . I think I like it.

Deimos eyes Uljen and I touch Uljen's arm. "It's fine," I say. "Deimos isn't a threat."

Uljen purses his lips and doesn't move back but nods.

"Now isn't the time," Deimos says. "As Eros said, if you'd like to discuss something political with him, it'll have to wait until we return to Asheron, which I assure you won't be long."

"My brother's *life* isn't political," I seethe.

"But what happens to him, and *where* it happens to him, is." Deimos shrugs. "The answer isn't changing. Enjoy the rest of your night."

And just like that he turns around and follows Eros and Mal out.

I clench my fists and bite my tongue. I could scream and rage and demand we speak now–but it wouldn't do any good. Eros has made up his mind. And making a scene here won't help my position.

"Are you all right?" Uljen asks carefully.

"*Naï*," I say. Then, with a sigh, "*Sha*."

Uljen grimaces but nods. "You're doing the right thing. I think Eros will cave, even if only to avoid a war. The last thing he wants right now is more conflict. I'm sure he's already overwhelmed with the responsibilities of his new role, not to mention the crisis with the nanites and sickness."

"I hope you're right," I whisper, but the truth is, I'm really not sure he is. Because maybe Eros wants to avoid conflict, but maybe he also wants to be able to claim a victory of some kind on *something*. And if that something happens to also equal getting revenge for what my brother did to him, all the better.

Eros has too much motivation to fight my request. And he must know if it comes down to it, Elja simply can't fight Asheron.

He would crush us, and me with them.

15

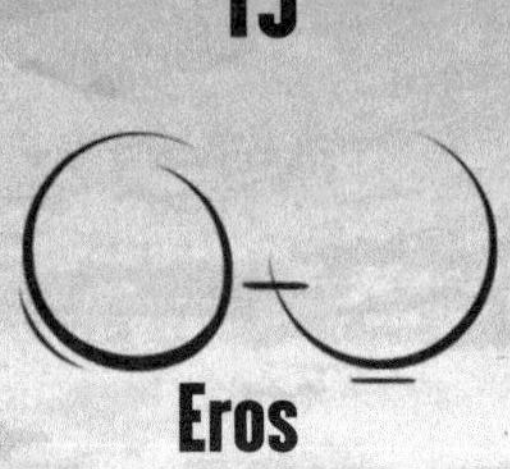

Eros

Deimos and I bring Mal to his guest room—we've had a long set and the poor kid is blazing exhausted. But after Kora confronting me like that, I'm anything but—I'm amped, and still kinduv blazed, and even if I weren't an insomniac, I doubt I'd have been able to get much sleep anyway.

Which is fine because Deimos doesn't seem too interested in sleeping either.

"We won't be here much longer," Deimos says, "so I'd love to show you around Vin Eja to see the night street performers the city is famous for. They're truly incredible and I think you'll like them." He smiles. "What do you say?"

I shrug. "Sounds good to me."

Deimos grins, takes my hand, and we're off with Fejn and Kosim at our heels. Down five sets of stairs (stars, the Daïvi fucken love their blazing stairs) and up to the front entrance with the enormous, thick double stone gray-blue doors. But then he pauses and glances at me.

"Is um . . ." He hesitates, then lifts our clasped hands a bit. "Is it okay for me to hold your hand in public? There will be orb guides out there following us around that'll likely broadcast everything we do."

I smile and lift a shoulder. "It's fine with me if it's fine with you. I don't mind people knowing you're more to me than my advisor."

The grin that takes over Deimos's face causes my breath to catch in my chest. He lights up like I just told him the best news in the world, and it feels so, so good to know I did that. I made him that happy.

"We're really doing this," Deimos says. It's not a question, not really, not anymore. But I grin and squeeze his hand and answer anyway.

"*Shae*. We're really doing this."

Deimos hugs me so fast I can't prepare for it. It's a quick, tight hug with his face pressed into the crook of my neck and his smile imprinting into my skin.

Then he lets go and pulls me into the night.

Vin Eja is nothing like Velja or Asheron. There aren't spires and mosaics, slanted roofs and sand. Here, every building is like a mini mountain–made of stone of all colors, textures, and sizes, every building a different shade. There's so much *color*–even the streets go from bright blue to neon green to light purple to suns-tinted orange. The walking paths alongside the road are the same way–a riot of color, except mixed together, with bricks of pink, blue, green, yellow, red all laid next to each other in no apparent pattern or order. It's so unlike anything I've ever seen, like someone built the city out of every color available in the universe.

And even at night, the city is alive with light, with laughter, with music. Everything is so energized, so awake, it's like the air itself is dancing around us. The energy is contagious—it gathers on my lips and has me tapping the fingers of my free hand on my thigh.

"This is amazing," I say. "Everyone seems so . . . happy."

"*Shae*, they smoke a lot here," Deimos says, and I'm not sure if he's joking. "I do love this city. Never fails to put me in a great mood. Come."

We take a few turns around vibrant buildings selling herbs, instruments, food, herbs—actually, come to think of it, there really *are* a lot of people smoking all over the place, which is kinduv hilarious—until we reach a long, extra-wide street full of people instead of ports. All along both sides of the street are people gathered in groups around performers; a group of dancers performing some kinduv traditional stomping chant dance thing; a woman blowing rainbow fire; two men balancing on their hands and bending their bodies in ways that should be impossible, mirror images of each other. The crowds cheer and clap and shout their approval.

But the thing that catches me most is Deimos and I aren't the only two of the same gender holding hands. There are men and women and people in between walking with their arms around each other and their fingers tangled together like it's the simplest, most natural thing. And it is—nothing has ever felt more natural than being with Deimos—but seeing so many like us out in the open, unafraid is just . . .

I haven't seen that before. And it feels so fucken freeing to see it casually like this. Like I can breathe—really breathe—for the first time in my life. Like I have nothing to hide or be afraid of.

It's amazing.

Deimos and I watch more performers than I can count, and he showers them all with more credits than I've ever seen in my life. People grin at us wherever we go–bowing and nodding and glancing at our held hands with bright smiles. Several not-unattractive people of various genders wink or whistle at Deimos and he grins and winks back which . . . I'm not sure how I feel about, but it seems like a casual, meaningless gesture to him. A group of kids run over and ask if they can take a picture with us, and though Kosim and Fejn step forward, I tell them it's fine, so the kids' personal orb guide takes a picture for them. Which then leads to like fifteen mos of people taking pictures with us until Deimos laughs and says that's enough and we keep moving through the crowd.

We've just broken away from the picture-takers when a really tall woman–like, she even towers over Deimos–steps in our path. Her face is painted with stripes of every color and her eyes are bursts of white around her pupils, to gray to black.

"*Ol Sira*." She bows and extends her arm, moving her light, flow-y robes. "And *Avra-kaï* Deimos, how wonderful, how truly wonderful to have you both gracing our humble place of performance tonight."

Kosim steps forward again, but I lift my hand and nod at her. "Thank you. We're having a great time."

"I'm delighted to hear that." She grins and my stomach lurches–her teeth are filed to points. "If I may, your majesties, I'd be honored to read your futures."

Read our . . . futures? I glance at Deimos, who glances at me. "It's fine with me," he says with a lifted shoulder. "What do you think, Eros?"

"Uh . . ." I glance at her again, still smiling with those unnerving teeth. "I . . . guess?"

"Wonderful! How wonderful. Please, please, come this way." She leads us through a group crowded around a white circle drawn on the ground. Kosim and Fejn follow us into the circle, but she stops and holds her hand out. "Please, if you could stay outside the circle. Right there in the front is fine, but I need this air clear to accurately read them."

Kosim's eyes narrow, but the circle isn't even that big and it's not like she can do anything to us in front of the quickly forming crowd anyway, so I say, "It's fine. We're right here."

Kosim purses his lips, but he doesn't protest.

"Wonderful, wonderful," the woman says. "Now please, everyone, quiet as you can, please. Quiet, *sha, sha,* just like that, thank you." She turns to Deimos and me again. "Now, if you two could face each other and hold hands."

Deimos shifts in front of me, takes my other hand, and wiggles his eyebrows with a grin. I laugh as the prickle of hundreds of eyes settles on my skin. The crowd is getting bigger by the breath. Which is probably why she wanted to read us or whatever, come to think of it, but no harm done, I guess.

"Beautiful, beautiful. Now stand perfectly still, please. Just like that, *sha*, thank you." She closes her eyes and holds her hands behind each of our backs. The crowd is so quiet I swear everyone is holding their breath. Deimos lightly squeezes my hands as we look at each other, smiling—and this *should* be awkward, staring at each other while people stare at us—but all I can think about is the warm glint in his mismatched eyes and the way his soft hands feel in mine. And how do my hands feel in his? Mine aren't nearly as soft—they're callused and usually dry and nothing like his silk-soft skin. Does that bother him? Does he even notice it?

I'm thinking too much.

"*Sha, sha,* I see it now," the woman says suddenly. "*Sha*, it's so clear. There are many changes ahead, my young *Sira*, and some of them will be difficult. People will come and go in your life, people you care for, but you must let them go when the time comes. No matter how much you love them, you can't tie them down."

Something inside me sinks as I look at Deimos. She can't mean—she's not talking about Deimos, is she?

Would I believe her if she was?

"But *naï*, not the *Avra-kaï*." She smiles and the breath unhitches from my chest. "*Naï*, I see much happiness for you both. There will be good and bad sets, of course, but I predict many, many happy cycles together."

I grin and Deimos grins back. "I like the sound of that," he says with a wink.

The woman smiles, then leans close to Deimos and whispers something in his ear I can't catch. Deimos's smile widens though, so it must be something good. Then she pulls away and turns to me, opening her eyes. "You have some hard times ahead of you, young *Sira*, but this one will help you through it, if you let him. Keep him close."

"I will," I say, and she smiles, steps back, and bows as the crowd claps and cheers.

But while I'm smiling and like the idea of having a lot of time with Deimos, a part of me still stutters on what she said.

If she wasn't talking about Deimos leaving, then who did she mean?

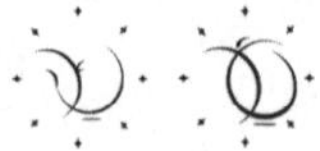

We're looking at glass statues lit on the inside with some kinduv solid, fluorescent mist or strings of molten glowing *something* when something warm and wet drips on my nose. I startle and wipe it off my nose—and whatever it is comes off clear on my fingers. Water?

"Oh," Deimos says. "Did you feel that?"

"*Shae*," I say. "Something dripped on me."

The words have barely left my mouth when water slams over us like a wall. I gasp and throw my arms over my head, but the water is warm and soft—not hard and cold, not like Dima's dungeon, this is different, this is different—and I'm crouching over the multicolored stone pathway and Deimos is gripping my shoulders and smiling as he blinks through the rain.

Rain. It's raining.

"I'm with you," he says. "Okay? You're not alone. We're soaked, but it's okay, *shae*?"

He's with me. My drumming heart slows just a bit, just enough to breathe, and the rain pours over us and drips into my eyes and mouth and soaks my clothes, and I can't remember the last time I've seen rain. Two years ago? Three?

I laugh. "It's actually raining."

Deimos grins. "That happens more often as you go up north. Come on." He takes my hand and pulls me up, but I tilt my face back and take a deep breath.

This isn't Dima's dungeon. This smells clean, fresh, nothing like the desert, nothing like anything I've ever smelled before, but it's actually–relaxing. I can separate this from what happened in the dungeon–that was cold, and solid, like a wall of ice hitting my head and shoulders so hard it hurt. This tickles my face with warmth and slips over my lips and I can barely believe it but I'm soaking wet and not throwing sand.

"I'm not panicking," I say with a laugh. "I'm actually–I think I'm okay."

Maybe it's the openness of being outside. Maybe it's the quality of the rain, the way it feels different. Maybe I'm finally learning how to separate what happened from today. I don't know, not really, but right now I'm laughing in the rain and Deimos is grinning at me.

Then he tugs my hand and we're running and whooping and laughing in the color-lit streets. Our feet splash over the soaked stones as the rain thunders around us and there's water in my eyes, on my tongue, on every inch of my skin. Deimos squeezes my hand as we run and grins at me and I grin back–

Then he pulls me against a building every shade of blue. My back hits brick. There's an overhang above us, so we're standing in this strip of dry with water pouring like a wall behind him. Deimos is radiant–smiling from his eyes, from his panting breaths, from every inch of his soaked skin, and the way he looks at me, *really* looks at me in a way no one has, like–like he likes every bit of me. Like he *wants* me. My heart drums in my ears as he leans close–closer–chest against my chest and hands slipping up my arms and to my jaw–

"Eros," he says softly, so softly I almost miss it. "I've never wanted anything as badly as I want to kiss you right now."

Heat blossoms in my stomach and tugs hard and low. Is he–I think he's *asking* to kiss me.

No one's ever asked before.

I take a shaky breath. His lips are barely a mo from mine, so close the water dripping off them almost drips onto mine. "Well, Deimos," I manage to say, "then I think you should kiss me."

He grins that smirky grin, shaking with laughter. "You just *think* I should? Or I should?"

"Shut the fuck up and kiss me."

Deimos is laughing as his mouth closes over mine. His mouth is softer than I expected—like his hands holding my face as he presses tight against me, chest to chest, hips to hips, one leg slipping between mine as our lips move together. I feel like I've been dipped into a vat of liquid sparks—my whole body thrills with his touch, his taste, the way he holds and kisses me carefully, like I might break even as he pins me to the wall. Deimos kisses me slowly, and so carefully, giving time to my top lip, my tongue, my bottom lip, the corner of my mouth and trailing kisses down my jaw and up to my ear, drinking the water off my skin.

His breath is hot on my ear when he whispers, "You're perfect," and I swear to the stars my eyes sting at those words coming from him as he kisses his way back to my mouth.

"You're perfect," he whispers on my lips.

"You're perfect," he whispers on my neck.

Hot all over and I'm fucken crying like a baby. Shit, that is *not* attractive, I seriously have to cut that out before—

"*Ej*, *ej*, what's wrong?" Deimos wipes the wetness from my eyes with his thumbs. "Am I doing something wrong? We can stop if—"

"I just have rain in my eyes," I say quickly. "It's—I'm fine. Seriously, I'm beyond fine. It's just the rain."

Deimos arches an eyebrow and smirks. "You're a *terrible* liar."

My face goes hot. "I am not."

"*Sha*, you are." Deimos kisses me lightly and laughs. "But that's a compliment. It means you're an honest person. I like that about you." Then he pushes off the wall and slips his hand in mine again. "Come on, it doesn't look like the rain is going to let up any time soon. We should head back before Kosim and Fejn get tired of standing in the soak."

The lack of his skin on mine feels like a hole in the universe. Like blowing cold air onto my damp, still-warm skin. But I take his hand and walk with him under the overhang, my pulse still thrumming in my ears, my skin still tingling with the echo of his lips.

Just before we step into the rain again, I pull Deimos back. He glances at me questioningly and I take a deep, shivering breath. "It's just–no one's ever said that to me before."

Deimos blinks. Frowns. "Said . . . you're a terrible liar?"

"*Naï, naï*," I laugh weakly and bite my lip. My ribs are clattering inside my chest. I want to say it, but I don't, but I do. "No one's ever . . . called me . . . perfect."

Deimos's eyes widen.

"I'm just–I hate the word, but I'm a half-blood, you know? The only one who ever really wanted me was Kora, and even then it was with conditions because of what I am, and it was with the reminder that it couldn't ever really happen because of course not, I'm a fucken–"

"Eros–"

"No one's ever wanted me, the way I am, without conditions." The words tumble out of me and my throat aches as I speak. "I was never enough."

Deimos drops my hand and holds my face again. He looks into my eyes and his breath tickles my face as he says, "You're perfect. I want you exactly as you are, no conditions, no changes, no alternate universes where you aren't exactly what you are, here, today." He smiles and lifts a shoulder. "I can only pray you want me back in the same way."

His words are liquid happiness filling me from the inside out. And he means it—he *means* it—it's in his eyes, in the gentle pressure of his fingers on my face, in the intensity of his voice.

I really never thought I'd get this.

"You don't have to pray for that," I answer. "You have it. I want you."

When Deimos kisses me again, it's a promise. From me to him, from him to me.

It's a promise I'll do anything to keep.

16

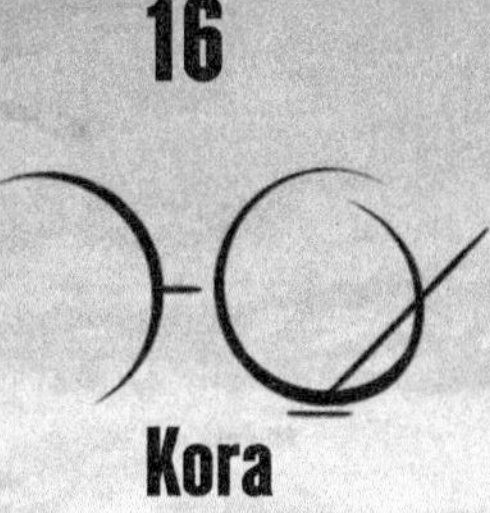

Kora

The halls are dark when Uljen and I walk back to our rooms, lit only by small white lights ensconced in partially transparent blue geodes. The light is cool and paints our skin in smooth ice, giving the whole hall the feeling of being–almost underwater, if water were blue-tinted rather than purple.

Uljen's hand brushes against mine–accidentally, I think–and a hot jolt races up my arm and into my chest. I glance at him and he glances at me. Did he notice that? The air between us is thick with–something. Like a charge crackling in the space where the air meets my body and his.

To put things plainly, Uljen is not an unattractive man. He's broad-shouldered and his smooth brown skin looks soft. Though long hair on men isn't common in Elja, it suits him–the strands that have slipped from his tie frame his face perfectly–and his jaw is strong and angled.

In the short time I've worked with him, I've noticed people seem to avoid looking him in the face–likely because of the scars marring his cloudy left eye and cutting through his brow and cheek. But it doesn't bother me, not really–if anything, the way he fearlessly wears his scars bolsters me.

Uljen showed me I don't need to hide my scars, something I'll forever be grateful for.

"Well, this is me." Uljen nods to the door leading to his room. "I had a really good time." He pauses. "Thank you for dancing with me."

I smile. "Thank you for inviting me."

"Naturally." His gaze dips to my lips before bouncing back to meet mine. My heart pounds as I step toward him, closing the space between us.

And when my lips taste his, he sighs.

Uljen and I are about the same height, which is different, but makes lining up a lot easier. I lean against him as my hands slide down his hard sides and I run my mouth over the stubble on his jaw. Uljen tilts his head back as I slowly work my way over his scarred cheek, then down his neck. Uljen's skin tastes like a smoky, sweet herb. Every catch of his breath makes my heart pound harder, makes me want more.

I don't want to think about Eros, about Dima, about the responsibilities and difficult decisions waiting for me at home.

Right now, more than anything, I want–*naï*, need–to lose myself. And Uljen makes it so, so easy.

"Kora," Uljen whispers, his voice strained. "Is this a good idea?"

I pause and lean back, running my fingers over his collarbones. "Probably not." Uljen looks at me, and I lift a shoulder. "I just don't particularly care at the moment. I'm tired of holding back."

Even in the blue-tinted light, the purple flush warming Uljen's skin is clear. He runs his tongue over his lips and looks me over but doesn't move.

Maybe he's right. Maybe this is a terrible idea. Maybe this is too much, too soon. Just because he danced with me doesn't mean he wants–this, whatever this is.

I stand up straight and force a smile. "I apologize, I didn't mean to make you uncomfortable. I'm not going to push you into anything you don't want to do so . . . good night."

I turn away and take a steadying breath, ignoring the prickle of a flush in my cheeks. That was–embarrassing. Maybe, if I'm fortunate, we'll both be able to pretend that never happened. *Kala*, I hope I didn't just completely mess–

A hand grips my shoulder–I turn–and Uljen's mouth crashes into mine as he grips my hips and lifts me. My gasp catches in my throat. I wrap my legs around his waist as he holds me tight, his mouth insistent, demanding on mine. He walks and doors slide open and closed behind us, and moments later my back hits a plush, rocking bed.

I yank off Uljen's shirt as he fumbles with unwrapping me out of mine. "*Kala*, why is this so complicated?" he asks with a breathy laugh.

I laugh and help him untie my top until his weight settles on top of me, skin to skin. Then Uljen slows. The hunger abates to something else, something tempered and rhythmic as he kisses my lips, my neck, his hands sliding down my stomach and into my skirt as he kisses my breasts.

I focus on the moment. On the heat waking in my legs, my stomach, my face and pooling between my legs. On his touches, his desert-tinted smell, the feel of his mouth on my skin. I focus on the now, because I can't lose myself in the past, I won't, not this time, not with Uljen.

His prosthetic leg touches my calf and my heart stutters—it's colder than I expected. But it's an anchor. A reminder this is Uljen, not Eros, not Midos.

I'm here, and I'm present, and this feels wonderful and there's something freeing in knowing this means nothing at all. Uljen and I aren't in a relationship. There aren't expectations. And even if we were, it would be permitted.

I have nothing to worry about. I can just enjoy this.

Uljen's skin is hot and slick against mine, his breaths heavy against my neck when he abruptly pulls back.

"Something wrong?" I breathe.

He shakes his head. "*Naï*, just . . . are you sure?"

Does he know I've never done this before?

Do I want him to?

"*Sha*," I say carefully. "I'm sure. Are you?"

His low laugh sends a thrill through me. "*Sha*, I'm sure. But I've . . ." He smiles weakly. "I've never done this before."

I blink. "You—really?"

Even in the dim moonlight, his flush darkens his face. But still, he says, "Really."

I truly wasn't expecting that. Uljen is handsome, and older than me, albeit not by much, and I just assumed—

Well. I assumed.

"Okay," I say. "Well as long as you know how *not* to impregnate me—"

"Ah, *sha*, that's . . . we learn that in schooling."

"Then it doesn't bother me." I pause. "I haven't before either. As we're being honest."

His eyes widen. "You . . . really?"

I laugh. "Is that so shocking?"

"Well, *sha*. You're beautiful and powerful. I assumed you could have anyone you wanted, whenever you wanted."

"*Sha*, well, that would require trusting people enough to let them into my bed."

Uljen nods and gently brushes hair out of my face. "And you trust me?"

"I trust you not to try to kill me, which is trust enough for now."

Uljen smirks. "I suspect even if I tried, you're likely more than capable of defending yourself against me."

"That's because you're smart." I sit up just enough to kiss him. "Now are we going to continue or talk all night instead?"

Uljen kisses me with a grin like a twist of shadow.

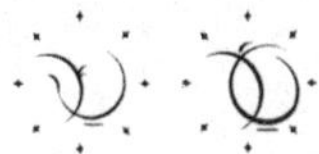

"Mamae, what is sex like?"

Mamae smiles and sits on the edge of my bed, patting the blanket beside her. I lie next to her as she leans back on her elbows and sighs. "Well, that depends who it's with. With yourself, it can be personal, exploratory. A way to learn what you like and what you don't. A way to get to know yourself. With someone you're attracted to, it can be fun and feel nice–a way to relax and be vulnerable with someone else. Sometimes sex is entertainment, just a way to satisfy a craving, like eating a sweet. Sometimes sex ends up awkward and disappointing, but you learn something–even if it's just not to have sex with that person again."

She laughs, and I snicker.

"And sometimes, my love . . . sometimes you'll have sex with someone you care deeply about, and sex is a way to open up to them. To be completely vulnerable and give all of yourselves to each other. That kind of sex is a way to show your love and a way to get to know each other in a personal way you'll never forget. That kind of sex is my favorite." Mamae grins.

I smile. "Is that what it's like for you and father?"

Mamae's grin fades into something tighter–flatter–like the way she tries to smile when people compliment Dima and ignore me right in front of us. "I think that's enough questions for one night, my love."

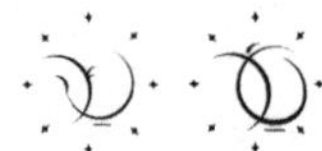

Sex with Uljen is like kindling a fire. Every touch, every movement stokes the flames from sparks to embers to a deeply burning flame. Sex with Uljen is also a little awkward, with neither of us really knowing what we're doing and just doing what feels good.

But it does feel good. And warm. And the pressure of his body on mine as we move together, again, again, is calming in a way I hadn't expected.

"Is this okay?" Uljen whispers, and my throat is too tight to answer so I nod and hold him tight as his lips find mine, and he moves, and I move, until the fire burns out and we cool, breathless in the dark.

17

Kora

I wake in my own guest bed with aching muscles I didn't know existed and the knowledge of what we did sitting like a boulder on my chest.

I sigh and sit up, running my hand through my loose hair.

I had sex with Uljen, my advisor, and it was his first time. And mine too. But I went in knowing it was just for fun and didn't mean a thing and he–

Well. I shouldn't assume it meant anything to him, either. It's probably fine. We were just acting on an impulse. That's all it was.

It's fine.

I close my eyes and take a deep breath, letting a smile play over my lips.

I had sex. And I don't *feel* any different–am I supposed to feel different?–but for once I didn't let fear or distrust get in the way and it was actually . . . nice. Quick. But nice nevertheless.

I wish I had a female friend to talk to about it. I miss the laughter of private conversations Anja and I once had late into the night. The understanding of one woman to another.

The knowing smiles and grimaces, the way Anja always knew what to say to make me feel less alone.

I miss her so dearly.

What would Anja have said? She probably would've thought sleeping with Uljen was a terrible idea, but I don't think so. I think it'll be okay.

After washing and getting dressed, it's time to head over to the dining room for the morning meal before heading back to Elja. And to my surprise, Uljen is waiting for me in the hall.

And his wide eyes as he looks at me send my stomach spiraling to my toes.

"What's wrong?" I say quickly. "Did something happen in Elja? *Kafra,* I forgot to check my glass this morning–what's happening?"

"What? Oh, *naï*, everything is fine in Elja." Uljen shakes his head. "Nothing's wrong, I just–we, you know, should probably talk."

I arch an eyebrow. "Talk?"

Uljen nods, then glances at the guards standing several paces down the hall and lowers his voice. "You know. About last night."

Something inside me twists. Maybe it was naïve to assume last night would mean as little to Uljen as it did to me. "It was just some fun, Uljen. We didn't agree to marry."

Uljen's face purples and he laughs a little. "I-I'm aware. I just thought we might want to . . . establish expectations?"

"I don't have any expectations." Uljen bites his lip so I place my hand on his shoulder. "Trust me. Everything is fine. And if it made you uncomfortable, then we don't have to do it again, okay? But you have nothing to worry about."

Uljen blinks. "Again?"

"We have no obligations. Let's just get back to Elja, *sha*? We have a lot of work to do."

I walk away with his gaze prickling my back and his panicked eyes burned into my mind.

Kala, I hope I didn't make a terrible mistake.

To say that the hovercraft ride back to Elja is awkward is an understatement. Uljen is silent the entire ride over, drumming his fingers on the windowsill as he avoids my gaze. But I'd rather his silence than him trying to make something of what we did last night, so I don't push him.

When we arrive back on the palace grounds, Jarek is waiting for us at the landing strip, wearing his characteristic grimace. *Kala* knows that man doesn't smile half as much as he should.

"*Avra* Kora." Jarek bows, glances at Uljen, and nods at him. "I'm afraid I . . . must speak to you before you enter the palace."

I frown. I'd checked the feeds over the morning meal and throughout the hovercraft trip back to Elja, and there was no new information about Vejla. The sickness has stayed in Asheron so far, and Eljans feel taken care of with the filter masks and boosters. For once, things are actually quiet in the Eljan city.

So why does Jarek look like he's about to give me terrible news?

Oh *naï*. My eyes widen. "Is it Dima? Is he okay?"

"Dima's fine," Jarek says quickly. "This has nothing to do with him, but unfortunately there's been . . . an incident."

"Incident?" I frown. "Nothing was reported on the feeds."

"*Naï*, not yet. I haven't allowed any guides in the throne room yet. I've ordered silence from the staff and guard until you returned."

My stomach churns. Whatever this is, it's sounding more serious by the moment. When Jarek doesn't continue, I step forward. "Well? Are you going to tell me or watch me sweat under the suns?"

"It's . . ." Jarek grimaces. "The servants. There's been a . . . protest."

That's . . . not the news I was expecting. I frown. "What are they protesting?"

"I think . . ." He sighs. "It's better if you see it for yourself."

I step past him and march into the palace, my heart in my throat as I step over the rough tile, every breath bringing me closer to the throne room, where the doors are closed and eight guards stand shoulder-to-shoulder, blockading the entrance, as though the closed doors and usual four guards weren't enough.

"*Avra*." The guards bow and part, clearing the way without my having to ask.

I stand in front of the heavy double doors, my heart thrumming in my chest. Whatever is in there, it has to be something truly serious for all of this build up, for all of this protection.

Part of me almost doesn't want to know. Part of me wishes I could rewind to last night when everything was warm, and nice, and the only thing that mattered was feeling good.

But whatever this is, I can't turn away from it.

This is my responsibility.

I am *Avra*.

I push the doors open. Inside are the servants, as expected, but they're all sitting. Side by side, holding hands, facing the doors–facing me. There are so many of them they fill the large room–I honestly hadn't realized we had so many on the palace grounds.

And as their gazes settle over me in the silence, as the pressure in the room settles over me, the woman closest to me says, "No more."

And then, like a wave, the others repeat it, the same two words: no more. Again, and again, their voices building, louder, an endless chorus until those words are the air, until their voices drown out my drumming pulse, until every repetition is a cry, is a shout, and those words thunder and clap and roar.

NO MORE.

PART II

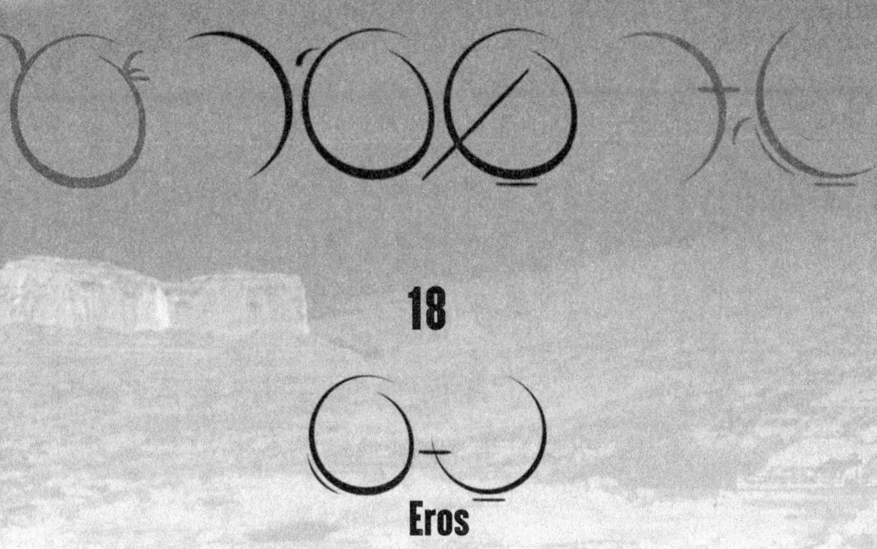

18

Eros

You'd think not sleeping would get easier. You'd think your body would get used to the routine of uselessly staring at your bedroom's shadow-painted mosaicked ceiling for six segs before rolling out of bed, your veins full of lead and your eyes endlessly throbbing in your skull. Or you'd think, at the very least, you'd shut down eventually and sleep more than a seg at a time and wake up—maybe not *refreshed*, but at least feeling a little better.

But no. Not even close.

Still, I've been productive. Kinduv. I recorded a launching message for People Speak, which is what we're calling the message system the people can access to make their wishes known. Deimos put together a team to filter through the messages—they'll write up daily reports sharing trends and general feelings, and Deimos will go through the most important messages himself before passing it over to me. I think it'll help. At least I'll get a sense of what people are thinking, if they use it.

I also handled the thing with Dima—or rather, let Kora handle it, telling the people I trusted the Eljan government to try him fairly which, honestly, was a lie. But that doesn't matter. I had too much to worry about already without fighting over this with Kora. And yeah, maybe it didn't look great on me–but Deimos pointed out it looked worse for Kora to publicly fight with me over it, so. It's over.

Two less things to think about. A mountain left to tackle.

The Remnant. The plague. The nanites. Too many problems without solutions and somehow I'm supposed to just–handle it.

Deimos rolls over, throws his arm over my chest, and buries his face into the crook of my neck, mumbling into my skin. "Did you sleep at all?"

I close my eyes and soak in this moment. This warmth of his skin on mine and the heat of him breathing on me. It settles the forever buzz behind my heart, vibrating in my chest, for just a couple breaths. Just enough that I can fill my lungs for an instant without feeling like someone is sitting on my chest.

"Sure." I don't bother trying to sound convincing. Deimos knows the truth.

He sighs, propping himself up on one elbow. "It's not healthy. No wonder you're having so much trouble with the stress of your position. How long has it been since you've had a full night's rest?"

I think back. The sets have all kinduv blurred together–probably at least in part from the not sleeping thing–so it's hard to count back. "I'm not sure. The night before Kora's lifecycle celebration, I guess."

Deimos groans. "That was the beginning of the term. Do you know what set it is?"

"Not really."

"The forty-fifth of Okona. You haven't slept in nearly a full term."

The nomads do dates differently than the Sepharon—we separate the year into seasons, rather than terms—so it's hard for me to really parse out what that's supposed to mean. But I guess it sounds like a lot. Especially since I'm pretty sure they have fifty sets a term or something. That's a lot of not sleeping.

Makes sense, though. It definitely feels like I haven't slept in forever.

"Come." Deimos rolls out of bed and stretches his arms over his head. His pants hang low on his hips and the mismatched markings on his arms continue down his chest, following the curve of his muscles and emphasizing the V-cut disappearing into his waistband.

Deimos smirks and lowers his arms. "I'm well aware I'm quite the specimen to look at, but I really think we should get you to a medic, *shae*?"

I blink. "Medic? I'm not sick."

"*Naï*, you're not sick, but you will be if you don't sleep."

I shake my head. "The medics have enough to worry about trying to figure out a cure for the *kafran* plague. I don't want to distract them from—"

"Eros." Deimos kneels on the bed next to me. "You're *ken Sira.* I appreciate your concern for the people, but there are *plenty* of medics and you're important too, *shae*? Look at it this way: you can't do your best as a leader if you aren't well. You need to take care of yourself, too."

We've had this conversation before—several times, since Deimos took to sleeping in my bed roughly ten sets ago and it became impossible to hide that I'm not actually sleeping. The first night I blamed it on nerves–which wasn't totally wrong since Deimos was sleeping *in my bed*, and even though we weren't really doing much of anything besides kissing, I still had an impossibly attractive guy in my bed and the knowledge that one set probably soon we'd be doing more than kissing and I had literally no clue what to do with a guy–

Well. The nerves were real even if I was well aware I hadn't been sleeping long before Deimos joined me in bed.

Since then we still haven't done anything more than kiss and touch above the waist, and, humiliatingly, I have a sinking feeling it's because Deimos has picked up on the fact that I have no fucken clue what I'm doing and is taking it slow with me.

Which–I appreciate but also kinduv wish he didn't take it *that* slow. But I guess it's only been ten sets. Still.

Anyway. My not sleeping isn't nerves–we both know that. And if I'm being honest, he's right, I guess. I need to sleep–I know that, I've *known* that.

But sleeping means dreaming, and dreaming means reliving the worst sets of my life.

Deimos takes my hands and rubs his thumbs over my skin with a small smile. "Do it for me, *shae*? I'm worried about you. I want you well."

And with those wide eyes staring me down and his light grip on my hands, it's impossible to say no to him and he knows it.

"Fine," I mumble.

Deimos leans forward and kisses me lightly. "Thank you."

Twenty mos or so later–after Mija takes ten to make me look "presentable"–Deimos and I are walking down the hall to the palace's personal medical center—not the larger one in the palace complex, but a much smaller version reserved for my advisors, Mal, and me—with Kosim and Fejn on our heels.

"He'll likely just give you something to aid your sleeping," Deimos says. "It'll knock you out for six or seven segs at a time. So you don't have to lie awake in bed anymore."

A cold trickle crawls down my spine and burrows into my stomach. What if whatever they give me traps me in my dreams? What if it knocks me out, but in the process I can't wake up when the nightmare gets bad?

Could that happen? Is that a thing?

Fuck, maybe this is a bad idea. The dreams are bad enough when I wake up in a cold sweat, panting, a scream frozen in my throat. If I was trapped in them, it'd be an endless torture in my own mind.

I don't want to sleep if it means getting trapped in Dima's dungeon again, or watching Day die again, or killing Lejv even though I didn't kill Lejv, or drowning in the blood on my hands until—

"*Ej*. Eros. Look at me." Deimos is standing in front of me, holding my shoulders. When did that happen? We're under an overhang with white sands scattered over the black stone. Wait—when did we get here? Where are we?

"*Breathe*," Deimos says. It's not a request. Breathe. I breathe in and out and in and out and Deimos nods, but the set of his jaw, the gleam in his eyes—I'm freaking him out.

I'm freaking me out.

Did—did I black out?

"Okay?" Deimos says.

I shake my head. "I think this is a bad idea."

"Really? Because I'm more sure than ever that letting you convince me you were fine and the sleeping thing wasn't a problem was the worst idea I've had in ages."

"I can't get stuck in the dreams," I blurt out. "I can't do it. If–if I can't wake up because of something I'm taking, I'll be trapped and–I can't, Deimos. I can't do that." My breaths are stuttering in my chest. The heat of the suns is overwhelming and my chest and face are fire and Deimos's frown deepens and I'm scaring him–stars, when did I get so fucken panicky?–and he opens his mouth–

"*El Sira*." It takes half a mo for me to a realize the voice doesn't match Deimos's lips because Deimos didn't speak.

I glance back. Kosim and Fejn are both frowning deeply. I'd forgotten they were there. Come to think of it, I'm pretty sure they haven't seen me melt down like this before either. I want to crawl into a hole and never come out. What'll happen if they think I can't handle my position? Can I be removed from being *Sira* for being a panicky little–

"I apologize for interrupting," Kosim says. "But we just received word about something serious. Kantos needs to speak with you in the conference room."

Kantos is the head of the guard, right, I remember that. I don't think he likes me very much–the few times I've spoken to him, he always looked like he had something that tasted terrible stuck in his mouth–but he does his job, which is all that really matters.

"Can it wait?" Deimos says. "I really think it's of vital importance Eros see a medic immediately."

"This is very serious," Kosim says.

I take a hot, shaky breath. "I'm fine." Deimos starts protesting, but I talk over him. "We'll see what's going on, then go to the medic, okay? I'm not about to take something that'll knock me out in the middle of the set anyway."

Deimos purses his lips but reluctantly nods. "We're going to the medic *immediately* after. No excuses, Eros. I won't allow you to avoid this any longer."

My stomach twists at the thought of getting trapped in those nightmares, but I nod anyway. "Let's just get this over with." I look at Kosim. "Lead the way."

The conference room is small. Well, small in comparison to the rest of the rooms but not a space I would've called small a couple terms ago. A large floating table—that I'm pretty sure is actually a huge glass—fills up most of the space. Kantos, as expected, is already there waiting for us, as are ten or so other guys who all look as uptight and reluctant to see me as Kantos does. All in military uniforms and enough markings to indicate they're probably all important or high-ranking or something. I haven't quite figured out the marking system thing yet, but generally the more there are, the more status someone has.

Except for me, which Deimos says I should change if only to show I'm embracing tradition, but embedding ink under my skin isn't really high on my list on priorities given the way everything's gone to shit so quickly.

"*El Sira.*" Kantos and the others bow as we enter. "I'm afraid I have some terrible news."

It hits me all at once I haven't seen Mal yet this morning. Not that that's unusual—he usually sleeps in well into the set and moseys over to the morning meal around noon—and this probably has nothing to do with Mal, but my mind jumps to the worst at "terrible news" and the worst right now would be something happening to Mal.

I can deal with just about anything as long as Mal and Deimos stay safe.

But this probably has nothing to do with Mal, so I force myself to keep those fears to myself and instead say, "Go on."

Kantos taps the table and it lights up with the feed interface I've gotten used to. But he clears those away with a wave of his hand and opens a file that he unlocks with a palm print and eye scan before he gestures the glass to project an image over the table.

It takes me a mo to process what I'm fucken looking at.

Three Sepharon men, hanging upside down with–with no faces.

Like, their faces are bloody, flat, purple pulps because their faces have been cut off. They're dead, obviously, and I can only hope the mutilation happened after they died because fuck.

I force myself to look at Kantos and not that dripping mass of purple flesh, glinting with bone. "What is this?"

"That's an image from the city square this morning," Kantos says. "Redbloods have taken credit for the attack." He swipes his hand through the image and it adjusts, like a turning camera, to a nearby wall painted with purple blood. There are words on the wall, in English and Sephari, and these guys don't know I can't read. I recognize one word though: NO.

Still, even if I can't read the whole thing, that there's English on there at all definitely means humans were involved, since most Sepharon don't understand a word of English.

"Does this mean anything to you?" Kantos asks. "Do you know what the Remnant is?" My heart jerks at the word. Kantos must see the change in my face, because he grimaces. "You do."

Fuck. Rani swore she'd ruin my life if I didn't give them what they wanted once I became *Sira*. And Shaw came here to warn me himself and–I can't. I can't handle this right now. But I have to. Fuck.

"I've met the group who calls themselves the Remnant, once. We aren't really on friendly terms."

"I see. Do you know what they want?"

The room is hot. They left a message in fucken Sepharon blood in the middle of the city. This is going to get worse. This is going to get worse but I can't just overhaul this government in a set. I can't throw away their ages of tradition, and I said I'd try to help them but how can I focus on that when people are fucken dying? First the sickness, now this? "Nothing I can give them right away," I say with my heart in my throat.

"You realize this is a threat." Kantos points to the projection. "'No more. The Remnant will rise.' This is an insurrection. We must put them down before this catches on and becomes a problem we can't easily control."

The Remnant will rise. They're coming after me. They'll start a war.

"Do you know who did this yet?" My voice is tight. I can barely breathe. It's really fucken hot in here and Kantos sounds far away when he speaks.

"We have footage of the perpetrators, *sha*."

So far away. Like he's speaking in another room, like I'm not even here, like the air is turning solid in my lungs and clinging to my skin and pressing in on all sides. It's getting harder to breathe. To focus. To stay here, in this moment, in this room of Sepharon men staring at me for some kinduv answer, some kinduv leadership, *something*.

"And do you have them in custody?" Deimos asks for me.

Kantos purses his lips. "Not yet."

"Then I think we should focus on that." Deimos looks at me. "Right, Eros?"

"*Sha*." My voice is tight. I can't breathe. I can't breathe. They cut their fucken *faces* off. What am I supposed to do? How am I supposed to stop them?

The door opens next to me. It's Varo. Isn't he supposed to be watching Mal?

"What is the meaning of this?" Kantos scowls, stepping toward Varo. "You know better than to disturb such an important meeting."

"*El Sira*." Varo bows and stands stiffly, his fists at his sides. "My sincerest apologies for interrupting to bother you with this, but it's urgent. I–I'm afraid I can't find Mal."

The thunder of my heart is a roar, drowning out everything else. He can't find–what does he mean he can't find Mal? His fucken job is to watch over Mal, what does he–what does that mean?

Mal is missing?

No. No no no. Mal can't be missing–where would he have gone? The palace complex is big, but he never goes *that* far, he's still getting to know the place and–and–

Stars above. What if the Remnant got him?

Could they have done that?

Could they have gotten in here?

"Eros, it's okay, we're going to find him. I'm sure he's fine; he's probably just exploring again." Deimos's voice. Deimos in front of me. Really close. I'm crouching against a wall and gripping my hair tight–tight–and the pain isn't grounding me, the pain isn't doing anything, and my whole body is hot and prickling and I can't breathe I can't breathe I can't lose Mal I can't I can't I–

"Everything is going to be fine." Deimos is holding my face. My head is throbbing, my heart is screaming, my lungs are aching.

"Find him," I whisper. Kantos and the guards are staring at me. Everyone is watching me break to pieces. I'm losing it in front of them and I don't even care because no one is moving and Mal is missing.

"Of course," Deimos says. "They'll find him, don't worry, I'm sure he's fine–"

"FIND HIM." The words explode out of me, but I'm not looking at Deimos, I'm looking at Kantos and Varo and all these other useless assholes staring at me instead of doing their fucken jobs.

Deimos winces, but it's enough. They file out of the room.

And I crumble into Deimos's arms, everything pouring out of me, a storm I can't contain, as he pulls me into his arms and holds me tight.

Holds me together.

19

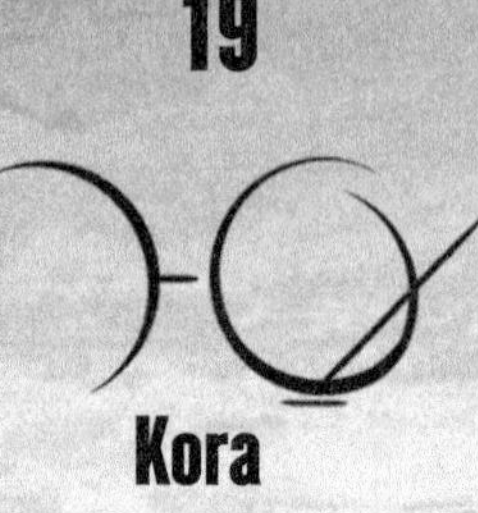

Kora

It's been twenty-four full sets since Eros was coronated and nineteen since slavery was abolished in Elja.

I'd expected the complaints and outright disrespect from upper-crest individuals displeased with the new law Eros established–and of course they made themselves known, through a wave of calls and pulled support and claims that I was somehow doing the freed people a disservice by supporting Eros's law. But the shameful truth is I should have done this in Elja cycles ago.

I was just too scared to make a move that might upset some people–and worse, I ignored the need to overcome that fear while others were treated as property instead of people. Nothing erases what I overlooked. Nothing excuses what I allowed with inaction, what I benefited from in silence.

I can't erase that and I'm ashamed I waited for someone else to do it for me.

But now, nineteen sets later, the displeased calls have died away. The former servants who wanted to stay behind for pay are now getting a living wage. And the halls are emptier, of course they are, but it's a peaceful kind of quiet.

"You look nervous." Lira, my new personal assistant–a redblood girl–weaves the brush through my hair. Her dark eyes meet mine in the reflection of the mirror, and her lips quirk with a tilt, almost daring me to lie. "Is it because of the trial tomorrow?"

My stomach twists tight and I press my lips together as I brush my fingers over the chain of my earring. The one Mamae gave me. The one that makes me think of her.

Dima's trial.

I've made it through the last many sets by thinking about the trial as little as possible. But now with only segments separating us from the set my brother faces Elja to get tried for his crimes, I can't really do that anymore.

In the end, Eros let the matter of Dima's trial go, I suspect in large part because he has his hands full with the plague–and now newly reported redblood violence–in Asheron. The quarantine has managed to keep the disease contained in the city, but I can only imagine how stressful it must be to watch helplessly as your people die until the medics discover some sort of cure or preventative. And now the recent attacks against Asheron officials aren't going to help matters.

So while I do feel somewhat bad about what Eros must be going through right now, part of me is glad he's had enough distraction that he let the case of Dima go.

But of course, the Eljans aren't going to let it go. And I shouldn't either. Dima has to stand trial for what he did–I just hope they don't kill him for it.

Even if a part of me whispers that if he weren't my brother, I might think he deserved it.

"The trial worries me, *sha*," I say.

Lira nods and begins braiding my hair.

"You're doing the right thing, though," Uljen says from across the room. He's lying back on my bed in a way that's way too familiar–does Lira notice? Does she know we've been fooling around?

Do I care?

"I know," I say. "It just doesn't really feel like the right thing."

"The right thing doesn't always feel good," Lira says. "Sometimes the right thing feels downright terrible. But how we feel about something doesn't change whether it's right or wrong–at least, not when it comes to someone else's crimes."

I sigh and close my eyes. "Am I terrible for hoping they'll go easy on him?"

"I wouldn't say terrible," Lira says. "Just naïve."

Uljen sighs and sits up. "You really want them to go easy on him? After everything he did?"

"He's my brother, Uljen. I don't want him to die."

"What if the choice were between a quick execution or living the rest of his sets in an underground prison, never seeing the suns again? I think I'd rather death, to be honest." Uljen shrugs.

I scowl. "You're not helping."

"I'm just saying–there are worse things than death. Death could be merciful compared to some other options."

"*Sha*, I'm sure she feels *much* better now." Lira rolls her eyes. "Why are you in here again?"

"I'm her advisor."

"*Sha*, you're her advisor, not her stylist. I don't see why you need to be here while she prepares for the set."

"Okay," I say loudly. "Stop fighting, the two of you. *Kala*, you're worse than–" I bite my lip. I almost said they were worse than Dima and I used to be, but I'm really, really, trying not to think about my brother right now. If I think about him too much, and think about how we used to be, and how *nice* the last many sets have been with him–

"Oh, great, now you've made her cry." Lira quickly ties off my hair and slips in front of me, dabbing my cheeks with a soft cloth.

"*I've* made her cry?" Uljen scowls. "You're the one who said it was naïve to hope the Eljans might be merciful to Dima."

"Right, because that was *so* much worse than telling her all the terrible things they might do to him that *doesn't* involve killing him–"

"You two are impossible." I cover my face with my hands and take a deep, shaky breath. My eyes still sting and my throat still aches but I have to pull myself together. I can't get emotional, not now. I have to get through this set like an *Avra*, like I'm confident in our legal system and sure whatever happens tomorrow will be *Kala*'s will. And I do believe that. Somewhat.

But when *Kala*'s will could easily involve my brother's execution, it's not really a comforting thought.

"Can you two try *not* bickering for a set? Or a segment, even? I really"–I lower my hands and carefully wipe my eyes, taking another careful breath–"I don't have the energy for it right now."

Lira bites her lip and gently touches my shoulder. She looks genuinely apologetic. "I'm sorry Uljen is such a *sko*."

"Excuse me?" Uljen says at the same moment I laugh. I didn't think it possible, but her serious expression and gentle voice coupled with–with *that*. She's bold, and I can't help it. I laugh.

Lira grins and Uljen's scowl deepens.

"Fine," Uljen says. "Then I'm sorry Lira is so insufferable."

"You're not cute enough to get away with that," Lira says. "It's only adorable when I do it." She grins and her dimpled smile is undeniably precious.

Uljen huffs and stands. "Perhaps we should just focus. Kora, I understand this is difficult, but you're doing really well. The people have responded positively to freeing the servants and offering paid positions in the palace complex, and they seem to be more convinced every set that you're listening to them and trying to be better."

"Which you are," Lira adds. "So it's good they can see that."

Uljen nods. "The trial isn't going to be easy for anyone, but that you're going through with it is a huge show of faith. The people are much happier and are beginning to trust you again. This is all good news."

I want to agree with him, I do. I want it to be easy to say that things are getting better, that I'm headed in the right direction. And I *know* I'm doing better, I know the people are responding in ways I'd only ever dreamed of before.

But I'm terrified.

"Whatever happens tomorrow will be for the best," Uljen says.

Lira rests her hand on my shoulder and I slip my hand on top of hers as we glance at each other in the mirror. And she doesn't say it, but she doesn't have to.

The doubt is clear on both of our faces.

20

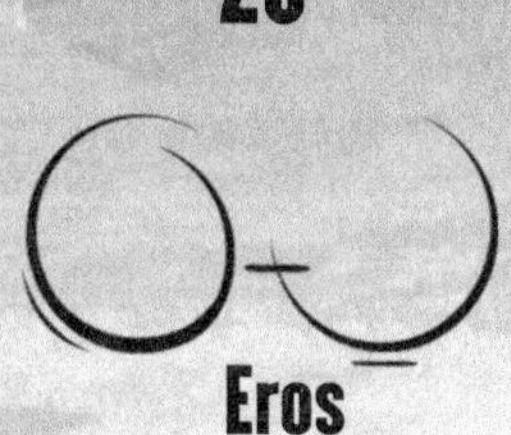

Eros

"This is ridiculous." Kantos is looking at me as I'm just starting to breathe again in Deimos's grip with a disgusted curl of his lip. "We have a crisis to address immediately and *el Sira* is blubbering on the floor like a child."

I'm not sure when Kantos got back–I didn't hear him come in–or how long Deimos and I have been sitting on the floor in the meeting room. My body aches like my soul is bruised. My face is crusty with what I'm pretty sure are dried tears and if my eyes are half as puffy as they feel . . .

Well. I'm wrecked.

And now the fucken head of the guard is taunting me. Because apparently he has time to be doing that since he's here and not doing his blazing job.

"Did you find my nephew?" My voice is steady. Hollow. Already tired of this conversation.

"*Naï*, but I assigned ten men to the job–ten men who, by the way, could be better served doing *something* in the square, where we still have Sepharon blood on the streets. And now I return for orders to find this? You're not a *Sira*, you're a child." He scowls at Deimos. "And if you were a halfway decent advisor you'd never coddle this behavior. Not that I'm surprised, as you clearly were only selected for your . . ." He gestures to us.

Everything pares down to glass-like clarity. My blood boils. Deimos stiffens behind me. I stand.

The military leaders who were in the meeting room earlier are all behind Kantos, glancing at each other with varying degrees of frowns and uncertain looks. I look Kantos in the eye and roll my shoulders back. "Is that what you think? I'm a child who doesn't deserve your respect, is that it?" I step closer. "And you think Deimos was selected because . . . what, exactly?"

The room is deathly quiet. Kantos doesn't speak, but he doesn't back down, either. His glare is anything but apologetic.

"Not that I have to justify myself to any of you, but Deimos was selected because of his experience, and *sha*, because he was one of the only ones who supported me long before I had a chance." Still silence. I shake my head. "Lock Asheron down. No one out after dark, all businesses close two segments before the suns set. It's the hot season and the suns are up for long enough that it shouldn't be problem. Make it clear this violence won't be tolerated, find the ones responsible, and make an example of them."

Kantos snorts. "And why should I listen to you? Why should any of us listen to you after finding you like this? You're weak."

I smile. "I don't give a shit what you think of me. I've heard every insult under the suns. But this *weak*, *childish* half-blood is your *Sira*. And you'll follow my orders because if you don't, you'll leave here without a title or a job."

Kantos glares. "I will never serve a pathe–"

My fist hits his nose with a satisfying crunch. Kantos stumbles back so hard he rams into the guy behind him before falling to his knees, blood streaming down his face. He looks up at me, wide-eyed, his mouth opening and closing like he can't believe I just hit him. Even Kosim and Fejn are staring at me open-mouthed–until Kosim turns his head slightly and covers his mouth with his fist, hiding a smirk. His shoulders even shake slightly.

I grab a fistful of Kantos's uniform, yank him to his feet, and brush off his shoulders. "I'm not going to tell you again. Go do what I *kafran* told you."

Kantos stares at me. Blood drips over his lips and onto the floor. The rest of the military men are just as stunned, some outright gaping, but still, no one is moving.

"Am I not speaking Sephari? Should I repeat it in English?" I take a quick step toward Kantos and he stumbles a step back, finally bowing before the others follow suit.

"I-I apologize, *el Sira*," Kantos mutters, wiping his nose with the back of his hand. "I'll relay your commands to the men immediately."

"Good."

Kantos and the others leave, dripping a purple mess in their wake as they go. My head is buzzing and my fist aches and I just punched the head of the military in the face.

And I'm pretty sure it worked.

"*Kafra,* Eros." Deimos laughs and claps his hand on my shoulder. "That was–you shocked even me. And I'm not easy to shock."

"He didn't respect us," I answer. "Guys like him tend to respond to fighting faster than anything else."

"Oh, he responded." Deimos smirks, but it quickly fades as he glances at me again. "Are you okay?"

"*Naï*." I glance at him. "Are you?"

"I'm fine, but . . ." He sighs. "Of course you're not okay, I apologize, that was a ridiculous question. Let's look for Mal, *shae*? I'm sure Kantos will let us know if he needs anything else from you."

"*Shae*." I swallow the hot lightning zipping around my throat and ramming into my chest. The panic roaring to set me off again, to send me into a spiraling mess on the ground but I can't, I won't.

I can't keep falling apart like this. Deep breaths, chin up, focus. Mal needs me.

"Let's go find him."

21

Kora

The suns are more than halfway to the horizon when the trial begins.

The capital house of justice is packed with people. I'd never actually been in the building before—the whole thing was renovated sometime during my father's reign, back when Vejla had money to spare. It's all angles and metal and glass—the floor, impossibly, seems to be made of a single smooth sheet of white, shiny stone speckled with red. It's supposed to be reflective of Elja's colors, I suppose, but I can't help but think it looks like specks of red blood are embedded in the stone.

Six guards escort Uljen, Jarek, and me through the dense crowd and into the large hearing room. Rows of already-occupied benches create an aisle down the center. The room is three stories tall, with two floors of balcony seating along three of the four walls, before the angled glass ceiling pitching into the sky.

But the worst part: it's stifling. Without the nanite-powered cooling units, and with the room so packed full of people, the room is an oven. Sweat beads on my forehead and drips down my back as we walk the aisle and I do everything I can to swallow the edges of panic gathering in my throat and jump-starting my heart. I have to look confident. I have to look absolutely sure that whatever happens is *Kala*'s will.

And yet, if I'm being entirely honest, if *Kala*'s will means my brother dying, I don't want *Kala*'s will at all.

I've obviously never lived a set in a world where I was alive and he wasn't. And despite everything he's done to me, everything he's done to Eros, all the pain and suffering he's caused others—I don't want to experience that reality.

We sit at the front, just before the empty space where Dima will stand before the row of eight judges who will hear his case. I resist the urge to touch my earring. It's a tell, a nervous crutch. I probably shouldn't have worn it.

I don't even know if Dima plans to defend himself. Would it be better if he didn't? I suspect it might—it could be a way for him to show remorse, to prove he understands the gravity of what he's done. But what if that backfires? What if presenting what he did without a defense seals his fate?

And yet, there isn't a defense for what he did. Trying to make excuses for his actions would probably only make things worse.

The hum of chatter quiets for a breath, then explodes. I startle and glance back—

My brother is here.

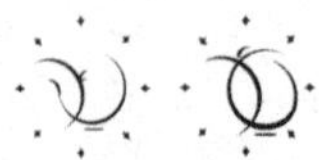

"You seem so . . . calm."

I'd visited Dima last night, smothering the terrifying whisper that it might be the last time I see him, aside from the trial. I'd expected him pacing, sweating, shaking–maybe even drinking. I would've understood if he was drinking.

Instead, he was quiet. Lying on the bed with his head on Jarek's stomach, his hands clasped over his chest. And he smiled as I entered and patted the bed next to him.

"I'm scared," Dima admitted with a weak laugh. "But . . . that's okay. I've earned the fear, and whatever happens tomorrow, it'll be *Kala*'s will."

I grimaced. "Everyone keeps saying that."

"Do you not believe it?"

"I do . . ." I sighed and ran a hand through my hair, let loose after being up all day. My scalp was still sore from having it pulled back so tight. "I just . . . don't know that I'll agree with *Kala*."

Dima smirked. "Unfortunately, whether or not you agree with our deity doesn't really matter."

I glanced at Jarek. For all of Dima's apparent ease, Jarek seemed–stiff. He was always quiet, but his silence was different this time. He ran his fingers absently through my brother's hair while burning holes into the ceiling with his intense stare.

It was possible Jarek was just as unsettled as I was.

"I'm sorry for putting you both through this," Dima said. "Although, if I'm being transparent, Kora, I'm somewhat surprised you're not . . . more at ease with this."

I arched an eyebrow at him. "Did you expect me to be happy about your probable suffering?"

Dima lifted a shoulder. "I expected you not to be bothered by it, at the very least, especially given what I did to you and Eros. And . . ." He hesitated, but then nodded, as if he'd decided something. "I probably shouldn't be telling you this, but I . . . I hired someone to kill you. The redblood attacker that night, that Eros defended you from–"

"I know."

Dima's eyes widened. "You–what? How?"

I sighed and dug my fingers into the silky sheets of his bed. "Eros met the redbloods you hired. They said you offered them credits and technology in exchange."

Dima winced, like I hit him, which was ridiculous because he was the one who *paid* people to *kill* me. If anyone should have been acting wounded, it was me.

"I . . . *sha*, that's true."

I purse my lips. I wasn't expecting him to deny it, and even if he had, I'd known the truth–after all, Eros had no reason to lie to me about it, and that assassin didn't hire himself. Not that I doubt he needed much motivation to hate me, given he was a redblood and I was Sepharon.

"Well. There you have it," I said with a sigh. "I've known."

"Did . . . Eros tell you father did as well?"

My heart stumbled. "Father?" The word squeaked out of my mouth. The room blurred. Father–father tried to kill me, too?

"The . . . explosion at your coronation. I-I can't say for sure–he didn't outright tell me–but the night before, he'd given me the impression that I would . . . be *Avra* very soon." Dima grimaced. "I'm so sorry, Kora."

My own father. I'd known he had never wanted me to be *Avra*, known, even, that he'd attempted to sabotage my reign before it even began. But to try to kill me? To almost succeed? To kill so many in the process of–of targeting your own child?

"Oh, Kora." Dima pulled me into his arms and the embrace was so natural yet so foreign. We hadn't hugged like that in—I couldn't even say how long.

It could have been the last time we would.

I closed my eyes tightly, pressed my tear-streaked face into his shoulder, and took a long, shaky breath.

"Maybe I shouldn't have said anything," Dima said so softly I almost didn't hear him. "Maybe I should have taken that secret to the sand and winds."

"*Naï*." My voice croaked as I sat up and wiped my face, forcing calm into my lungs. "I'd rather know the truth, even when it hurts. Thank you, Dima."

My brother shook his head, his frown deep. "I truly don't understand why you've been so civil to me."

"Because at the end of the set, Dima, you're my brother." I shook my head. "Obviously I wish we weren't here, and you hadn't tried to kill me and frame me, and you hadn't tortured Eros, and you hadn't put those boys to death or thrown those innocents in prison. But the terrible things you did doesn't erase that I care for you and always will."

Dima frowned. "And if I hadn't apologized? If I hadn't shown remorse?"

I lifted a shoulder. "Then you'd likely be in the cells, and whatever happens tomorrow would have been slightly easier to watch." I glanced at him. "But I also would have been convinced you hated me, and that's a pain I don't relish reliving."

"I don't hate you." Dima paused. "I never did. Even when I—when I wanted you . . . out of the way. I was twisted by jealousy and I thought life would be better without you, but I didn't hate you."

"I'm not sure that's much comfort given what you did anyway, but I suppose I appreciate the attempt."

Dima's smile looked like a grimace. "Well. Thank you for visiting me tonight." He bit his lip and took a shaky breath. "I hope . . . I hope the trial isn't the last time we see each other. But if it is, I want you to know how sorry I am for everything, and how much I wish I could take it back–all of it."

"But you can't," I whispered.

Dima stared up at the ceiling. "*Naï*," he answered softly. "I can't."

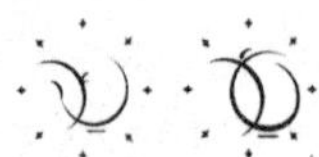

"Your crimes are extensive."

My brother stands before the panel of eight, shoulders pulled back, hands cuffed in front of him. It occurs to me, watching silently from my bench, that my brother has grown. Which I knew, obviously, but I hadn't noticed before how his jawline mirrors father's, or the way his hair curls just slightly at the edges just like his.

Standing up there in front of everyone, Dima doesn't look like a boy. He looks like a man.

"They are, *sha*," Dima agrees.

"And do you have any defense?" a woman sitting in the center of the panel asks.

Dima pulls his bottom lip into his mouth for a moment. Beside me, Jarek taps his finger on his thigh, taking careful, steadying breaths. I imagine he feels just as ill as I do right now.

"*Naï*," my brother says. "There's no defense for what I did. I was power-hungry and lusting for a position that was never meant for me. I made terrible decisions, decisions that hurt and even killed people, in my quest for power. I can't take that back, and I deserve to be tried and punished for those crimes."

The room is deathly silent. I'd expected some murmurs, whispers, *something*, but if I closed my eyes I could almost imagine I was alone in the room for the lack of sound. The panel confer quietly among themselves before the woman in the center nods and turns to Dima again.

"Any one of your crimes–framing your sister to take her position, lying to the former *Sira*, inciting wide-scale violence with your treachery, killing and imprisoning innocents–any one of those alone would warrant very serious consequences."

"I understand," Dima says softly.

"And you understand some of those crimes alone warrant consideration of execution?"

The bulge in Dima's throat bobs. My chest hurts. I force myself to keep breathing–deep breath in, deep breath out. "I understand," Dima says.

The woman leans forward, clasping her hands in front of her. "So tell us, Dima. Why should we keep you alive, given the enormity of your crimes? Why should you be permitted to continue with your life when you've stolen the lives of so many?"

Oh, *Kala*. I can't breathe. The room is stifling and they're seriously considering sentencing my brother to death and I can't breathe.

Dima's voice shakes, but even so, he keeps his head high as he speaks. "Truly, I don't have an answer. I'm not any more deserving of life than those that I–I killed, directly or indirectly. I'll live with the guilt and weight of their deaths on my shoulders for the rest of my life, however long or short that may be. All I can promise is if the panel decides to let me live, I'll pay penance for the rest of my sets. I can't erase what I've done, nor will I ever forget it."

The woman nods and turns back to the rest of the panel. Their whispers are impossible to decipher, even through the thick silence stoppering my throat like a mouthful of sand.

Please, I pray. *Please don't let them kill him. I don't care if he deserves it. I can't watch them kill him. Please. Please please please–*

The woman turns back to Dima. "The panel has come to a decision. Dima Kuru Orolen d'Elja, the seriousness of your crimes is too much to ignore. While this panel acknowledges and appreciates your apparent remorse, there's only one sentence we feel is appropriate to atone for your actions."

Dima's voice cracks when he says, "I understand."

I'm going to be sick.

Don't do this. Please don't do this.

"This panel has determined you will be executed in two sets time, by beheading in the main square."

"*Naï*." The word is out of my mouth before I can stop it. I clamp my hand over my lips and hold back the scream crawling up my throat as Jarek sinks to his knees with a deep groan, covering his face as he begins to shake beside me.

"You will be taken to the cells," the woman continues, ignoring our outbursts. "And over the next two sets, you will be permitted to spend time with your loved ones to say good-bye."

"*Naï!*" Jarek is sobbing on the floor as guards approach my brother to take him to the cells. The room blurs with tears and voices fill the room as Dima bows to the panel. When he turns to us, his jaw is set, eyes shiny as the guards escort him down the aisle and out of the room. And it's too loud in here, too hot, too full of people and I'm going to drown in Jarek's inconsolable sorrow if I don't get out of this room, if I don't get air. I need to be anywhere but here, anywhere at all.

They've sentenced my brother to death.

They're going to kill him.

And I can't–I can't do anything. I'm *Avra* and I can't do a *kafran* thing to stop this.

The suns beat on my shoulders and the desert air is dry and familiar, but it does nothing to stem the tears flowing freely down my cheeks. I close my eyes and choke back the sob shaking my chest. I should have known. I should have known he didn't have a chance, not even here, not even in Elja. Why did I let myself believe otherwise, even for a moment? Why did I let myself hope when I knew that in Elja, taking a life means losing your own?

Kala, I have never wished so badly to live in another territory, like Invino, where they no longer do executions. Why couldn't he have committed his crimes there?

"Kora."

Even without opening my eyes, I know Uljen's voice. I wipe my face with the back of my hand and force myself to look at him. Lira looks at me warmly, glassy-eyed beside him. "We should get back to the palace," I say softly. "For privacy. The guides probably have plenty of footage of me crying out here as it is."

"You're allowed to be upset," Uljen says. "He *is* your brother. But you're doing the right thing, you know that, *sha*?"

Am I? Is letting them execute my brother the right thing?

I've taken lives, too. I ordered a raid on Eros's camp. I may not have shed blood myself, but I may as well have. How is that different from Dima's lying to Roma and giving him an excuse to commit genocide? What's to say Roma wouldn't have done the same without Dima's prodding?

I told Eros I wouldn't let Asheron hang Roma's crimes on Dima's shoulders, but Eljan court did exactly the same.

Then again, even without the lying to Roma thing, he executed innocents. His fate probably would have been the same.

"I couldn't do anything," I whisper. "What use is being *Avra* if I can't even save people I care about?"

Uljen grimaces and touches my shoulder. "You can't save people from themselves." I should shrug him away–after all, touching an *Avra* in public sends all sorts of implied messages that aren't entirely inaccurate but I don't necessarily want broadcasted–but I don't. I don't really care what people think. Not right now.

I open my mouth to answer, but an agonized scream rips through the relative quiet before I can speak.

Jarek marches toward me, tears streaming down his purpled face, fists clenched at his sides. His devastation brings fresh tears that blur my vision before I quickly wipe them away. He hasn't spoken, not yet, but I know what he'll say: I failed him. I swore to protect Dima, and in the end I couldn't do anything. My brother–the man he loves–is going to die in two sets.

Lira moves next to me and Uljen takes half a step forward, shielding me from Jarek, I suppose, but it's not necessary.

Jarek isn't going to attack me. He stops a couple paces before us both.

"You promised!" he sobs. "You said you wouldn't let them kill him and you sat there and did *nothing*!"

"I'm so sorry." I'm crying again. "I thought holding the trial here in Elja instead of Asheron would shield him, but–"

"You *swore* to us! You *swore*!" He's inconsolable and I have nothing to help him. No way to make this better. I can't fix this, I can't make it go away, I can't save my brother or Jarek's heart.

He tried so hard to save Dima and it didn't do an ounce of good. It was too late. Dima had already doomed himself.

Jarek collapses to his knees in the sand and some guards come over and gently help him up, speaking to him quietly as they usher him away. I don't know what his friends could possibly say to him to help right now, but better that he spends time with them than with me.

I'll never recover from this.

"I'm sorry," I whisper to the air, to no one, shivering in the heat.

"You've done the right thing," Uljen says softly. "I know it doesn't feel like it right now, and it never may, but you've done the right thing. You let the courts handle it and you didn't interfere. This is what needs to be done. You know that."

He's right–of course he is. But the pain of knowing I couldn't stop this, of knowing the courts and my people think Dima deserves this, of knowing if he wasn't family I'd likely agree with them, of knowing in two sets I'll be the only remaining member of my immediate family–

It's so much.

Too much.

And I wish more than anything I could turn the suns back and wind Safara back in orbit again and again and again to a time before Dima despised me, a time before his jealousy and thirst for power poisoned the good in him, a time when my brother and I were the closest of friends and nothing, not even the throne, could drive a wedge between us.

22

Eros

"*Kafra*," Deimos says, which about sums up what I'm thinking. The wall-mounted glass in my room keeps streaming the Eljan feed. Someone on the feed starts screaming and Deimos mutes it with a wave-like gesture. "I didn't think they'd actually agree to execute him."

"Neither did I." I rub my thumb over Aren's bracelet. And honestly? I'm not sure how to feel about this. Kora's going to be devastated, obviously, but I fucken hated Dima. He deserves this. Pretty sure *he* even knows he deserves this.

Only thing is Kora doesn't deserve to go through this. Even if Dima doesn't deserve to have a sister like her.

So. Basically. *Kafra*.

"All right, I obviously have to call her, but first." I glance at Deimos. "How does this change things? Politically, or whatever."

"Well, look at you, speaking like a *Sira*." Deimos smiles weakly and sighs, flopping back on the ridiculous mountain of pillows propped up on my bed. The bed rocks a little with the movement and Deimos smirks a little. Pretty sure he does that on purpose. "As much as this is terrible for Kora, I think it will actually help you."

That's not the answer I was expecting. "It . . . will?"

"*Shae*. This is the verdict the people in Asheron would have wanted and inevitably would have come to. So this gives credence to your claim of generosity and the whole bit about how you trusted the Eljan government would make the right decision."

"Even though that was a total lie."

Deimos shrugs. "They don't know that. Now it just looks like you were right."

I grimace. "Somehow I don't think Kora's going to appreciate my getting political points over her brother's death."

"Which is unfortunate for Kora, but irrelevant." Deimos sits up. "You aren't going to talk to Kora about politics now, regardless." He hesitates. "It's going to be difficult to speak to her now. She'll be understably emotional and you need to be prepared for that."

I grab the glass at my bedside table. "Don't worry about me. I have more experience dealing with grief than anyone needs."

23

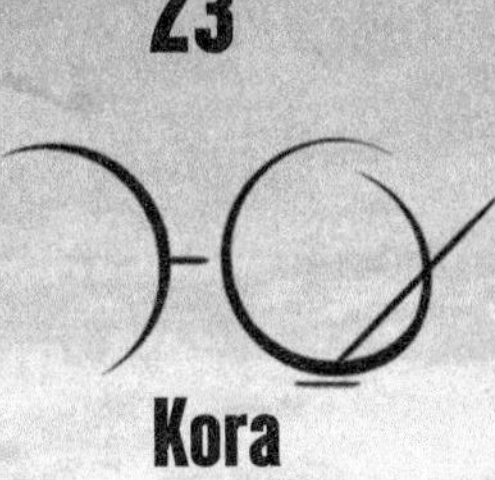

Kora

I've barely made it back to my room—sweating, but shivering, Jarek's screams echoing in my ears—when my glass informs me Eros is attempting to call me.

To be true, I'm not in a proper state of mind to speak to anyone, but maybe that's exactly why I tell the glass to allow the call.

"Go ahead," he says after his face appears on the screen.

I wipe my eyes with the back of my shaking hand. "I don't know what you mean."

"You know what you need to do," Eros says. "Let it out."

There's a moment of quiet when he looks at me, and I look at him, and there's no question in my mind he knows what I'm feeling. He knows loss—and it's my fault he's so familiar with this pain—but I can't deny that he's been here. That he's right.

I don't know how long I cry, face in my palms, the glass propped up in front of me, shoulders heaving again and again until I ache with it. Until I physically can't continue. Until my body is an echo of grief.

"I know things haven't been perfect between us," Eros says, at long last. "But I want you to know I'm here. Whatever happens, I'm here."

I didn't realize how much I needed to hear those words until he said them. Something inside me shifts–it feels like release–and though everything still hurts, I can breathe a little easier. Not much, not now.

But it helps.

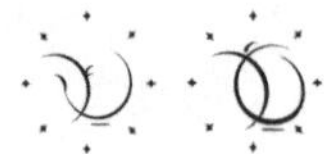

Uljen is fast asleep, his chest rising and falling peacefully beneath my ear. He always falls asleep after we have sex. It'd almost be funny if I wasn't still devastated by the set. And if the actual *having sex* part of having sex wasn't over so *kafran* quickly. Though I'm not sure if that's an Uljen thing or a sex thing. Not that it hardly matters right now.

The point is he's out for the night, and no amount of lying there listening to him breathe is putting me to sleep. My mind is buzzing, humming; my bones are vibrating with the need to move.

I roll away from him and throw a night wrap on. My feet pat softly over the cooling tile as I comb my fingers through my hair. I'd already dismissed the guards usually standing outside my room as Uljen and I entered my bedroom–I told them I wanted privacy and to patrol outside tonight instead–so the hall is dark and empty as my bedroom doors silently slip closed behind me.

My brother is going to die.

What was once a terrifying possibility is now an undeniable truth. I will be the last of my immediate family. Alone.

And even now, as the ruler of a nation, I'm powerless to stop it.

And the truth is I shouldn't *want* to stop it. The truth is, if anyone deserves to die, it's my brother. But for all the awful he's done, I can't unwed that from the reality that he's my brother. My twin. We were close once, and now that he seems truly repentant for his horrible actions, I think we could become close again, with time.

But we don't have time, not anymore.

Dima will die the set after tomorrow. And I will have to watch and act stoic. Like a ruler. Power, strength, respect–but *Kala*, those words are meaningless as I walk the edge of breaking.

"Think they'll sharpen the blade?"

The whisper stills me mid-step. The hallway turns sharply to the right just ahead and I'm close enough that the voice carries. Guards. I silently slip over the bare tile until my back hits the mosaicked wall.

"Why wouldn't they?" a second voice asks. They don't seem to be getting any closer. I've wandered farther from my room than I realized–the throne room around the bend is guarded at all times, as is that entire hallway. The guards are stationed in pairs there in four spots along the long pathway. They don't move until their relief arrives. Which means I can listen here around the corner without fear of them discovering me.

"I saw an execution once where they didn't. The first time didn't cut all the way through. I'll never forget those screams–or the blood . . ."

I cover my mouth and press hard with my palm, stifling the bile-hot horror climbing up my throat. I'd heard of butchered executions–even heard whispers they were sometimes done on purpose to especially vile criminals. I'd never given it much thought before, always assuming someone sentenced to die had done something deserving of such a violent end.

But imagining Dima with his head on the block, suffering. It's agony.

"*Kala*," the second guard hisses into the darkness. "I did *not* need to imagine that."

"*Sha*, well, I didn't need to see it and yet here we are. I just hope I don't have to see it again."

"I don't think you will. Dima's fate may be decided, but he's well-respected. They may even sharpen the blade extra. Make it quick."

"Maybe."

I close my eyes and breathe deeply through my nose, trying to still my quivering breaths. I don't know how I'm going to hold myself together at the execution. I can barely keep from shattering just imagining it. *Kala*, why did this have to happen? And why did it have to hurt so severely?

"I wonder if Jarek will take his position as second. I think it more likely he might just leave," the second guard says.

"*Sha*. He hasn't been himself since the trial was announced–or before that, to be true. Seemed distracted, but with Dima dead . . . I don't know he'll be able to handle staying here."

"It'll be hard for everyone in the guard."

"*Sha*, but . . . you know."

The first guard sighs. "I know."

I can't listen anymore. I turn around and retrace my steps, back into my room, holding my breath as I cross my room where Uljen is still asleep, then out into the warm night through my garden. My steps carry me quickly with that conversation echoing in my mind. With the image of my brother on his knees. His purple blood staining the sand, spilling so much it leaves a near-black slick–

I won't think it.

I need to see him.

I cross the sands with my fists at my side and my eyes stinging, daring someone to question me. But as I enter the nondescript building that marks the entrance of the tunnel down to the dungeon, there's no one there to ask me what I'm doing. Which is . . . odd.

I pause in the small, empty, brightly-lit room, glancing around just to make sure I haven't overlooked someone standing in a corner, but the room isn't large enough to hide anyone, even if it were dark enough to do so. It should likely concern me at least two people are not at their very important post, but it saves me an argument so at the moment, at least, I don't care. I won't waste any more time worrying about it–instead, I continue forward down the steps and into the belly of the dungeon.

The dungeon is a single, long hallway with doors spaced evenly on either side. Everything is too bright down here. And white–uniform, uncomfortably so, which I suppose is the point. Down here there are usually orb guides patrolling and recording, along with two guards in addition to the two upstairs. And there *are* orb guides–three of them on the floor, facing the walls, turned off. Something grips my heart and squeezes–this isn't right, something is very wrong. But then the door at the very end of the hallway opens and four guards walk out with Jarek and my brother and it all makes sense.

The six men stop abruptly and stare at me, wide-eyed.

"Oh, *Kala*," one whispers just as Jarek grabs his shoulder to keep from running into him.

"What's . . ." Jarek's gaze meets mine. His shoulders slump slightly, like the release of a long-held sigh. While the four guards are looking at each other with something like terror, Jarek just looks sad. "You know I had to try."

"Of course you did." My words come out even, tempered. Of course Jarek had to try to release my brother, of course the guards—who are loyal to Jarek and Dima—would risk their jobs and their lives if Jarek asked them to. And of course Jarek asked.

Dima laces his fingers with Jarek's. Is this the last time they'll be able to do that? Dima has a set left to live; I imagine he'd like it best spent with Jarek, but his final segments are slipping away. In a set and a half, the executioners will arrive to take him to the city square.

"I know what you have to do," Dima says softly. "It's okay, Kora."

But it's not okay. My heart beats against my ears and I can barely see through the sting and it's not okay. Nothing about this is okay. I'm falling apart and I haven't even said good-bye yet.

"I'm going to turn around." This time my words shake. I squeeze my shivering hands together behind my back and straighten my shoulders. "I'm going to turn around and walk out this door. I wasn't here. I didn't see anything." I look at the guards. "I hope you four have excuses prepared for how you let my brother escape."

Jarek's eyes widen just as a guard steps forward and nods. "We do. Jarek will—"

I hold up a hand. "The less I know the better." I step forward and wrap my brother in a tight embrace before I can think better of it. For a breath, Dima stiffens—but then he relaxes and holds me in return. I close my eyes and, for a moment, I can almost imagine the way things used to be, when we were young, before the jealousy and anger and hatred. Before my brother turned against me and started down the path that led us here.

I miss it dearly. I miss him—I never had the chance to reunite with that Dima again, and now I won't.

Then I force us apart and wipe my eyes before they see the tears. "I love you." It hurts to speak. "Be careful. Be safe. Both of you, please."

"We will," Dima says with a soft smile, confirming what I'd guessed: Jarek will run with him. Good. At least he won't be alone.

"*Kala's* fortune," I whisper, and then I turn around and force one step after another, down the long, cold hallway. And I don't look back, not when I climb the stairs, not when my feet brush against the soft warm sand, not when I enter the palace again, tracking sand over the smooth tile.

"Kora?"

I startle to a stop, the gasp caught in my throat.

Lira steps through the shadows, frowning as she crosses her arms over her chest. "Are you all right?" she whispers.

I hesitate. "*Naï*," I admit quietly. "Not really."

Lira nods. "I'm sorry about Dima. I can't imagine what you must be going through right now."

Naï, she can't. Because she doesn't know, because she can't know. I swallow hard. "Why are you awake? It's late—or, early, I suppose."

"I was thirsty." Lira smiles weakly and shrugs.

Does her bedroom not have a washroom? I can't remember what room she was assigned to. Is it even in this hall? I thought the rooms here were all larger—generally what guests and high-ranking officials get, but—

"You're not just taking a walk because you're upset, are you?" Lira asks.

I shouldn't answer that question. I despise lying, but if there was ever a time to lie, it's now. I shouldn't trust Lira with the truth—she's a redblood, and formerly a servant, and there isn't a chance she'd agree that Dima shouldn't face his sentence. Why would she? Dima never mistreated the servants, but he's Sepharon and . . .

And I'm making a lot of unfounded assumptions about Lira just because she's a redblood.

"I take your hesitation to mean *naï*," she says with a soft laugh. "Do you need help?"

I frown. "Help?"

"Well, *sha*." She steps toward me and lowers her voice to barely above a whisper. "You're freeing Dima, aren't you?" My eyes widen and she smiles. "I'm not going to tell anyone, don't worry. But I understand. I'd do the same for my brother, even if he *was* a *sko* who probably deserved it."

I should deny it. Lie. Claim I don't know what she's talking about. Tell her what she's talking about is a crime. Make it impossibly clear I would never consider such a thing—even if it's exactly what I just allowed.

But I'm exhausted. Keeping everything in, refusing to trust, it's draining. I want someone I can confide in, someone I can turn to. I may have lost Anja, and it's clear Eros and I will never have that kind of closeness again, but why not Lira? She's offering to help.

"You have a brother?"

Lira nods. "So do you need help?"

"I–*naï*." I run my hand through my hair and inhale deeply, stilling my breaths and forcing back the tears.

"Are you sure? I don't want to miss out on something exciting–insomnia is a boring bitch."

I glance at her. "I'm not sure I would call this exciting."

"Well you may not, but I sure as sand would."

Something twists inside me–the way she speaks, the phrases she uses and the lilt of her Sephari–it reminds me of Eros. "You didn't grow up in Vejla, did you?"

Lira blinks, then tilts her head and smiles slightly. "How could you tell?"

"The way you speak. It–reminds me of someone."

"Eros, right? I guess that makes sense."

"Did you know him?"

"Nah, I wasn't a nomad like him. But everyone knows your relationship with Eros, so wasn't a big leap to guess."

I frown. If she wasn't a nomad and she didn't grow up in Vejla, then–

"Well, good night, Kora." She pushes off the wall and smiles, nodding at me through the darkness. "And best of luck. To all of you."

I nod as Lira makes her way past me down the hall. We need all the fortune we can get tonight–especially Jarek and Dima.

I don't know if they'll make it out of the city. I don't know if they'll make it out of the territory. I don't know if they'll last a few segments or a few sets or a few terms or cycles.

But it's out of my hands now. I did what I could.

And I don't doubt I'll have to pay for it.

24

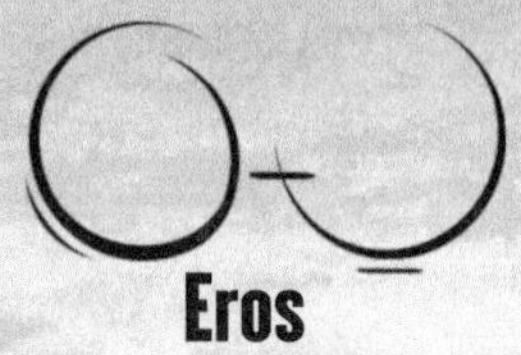

Eros

We looked all fucken set and we couldn't find him. Not in his room, not in his usual hangouts like the garden or the library audio archives or the dining hall. Not wandering the halls, or wandering the complex—which he technically wasn't supposed to be doing anyway but I wouldn't have cared if it meant we found him and he was okay.

He's missing.

My nephew is missing.

Missing in a city where people hate him, a city where people are literally losing their minds with illness, where a contagious disease is spreading—albeit slowly now—but still. We checked the whole fucken complex—even Mija's been looking for him and that's not even her fucken job—and now I'm standing at the edge of the mostly abandoned palace complex merchant square, Mal is still missing, and if anything happened to him—

"You're about to panic again." Deimos rubs my back, his eyes narrow in the harsh warm light of the setting suns. "Don't panic. Breathe. Just breathe."

"Easy for you to say." I press the heels of my hands into my closed eyes, taking a slow, shivering breath of hot desert air. I lower my hands and run my thumb over Aren's bracelet, which is wearing out a bit from all the times I've rubbed it. "It's not your nephew who's missing."

Deimos's hand stops moving on my back, just for a mo. "I'm . . . going to choose not to let that comment bother me, because I know you're upset. But I hope you realize I care a great deal for Mal, too."

" . . . Sorry. You're right, I'm just–I'm trying to imagine a situation where he'd be missing for this long but still be totally fine and it's not working."

"I know." Deimos sighs and slips his arm over my shoulders. "It's completely reasonable for you to be worried, but I swear to you we'll find him. And I'm choosing to believe he's fine and just . . . lost track of time, doing whatever he's doing."

I wish I could do that. Just choose to believe something and believe it so easily. I wish I could tell my brain to think a certain way, to be a certain way, and it'd just happen. Instead, my insides are trying to crawl out of my throat and every breath shudders in my lungs and it's too hot to focus and my skull is pounding endlessly with the second-worst brainblaze of my life and I just want to curl up in a ball and sleep but I can't, not while worrying about Mal, and not even if he were fine.

"Sure," I say, but my voice sounds hollow, even to me.

"We should get inside." Kosim nods back toward the palace behind us. "I don't like being out here. We're too exposed."

Deimos frowns. "We haven't left the complex. Surely we don't have to worry about a threat in here . . . do we?"

"There are always threats," Kosim answers flatly.

Fejn nods. "It would be best to go back inside. And I'm sure the border guards wouldn't have allowed Mal to leave the complex alone, so it's only a matter of time before we find him."

It hurts to agree, but there's no point in looking out here anymore. Not when we've looked as thoroughly as we have and come up empty.

At least Varo and Kantos and the rest of them are still looking for him, too.

Doesn't stop me from glancing around on the off-chance I might see him as we wind around the mostly empty streets, where closed stall and store after stall and store stare glumly back at us. I run my fingers over the mark of *Sirae* snaking over my hand—it doesn't itch anymore, but the dark pathways over my skin of tight, clean writing I can't read still feels kinduv like someone else's mark—and turn Aren's bracelet over my wrist again and again as our feet trudge over the sand-strewn stone.

And then a flash of rust-orange stops me so dead Fejn stumbles into me. "What is it?" He peers down the empty alley I'm frowning into, cupping his hand like a visor over his eyes.

Sweat drips down my back and I try to keep my breathing even—don't get excited, don't hope, not yet. "Hold on." I break from the group, feet pounding over gritty, sandy stone as someone curses behind me—Deimos, or Kosim, probably, I don't care. I race down the alley and around the bend to a narrow space between buildings, barely wide enough for me to stretch out my arms.

A boy is standing there, arms-length away, back to me, orange head-wrap tied around his head. Breathing heavy, holding his middle, head lowered, like crying, or in pain. His skin is lighter than Mal's, and lighter still pathways swirl down the back of his neck and over his back and arms. A Sepharon boy.

Not Mal.

My stomach sinks. Something hot and tight crawls up my throat as footsteps settle behind me—the group catching up, I guess. I turn to them and shake my head, blood heavy as I mutter, "Sorry, I thought—"

A scream behind me jolts me into a turn as something heavy slams me to the ground. Pain rips through my shoulder—hot and deep—as the kid sits on my chest and digs his grimy fingers into my mouth and—

The pain tears through wet and burning as the kid is yanked off me. I slap my hand over the wound pouring blood over my chest and back and my skin is instantly slick with the stuff. Stars above it fucken *hurts.* Kosim grips him in a tight body hug as the kid writhes, kicking and screaming and bucking his head and it's then that I see his eyes: shiny and black.

He's diseased. He's diseased and he just bit a chunk out of my shoulder and Kosim is wrestling with him and—

The kid twists around and spits pink and purple-red on Kosim's face. Kosim throws the kid to the ground before the blast of a phaser burst turns the rabid kid into a—a corpse. He's dead.

Fejn is shaking as he puts away his phaser. He looks at Kosim and me. "You both need to see Zarana immediately."

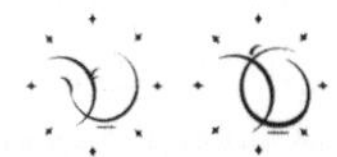

I'm still shaking after Zarana has finished patching up my shoulder and had me breathe in so many boosters my mouth has gone numb. I can still feel that kid's teeth sinking into my shoulder—the ripping sensation as Kosim yanked him off—his dead eyes staring into the suns. He couldn't have been much older than Mal, and his eyes were black and this fucken disease–

What if I get sick? Or Kosim? What if we already are?

"Kosim and I should be quarantined." My voice is flat. Hollow.

"I agree," Zarana says. "The symptoms usually appear within a couple segs, so we'll quickly know if there's anything we need to worry about."

Kosim just leans silently against the wall and nods. He wasn't hurt, but the kid spit my blood and his saliva all over his face. I'm probably more at risk of being sick seeing how the kid bit me and all, but we need to be safe, especially since they say the disease is passed on through body fluids. I won't risk infecting everyone.

Kosim and I settle in small glass cube-like rooms, next to each other so it's almost like we're not alone. And I mean, we're not alone–Deimos leans against the opposite side of the wall in the hallway and Zarana sets it so we can hear each other through it, so there's that. The rooms are pretty empty: just a bed, sink, and offshoot to a not-glass washroom, but they also gave us each our personal glasses and set up larger glasses on the walls, which I'm decently sure they're only doing because it's us. I'm not complaining, though.

I'm honestly less concerned about getting sick than I probably should be, mostly because Mal is still missing. As far as I know, he could be sick, too. After all, if that sick kid was somehow in the complex, it means there are other sick people in the complex, too. Which means none of us are safe, not really.

Deimos does his best to distract me for stars-know-how-long, mostly through reading off People Speak reports.

Ignoring "general unpleasantness" as Deimos put it, that they filtered out, it sounds like people's main concerns are a cure for the plague and fully restoring the nanites. I got a couple nice messages from humans, though, saying they're glad to see *someone like me* in power and they hope I won't forget them.

I won't forget them.

More of a problem, though, are reports filtering both through the network and other channels of some people ignoring the slavery abolishment law. Deimos agrees to send instructions to security across the globe to enforce the new law as strictly as possible and arrest those who try to defy it.

There are other messages, too, from formerly enslaved people skeptical the law will hold. Or worried they won't be able to support themselves, even with the programs set in place meant to help them build their new lives. Which is obviously fair, and all we can really do is make sure the programs set in place to help them are running smoothly.

A lot of the messages are videos, which Deimos and I watch together. One, from a formerly enslaved woman, really stays with me.

"I want *el Sira* to know while we're all glad he's finally changed the law, it's not going to be as simple as declaring slavery over and moving on to the next problem." She twists a little and gestures to her arm, where a band of black text is inked into her skin. "This mark will never go away. Neither will our memories, and we won't get the cycles of our lives back that were spent as property. This is a good step forward for human rights, and I'm so glad for it, but please don't let this be the only step."

I rub the almost identical marking on my arm, the one declaring me Kora's personal bodyguard. Telling the world I was hers.

I may have not spent cycles as someone else's property, but I know what it's like to lose everything, even your own right to freedom. And she's right. It doesn't just go away with a few words. I'll be working to give humans equal standing on Safara for as long as I'm *Sira*—and if I have anything to say about it, so will whoever comes after me, and whoever comes after that.

None of this will go away quickly. We all have to work to be better together.

Eventually I tell Deimos he should probably get some rest.

"You don't have to stay all night," I say. "I'll be fine in here."

"I know I don't *have* to, but—"

"Deimos." I smile weakly and press my palm against the wall. "Really, I'm going to feel bad if you end up sleeping in the hallway. I'll see you in the morning, okay?"

Deimos hesitates, but before he can answer, the giant glass hanging on the wall and my personal glass lying on the bed lights up blue with a low beep before an image of an empty room appears with a sound like a mic getting shuffled around.

I frown. "Did you turn those on?"

"*Naï*," Deimos says slowly. "I'm not even in the room, *shae*?"

Kosim jerks up in the room next to me and scowls at the giant glass in his room, displaying the same blue image. He clenches his fist and touches his ear with his free hand, probably talking through the coms to the other guards.

Then a woman steps into the frame and my stomach bottoms out as Deimos stiffens. Rani looks exactly the way

I remember her: perpetually blazed and determined to do something about it–something that'll probably leave someone dead.

"My name is Rani Jakande," she says, and her voice echoes just slightly from the delay on the smaller glasses, making it sound like there's three of her in the room. "I'm the leader of the Remnant, a widespread network of humans fighting for equal representation and freedom."

I glance at Deimos. "How is she doing this? Is this broadcasting everywhere or just here?"

Deimos shakes his head. "I don't know how. But judging by the way she's introducing herself, I'd guess it's more widespread than just here. If she were just trying to contact you, she wouldn't need to introduce herself again."

He has a point.

Fejn rushes down the hall, pale-faced and frowning.

"*El Sira*, we have a situation," Kosim says through the wall.

"I can see that." I gesture to the glasses.

"We're in the middle of a revolution as we speak," Rani continues. "We will stop at nothing to get our rights, and if *ken Sira* won't cooperate and give us what we deserve by virtue of being living, rational beings, then we'll take it ourselves."

"Our techies are trying to shut it down," Kosim says.

"It's streaming planet-wide," Fejn adds with a grimace.

Prickling heat drips down my spine. Rani warned us, but she didn't exactly give us a lot of time to try to make things happen, either. And now she's addressing the whole fucken planet with–with whatever this is.

"We, the Remnant, commend *ken Sira* for taking a step forward and abolishing slavery. It was far overdue, but we acknowledge the move is in the right direction. But it is not enough.

"We, the Remnant, take full responsibility for the plague spreading across Asheron–and we can, and will, make things much worse if humans aren't given fair representation in the government, and *ken Sira* doesn't take steps toward reorganizing the current system to make it equitable and chosen by the people–*all* the people. The times of royal bloodlines must end or we will take matters into our own hands.

"Any deaths from here on out are on your head, Eros."

And just like that the glasses turn off.

And we are so fucked.

25

Kora

I suppose if I was going to choose the perfect night to aid my brother and his boyfriend to escape the cells and run from the territory, the night to do it would be a night like tonight: when redblood rebels created global chaos by hacking the world feed to threaten Eros and the people. In a way, this perfect chaos almost feels like *Kala*'s blessing on the whole matter.

As a bonus, it distracted me from dissolving into an anxious mess imagining all the horrible ways it could go wrong.

Uljen puts on his prosthetic leg and throws on pants as he stumbles out of bed, his mussed hair slipping in front of his eyes as he grumbles under his breath about it being the middle of the night.

"*Or'jiva* to ruling," I say dryly. "The world unfortunately doesn't stop so the rest of us can sleep."

Uljen stands up straight and brushes his hair out of his eyes with his hand. "How are we going to respond to this?"

"I'm not sure we have to," I answer. "We've already done what the Remnant wanted—they even *commended* us." I lift a shoulder. "I think this is on Eros. All we really have to do is see if we can safeguard our feeds so they can't force their way on again, but the rest is up to *ken Sira*."

Uljen nods. "Do you think he'll do it? Abolish it globally?"

"I know he's certainly wanted to. This gives him a good excuse to do it more quickly than he may have otherwise."

"That's true." Uljen frowns. "So you think we . . . should do nothing?"

"I think we should wait and see how the situation develops before we respond."

A frantic rap at the door startles us both. My heart is thrumming in my throat. Either someone is here to brief us on the broadcast, or they've "discovered" Dima's empty cell.

I want it to be the former–I'm not sure I'm ready for the vital deception I need to go along with, I need to perpetuate, to save my brother's life and protect my own. But I knew all along the only way to get Dima to safety was to tell an enormous lie again and again and pray that enough people believe it to overlook it.

"*Sha*," I say, and I'm proud of how steady my voice is.

Two guards enter, wide-eyed and breathless. I'm assuming these aren't the two who helped Dima escape, or else they're exceptionally good actors. They bow low. "*El Avra*," the shorter of the two says. "I-I'm afraid I have terrible news."

I purse my lips. They're definitely here about Dima. "Aside from the rebel broadcast we just watched?"

He winces. "*Sha*, unfortunately so."

I cross my arms over my chest and summon my sternest face. I can pretend to be irritated and surprised when they tell me what I already know. I can act like I have no idea what's happening. "Go on, then."

"It's—it's Dima, *el Avra*. I-I'm afraid he's . . . he appears to have escaped."

I let the moment wash over us. Stare at the guards, already grimacing with the weight of what they imagine my reaction will be. "Excuse me? What do you mean it *appears* he's escaped?"

"He's not in his cell," the taller of the two finally volunteers. "We're searching the grounds as we speak, but we wanted to inform you—"

"How could this have happened?" I cut in. "He hasn't been there for all of a set and you've already lost track of him? He was locked in a cell, for *Kala*'s sake!"

They wince. I'm a terrible ruler for berating them when this is entirely my fault.

"Unbelievable," I say before either of them can answer. "Find him. Now."

They bow and quickly leave the room, leaving Uljen and me in silence. My heart drums steadily in my ears and my stomach twists so tightly it'll be a miracle if I'm not sick by sunrise, but I've done it.

I think I was convincing. I'm relatively sure I convinced those two guards, at least. Maybe this won't be so difficult after all.

Kala, I hope Jarek and Dima have had enough time to get out of Vejla.

"Incredible," Uljen says flatly.

"It truly is unbelievable. I know we don't have prisoners often, but to lose him so quickly . . ."

Uljen crosses his arms over his chest and narrows his eyes. "*Sha*. Unbelievable is exactly the word I would use. *Entirely* unbelievable, in fact."

Oh no. A burst of cold washes over me as Uljen shakes his head with that disappointed scowl. He hasn't said it, not yet, but he doesn't have to.

He knows. Somehow, he knows.

"You've just made possibly the biggest mistake of your life," Uljen says. "You realize that, don't you?"

"I have no idea what you're talking about," I say stiffly. "Surely you don't think I have anything to do with this?"

Uljen scoffs. "What could *possibly* make me think that? It's not like you were against this trial from the beginning, it's not like you wanted to protect your brother for unfathomable reasons, *especially* given everything he did to you and to your friend–even ignoring the whole *inciting genocide* and *murdering innocents* bit."

"I did my duty. I let the trial play out and I didn't interfere–"

"You can't seriously expect me to believe you had nothing to do with this."

"I do!" I burst out, glaring at him. "Because it's the truth. I had nothing to do with this."

I'd expected lying to be difficult. I'd expected the words to taste different, to feel different as I spoke them into the air. I'd expected an ever-present sense of *wrongness* to slow the lies on my tongue so I had to fight to get them out.

But I was so wrong. Lies slide off my tongue, slippery and sweet like *ljuma* syrup. It's a little frightening how easy they are to tell, how simple it is to speak them like I believe them.

But even as I speak them, I wish I could yank them out of the air and swallow them back again. Because the hurt on Uljen's face is a physical ache in my chest, and it's a pointless hurt–he doesn't believe me anyway. Even before he speaks, there's no doubt in my mind he doesn't believe me for a breath.

Uljen takes a step away from me—and his face, it's the same expression Eros had when I I turned away from him after our kiss.

Betrayal.

"I had many worries about working with you before I accepted this position. But I never thought you were indecent enough to look me in the eye and lie to my face." He shakes his head and walks toward the door. "It appears I was wrong."

And then he's gone and I've ruined everything.

Again.

26

Eros

Trying to process Rani's message on no sleep—when I was already stressed as fuck from Mal missing, and the plague, and getting attacked and possibly infected, and the still out-of-commission nanites, and trying to be ruler of a fucken planet that doesn't even like me very much—is like . . .

I don't even know. My skull is throbbing and trying to think through the endless hammering behind my eyes and the fog that wants to pull me under and drown me in blood-soaked memories is next to impossible.

"I think it's time we consider Mal's disappearance is less innocent than I'd originally hoped," Deimos says.

We're sitting almost next to each other, backs against the glass keeping us apart. Keeping Deimos safe. From me.

"You think?" My voice comes out colder than I mean. I'm just so tired. So sick over what could be happening to Mal.

Deimos sighs. "The good news is Asheron is locked down because of the disease, so it's highly unlikely whoever took him was able to leave the city with him."

I lean my temple against the cool glass, turning toward him. "Deimos."

He glances at me. "Eros."

"Just say it."

Deimos opens his mouth and then closes it, probably considering a joke then thinking better of it, if I know him—and I think I do. Instead, softly, he says, "Say what, *mana Sira*?"

Mana Sira. The formal way of saying "my ruler" is with *el. Mana* is the informal version of "my," like what you'd say to a sibling, or loved one. Combined with *Sira* it feels . . . closer. Like he's calling me his, but not in the way where I'm everyone's *Sira*—it's more possessive.

Deimos is literally the only one who could get away with calling me *his* like that.

And I wish I could focus on that, I wish I could slip right through this glass and show him I know how much that means, but I can't, because Kosim and I might be sick, and worse—worse—Mal is missing.

"Say the Remnant has my nephew."

We're both quiet for too long. Then Deimos sighs. "It's . . . a very real possibility I've been considering as well, *sha*."

"I'll fucken kill them if they hurt him."

"Eros—"

"I will."

Deimos grimaces. "I know. But let's find him first, *shae*? I know how to track people down. Whoever has him won't for much longer." He stands. "I'm going to find Zarana about discharging you. It's been long enough that we would've noticed symptoms by now and you seem fine to me."

"Thank you." I turn to the glass wall separating my room from Kosim's. He's lying on his bed, arms crossed behind his head, staring up at the ceiling as he's been doing for most of the night. "I bet you're getting tired of being in here, too," I say.

Kosim looks over and my stomach plummets.

The whites of his eyes are gray.

"*El Sira*," he says softly, "I'm so sorry."

27

Eros

Zarana clears me as disease-free but Kosim definitely isn't. And it's shitty, because this is my fault. He got sick because he was defending me, and he only had to defend me because I got distracted and thought that kid might be Mal and–

It's not fair to blame myself, I know that, I do, because it's not like I could have known that kid was sick. But I'd do anything to take back that moment so Kosim doesn't have to endure this.

We still don't have a cure. And if he dies, it'll be on me.

"I don't get it," I tell Zarana after she releases me from quarantine and gives me yet another immune booster. "The kid *bit* me and I'm fine, but he spits in Kosim's face and Kosim gets sick? How does that make sense?"

Zarana lifts a shoulder. "You have a different immune system than Kosim does. Evidently your body was better prepared to fight it off than his was."

"Do you think it's because . . ." Deimos hesitates and glances at me. "We haven't heard of any humans getting sick, right?"

I frown. I hadn't thought of that–but he's right: so far all the patients I've heard of were Sepharon. But I figured it was mostly because there are more Sepharon in the city than humans, and because humans probably wouldn't turn themselves in to a Sepharon hospital. But still . . . especially since we know now the Remnant is behind this whole mess, I guess it might make sense that it wouldn't affect humans.

"There haven't been any reported, though that doesn't mean there aren't any." Zarana pauses. "Still, I'd like to take a sample of your blood, if it's okay, *el Sira*."

"Fine by me."

After that's done, I visit Kosim one more time. "We're going to get you better," I say with enough conviction, I hope, to convince us both. "You'll be back on the job in no time."

Kosim grimaces, nods, then looks over my shoulder to Fejn, standing beside Deimos a step behind me. "If I become rabid," he says softly, "please."

Fejn presses his lips into a thin line. Runs his thumb over the beard on his chin. But then he says, "I will," and I hate that he has to make that kinduv promise at all.

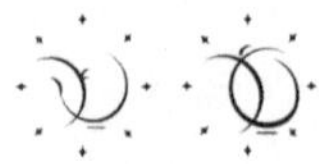

The long, floating glass table in the meeting room I usually talk to my advisors in is an enormous, interactive map of Asheron. Projected buildings are propped up on the surface, like a miniature version of the city is floating in front of us, with every building and street labeled, not that I can read it, but Deimos can and that's what matters. I run my finger through a short, square-ish building and crouch to peer into the building. I can't see faces, but it almost looks like–

"Are those people in there?" I glance at Deimos. "Is this live?"

Deimos nods. "It's all based off the guide feed running in the city. Guides don't usually go into buildings unless we manually order them too, and there are projections to fill in the gaps, as they can't be in all places at all times, but it's generally relatively accurate."

I stand. "So . . . can they find people?"

"Sometimes. They can *look* and they've been known to identify people, but there are absolutely ways to hide from them. Which is usually about when bounty hunters are called in." Deimos smiles, just barely, as he looks at me. He wants me to say it.

"Like you," I say.

His smile widens. "Like me. When I was in the business anyway. I left officially when I began advising you–and my departure was a great loss to the bounty hunting community, I'll have you know–"

I snort.

"But the important part of all this is you're fortunate enough to know me."

I don't know how he does it–I don't know how he gets me to a crack a smile or even laugh when I'm feeling at my worst, but he does. I laugh. "*Shae*, that's definitely the most important part of all of this."

"It is, because before I retired I was one of the most highly paid hunters and not just because I'm easily the most attractive of the bunch."

"Why would you being attractive make you a more highly paid bounty hunter?"

Deimos scoffs as if the answer is obvious, then waves his hand and gestures to the map again. "Anyway, I have some ideas about how to find Mal." He makes a motion like pinching the edges of the map and pulls, dragging the map over until the projection of the palace complex sits in front of us. "So we're here." He taps a building and a red spot appears inside, where we are, I guess. "And as I'm sure you can imagine, the guide footage is much more complete within the complex than it is in the streets. There are places the guides don't go, of course, like the bedrooms and washrooms for obvious reasons, but by and large there is *always* a recording of what goes on. Very well-protected footage, by the way, this is difficult to access even if you work here."

"Okay. So you're thinking . . . there might be footage of Mal?"

"Well there's certainly footage of Mal—the question is when we *lost* footage of him. So let's see how far back we have to go. His bedroom is . . . here, *shae*?" He's moved the map again and somehow wiped off the roofs of buildings so we can see inside. The hallway he's gesturing to is right outside of Mal's bedroom.

"*Shae*," I say. "That's it."

Deimos nods. "As I said, we can't see into bedrooms, however . . ." He places his thumb and forefinger at the edge of the map, then slowly rotates them left, like turning a dial. People quickly move through the hallway, but backward, speeding through time as we fly through hours of footage.

"There." I point as Mal exits his room, stick in hand and his other hand trailing the wall before he steps more confidently away from the wall.

"Good, so this was"—he glances at something written along the border of the map—"Okona 47, so two nights back."

"Where is he going in the middle of the night?" I frown at the footage. "What time is this?"

"22:14," Deimos reads off. "After we'd said good night and Varo had gone to bed."

Mal walks out of the main building then heads toward the lab. At least, that's where I'm guessing he was going since Varo had mentioned Mal was spending a lot of time with the techies, but I can't say for sure because he doesn't actually get there. Because instead, a kid runs up to him and the two stop to talk.

I lean forward. "Can we get closer? Who is that kid?"

Deimos presses both of his hands flat against the map's border and slides them apart. The map zooms forward until we can clearly see Mal and this kid–human, probably around his age, pale skin and dark hair. The two are smiling and chatting and we don't have audio, so I don't know what they were saying, but Mal is laughing and they seem familiar. I guess Mal made a friend?

I should have known that. I should have checked in with him more. I figured he was handling himself fine, that he didn't need me hovering over him and it was easier to think that–one less thing to worry about–but I–

I close my eyes. Take a deep breath. Open again.

I can't change the past. And I can't keep focusing on it, not if I want to be a good ruler, not if I want to save my nephew. Forward. I have to respond to now.

Mal and that kid turn around and walk right out of the complex. Right past two guards who barely look up at them as they leave.

"I want their names." I point to the guards as the footage glides past them. "They can't let people come and go without acknowledgment like that. Security aside, there's a fucken *plague* and they didn't even check to make sure Mal and that kid have masks–which they don't–"

"I'll find out," Deimos says, gaze glued to the moving map. "They won't have jobs when I'm through talking to Kantos."

The boys walk deep into the city, past empty streets and closed shops. Everything is lit and there are guards posted—all in masks, all standing sentry—but if they notice one of the human boys walking past them is the *Sira*'s fucken nephew, they don't show it.

And then the kid turns into an alley between two tall buildings and I want to strangle Mal for following. For not thinking *hey, this is kinduv dangerous maybe I should fucken not.* For not hesitating, not even a mo, while this kid walks him to an area where there aren't guards, where no one can help him, and it's too late by the time Mal stops and realizes how badly he fucked up.

Four men step out of the shadows, two in front, two behind. And none of them pay attention to the kid—they go right for Mal.

I'm going to be sick. It's already happened—I know, I know—but watching this while I can't do anything, while I wasn't there to help him, while he was alone, and terrified, and I should have been there, I should have protected him.

To his credit, Mal fights.

When one of the men grab him from behind, he bucks his head back right into the guy's nose. Blood spurts, the guy drops him, one of the men in front lunges forward just as Mal swings his stick between his legs. That blazing hurt just to watch—good—but in the end, there's too many of them. They're four fully grown men and one skinny, partially-blind thirteen-year-old. And as three wrestle Mal into submission, as the human kid who lured him out there watches silently, to the side, hand over his own mouth like trying not to make a sound–

The leader, who hasn't fought, who's watched this whole time, hands in pockets, almost bored, steps into the light.

And I swear to the blazing suns I'm going to kill Shaw when I find him.

28

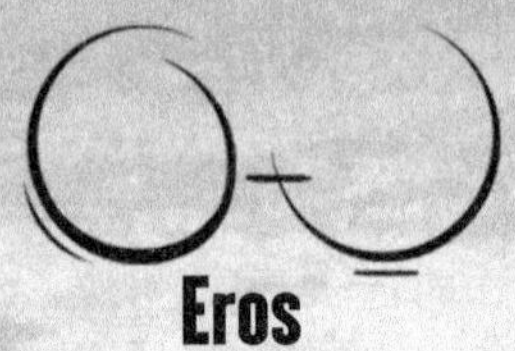

Eros

The footage stops being useful after the four men and Mal disappear into a small building in an offshoot of the alley. Deimos speeds through the rest of the footage until we're caught up to live and no one goes in or out between there, so they're either still in there or that building is a front for a tunnel system.

I'm assuming tunnels. But either way, we know where we're going next.

Kantos creates a rescue team–twelve people including himself and Varo, who insisted on being part of the team because it was his job to protect Mal.

"I'm going with you," I say, and no one argues with me because they can't.

"Then so am I," says Deimos.

"And so are we." Lijdo–Kosim's replacement–gestures to Fejn and himself.

And while it's probably not the best strategy to put the blazing world ruler and his closest advisor on a dangerous mission that could end with everyone dead, I don't care.

I've failed Mal too many times. I won't again.

We get to the building just as the suns begin to rise, painting the deep purple dawn with orange, pink, and red. It's a small house, two stories, sand brick and metal paneled, dusty black floors. Looks like a family probably lived here at some point—there's a kitchen, eating areas, bathroom, rooms I guess were bedrooms. But not now. The place is empty.

"It's secure," Kantos says, as if that weren't obvious.

We all got here on sandbikes, and I kept my helmet tucked under my arm. I put it on again now—which feels weird over my filter mask, but still fits—and everyone but Deimos stares at me like I've lost all sense, but Deimos knows what I'm doing because he's the one who taught me how to do this to begin with.

"*Shae*," Deimos says. "I was thinking tunnels as well."

I flip the filters on my helmet until I've got heat signatures flaring like pillars of fire below us, hidden deep in the sand but not deep enough. "Below us." I pull my helmet off. "They're probably watching."

"Okay, my turn." Deimos pauses and glances around, then looks more intently at the smooth kitchen floor. "There *was* a dust covering," he murmurs, crouching as he runs his fingers over the glossy ground. "But we've ruined that. Still . . . everyone move to the walls."

We do. Deimos inspects the floor, muttering under his breath as he works, stepping softly, slowly, like we're in danger of the floor moving beneath us.

"Here," he announces, tracing parallel lines over the stone. I move closer, squinting at what he's pointing at, and it's not until I'm crouched next to him that I spot the faint scratch marks, perfectly straight, marring the otherwise smooth black surface. "Which means . . ." Deimos traces the barely there indents back with his fingers. "Here. Feel the lip?" He takes my hand and presses my fingers where he's touching. It's barely there–I honestly wouldn't have noticed it without Deimos pointing it out–but we trace out a perfect, large square, about the size of what you'd expect a hidden door in the floor to be.

"Okay," Kantos says. "So now do we have to find the control panel to open it?"

"We could." Deimos stands, wiping his hands together to brush the dust off. "Or we could skip that and blow it up."

Ten mos and one small, controlled explosion later, we re-enter the room wearing our sand bike helmets to see through the dust-filled kitchen. The masks meant to protect us from plague also does a great job filtering the cloudy air. The explosion was small enough–and controlled enough–to barely touch the walls of the empty room. But it incinerated the hidden door, leaving a gaping maw in the middle of the room, which leads into a long, empty tunnel with ladder rings welded into the walls.

"Well!" Deimos says cheerily. "That was fun. Now, who's going first?"

We can only go one at a time, which is an obvious tactical disadvantage, but so be it. Kantos and four other team members go first, followed by Lijdo, then me, then Varo, then Deimos, then Fejn, then three others of Kantos's team. The remaining three stay up top, guarding the entrance to make sure no one sneaks up on us.

Thankfully, the tunnel is wide and the ceiling is tall–this one seems more clearly built for Sepharon to easily move in and out. Everyone wears portable torches both on their helmets and at the end of their phasers, which are held out, ready.

Unlike the extensive system at the Remnant base in Elja, though, this one is simple: one short tunnel leading to one metal, locked door. Not reinforced though. Decently sure it wasn't built to keep out a small army.

Deimos runs his hand over the door, taps it lightly, then licks it and spits at the ground. "Simple, uncoated," he announces. "It'll corrode with phaser bursts."

Kantos nods. "Step back." He gestures to the two on his either side. "You two with me."

Everyone but the two Kantos pointed to step back. And the three of them unleash a storm of phaser bursts over every inch of the door, filling the tunnel with the thick smell of burning metal and something sharp as the door slowly turns to an eye-burning red, like the inside of a superheated coal.

The screech of phaser bursts almost brings me back to the day Kora blasted into my life. The day her army ripped apart my home, my family, everything I thought I knew. Day looking at me, on his knees, hands behind his back, knowing–

I dig my nails into my palm and take a deep breath of burning metal–not fire–not home. I'm here. And I'm staying here until I get my nephew back from that asshole.

Hang on, Mal. I'm here.

The phaserfire stops all at once. And the silence is loud, so loud, stuffing my ears with pressure. The fire-red door dulls to a less-intense orange, then a dull, almost brown, until–finally–dark gray. The shine is gone. It looks impossibly old.

And perfectly brittle.

Kantos nods to us and we all get ready. Phasers up. Ready to move. Heart thrumming, cool air painting me in sweat.

"Just be careful," I say. "If Mal's in there I don't want him getting hit."

"*Sha*, *el Sira*," Kantos says, and the rest nod.

I'm in the midde of the pack, which I don't love, but I get it–I need to be protected, even if I can take care of myself. But since I'm definitely not the tallest guy here, it also means I can't see everything going on up front. I don't need to, though.

Someone up front slams their elbow into the door and the whole thing shatters like razor-thin glass. Then we're surging forward, and Kantos is screaming, "On the floor! Faces on the ground! Hands over your heads!" and then I'm in.

The room is more like a large closet–or small closet, by Asheron standards–barely big enough to fit us all. Shaw is on his knees, hands raised, smirking as his three men splay themselves on the ground as instructed. And Mal–Mal is lying on the ground behind him, and he's across the room and it's clear from here he's shaking, and fuck, he's terrified, of course he's terrified–that fucker dragged him down here and stars know what they've done to him and–

I push through the crowd, pass Shaw, who has the arrogance to smile at me like this is all going to plan, and crouch next to Mal.

"Hey." My voice is soft while Kosim keeps yelling at Shaw. "Mal, it's me. I'm here."

Mal lifts his head and squints at me. Too pale. "Can I get up?" he whispers.

"Of course you can." I help him up and he hugs me–tight.

"I knew you'd find me," he says into my chest. "I knew it. Okay." He takes a deep breath and lets go. Then brushes himself off. "Sorry."

"You have nothing to apologize for." Deimos steps up to us and wraps Mal in a hug. "Are you okay?"

"Yeah." Mal's voice shakes, and he nods, and I believe he wants to be okay, at least, but his face, his chest is bruised. They hit him. They hurt him.

Then someone laughs behind me and it's a bucket of cold water over my head.

It's Shaw. On the ground, with Kantos's knee on his spine and his arms pulled back, cuffed. But he's laughing, enjoying this, watching me with too-bright eyes and a full white smile.

He fucken abducted my nephew. For what, fun? To say he could? To remind me no one's out of reach? To laugh in my face, even when I've got him plastered to the sandrock, even when he's lost?

Kantos looks at me and I say, "Pull him up."

Kantos does, bracing Shaw's cuffed arms behind his back. Shaw snickers and spits to the side. "That's right, Eros. You know what you want to do."

I do.

The first punch cracks across his jaw and down into my elbow.

The second his opposite cheek.

The third his nose, spurting blood, slickening skin like warm oil.

The room is roaring with the song in my ears, the endless drum. I think there are voices–someone saying something–but Shaw is laughing, and I don't care that my fists hurt, I don't care that I was done with this, this fighting, this bleeding, this killing.

I hit him again. He took Mal.

I hit him again. He hurt Mal.

"UNCLE EROS," Mal screams, and it's the first time a voice has cut through the dull thunder in my head, and he's crying, he's crying.

I'm panting. Shaking. Itching to move.

But Mal is crying. "He's human!" he says like it should mean something, and maybe it should. "He's human, please, please, stop . . ."

Shaw grins at me with blood-painted teeth. "That's right, Eros. I'm human. Mal's human." Then he spits. In my face. "But you?" He leans close, leering, sweating, smiling. "You're just a fucken mutt. No better than an animal."

He slumps in Kantos's arms, out before I register my smarting knuckles. His blood on my skin. Wet. Warm. Cooling.

I wipe it off on Shaw's shirt. Turn to Deimos, to Varo, to Fejn, and Kantos, and Sepharon men watching me grimly, with something like respect.

It's true I'm human. It's true I'm Sepharon. And it's true the language of violence is one the Sepharon have honed bone-shard-sharp, and I know it too well and I hate that I do.

Call me what you want. Call me a half-blood, a mutt, a murderer, a victim, disgusting, a waste of air, an animal–say what you want about me, I've heard it all.

But hurt the people I care about and I will fucken destroy you.

"Take him."

29

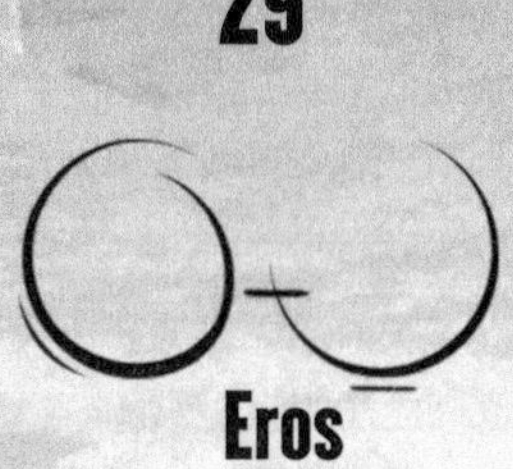

Eros

"What are you going to do with him?" As my bedroom doors close behind Deimos and me, Kora is looking at me through the glass, brows furrowed, not really disapproving but more like–concerned. I would have expected the whole *we saved Mal and arrested Shaw* thing would've gotten at least one *congratulations* or at least a *I'm glad Mal's okay*, but instead, that's the first thing she says.

What am I going to do with Shaw?

"I don't know." I stifle a yawn. It's the dead segments of the morning, still technically night and I probably shouldn't have called Kora so fucken early, but it turns out she was up anyway. And I just–don't know. Needed to talk to someone separated from it all. "I haven't had enough time to think about it. We only just got back."

"You'll need to come up with an answer quickly," Kora answers. "I imagine it won't be long before Rani contacts you, demanding the same."

Deimos glances at me with a *look* and he doesn't have to say it. So, yeah, she's probably right. But stars, it'd be nice to have a mental break from all this for, like, I don't know, a couple breaths, even?

"We'll strategize a response." Deimos sits on the edge of my bed as I settle next to him. "But I imagine you're right. I expect we'll hear from Rani and I suspect she won't be at her most charitable."

I snort. "You say that like she's ever been charitable."

Deimos just waves his hand in response.

"You realize she'll be reacting the same way you did upon realizing Mal was missing, right?" Kora says. "She took your family, and now you've taken one of hers. Her primary concern will be getting him back *immediately*, and by whatever means necessary."

I hadn't really thought about it that way, but, yeah, that's probably true, too. I run my hands over my face and take a deep breath, trying to fight off the impending brainblaze. "Maybe I can use it as leverage. Force them to negotiate."

"Or," Deimos says, "in the highly likely event that she still won't want to negotiate, you could try him, because he's a criminal, and criminals should be processed through our justice system."

"You mean our execution system," I answer flatly.

Deimos just grimaces.

"Whatever you decide matters less than making sure you decide *something*. The world is watching, Eros, and you need to have a strategy ready to handle the Remnant's response."

After ending the conversation with Kora, Deimos and I check on Mal to make sure he's asleep. Except he isn't, not even close, which I guess shouldn't be surprising despite the stars-cursed time, all things considered.

Mal's lying on some pillows tossed on the floor, arms crossed behind his head, in his dark bedroom. He doesn't turn his head when the doors open, so for a moment it almost looks like he *is* sleeping, except his eyes are open, and I've barely taken a step in the room before he says, "I've been thinking."

Deimos and I sit on either side of Mal. We haven't really talked to Mal about what happened yet, though Zarana told us he'd said the bruises were from when he was initially taken and after that "nothing happened," whatever that means. But I know what it's like to go through shit and not be ready to talk about it, so I don't want to force Mal into a conversation he isn't ready for.

So instead, I let him lead.

"What about?"

Mal takes a deep breath. "I've had this idea. I've been talking to the techies and you know how we got here–humans, I mean–on a giant ship, right? Just like the stories said, from Earth, where there are other humans like us, like, a whole *planet* of just humans." He's smiling now, and this is not at all what I was expecting this conversation to be, but if this is what he wants to talk about . . .

"Uh. Sure?"

"So, right, I've been with the techies in the lab a lot–they're super nice and even let me kinduv help a little. Oh, oh, one of them even gave me this." He lifts his wrist and points to a shiny black band I hadn't noticed. "It reads stuff for me since, you know, I can't really see anymore and I never learned how to read Sephari anyway and it also like–it tells me if I'm going to walk into something or someone and gives me directions. It helps a lot."

"That was . . . nice of them." I glance at Deimos and he glances back at me with a bemused shrug.

"Right, so anyway, they have the ship!"

I'm really struggling to keep up with this. A mo ago, Mal was missing and I was trying to handle the Remnant thing and ignoring my fucken endless brainblaze through an exhausted fog before I took more painkillers and then I got fucken bit and Kosim is sick and now we found Mal and took Shaw and Mal seems to be fine and is excited about some ship and dammit, I wish I could be excited with him. I wish I could get where he was going with this, but I'm just so fucken exhausted.

I really need to sleep but the thought of it makes me sick.

"The ship humans arrived on?" Deimos says. "It would be ancient at this point, wouldn't it? That was, what, several hundred cycles ago?"

"Well, *shae*, it's old as fuck," Mal says. "But they've preserved it and they said with some upgrades they could easily get it working again and it still has all communication stuff intact, like–they didn't damage the ship at all when they took the first humans captive. They just took the ship for themselves and the humans never got it back, which was shitty, but, like, they have it!"

I'm not sure if he's supposed to be implying something obvious and I'm just too tired to get it or if he's actually being too vague to really follow, but either way I have no idea what's going on.

"Okay," I say, more flatly than I mean to.

Mal frowns at me. "Okay? That's all you have to say?"

I close my eyes and rub my temples. This throbbing brainblaze is getting bad and now that the adrenaline is long gone, my shoulder is burning again. Maybe I should ask for those painkiller things they gave me after Lejv's guys attacked me. That thing worked so well it was like a pain eraser.

"I'm just–not sure where you're going with this," I manage, opening my eyes again.

"Well it's obvious, isn't it? We could go back!"

Deimos arches an eyebrow. "Go . . . back?" he says carefully. At least I'm not the only one totally confused.

"To Earth! The humans could leave, and then there wouldn't have to be any more fighting about humans and Sepharon sharing the planet. We could go to Earth where there are only other humans."

I frown. "I don't think it's that easy."

"Sure it is. We take the ship, and we–"

"Mal." I sigh and press my palms against my eyes. "There are a lot of problems with that plan." When I lower my hands from my face, Mal is scowling and crossing his arms over his chest.

"Like what?" he demands. "Name one problem."

"Well not everyone's going to want to go, for one," I say. "The Sepharon haven't made human lives easy, obviously, but generations of humans were still born here. This is just as much their home as it is the Sepharon's."

Deimos nods. "Not to mention there are *many* more humans here now than those who arrived here hundreds of cycles ago. There have been generations upon generations of humans who were born here, descended from that original group of humans. They likely wouldn't all fit on a ship designed to hold a fraction of them."

"*And* like you said, that ship is old as fuck. Even with upgrades, it's pretty risky throwing thousands of people on a hundred-cycles-old ship and hoping it'll just work."

Mal frowns. "Okay but you've already solved, like, one of those. If not everyone is going to want to leave, then the ship doesn't have to hold so many, right? Maybe there will be enough room. And maybe it'll be enough to show the Remnant that you're doing *something.*"

"And if there isn't enough room?" I ask. "What then? I don't want to introduce a new thing for humans to fight over. And I'm not sure suggesting humans leave is really what the Remnant is looking for. That's probably the opposite of what they want, really."

"Well, for the room thing . . . then we send them on Sepharon ships, too. It doesn't have to be just the one ship. And it's not exactly what the Remnant asked for but they said you had to show signs of taking steps to *reorganizing the current system* and this could be a step if you present it right."

"I think they more meant reorganizing the government but . . . maybe." I glance at Deimos. "We have ships?"

"Well, *shae*." Deimos lifts a shoulder. "We don't use them all that much because we're a rather . . . reclusive race, but the technology is there. My father used to tell me about the space program we had once. It was grounded and defunded because we weren't really interested in interacting with other races, but—"

"Hold on, hold on. *Other* races?"

Deimos smirks. "Well you didn't think it was just Sepharon and humans in the whole universe, did you?"

If I were being honest, I'd say *sha*, mostly because I never really thought about it, but the way Deimos is looking at me kinduv makes me feel dense for ever thinking that. So I just turn to Mal instead. "You said the techies know about this?"

"Well obviously," Mal says like I actually am the densest

person in the room, which maybe I am. "They're the ones who told me."

"Are they still there?"

Mal nods. "There's always people there. The lab never sleeps."

"All right." I stand and stretch my arms over my head, willing this brainblaze to go the fuck away. "Does Varo know you're okay? He was worried about you earlier."

"*Shae*, he stayed with me when Zarana was checking on me."

Deimos nods. "Good. From now on, don't go anywhere without Varo, *shae*? He's our way of knowing you're safe. And he's there to protect you."

Mal grimaces and sits up, lightly wrapping his arms across his chest. "I know, I . . . I messed up." He glances at me. "I just . . . wanted to hang out with someone like me, you know? Human. And my age."

I sigh. "I know. I wish I could give that to you but . . . you know."

Mal just nods.

"Relatedly . . ." I tug on Aren's bracelet around my wrist then force my hands flat on my lap. "Do you want to talk about what happened? Any of it? I know I . . . I know I lost it a bit back there."

Deimoes touches the small of my back, just a bit, to say he's there. And it helps me breathe deep, steady, as Mal frowns. He's quiet for a long time–so long I almost open my mouth to say forget it, he doesn't have to talk about it–but then, finally, Mal says, "I thought you were going to beat him to death."

A chill rolls down my back. What happened back there–it's exactly the kinduv thing that's made it impossible for me to sleep. The nightmare where I kill Lejv, where I don't hesitate—except this time it was reality, and it was Shaw, and I don't—

I don't know. I don't think anyone else would have stopped me, and if Mal hadn't called out . . .

I don't regret beating the stars out of Shaw after what he did to Mal. But a part of me is glad Mal snapped me out of it because I don't think I would have stopped if he hadn't.

"I think I might've if you hadn't said anything." I glance at Mal. He isn't looking at me, but he doesn't look—I mean, he doesn't seem scared or disgusted or anything. "I'm glad you stopped me, though. Even if he probably deserves it."

Mal shrugs. "I don't know that anyone actually deserves that. And if they do, I don't know that it's really our call to make." He pauses and faces me. "I'm not, like, judging you or anything—I know you've had to make hard choices and everything. I just, I don't know. I feel like people hurting each other doesn't usually make anything better."

The thing is, I don't disagree with him. But that doesn't change that I've had to kill. And it doesn't change that despite wanting to leave that violence behind, buried deeply in my past, I was ready to do it again. And maybe I don't feel bad about how I reacted to Shaw after he hurt Mal, but maybe I wish Mal hadn't seen that side of me ready to take someone else's life. Because no one else did that. I did.

"I'm sorry I reacted like that in front of you."

Mal shrugs. "You were just angry and scared. I get it. I'm not mad." He stretches his arms over his head. "I'm kinduv done talking about it though, okay? Can we move on and talk to the techies about that old-as-fuck ship?"

I ruffle his hair and try to force a smile. "Sure. Whatever you want."

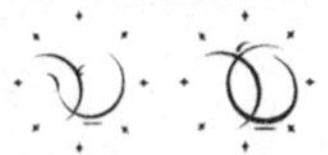

The "old as fuck" human ship is enormous.

I knew, I guess, in theory that a space ship that carried people from one planet to another would have to be pretty damn big–I mean, people *lived* in there. But I guess it hadn't really occurred to me that ships would be so big they couldn't actually land on the planet.

"So it's just been floating out there?" I ask. "All this time? Hanging out in space outside of Safara?"

"We've kept it with our other ships, *sha*." Dara says. "As I'm sure you're aware, our space program was pretty severely defunded several decades ago. It's basically been cut down to just maintenance and weaponizing research to make sure we don't fall behind, technologically, just in case we ever need to mobilize our ships in force."

I didn't know until thirty or so mos ago, but she doesn't need to know that. I just nod like I knew all along. "This is probably an obvious question, but how did the humans get on planet if the ships can't actually land?"

"Shuttles," she says. "Same way we get to our ships to maintain and upgrade them. We still have the ones the humans used if you'd like to see them."

"Do they still work?"

She lifts a shoulder. "They're slow and clunky, but *sha*, they work. We can upgrade them relatively easily, as well."

"See?" Mal says. "No one has to be stuck here. People could leave if they want to. And I bet a lot will want to. The nomads aren't the only ones who don't really have a home here."

I frown. He has a point–maybe I should consider extending the shelters we're setting up for freed enslaved people to others, too. How many people would the shelters be able to take?

"Do you think it would work?" I look at Dara. "Sending humans back to Earth on that old Earth ship. Would it make the trip?"

"We've maintained the ship and upgraded it over time—it was already pretty severely outdated when we first confiscated it. It's been a sort of curiosity project for us, to see how we could integrate our technology with theirs. If you could call theirs technology—it was rather rudimentary."

"So, that's a *sha*."

"That's a *sha*. But first we need to eradicate this disease—last thing we need is an outbreak on a ship or introducing a deadly virus to another planet. And then we'd require funding for food and supplies. It's a long trip to Earth—we've calculated and with our current technology it'd take four cycles at best. And even before that, you'd need to make contact with the Earthers. I can't imagine a ship appearing out of the blue full of unannounced redbloods who grew up on another planet would be well-received. I have no idea what their relationship is like with the other races, but if they're anywhere near as reclusive as we are, a ship just appearing in their orbit would likely be seen as a threat."

I hesitate. The thought of speaking to people on another planet—*humans* on another planet, who have never had to worry about integrating with Sepharon, who probably know very little about us because of the way the Sepharon have shut themselves away from everyone else.

Honestly, this all feels artificial. Like I can't completely swallow it because it's not completely real. Like this is a bizarre dream.

Although that's probably the lack of sleep talking.

"So, if we wanted to contact them . . . how would we do that?"

Dara smiles. "Like I said, we still have the shuttles. And we've maintained those, as well, so the communications systems are all still intact. It might be a little difficult to establish contact again, but I'm sure I could get a team on it to figure it out, if you wanted."

Mal is grinning at me like this is the best thing that's ever happened, and maybe it is good. Maybe this could be a solution for those who have nothing left. For those who are tired of fighting to live, tired of fighting to be equal.

We know nothing about Earth. For all I know, it could be just as bad there as it is here. But Mal might be on to something. This could be worth looking into, even if just a vague possibility.

"Go ahead and get a team on restoring communications with the Earth humans," I say. "And let me know as soon as it's working. I want to be the first to talk to them."

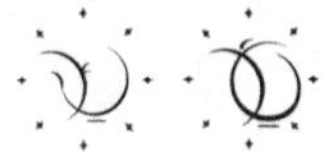

While apparently, if I wanted to, I could just feed myself explaining whatever new laws I wanted to establish and that would be the end of it, Deimos and I agree that talking over all this new information with the Council would be the best first move. Especially since everything is still rolling around sluggishly in my head and it's getting harder by the mo to process it all.

It doesn't take long for the Eight to arrive. They each

bow to me as they enter then sit at their appropriate places at the table. Tol is the last to arrive, which makes sense since they're coming from the lab decently far from the palace, like we just did.

"Thank you all for joining us so early," Deimos says with a casual smile. "It's been quite the set already and the suns have barely risen."

"Thank you for calling the meeting," Tol says. "I was about to contact you both anyway to let you know the techies have tracked down the source of the feed hack and are in the process of coding new defenses to ensure it doesn't happen again."

"Wonderful," Deimos says, and I nod.

"As you probably guessed, the feed hack and arresting Shaw are a big part of the reason we're here right now."

"But not the only reasons?" Kenna says with an arched eyebrow.

"Uh, not the only reason, *naï*," I answer.

"How is Kosim?" Rion asks. "And how are *you*? We heard about the attack and that Kosim fell ill."

I grimace. "My shoulder will scar but I'm fine. Kosim . . . I don't know. Zarana is doing everything she can to try to save him."

All eight Council members lower their heads. I think it's their way of showing condolences or something.

"Any news of a cure?" Kenna asks.

"Humans don't seem affected, so Zarana took a blood sample from me, but that's all I know so far. I'll make sure the eight of you are kept updated."

Kenna nods.

"I imagine you've seen the news about Dima's sentencing and subsequent escape," Rion says.

It takes me a mo for those words to sink in. The sentencing I'd heard about briefly, but . . . "Dima escaped?"

"Unfortunately." Rion purses his lips. "He and his boyfriend ran sometime last night and haven't yet been found. I imagine they're both halfway out of Elja by now. *Kala* knows where they plan to run to."

I scowl. Really? I just blazing talked to Kora and she didn't say a fucken thing to me. I can't imagine she's torn up by the escaping news after being so adamant that Dima be tried in Elja to give him chance or whatever. As if he deserved an ounce of mercy. As if he didn't kill innocents.

Stars, I wouldn't be surprised if she *helped* him escape.

"Great," I mutter. "I didn't know that, but I can't imagine there's much we can do about it now."

"Elja should be punished for their transgression. The refusal to hand over Dima was bad enough, but to botch the process like this makes a mockery of the system, and by extension, a mockery of you, the *Sira*, who demanded a free and quick trial."

The brainblaze pushes harder against the backs of my eyes. I can't focus on Dima, not now. There's too much to think about. Too much that needs some kinduv action or attention, but I can't do it all. I have to focus on one thing at a time, and right now that thing has to be answering the Remnant.

"I'm going to be honest with you," I say. "I can't prioritize punishing Elja right now. We need to talk about the Remnant's threat last night, and Shaw's arrest, and what we're going to do when they inevitably contact us again. And I do have some ideas." The Council members nod and no one protests the whole skipping-over-Dima thing, so I plow ahead and tell them about the ship, and Mal's idea, emphasizing the part where it's *optional* for humans to leave. "But it's an option I think a lot will be open to," I finish. "Especially given everything they've suffered here for generations. And if I present it right, I might be able to play it off as a . . . *reorganization*, like the Remnant wants, without caving to exactly what they're demanding."

Tol smiles. "That's brilliant. I think the people will really respond to that."

Kenna looks a little less enthusiastic, but she nods nevertheless. "You'll definitely want to be careful with how you word it–you don't want to give the impression that humans *should* leave, which is a message you risk sending not only to the humans and Remnant, but to the Sepharon as well who might take it as an excuse to be even more hostile to humans."

My heart sinks a little at that. I hadn't thought of that–which is ridiculous because I should have thought of that. It's so obvious. Of course assholes will take it as a way to harass humans even more. Bigots will *want* humans to leave.

But if we have the option to give humans a chance to live somewhere the Sepharon won't follow, wouldn't it be wrong not to present the possibility just because some people might be assholes about it?

"That's a good point," I say. "I don't think that should stop us from looking into the possibility of getting humans who want to leave out of here, though."

"It shouldn't, I agree," Kenna says. "But I do want to caution you to think carefully about the way you present it."

"How do you know the Earthers will take them back?" Rion asks. "You don't want to go through the trouble of sending them there just to have them turned away."

"I've already talked to the techies about that. They're in the process of setting up a communications channel so I can talk to . . . someone there."

Rion nods. "And if they say *naï*?"

"Then I won't say anything to the people here, I guess. I'm going to talk to the Earthers first before I make any announcement."

"Good. And when will this conversation happen?"

I open my mouth to answer but Tol beats me to it. "I'm sorry to interrupt, but we're dealing with another hack this time in the personal communication interface." They glance at me with tight lips and a lifted shoulder. "It sounds like you were expecting this given Shaw's arrest, and you were right. The Remnant want to speak to you, *el Sira*."

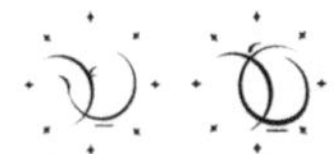

Unlike every other time so far, this hack isn't broadcasted on every feed–probably because Rani doesn't want to admit to the world that they blazed things up and now I have their guy.

So even though it's probably bad for diplomacy or whatever, I'm smirking a bit when the techies feed her through to the glass in the Council room.

"You're a smug little shit, aren't you?" Rani's glare is so sharp her face looks carved. "You think we won't get Shaw back?"

"Good morning, Rani," I answer calmly. "So nice to see your face twice in under twelve segments."

"I swear to the stars, Eros, if you hurt Shaw–"

"Oh, we're way beyond that." I laugh. "I beat the sand out of him when I found him. You know why?" I stand and step closer to the glass recording me back to her. "Because he and his friends abducted and beat my thirteen-cycle-old nephew. So do us both a favor and skip the self-righteous shit about how I've gone too far, taking your man, when you've been fucken terrorizing my people and attacking my family. You started this war, Rani, but I'm not afraid to finish it."

"Terrorizing your people." She laughs–a hollow sound. "You think what we've done so far is bad? I swear to the suns, and the stars, and every grain of sand on this stars-forsaken planet, if you don't release Shaw immediately, I will burn Asheron to the ground if that's what it takes to get him."

"You think I'm thick?" I shoot back. "I'm not going to just *free* him without you giving us something in return. That's not how a fucken negotiation works."

"Oh, you think this is a negotiation? That's cute. Borderline adorable, even."

"You seem to be forgetting I have your man."

"No, Eros." She leans forward, her gaze drilling holes into the glass. "You seem to be forgetting I have the means to destroy you. You can't hold Shaw, not for long, and you know it."

"Weird. Almost like you think I'm too thick to realize if you really could get Shaw so easily you wouldn't ask–you'd just take him, consequences be damned."

Rani sits back. Laces her fingers together. "Asking was a courtesy. But you know what? You're right. I'm not feeling so courteous anymore."

And that's it. The feed blacks out.

And I may have just really fucked this up.

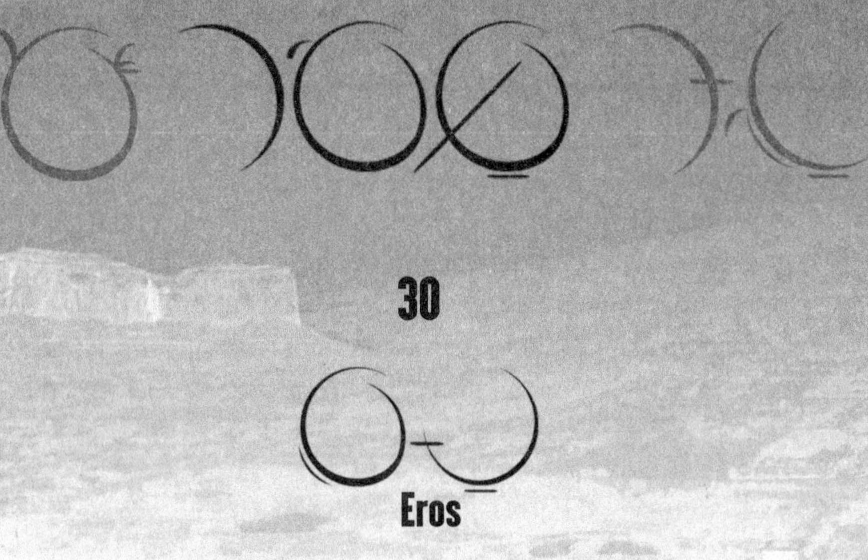

30

Eros

I've barely had time to process the enormity of what just happened with Rani when Tol says they're sorry about the timing, but the techies have set up contact with the head of an Earther organization called *Inter-Nassa*. And apparently, they're eager to talk.

Which is great because I'm definitely not in the right state of mind to talk to Earthers for the first time about a really fucken important issue that could change thousands of human lives forever, but you know, sure, whatever, let's do it right now, why not? Can't possibly go any worse than what went down with Rani.

The human Earther representative they've chosen is a guy who reminds me of Gray. They have the same sharp, dark eyes and shadow-black stick-straight hair. Main difference is this guy is at least four shades paler than Gray and obviously their faces are different, but the resemblance to someone so far away, someone who's never stepped foot on Safara . . .

I mean, it makes sense since humans are all the same species, but it's still weirdly unsettling.

The rep's face is blown up on a glass the size of half the enormous wall in the lab. I'm not sure I really like this set-up—I'm sitting with a guide hovering in front of me while he looks like a giant peering at me through the fucken sky. It makes me feel small. At least with a regular glass-to-glass communication, the glass just kinduv floats in front of me like looking through a small window but this . . . well. He can't know what my set-up looks like, so I play it calm. Like I talk to humans from another planet all the blazing time. Like I've been ruler of the fucken world forever and I don't still feel like a kid playing pretend.

I start our totally normal, everyday conversation with, "Do you speak English?"

The guy arches an eyebrow and his eyes widen—then he laughs. I'm not sure what was funny about asking if he speaks English. I glance at Deimos, standing beside me out of the guide's view. Deimos obviously doesn't speak English—no one in this room does except for me—but he lifts a shoulder at the guy's laughter with an expression like *who knows*?

"Yes, I'm sorry," the man says, drawing my attention back to him. "I didn't mean to laugh—I just—we just spent a good forty minutes trying to figure out which translation software would be best and seeing if we had any information on the Sepharon language—which, turns out we don't—and there you are, speaking English."

His English is weird. Fast, and kinduv hard to parse with the way his words come out all chopped up like a knife rapidly hitting a cutting board. But though it takes me an extra half-mo to process, and I'm not really sure how long a *minute* is, we do understand each other, which is a good start.

"Let me start over and introduce myself," the guys says. "My name is Koji Issen. I'm head of communications at the

Earth branch of the Interplanetary Alliance. You've probably heard of us."

I hadn't heard of them, but he doesn't need to know that. "Sure. I'm Eros . . ." Do I introduce myself the Sepharon way? The human way? He used a first and last name like the Kits. Would it be better to show him I'm somewhat like him? Does he know I'm part human? "Eros Kit d'Elja," I finally say, combining the two. It feels the most fitting, seeing how I *am* both. "I'm *Sira*." I pause. He probably doesn't know what that means—after all, it's not like the Sepharon share information with people off-planet. "Uh . . . world monarch, I guess."

"World monarch you guess, huh?" He grins, and I kinduv get the sense he might be making fun of me. "Well, that's a pretty impressive title, ruler of the world. I feel more important just talking to you."

I'm not really sure what I'm supposed to say to that, but I guess we should just move on. "Right, so, I'm sure you're aware we have a lot of humans here on Safara."

"We weren't aware of that, actually," Koji says. "We never really knew what happened to the OC that went over there forever ago. It was considered a failed mission and we assumed everyone was dead."

"OC?"

"Sorry—original crew. The group of humans that tried to settle there back in 2150."

I nod. "The way I understand it, many were killed but there were a lot of survivors. And now generations later, they live all over Safara. I'm not sure exactly how many there are, but it's got to be more than the . . . the OC."

"Makes sense." Koji crosses his arms over his chest and leans back in his seat. "So tell me, Eros, Ruler of the Free

World: why are you contacting us out of the blue five hundred years later? You guys made it pretty damn clear we weren't to contact your people ever again if we wanted to stay at peace."

"Things haven't been great for humans here," I say. "There's a lot of discrimination and persecution just for being human. But it was recently brought to my attention we have the ship that brought the humans here to begin with, and we've got other ships, too, and I think some humans would be open to the idea of going back."

Koji tilts his head slightly. "Going back?"

"To Earth. Where they'll never be attacked for being human again."

Koji's face softens as he glances at someone out of the frame. He nods and looks back at me. "That's a real interesting proposal, and if you're serious, I can definitely bring it to my higher-ups who'll talk it over with others and seriously consider it. But I think you should know coming here won't mean they won't ever face discrimination again. We've got a host of our own problems here on good ol' Earth."

I frown. "I thought Earth was all humans."

"We are–well, mostly, there are some other friendly species here, too, but for the most part, yeah. But everyone being human doesn't stop prejudice and discrimination. Humans will always find reasons to hold some higher than others–I imagine, in the case of your sending humans over, they'd face a new kind of anger from people who won't consider them *really* human because they were born over on Safara instead of Earth. We've already got that kind of nastiness from ship-born and base-born people. So they won't be discriminated for being human, per say, but there will always be something."

He shrugs. "I just don't want to give you the impression everything will be perfect here. We're no paradise, either."

I nod slowly. "I guess that makes sense. But do you think it'd be possible to send some humans over there?"

"Maybe." Koji pauses and looks away from the camera again before he nods and addresses me. "Let me talk to my people and we'll get back to you. This isn't going to be a slam-bam process, but I'll get the ball rolling and see where it goes, feel?"

I frown. "Feel what?"

Koji is laughing again when the camera blinks off. And I guess . . . that was that.

We talked to some Earth humans. One Earth human. And I represented Sepharon and humans here on Safara and I think it actually went somewhat okay.

I take a deep breath and smile. I did it.

And now we wait.

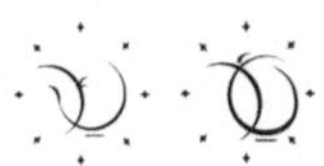

The next couple sets are a lot of back and forth. I tell Koji on our second chat that we have a deadline–though I don't tell him the deadline is because the Remnant is getting ready to unleash sunsfire on us for not moving fast enough, and also for taking Shaw. I consider making the freedom announcement separately just to placate them, but I don't want to do two major announcements like that back to back. Better to blend them into one announcement to help buffer the reaction.

Plus as long as we have Shaw, I'm pretty sure nothing short of letting him go will satisfy Rani. So we wait.

On the third set, the set we have to get back to the Remnant before they fuck everything up even worse, assuming Rani hasn't changed her mind about that whole timeline anyway, I've all but given up on Koji getting back to us to us on time when I get another call to come back to the lab for another meeting.

"This better be it," I mutter to Deimos as they set up the guide. "We can't keep waiting along for them to make up their damn minds like this."

"*Kala* willing, this will be it," Deimos answers.

I don't mention I doubt *Kala* gives a fucken blink whether the Earthers cooperate with us, assuming there is a *Kala* at all. Deimos steps aside and the guide whirls in the air, stabilizes, beeps twice, then a green ring lights up around the lens. I'm live.

"Eros!" Koji smiles at me from the giant screen he's projected on. "Good to see you. Thanks for your patience, I know time is of the essence over there. I can just imagine what a delicate situation it must be, with humans waiting to hear whether or not they can return home."

I never specifically said the humans knew of this potential plan–that's just an assumption I guess he's making. But he doesn't need to know it isn't true.

"Do you have an answer for me?" My voice comes out calm. In control.

"I do, yes. We've spoken to several leaders from all around the world, and our leading countries are each willing to take a limited number of Safaran refugees. Canada, Germany, and France are willing to take up to 2,000 refugees each. The United Kingdom, Australia, and the Philippines are willing to take 1,000 refugees each. China, India, Japan, Mexico, Egypt, and the United States are willing to take 500 each–which altogether brings us to 12,000 refugees total. How does that sound?"

Twelve thousand spots spread out over twelve territories. I honestly don't know if that's going to be more than we need or less–I haven't a clue how to begin estimating who is going to want to go and who is going to want to stay.

"If all goes well, we may be able to arrange for more to come in the future," Koji says. "I can't make any promises, obviously, but it's a start, don't you think?"

"Sure," I finally say. "It's a start."

"Good, good." Koji smiles. "So when do you think they'll arrive?"

I glance at Deimos and murmur the question in Sephari. He widens his eyes and lifts his shoulders as his lips tighten. He has no idea and neither do I, so I turn back to the glass. "I'll get back to you with an estimate. Thanks for your cooperation. I'm sure a lot of people are going to be happy to hear about it."

"I'm glad I could help negotiate," Koji says. "Now what do you plan to give us in return?"

I blink. Narrow my eyes. "Descendants of Earthers and your ship."

Koji laughs, then I guess he realizes I'm not joking because he abruptly stops laughing and his smile drops. "Oh. Oh, I'm sorry, you're serious. I didn't realize." I don't smile. Koji shifts in his seat and runs a hand through his hair. "I see. Well, surely you must realize we're doing you a pretty huge solid by taking these people. It's not a simple thing to coordinate resettling refugees all around the globe. It's only reasonable, I think, to expect some sort of tradeoff in return."

I'm not sure what he means by "doing me a solid"–a solid what?–but I let that slide. "I've opened up communications for the first time since your people came here," I say. "I'm sending back your ship and you'll get thousands of descendants of your . . . OC. I'm not sure what more you're expecting."

"Not *expecting*, but it would be *nice* to offer some sort of recompense for our cooperation."

Of course they want something. People always want something. I force myself not to scowl, but I can't imagine I'm hiding my irritation that well, especially given the way his smile takes a pained twist, like he knows he's walking a very thin wire. "Get it over with," I say. "What do you want?"

Koji's smile shifts into something smooth. It kinduv reminds me of Deimos's smile when he's putting on his *look how charming I am* thing that you'd think would lose its effect over time but definitely doesn't. It might have even worked with Koji if I wasn't so done with this conversation. "We'd like to set up an Alliance embassy on Safara. Or if that's too much to ask, one stationed just outside the planet. For us to further our diplomatic relations."

"No." I don't even have to consult with Deimos and the rest of the Council on that one. There's not a chance in the Void bringing *more* humans here will go well with everyone. And definitely not a whole building dedicated to humans–at least, not right now. "I don't know what our relations will be like in five to ten cycles," I say. "Maybe that's something we could talk about in the future. But right now there's no way that's going to happen." Koji frowns, but I press forward. "Look, opening up communications like this isn't a small thing. I can agree to keep the lines of communication open—both to you and to . . . to your alliance. It's a big step forward for Safara after we've cut ourselves off for so long, and it's all I can promise you right now."

Koji hesitates, then nods. "If you can promise to consider an embassy in the future—let's say we revisit the topic in seven years—then I think we can accept that."

"Fine. We'll talk about it again in seven years. But I'm not promising you a yes then, either."

"That's fine." Koji smiles. "So you let us know when you'll have the humans over here, okay? We'll be waiting to hear from you."

"I will."

And with that, I've actually done it. I've negotiated a place for 12,000 humans on Earth. I was too afraid to hope but this—this might actually work. This could be a really good thing. And it's all thanks to Mal.

The guide turns off and I stand, letting a smile slip over my lips as I turn to Deimos.

"You're doing so great." He grins. "You were perfect talking to him, you know that? Completely regal and professional—I fully believed you were an experienced leader and I'm sure it's what he believes as well. Really well done, Eros. You're adjusting well to your new role."

I smile. "Thanks to you."

"*Sha*, I suppose I did have something to do with that." He nudges my side with a smirk and I laugh.

"*El Sira*." Lijdo steps forward with that frown I'm pretty sure is permanently embedded to his face. My heart sinks at the address. So far the only times my guards have ever made a point to address me was to give me bad news, and somehow I don't think this is going to be any different.

Can't even enjoy a victory for five fucken mos.

"*Sha*," I say with a sigh. "What's wrong?"

He almost looks apologetic as he speaks. "I'm sure you'll see this on a glass momentarily, but I've just been informed there's been a joint announcement from Inara, Kel'al, Invino, and Sekka'l."

He hasn't even said what this joint announcement is, but if Sekka'l is involved, I can't imagine it's going to be anything good. And I have a sinking feeling I know what it is.

Lijdo grimaces. "I'm afraid they've announced they're going to secede."

Sometimes I hate being right.

31

Kora

For four sets, Uljen barely talks to me—and when he does, it's official business only. Updates on the search for Dima and Jarek, or the planning stages for an infrastructure project to clean up the city, or our depleting stores of food as we become increasingly dependent on Daïvi, Ona, and Kel'al to send us food.

I've done something irreversible in aiding Dima and Jarek's escape—and lying to Uljen about it even when I knew it was pointless to deny I'd been involved. But admitting the truth to him would be trusting him with something that could ruin me.

I can't trust anyone with that. I can't give someone a weapon to destroy me with. Because even if I want to believe they wouldn't use it, even if I want to believe my closest allies would never betray me—how can I?

My own twin brother tried to kill me. My father tried to sabotage me. If I couldn't trust my own family, how could I possibly begin to trust a man I've known for less than a term? A man who introduced himself by threatening my reign, by proposing he be *Avra* in my stead, by calming an almost irrevocably angered people just to show me he could.

Uljen is here for the people, but I know what power does to people. I know what it did to me, to my brother, to my father.

With Dima and Jarek gone and Uljen not speaking to me, the morning meals are painfully quiet. It's been four sets but I still glance at the places where my brother and his boyfriend used to sit. Where they will never sit again. And yet, I keep expecting to see them there when I look across the table, stealing secret smiles and sharing quiet laughs over jokes only they know.

Instead, Uljen sits still as a stone beside me as Lira loads up her plate with food across from me. "I swear, the food is better every set–and it was already amazing to start with."

I force a smile. "I'm glad you think so."

"Don't you? Actually, you're probably used to the food since you've always had it. Uljen, then, don't you agree?"

Uljen looks up quickly, as if startled someone is speaking to him. He was reading something on his glass, though it's on his other side so I can't see what he was looking at. I suppose I should probably be catching up on the morning news, as well, assuming that's what he's doing.

"Ah . . . *sha*, the food is good." He turns to me. "Have you read the reports this morning yet?"

I glance at him. "You mean from the Council and new head of the guard? *Naï*, not yet."

"You should."

I pause. "Okay. Or you could tell me what it is that you think is so important I know. That's also an option."

He purses his lips and, for a moment, I think he might just turn back to his glass and continue ignoring me, as he's been doing as much as possible for the last four sets, but instead he nods–albeit clearly reluctantly. "They're saying Eljans want to join the secession with Inara, Kel'al, Invino, and Sekka'l."

My heart stutters in my chest. "The people want–*what*?"

"I'm not entirely surprised," Uljen says. "You know the Eljans are overall a rather conservative people, and having a half-blood as a *Sira,* well . . ."

"We're not seceding."

"I didn't think we were. But you'll need to talk to the people and justify staying if you don't want them to feel ignored."

I groan and pinch the bridge of my nose. Of course the people want to secede. Uljen's right, this shouldn't surprise me–Eljans are traditional and upheld the anti-half-blood laws stringently for generations. They still do. And as much as I hate to admit it, it wasn't so long ago that I agreed with them. So of course they want to leave now that we've actually had some progress in Eros taking the throne.

"Well," Lira says lightly. "At least it'll distract from the whole Dima situation."

Uljen grimaces and shakes his head. He doesn't speak to me again for the rest of the meal.

The silence is a thick, heavy thing by the time we return back to my rooms to strategize what to say to the people about this secession nonsense. I suspect even Lira can feel it–she fidgets with the hem of her skirts, with her hair, and passes me uneasy smiles every couple breaths.

As soon as the doors close behind us, I turn to Uljen. "Just get it over with."

Uljen arches an eyebrow. "Get what over with?"

"You've been holding back for sets. I'm not a child, I know you want to say something, so say it."

Uljen's eyes narrow. "Don't ask for things you don't truly desire."

"I don't desire being reprimanded, but I *do* desire you getting whatever it is out so we can continue our work as normal. This stony, silent version of you makes our work more difficult than it needs to be."

Uljen rolls his eyes. "And that's truly your concern, is it? That my *stony silence* is making your job more difficult? Well your *releasing your criminal brother* has made *my* job more difficult, so I think you can handle some *stony silence* in recompense, don't you?"

I grimace. There's no use denying it. I'm not trusting him with new information if I admit he's right–he already knows, and my denials have been useless. He already has a weapon of my ruination. He already has a truth that could destroy me, because the way he speaks it tells me he has no doubts.

So as much as it terrifies me, there's little use in denying it anymore.

"I swore to my brother and Jarek that I wouldn't let them execute him. I did what I had to to keep my word."

Uljen laughs, shaking his head. "And keeping your word to your traitor brother was more important than not betraying your people, was it? More important than justice? More important than making things right?"

"Killing him wouldn't have made anything right–"

"That wasn't for you to decide, Kora!" Uljen paces across my rug, his shoulders stiff, face incredulous. "Truly, I thought you understood that. What happened to Dima was never supposed to be your call–you were, and are, too close to the situation to be able to make an unbiased decision."

I snort. "Oh, and I suppose the rule of the Eight was unbiased, was it?"

"They were more impartial than any decision you could ever make." He shakes his head. "And even ignoring the morality of the situation–I can't *begin* to fathom why you'd put your own life at risk to save a man who tried to kill you. Brother or not, Dima is *not* a good person. Surely you must know that better than anyone!"

"I haven't put my life at–"

"Kora." Uljen shakes his head and stares at me, wide-eyed. "Surely you must realize if anyone ever learns of your involvement in his escape, you could be sentenced to death in his stead."

My blood turns cold. My breath freezes in my lungs. "Excuse me?"

"You really think such an action would go unpunished? Being an *Avra* doesn't protect you from your own crimes–Dima's sentencing should have been more than enough of a reminder of that."

I clench my fists and take a shivering breath. My voice comes out low and cutting. "Are you threatening me?"

Uljen blinks and his eyes widen like I've slapped him. "What? *Naï*, Kora–you, you must know I wouldn't expose you to anyone but . . . if someone learned of your involvement–"

"And how would anyone learn of my involvement if you didn't tell anyone?" I don't mention to Uljen he's not the only one who knows–that Lira knows, too. Because as sure as he has apparently been that I was involved in Dima's escape, he never once mentioned Lira or the guards, so I can only assume he has no idea how they were involved. And quite frankly, it's not something he needs to know.

"I'm not–I'm not saying someone *will* learn of your involvement." Uljen sighs and runs a hand over his face. "I'm not a threat to you, Kora. I'd never do anything to harm you. I couldn't even if I wanted to."

My eyes narrow. "And why is that?"

"Why?" He laughs weakly and shakes his head. "I know we're not in a relationship, Kora–we're just friends who enjoy each other, *sha*? But I still care and I thought the feeling was mutual."

I am, possibly, the worst friend on Safara because the feeling is mutual but I am terrible at trusting people. But could anyone blame me, after everything?

Still. Uljen deserves better. "I . . . I apologize. You're right."

Uljen purses his lips again and nods. "And I accept your apology. My point is merely I'm on your side."

And I want to believe him just like that, I do. And maybe part of me does.

But the other part of me can't help but wonder if it's truly wise to trust anyone at all.

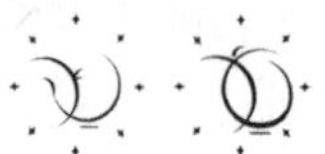

It's been a long while since I've addressed the people in the city square. For the longest time, my addresses had always been just outside the palace gates, because people were already gathered there, protesting, and I couldn't have ventured father into the city even if I'd wanted to. But this time I actually have a relatively normal address. This time there aren't protests, or screams, or tossed bottles and rocks. This time the people gather in the city square because they know

I'll be addressing them from there, and this time the murmur of the crowd is curious, uncertain, but not angry.

At least, not yet.

I take a careful breath, wipe sweat from my temple, and deliberately don't touch my earring. The suns, as always, are hot, but at this time of the cycle, they feel closer. The heat is more intense, like I'm sitting just breaths away from the surfaces of the suns. Like they're moments away from swallowing me whole.

But it's a familiar discomfort. It reminds me I'm home.

"Thank you all for joining me here today," I say to a quieting crowd. The guides hovering all around the crowd and in front of me amplify my voice, again and again. "I'm addressing all of you here today, because I've been made aware there's an increasing number of you who want to join Inara, Kel'al, Invino, and Sekka'l in the movement toward secession. Many of you, I imagine, are supporting the secession because of your mixed feelings regarding the new *Sira*, which I understand. But I feel it's important to remind you that unity of the territories under Jol eight hundred cycles ago has brought us the longest era of peace in our history. It was coming together and creating a single governmental system that works together with the territories that has allowed us to put down our arms and leave bloodshed and infighting behind as a thing of the past. And I truly believe *Sira* Eros intends to maintain that legacy.

"I trust *Sira* Eros to do what he must to keep the peace and keep Safara as we know it—a unified whole. And ultimately, that's the legacy I want to be a part of—and I believe it's the legacy you want to be a part of as well. For that reason, Elja will remain, and I truly hope Inara, Kel'al, Invino, and Sekka'l ultimately choose to stay as well. Generations of peace have taught us unity is the best way forward, and I intend to do my part in ensuring it remains that way."

Murmurs rumble through the crowd like thunder, but there aren't shouts of protest, at least. It seems they're listening. I can only hope it'll stay that way.

I nod and turn away from the crowd, just as someone shouts out, "What will you do about the fugitive, Dima d'Elja?"

I still and bite my lip. I take a deep breath and do everything I can to keep my expression as emotionless as possible as I turn back to the crowd. "Dima's escape is under investigation, and some of our best men are out looking for him and his accomplice as we speak. The investigation will not rest until they are found and dealt with accordingly." The words taste bitter in my mouth, even though I know they have to be true. I have to do everything in my power to appear as though I support the investigation. And I can't interfere in any way. And I won't.

But I can only pray they'll be unsuccessful. Because I can't save my brother a second time.

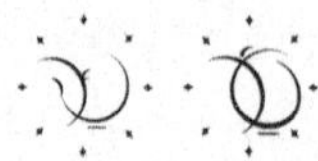

"You realize you've just effectively tied your fate to Eros's by supporting him publicly like that."

My bedroom doors have barely closed behind us before Uljen's criticism rains on my shoulders. I close my eyes and take a slow, steadying breath. "I'm aware."

"And you think that's wise?" Uljen steps around the room so we're facing each other again. The concern in his furrowed brow and deep gaze is genuine.

"I don't know what's wise or what isn't." I shrug and pull out the clips holding up my hair , letting it fall over my shoulders. "But I'm not going to betray Eros again. Not even to make my people happy."

"Interesting."

"Is it?"

Uljen shrugs. "You seemed perfectly fine with betraying him to try to save Dima."

I grimace. "Disobeying a ridiculous command that was devised only to make himself look better wasn't a betrayal. I don't have to do everything he says to support him."

Uljen smirks. "Technically you do. He's *ken Sira*, and ultimately who you answer to."

"An *Avra* answers to *Kala* above their *Sira*."

"Uh-huh. And I suppose you think *Kala* wanted a murderer to walk free, did he? That seems rather convenient."

I frown. "Dima hasn't walked free. He and Jarek have lost everything. And they're wanted fugitives. Even if they manage to stay out of shackles, they'll be hiding for the rest of their lives. I wouldn't call that *walking free*."

"Maybe so, but it's not the punishment he was sentenced, either."

"That wasn't *Kala*'s punishment. That was the Eight's punishment." I sigh and pinch the bridge of my nose. "Can we please not argue over this? What's done is done. I can't take back what I did, even if I wanted to. I'm exhausted of this conversation and we need to move on."

Uljen hesitates, then nods. "You do realize this isn't just going to disappear on its own, *sha*? This will be a continuous problem until Dima and Jarek are found."

"I'm aware. Now, if you don't mind, I'm going to take a relaxing bath and not think about any of this mess for the rest of the set."

"Understandable." He pauses. "Do you . . . mind if I join you?"

My heart trips over itself. I stare at him, wide-eyed. "You want to . . . in the bath?"

"Only if it won't make you uncomfortable. I do want you to be able to relax."

In a way, I'm grateful he doesn't state the obvious—that he's already seen me undressed multiple times, so sharing a bath shouldn't be a big deal.

"I'm just . . . tired of fighting, too, and I'd like to be able to relax with you," Uljen adds. "But only if you want to."

"Very well," I finally say, and Uljen smiles.

As we undress and slip into the large in-ground heated bath in my wash room, the whole experience feels—different. More exposed. Whenever I'd been this vulnerable with Uljen in the past, it was in the dark. We were painted in shadows and our eyes were frequently closed and it was more about touch and doing what felt good.

But there's nowhere to hide in my lit washroom, and the bath water is clear as violet-tinted glass.

"May I ask you a personal question?" Uljen asks, after we've sat in the warm water in silence for a few moments.

"You can ask," I say. "I can't promise that I'll answer."

Uljen smiles slightly. "I was just wondering why until recently you always covered your scars."

My heart sinks to my toes. I shouldn't be surprised that he's asking—after all, he's even more scarred than I am and he doesn't hide at all. But the question brings a hot prickle crawling up my throat and the room already smells like smoke as I consider how to answer. "It's . . . a reminder," I finally say. "It always felt like a judgment of some sort, for something so horrible to happen at my coronation. Like *Kala* himself was telling the world he was angry I was *Avra*. I'm not sure I still believe that, but the feeling of judgment is still there and . . . even without that, it's not a set I want to remember."

Uljen frowns. "That's understandable . . . but perhaps you could consider giving them new meaning."

I glance at him. His scarred skin begins on his face and reaches down his hip and to the remainder of his leg. It's on his chest, back, arm, and shoulder. It rips away *Kala*'s mark on his skin there entirely—Uljen was clearly much more injured from the attack than I ever was, and yet . . . his scars don't seem to affect him like mine do me.

"Did you never want to hide them?" The question is out of my mouth before I can think better of it. I grimace. That was hardly a question I should be asking. "Forget it—I apologize, I shouldn't have—"

"*Naï*, it's fine." Uljen smiles weakly. "I did—and for the longest time I didn't want to look at myself in the mirror because the scars made me feel . . . ill. But hiding them was never an option for me, not really. It's not like I was going to wear a mask, so I learned to accept it." Uljen crosses the space between us, stopping just in front of me. He gently takes my scarred arm and kisses my pink skin. "Our scars aren't a sign of weakness; they're a reminder of our strength. Of what we endured and walked away from. Of our survival." Uljen smiles at me. "And for that, I wear my scars with pride."

32

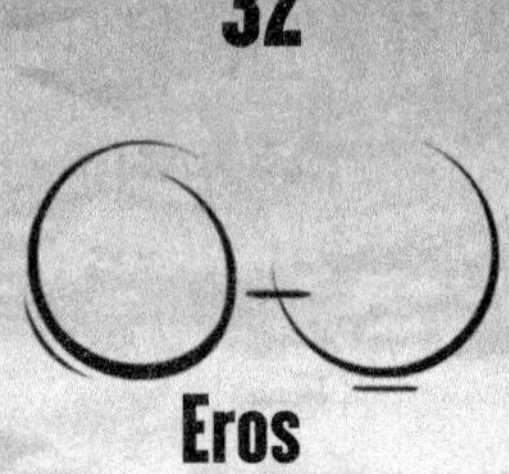

Eros

When Deimos wakes me for our morning run, I tell him I'm too tired and to go ahead without me today. It's not a lie–I *am* tired after another night of sleeping in fits and starts and feeling no more rested when it's over, but that's not the real reason I want him to go without me.

Mostly I need the privacy. Because if I'm going to do this boyfriend thing with Deimos, I need to research.

Are there more important things I should be thinking about right now? Obviously. Between the plague, and the Remnant threat, and Sekka'l wanting to secede, and taking care of Mal, and juggling blazing everything, I should be spending every spare mo I have trying to fix something.

And it's not like I'm not trying. I'm going to be addressing everyone about the Earth possibility later today. But I'm exhausted. I need a mental break. And through it all, as much as I'm trying to be responsible, I can't stop thinking about Deimos.

So I grab my glass and turn it on, my heart already thrumming in my ears in anticipation of . . . what exactly I'm doing here.

Fuck, how am I even going to research anything? I can't read.

I open up the feed, but that's mostly just news and not helpful. I need someplace I can search, like I've seen Deimos do on his glass, but I don't entirely remember how he got there. I try going through different pages on the glass–there's a pad thing I think you can write on, some random screens I assume are games, then a blank screen.

I bite my lip and glance at the door. This is going nowhere and I need to figure this out before Deimos comes back. Because I like kissing him–a lot–and I like holding him at night, but I think he knows I have no fucken idea what I'm doing because he hasn't really . . . tried anything more. And I want him to. But I also want to know what I'm supposed to do.

But this blank screen isn't exactly giving me any answers.

"Fuck," I whisper. "How am I supposed to Voiding do this?"

"Can I be of assistance?" the glass chirps in the same voice as the orb guides.

I arch an eyebrow. I can talk to it? "Uh . . . *sha*. I need to do a . . . search."

"What would you like to search?" it asks.

I bite my lip and glance around the room, my heart suddenly in my throat. Deimos isn't here. He only just left, like, five mos ago so I have plenty of time. No one is here. Relax.

I lean close to the glass and mutter, "How to . . . make men happy."

"Okay. Here are some videos on gift buying, popular men's hobbies, vacation spots–"

"*Naï, naï*." My face warms. "Not . . . not that kinduv happy. Like . . . how to . . . you know . . ."

"I'm afraid I don't understand," the glass says. And of course it doesn't. It's a fucken glass, not a person.

Fuck, I'm going to have to actually say it.

"I need to search how to have sex with guys . . . when you're a guy," I whisper, as if someone is actually going to hear me even though the room is totally empty.

"I'm happy to assist you," the glass chirps happily. "Here are videos on men having sex with men, pleasing men sexually, anal and oral sex for beginners–"

"Okay," I say quickly. "Got it, thanks." My face is on fire. Stars, it sounds so much more awkward with the glass announcing the search results to the room. But I've got it. Pages upon pages of videos. Which is good, because I don't have to read.

But I . . . also didn't really think about what exactly I'd be watching to learn this stuff. But since I can't read, there's no other way to learn it myself so . . .

I tap a video with a picture of a smiling young guy standing in front of a blank wall, which seems, um, less explicit than most of these other videos. He goes through tips on sucking guys off and stuff guys like and first-time tips using sex toys as examples, and just listening, even with ridiculously colored props and happy background music, makes me kinduv half-hard. So. Doubly glad Deimos isn't here.

I watch a bunch of videos, and, you know, it helps. There's stuff I wouldn't have thought of, like where and how to touch, and steps to take, and generally what to expect. And it's–reassuring, kinduv, to see random guys my age casually talk about sleeping with other guys. I feel a little more prepared already.

But then . . . there are a lot of videos of guys having sex. And even as part of me says *you don't need to watch this, you've already gotten the information you wanted*, I hit one of the videos anyway. I mean, what's the harm, right? I'm alone, and it might help me get a better sense of what it's actually like because stars know I'm not going to have Deimos describe it to me, and even if he did that wouldn't be the same anyway so . . .

Whatever. It's just a video.

It starts off ridiculous. The men–who, I'll admit, are unfairly attractive–flirt ridiculously and say stuff that would never work in real life and then they're kissing and moving to a bedroom and the clothes start coming off.

Like, really fast.

I swear I blink and it's suddenly two naked men on top of each other on a bed, and between the noises they're making and the way they're moving, I'm hard instantly. The room is an oven and I should probably stop watching this, but I can't. There's something–I don't know–something magnetic about seeing two guys just enjoy each other. And even as I'm throbbing watching them move together, I don't want to look away.

The ache is getting pretty bad, though, so I wet my palm, reach under the covers and grip myself.

And the door whips open.

I gasp and slam the glass face-down on the bed, but that doesn't turn it off and the moans are impossible to miss as Deimos blinks at me from the open doorway. Fuck. Fuck fuck fuck. Why is he back already? Wait–how long have I been watching this stuff?

Deimos's gaze slowly goes from me to the glass still groaning on the bed.

I thought the room was hot before but my face is absolutely blazing now.

"Is . . . that what I think it is?" Deimos smiles slightly and steps toward the bed, reaching for the glass before I snatch it up and try to turn it off—but I suddenly can't remember how to do anything and instead the volume goes up and the panting and cries get louder. If dying of embarrassment is a thing that can happen, it's definitely about to happen to me.

He kneels on the bed and plucks the glass out of my hands and I swear everything is happening in slow motion and I can't move a muscle. He wasn't supposed to—I didn't think—I just—

Deimos's lips quirk as he looks at the glass. "Ah, *shae*, I've seen this one."

I blink. Wait. "What?"

Deimos smirks and looks at me. "What, you think I've never watched sex videos before?"

My face is so hot it's tingling. "I . . . I don't know. Not like I . . . thought about you watching . . ." Suns and stars alive. Now I'm picturing him watching these. I shift uncomfortably to try to hide the fucken phaser barrel sticking up under the sheets but of course that only brings Deimos's gaze to exactly where I didn't want it to go and this actually couldn't get more humiliating.

When Deimos looks at me again, I swear it's like he wants to eat me.

"You know, I'm a little wounded you didn't invite me to watch with you."

My mouth opens and closes and opens and closes. "I . . . it's not like I planned—I mean, I wanted to do some research but—"

"Research, hm?" Deimos turns off the glass, tosses it off to the side, then fucken *crawls* up to me until his hands are on my shoulders, gently pushing me down. "You know, I'm *more* than happy to do that kind of research with you *any* time."

I can't breathe. "Deimos . . ."

Deimos's face softens. "We don't have to do what they were doing until you're ready—there's no rush. But if it's okay with you . . ." He trails his hand down my chest to the edge of the sheet. "I'd like to help you with this."

I gulp. He's so close I can practically taste the salty scent of his sweaty skin and his fingers are so fucken close and, I'm not gonna lie. I want him to.

"Okay," I croak.

"Wonderful." Deimos spits on his hand, then kisses and grips me in one smooth motion.

Look. I'm eighteen, so, yeah, I've jerked myself off before. And at this point, I've got it down pretty well exactly how to get off, not that it was ever all that hard to figure out to begin with. And in the end Deimos is pretty much doing the same exact thing I'd do to myself but this—

This is better.

And now that we've crossed this line, I don't think we can go back. And I don't want to.

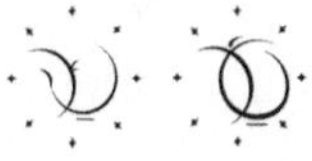

After Deimos has reduced me to a sweating, panting, blushing mess and we've cleaned up, I can't help but wonder how many times he's done this before. How many guys–and have there been not-guys? The truth is I don't really know because we've never talked about it, and I want to stop thinking about it but how can I when he seems so at ease with everything? When every heart-stuttering new step for me is just another knowing smile for him?

I'm not jealous of the people who've been with him before–well, maybe I am, just a little. I just mostly wish . . . I don't know. That I didn't have to wonder, I guess.

"Hmm." Deimos turns off the water and dries his hands with a cloth. "You don't look nearly pleased enough, given the *excellent* service I just provided."

I laugh and my face prickles hot again. "It wasn't–it's not that. You were blazing amazing."

Deimos snorts. "I know I was." His smile fades and he touches my shoulder. "I'm sorry, I shouldn't joke when you look so . . . concerned."

I shake my head. "I like your jokes, I just . . ." I take a deep breath. I should just say it. I can't know if I don't ask. And I can't be irritated that I don't know if I don't try to find out. "I know the . . . constant flirting with you is part of your personality, and it's fine, I just . . . was wondering . . ."

Deimos waits, watching. Fully serious. Waiting patiently for me to blurt it out.

"I mean, for one, are you . . . *just* into guys or . . .?"

"Ah. *Shae*." Deimos smiles. "It's just men for me, always has been. I *did* experiment some a few cycles back, just to see, but it only confirmed what I already knew."

I nod. It's not like knowing changes anything, but I don't know. It's . . . reassuring, to know, somehow.

"How about you? I have to admit I've been rather curious about it myself."

I blink. Deimos was wondering about me? Actually, I guess that makes sense given the whole thing with Kora. "I'm still working it out but I'm obviously *lijara*, as you well know. I've been into guys and girls so far. Haven't met enough other genders to be able to speak from experience but . . . I'm into more than one gender, *shae*."

"Okay." Deimos tosses me the cloth to dry my own hands. And just like that, I'm a little lighter, having said it. Establishing that so casually, so neither of us has to wonder, is a relief. And when Deimos grins at me, smiling back is easy.

33

Kora

Uljen, Lira, and I settle at the table with our morning meals placed before us, as the glasses in the room broadcast the feed from Asheron. Eros will be giving some kind of speech from the city square, and I don't know what it'll be about, but Eros publicly affirming his role as *Sira* isn't something I'll ever miss.

I sip my tea and stir dried fruit into my thick cream while watching the murmuring crowd on the glass. Fresh foods—especially fruits and vegetables—are rationed and much harder to come by now, but our stock of dried fruit is relatively extensive, at least. It's not the same as what I'm accustomed to, but it's a small price to pay to help keep Eljans fed.

Eros steps onto the podium, accompanied by guards. As he stands in front of the people and the crowd quiets, he looks—confident. At ease. And I'm sure he isn't, I'm certain he's terrified and hating the attention, but that doesn't matter because he's learned to hide it. He's learned to look like a ruler. And he does it so well.

"He looks good," Lira says softly.

I smile. "He's come a long way. He looks much more comfortable as *Sira* now, don't you think?"

Lira nods. "He looks like he knows what he's doing."

"Thank you, everyone, for coming out to listen to me this morning. It's truly an honor to serve the people." Eros inhales deeply and pulls his shoulders back, looking directly at the crowd and the orb guides hovering over everyone. "I want to start by addressing the recent admission from the Remnant that they are responsible for the plague affecting so many in Asheron–these attacks on our people are unacceptable and will not be tolerated. While what the Remnant are fighting for–equal rights for humans–is admirable and something I want to advocate for, as well, their methods are wrong and ultimately ineffective. We should be working together to make the world a better, more equal and accepting place, but if the Remnant continue to use violence and death to make their wishes known, then we'll only be taking steps backward, to the war-torn society our ancestors tried to spare us from."

Eros pauses to glance around, looking over the silent crowd. Then he nods, as if deciding something. "I also want to talk about a related topic many Sepharon seem reluctant to discuss–our human peers sharing this planet with us. Humans have been here for generations upon generations, but despite being here for more than long enough than it should take to integrate, they still find themselves persecuted. Enslaved. Treated as lesser. And it's long past time for that to end.

"In my short time as *Sira*, we've taken an important step toward ending that inequality with the abolishment of slavery. But I'm well aware that one move doesn't so easily wipe away generations of hate, and for that reason and more, I've been in talks with humans . . . on Earth."

Lira gasps beside me as my mouth drops open. Eros has been talking to Earthers?

The crowd murmurs and Eros raises his hand, effectively quieting everyone again. "I've negotiated a place for twelve thousand humans to return to their planet of origin *should they want to.* I want to emphasize this is an optional program—a way for humans to begin a new life somewhere else, because for so many humans, Safara has taken everything from them. However, I want to recognize that's not the case for all humans—for many, Safara is and always will be their home, and those humans are absolutely welcome to stay as we try to improve life together here. But for those who would be interested in learning more about potentially going to Earth, information will be sent to all public and private glasses at the end of this address."

I glance at Lira, who has her hand over her mouth, gaze caught on the glass. This is enormous—not only because Eros re-established communications with other peoples, but because people haven't come or gone to or from Safara since the arrival of humans ages ago.

But Eros is changing all of that. And I couldn't be prouder.

"Wow," Lira says. "I never imagined . . . back to Earth?" Lira laughs and looks at me. "Kora, this is amazing."

"It is," I agree, and when Eros ends his speech and steps away from the podium, it seems the people agree, too.

They cheer.

34

Eros

After successfully broadcasting plans for twelve thousand humans to return to Earth, should they choose to do so, Deimos says the People Speak network flooded with comments, especially from humans. A lot of it is good–people interested, or even excited to leave–and some of it is understandably hesitant, or even outright disapproving, which is fair. But it's encouraging, at least, to see some humans are happy about the suggestion.

With that going so well, though, I guess I shouldn't really be surprised the second important thing I need to do doesn't go half as well.

The large blank screen in the meeting room, for the fourth time, tells me what I already know.

"Inara's ignoring our summons, too," I say flatly. "Just like Kel'al, Invino, and Sekka'l."

Deimos and the rest of the Council grimace. "It would appear so."

"So what now?" I turn away from the screen and face everyone. They all look equally grim, and the way they glance at each other with pursed lips and uncertain expressions tells me something else, too. "This doesn't usually happen, does it?"

"Not to a *Sira*." Tol sighs and leans back. "It's highly disrespectful to ignore a summons, and to do so to a *Sira* . . ."

"It means they don't accept you as *Sira*, in essence," Deimos finishes.

"That's hardly new information though. I'm pretty sure I got that with the whole *we're leaving the fucken union that's been around for hundreds of cycles* thing. Seeing how secession only interested them after I became *Sira*."

"Well, *shae*." Deimos sighs. "That's unfortunately true. But this confirms it."

"So again, what now?" I point the glass. "Apparently I can't even get them to consider hearing me out. If I can't talk to them to try to convince them not to leave, what am I supposed to do? Let them go?"

"You could consider sending a military envoy to retrieve them," Rion says. "But that would mean risking war, particularly if they refused to cooperate, which I suspect at least some of them would."

"I thought the whole point of trying to convince them to stay was to avoid war."

Rion grimaces. "It is."

"Then that sounds like exactly what we shouldn't do." I shake my head and glance at Deimos. "Do you have any ideas?"

Deimos drums his fingers and chews on his lip as he looks at me. "This doesn't solve everything, but with Sekka'l's secession we could frame it in terms of their displeasure with the slavery abolishment—say it's Sekka'l holding on to a terrible practice, rather than because you're a poor leader."

"That *would* work," Rion says, "except Kel'al, Invino, and Inara are evidently considering the same, even though they haven't argued against the abolishment."

"And either way doesn't answer how to convince them to stay." I hook my finger under Aren's bracelet and take a deep breath. "Okay. So what happens if I let them leave?"

Deimos's eyes widen and Rion sits forward, pressing his palms against the table. "*El Sira*, surely you can't–"

"Just–tell me what would happen. Walk me through it."

"Well, you'd lose the confidence of the people, to start with," Tol says. "If one leaves, so will the other three–so that will leave you with other nations who will consider leaving as well. The union will fracture, territories will become independent, and you risk wars like the old sets as territories focus on only their own interests and damn everyone else."

"Not to mention the ramifications of losing the people's confidence," Rion says. "If the people see you can't keep the union together, they won't support you. And they'd likely call for you to step down. You'd be viewed as a failure and any progress you've made would be erased."

"Including any laws you made," Deimos says softly.

Rion nods. "A *Sira*'s first cycle is . . . probationary, in a sense. The laws you make become law, but if you don't last a full cycle, the next *Sira* could wipe out your changes."

Which means all the people I managed to free would lose their freedom again. Just like that.

I run my thumb over Aren's bracelet and bite my lip. "This is impossible. How am I supposed to convince people who don't want to be here not to leave if they refuse to even speak to me?"

No one has an answer for me. And the silence is damning.

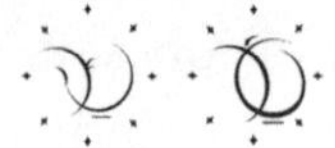

Deimos and I take a walk—with Fejn, Lijdo, and six other guards because no one wants to risk what happened last time happening again. And this time, despite Fejn and Lijdo's protests, we leave the complex.

After all, we got attacked *in* the complex last time, so the way I see it, we're not really safe anywhere we go anyway.

So with filter masks on, extra immune boosters given to us all, and a contingent of eight guards surrounding us, we take a totally casual, normal, not-at-all noticeable walk through the city streets. Right.

I shouldn't complain. I know the danger—obviously—especially after what happen with Kosim, and my shoulder still blazing hurts from that fucken bite. But staying in the palace, in the complex all the time, is suffocating. I grew up with a people who were always moving, making our homes in new places two or three times a term. Staying in one place is hard enough without the extra restriction of being trapped behind walls.

We visited Kosim before we left. He looks miserable—feverish and barely eating, eyes slowly darkening, but Zarana says his body is fighting it, because his progression isn't as quick as some other patients she's had. He still recognized us. Still knows what's going on.

Still knows he might die if we don't figure out a cure quickly.

I wish I could do more than wait for someone else to figure out a cure. I wish I could tell Kosim—or Fejn, even, who's constantly worried about him—that he's going to be fine, that a cure will be ready on time.

But I can't. *Sira* or not, I'm powerless to do anything but make sure he's comfortable and has the best medical care available.

People glance at us and bow as we walk by, their expressions mostly covered by filter masks. It's almost eerie seeing person after person–adults and kids alike–all wearing the same identical masks, all watching us with impossible to interpret gazes. Do they consider it an invasion for us to walk through like this? Or is it like what Deimos told me back when I was trying to get chosen as *Sira*, where the people see it as a way for us to say we don't think we're better than them?

I assume the worst but hope for the best.

While some shops are closed and the streets are a little emptier than usual, it's a relief to see people still going about their lives. At least the city hasn't come to a complete standstill–at least there's still an echo of normal, even with an unprecedented disease setting people against each other.

Of course, the increased guard presence stationed at every corner can't feel especially normal to anyone.

Eventually we reach the main square, which is still as full of people as always. But instead of the regular steady flow of people moving in and out, there's a gathering in the center in front of a golden statue of enormous stacked letters I can't be bothered to try to parse out right now, because shouting and all-too-familiar grunts turns my blood cold as I stop in my tracks.

My heart races. Prickles crawl down my back, sharp and radiating.

"Eros, what's wrong?" Deimos frowns at me, and he doesn't hear the dull *thump* of impact, the coughs and ragged breaths, the sounds through the cheers that I know too well.

“We’re going through the crowd,” I say stiffly. “Now.”

Our guards push through the people, clearing a path to the break in the center where two human men are passed out on the glistening, blood-splattered stone and a third is held by two Sepharon men while another Sepharon guy punches him in the jaw, the ribs, his stomach–

I don’t have to tell the guards what to do. They yank the Sepharon guy throwing punches back and wrestle him to the ground as Fejn frees the beat-up human from the two holding him up and more guards arrest them, too.

“You said you wanted them to leave, *el Sira*.” The Sepharon man on the ground laughs as guards twist his arms behind his back and activate magnetized cuffs on his wrists. “We’ll help them leave, *ej*? One *kafran* redblood at a time.”

It takes everything in me not to rip him from the ground and beat him like he beat these men. My heart is screaming against my ribs and my blood is broiling as I check the human men passed out on the ground–alive, thank the stars–then crouch in front of the guy Fejn is checking over.

“Are you all right?” I ask, hating myself for asking as soon as the words are out of my mouth. Of course he’s not okay. He and his friends were just beaten within a breath of their lives while a crowd of people watched and cheered. While guards in the square did nothing to help them.

The man wipes blood off his mouth and chin with the back of his hand and spits red on the ground beside me. And as he looks right at me with a heated, cutting glare, he doesn’t have to say a single word for me to understand.

This is my fault.

35

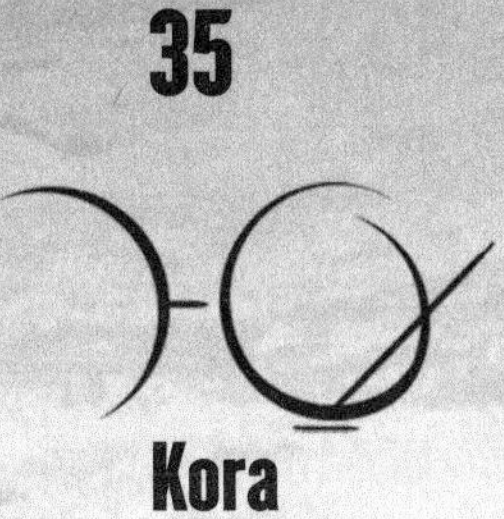

Kora

With the suns rising over the crimson sands, painting the purple sky with streaks of pink, orange, and gold, with my mind thrumming and blood buzzing, Lira finishes my hair and sets out my clothes for the set.

I dress and don't think about Uljen and face Lira with a thin smile.

Lira's smile in return is genuine and unforced. "Beautiful as always."

I nod and face myself in the mirror. My loose skirts and the wrap over my chest are customary enough—today my colors are light purple, pink, and silver. But even though I've been mostly leaving it uncovered, I haven't looked at my scarred arm in earnest in a while, and the splash of shiny, warped skin still churns my stomach. But what am I so afraid of? If I'm being honest with myself, I sincerely doubt anyone else cares about this as much as I do—certainly no one has commented.

This is my skin, and Uljen was right all along. There's no sense in hiding it.

I close my eyes and take a deep breath. I'm not thinking about Uljen yet.

"You seem distracted."

I open my eyes and glance at Lira. "That obvious?"

"Mostly because I've grown to know you." Lira smiles softly. "Do you want to talk about it, whatever it is?" She lowers her voice. "Is it Dima?"

I shake my head. "For once, *naï*. It's . . ." I sigh and tuck some loose strands of hair behind my ear. "It's Uljen. He . . . confessed his feelings for me and I have no idea how I'm supposed to respond. Or feel."

"Well . . . do you like him?"

I press my lips together. "I do. But I'm not sure how deep those feelings run right now. And I . . . I'm not sure I want our relationship to develop into anything more than friendship. I've already lost Serek and Eros and I'm—I'm not sure I could go through that a third time."

Lira tilts her head. "You haven't lost Eros. You're still friends, aren't you?"

"*Sha*, but . . ." I sit on the edge of my bed. "We had the potential to be more than friends, once. He had feelings for me, and I him, but it . . . it wasn't appropriate, given my position and his, and I was terrified of what a relationship with a half-blood would mean for both of us, and so I turned away from him. And he felt betrayed, so he moved on. And then Serek died and—" My voice croaks and I press my fist to my mouth.

Lira gently rests her hand on my shoulder and squeezes lightly. "You know, even if things with Eros had progressed initially, I don't think it would have lasted."

I glance at her. "What makes you say that?"

She lifts a shoulder. "Well now that he's *Sira* and you're *Avra*, it isn't permitted to begin with, *sha*? And even if it was, a relationship dies when you can never see each other. And it's not like you could ever permanently leave Elja or he could permanently leave Asheron. And then there's Deimos, who is with him every moment from what I gather off the feed, and it seems the two of them are rather close."

"*Sha*, I . . . I noticed that."

"So I don't think it would have worked out anyway. But the two of you still share a bond, and if I'm being honest, a friendship with the *Sira* is a very valuable friendship. So I don't think your time together was wasted at all."

She has a point, I suppose, though I'd never thought of it that way. I nod and she smiles.

"Besides, do you regret your time with Eros and Serek?"

"*Naï*, of course not."

"Then what are you afraid of with Uljen? I mean, take your time–you don't have to rush into anything. But I don't see any harm in seeing where it goes. If being with him makes you happy, great, and if not, you move on with new memories."

I laugh weakly. "You make a compelling argument."

"Thank you. My mother used to say if winning arguments and debates were a profession, I'd be a wealthy woman." I laugh. Lira smiles and pats my shoulder. "We should head out to the morning meal, *sha*? I'm sure Uljen is wondering what's taking us so long."

I nod and stand. "Thank you, Lira."

"You don't need to thank me. You pay me to help you, after all." She winks and I laugh again. And we leave my bedroom with giggles on our lips and walk right into four guards in addition to my two sentry guards, apparently waiting outside my bedroom.

"Oh," I say, stopping abruptly. "What is it? Is something wrong?"

"We have new information regarding Dima's escape," one of them says, and it takes every ounce of my self-control to keep my face neutral as my stomach plummets to my toes.

"I see," I say carefully. "What sort of new information?"

"Regarding . . . someone who may have been involved in aiding the escape."

Oh, *Kala*. What if they know? It sounds like they know. Who else could they mean? We obviously already knew Jarek was involved as he disappeared as well–unless, maybe they're here to report about the guards who feigned ill and claimed to be asleep?

But then why would they send four guards to do it?

"Well?" I say, trying to sound impatient and not panicked. "Who is it? Who was involved?"

The guards all look at Lira and my breath catches in my chest. *Naï*.

"Lira d'Elja, you need to come with us for questioning regarding the escape of the criminal Dima d'Elja. Immediately."

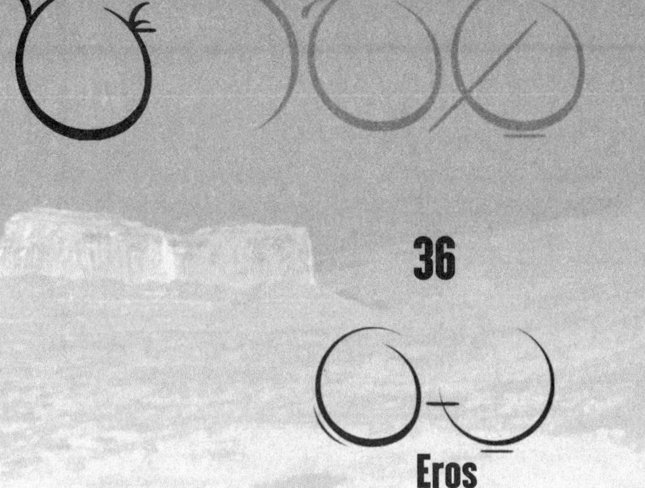

36

Eros

After ordering the military to disperse the crowds, establish an early curfew, get the humans medical attention, and put the guards who fucken *watched* and didn't do a blazing thing on permanent leave; after watching the feeds with my eyes throbbing in my skull and my blood running heavily through me like liquid rock; after trying to juggle this secession shit, and the spreading disease, and restoring the nanite production, and getting the ship up and running, and figuring out how we're going to keep track of humans who want to leave and where we'll tell them to go, and trying to do all that while learning all the menial stuff I have to do to keep the city, the territory, the world running smoothly–

I'm not panicking. I'm not. Deep breath in, deep breath out, I'm okay, and one way or another we're going to handle everything. One thing at a time. One step at a time.

But I don't feel right, either.

Everything is fuzzy and Deimos is talking to me but his voice sounds far away. And I don't remember walking to the dining hall to eat but we're here. And food is out–some rice, veggie, meat mix–and there's some moved around on my plate like I've been eating but I don't . . . I don't remember that.

How long have we been here?

"Maybe I shouldn't have announced anything." The words come out of my mouth but they feel wrong. Sound wrong–muffled.

My head is heavy and this brainblaze won't quit and I don't know what's wrong with me.

"What do you mean?" Deimos is frowning at me–at least, I think he is. His face is kinduv blurry. Which is weird because I don't have eyesight issues–at least, I don't think I do.

I blink a couple times to focus on his face. Better. "Just . . . with the Earth thing. Exactly what I didn't want to happen happened. Sepharon are attacking humans now like–to make them want to leave even more. That's not . . ." I rub my palms over my eyes. It's so hard to focus on words, on anything.

But this–this too is familiar. I know this bone-deep exhaustion. I've been here before, in Dima's dungeon–

The burning the pain the screaming–

"Eros? Eros, *ej*, look at me, *shae*? What's wrong?"

Nothing. Everything. I need to sleep–really sleep–but I can't because if I do I'll remember everything again and again, and stars and suns above I don't want to relive that dungeon and the death and the blood and please, I can't, I can't–

"Fejn, get a medic please."

"*Naï*," I say. "I'm-I'm fine. I don't need a medic. I'm not panicking. I'm okay."

Deimos shakes his head. "I've let you convince me to put this off for too long. You need help, Eros. The exhaustion is killing you."

"I'm fine."

"Eros–"

"I said I'm fine, Deimos!" My voice comes out louder than I meant and Deimos's eyes widen. Fuck. I didn't mean– "I'm sorry. I wasn't trying to yell."

Deimos purses his lips. "Okay. But please put the knife down."

Knife? I'm gripping a knife. My fingers are wrapped so tight around the hilt my knuckles are pale and my hands are shaking. When did I grab a knife?

I release it and it clatters on the table. The shivering in my hands travels up my arms and into my chest. My teeth chatter and I grit my jaw and clench my fists and nothing is helping and fuck. I'm falling apart. I'm shaking to pieces and I can't stop it. I can't hold myself together.

"He hasn't slept a full night in *Kala* knows how long," Deimos is saying to someone. A man in a familiar uniform but I don't remember what it means. When did he get here? I don't remember him walking in here and he definitely wasn't in here a mo ago. I'm losing time. Did I fall asleep or something? If I did, wouldn't I remember waking?

The guy is frowning down at me deeply. "I should have asked for you sooner, I'm sorry," Deimos says. "This is my fault."

"I'm sure it's not your fault, Deimos." The man crouches in front of me and puts his hand on my shoulder, smiling gently. "*El Sira*, can you hear me?"

Why is he asking me that? "*Sha*." I resist the urge to say *obviously*.

"Good. Do you remember the last time you've slept a full night? Deimos tells me it's been a while."

The answer is before the dungeon but I've lost count of the sets. "I don't . . . I don't know."

"He was having sleep issues during the campaign, too," Deimos says. "He told me this has been going on since *Avra* Kora d'Elja's lifecycle celebration, at least."

The medic arches an eyebrow. "That's over a term ago." He frowns at me, then looks at Deimos again. "Can you bring him to his bedroom? I'll meet you there shortly. Thank you for calling for me. You did the right thing."

Deimos gently pulls me up by my arm and I'm too tired to protest. Even walking feels funny. Heavy, like boulders are tied to my ankles.

But when I lie back in bed, I don't want to dream. "This is a bad idea," I mutter.

"It'll be a dreamless sleep," Deimos says. "Right?"

Oh. I guess the medic is here. Did I lose time again?

"*Sha*," the medic says. "You won't dream. To you, it'll likely feel like you wake up as soon as you fall asleep, but in the meantime your body will get the rest it desperately needs." He unpeels a wrapping off one of those sticky gel things and places it on the side of my neck. It stings a little. Barely. But the pain is a distant thing, easily ignored, and as Deimos slips his hand in mine, I drift away, holding on to him like a lifeline.

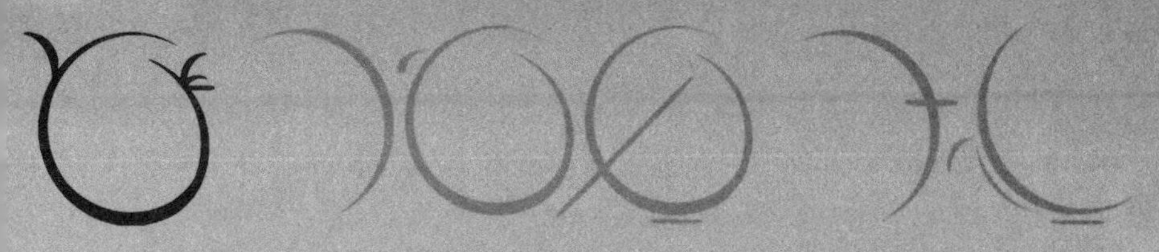

37

Kora

"We can't just leave her to them!"

Uljen sighs and leans against the wall, crossing his arms over his chest with a grimace as I pace the space in front of my bed. "We can't do anything."

"*You* can't do anything, perhaps, but I–"

"Kora, *naï*." Uljen drops his arms and shakes his head. "Lira may not have been involved, but *you* were. You can interfere with this investigation or bring attention to yourself right now. If anyone learns–"

"No one is going to learn–"

"Lira is innocent, so they'll find her innocent. You have nothing to worry about–they'll interview her, go through the evidence, then let her go." I stop pacing and bite my lip. When I glance at Uljen he frowns. "She . . . *is* innocent, isn't she?"

I sigh. "She . . . we saw each other right after I allowed Dima and Jarek to escape. I don't know what she was doing up, but she *was* awake and walking around."

Uljen pinches the bridge of his nose. "Well. Have you considered she might not actually be innocent?"

"She didn't even know Dima had escaped. She guessed but I never confirmed it."

"Or she was *pretending* not to know and her so-called guess was conveniently right."

I shake my head. "She didn't know. And she had no motivation to help him. Not to mention I would have seen her there with the guards that *did* allow her to escape." I frown. "They're likely putting the blame on her to protect themselves." I stop pacing and take a deep breath. "I'm not going to let her take the blame for this."

"*Nai*? Then what will you do? Confess? They will *kill* you, Kora."

"*Naï*, I'm not going to confess." I bite my lip. "But I don't think I have to."

"Whatever you're thinking, it's a terrible idea. You should let the sands uncover this as they will. This is too risky for you, especially given your involvement."

I scowl at him. "How could you just let her take an undeserved punishment?"

"Well she was doing *something* that night."

"She was thirsty and got a drink and ran into me, Uljen. That's it. She doesn't deserve to take the blame for this!" I take a deep, calming breath. "And if you insist on being cynical, then you should probably consider Lira saw me that night and could mention that to the guards to save herself."

Uljen makes a low noise like a growl, turns away and clenches his hair as he curses into the quiet. When he turns back, he looks about ready to commit a crime himself. "I can't believe you put yourself in this position. You're too important to be implicated in this, Kora. How could you?"

"I wouldn't take this back even if I could." I pull my shoulders back and look Uljen in the eye. "I won't sit back and allow her to suffer for this. It's my duty to protect her."

"*Naï*, Kora. It was your duty to accept *Kala*'s decision whether you liked it or not."

I turn away from him and march for the door. "Last I checked, I don't worship the panel of Eight."

Given that the cooling system still isn't working due to the damaged nanites, the cells are cooler than I expected. Though I suppose that makes sense, as the entire complex is underground.

I walk through the halls with my head held high, my simmering anger boiling over my shoulders. I want everyone to see me coming. I dare them to try to stop me.

Of course, no one does, which is just as well.

There are two guards standing outside the main dungeon entrance. They glance at each other uncertainly as I approach like a whirling sandstorm. I storm right up to them and look them in the eye. "I demand Lira is released immediately. She wasn't involved in Dima's escape and it is unlawful to detain an innocent."

"That's . . . *el Avra,* with all respect, how can you be sure?" one guard asks. "We've received evidence that indicates she may have been involved, and while we can't yet be sure—"

"What evidence?"

The guard blinks. "I . . . I'm sorry?"

"What evidence do you have that Lira was involved in the escape?"

"*El Avra*, you know we can't discuss that," the second guard says. "It would threaten the integrity of the investigation."

"Fine. Well whatever evidence you think you have is irrelevant because I know Lira was nowhere near the cells the night of the escape."

Both guards frown. "How could you possibly know that?" the first asks.

I take a deep breath. "Because she was with me the entire night."

They glance at each other. "And . . . where were you, *el Avra*?"

"In my bedroom, naturally. Where else would I be in the middle of the night?"

The first guard's frown deepens. "What was she doing in your bedroom in the middle of the night?" But I think the second guard understands what I'm implying, because he nudges his partner. Just to make a point, though, I make it utterly clear for them.

"We were together," I say firmly. "The entire night. So I know for certain she couldn't have been in the cells, because she was in my bed with me."

They stare at me, wide-eyed, as the first of the two slowly purples. But the guides aren't permitted in the halls near the royal bedrooms, and the ones in the dungeon were disabled, so there's absolutely no footage of us anywhere near the cells that night.

It's my word against theirs. And I'm *ken Avra*.

"So," I say. "Are you going to release her? Or shall I do it myself?"

PART III

38

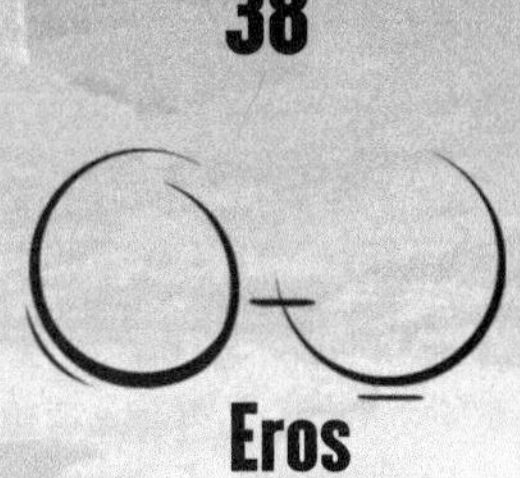

Eros

Sixteen sets have passed since I started medicating nightly to sleep–which has, gratefully, been working–and I would've hoped half a term ago that things would be better by now, but I guess that was hoping for too much because–well.

With the capital under curfew, territories still preparing to secede, humans getting impatient on updates on the ship, the plague worse than ever even with the medics swearing they're on the verge of a cure, and having to quarantine and test everyone who enters the palace grounds, Kosim hanging on, but just barely, not to mention not being any closer to figuring out how the hell to handle the Remnant since we can't exactly just throw out the whole damn monarchy–

I'm finally getting enough sleep and I'm still fucken exhausted. But at least Mija has less to complain about even if I still feel blazing awful.

"You only look half-dead instead of completely dead these sets," she says cheerily as she paints skin-toned whatever under my eyes. "At this rate, you'll look almost alive without my help in no time."

I laugh weakly. "Won't be long after that before I look completely alive and then I won't need you to paint my face. What then?"

Mija snorts. "You think this is all I do? Who do you think picks out your outfits every set?"

I hesitate and glance up at her. "Uh. Deimos?"

"He helps sometimes, but he's been pretty busy with his advisor duties. You know, like helping you run the planet and also keeping you warm at–"

"Mija."

She snickers. "Don't worry, *el Sira*. I have plenty to keep me occupied. You won't get rid of me so easily." She winks.

Today's meeting with the Council is in the throne room since our regular meeting room is getting decontaminated, which we're doing to every room every three sets now. It's not exactly convenient, but all the precautions we're taking seem to be working, because none of the palace staff who stay within the complex have gotten sick yet.

"As the techies have had to split their attention on renovating the ships and fixing the nanites, it's taking longer than we originally expected," Tol says. "Which is understandable, but we need to make sure the ship project doesn't delay the nanite fix for too long, or we'll start to run into issues with famine in the south."

"I thought the southern nations were getting food shipments from us and Daïvi and . . . somewhere else to avoid that," I say.

Tol nods. "They are, *sha*, but we only have so much excess food in store. Like I said, if this goes on for too long, everyone's resources will run thin."

"Do we have some kind of estimation of how long it'll take with their attentions split as they are?" Rion asks.

Tol shrugs. "Not a full term for the ships—maybe a couple spans. The nanites will take several terms, however."

"Well as soon as they're done with the ships, they can refocus on the nanites," I say. "At this point a lot of humans on People Speak seem eager to go so . . . they're equally important."

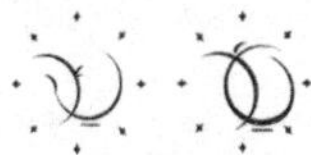

Partway through the mid-set meal, Deimos stops eating altogether and frowns at his glass. He doesn't even notice when Mal swipes a roll off his plate, which is probably the most concerning sign of all.

"Everything okay?" I ask.

"*Shae*, just . . ." Deimos drums his fingers on the table and leans back a little. "The team I have monitoring the People Speak feed flagged this message for me to look at." He looks up at me. "It's from someone claiming . . . well, let me just show you." Deimos passes over his glass. The image he has up is of a guy, or, actually, I'm not sure. But the person has short, curly hair just long enough to cover their ears, brown skin slightly darker than mine, and rigid, angled markings. But no tattoos. Interesting.

My marked hand tingles. Still feels weird to have something so intentional—something respected that I once hated—permanently on my skin.

There's something about them that feels—off. Not necessarily in a bad way, but . . . maybe it's their eyes. As far as I can see from here, they seem to only be one color: an orange-tinted brown.

Deimos taps the glass and the video message plays. "Thank you for your time, *el Sira*." The person bows their head. "My name is Ven. I wanted to contact you, *el Sira*, because for the longest time I thought I was alone. It wasn't until recently that I met others like me, others in hiding. And that knowledge completely changed my life, but I . . . I don't think you know it yet, and seeing how important the information was to me, I thought it was important to share with you, too."

What is this kid Voiding talking about? I glance at Deimos, but he's just tapping his finger on his chin. "Keep watching," he murmurs.

I look back at the screen.

Ven smiles. "The message I carry is about you, *el Sira*. You're not alone."

What is that supposed to fucken mean? I'm not alone? I'm not alone in what? But then Ven takes a deep breath and speaks again.

"You see, I'm just like you. I'm a half-blood, too."

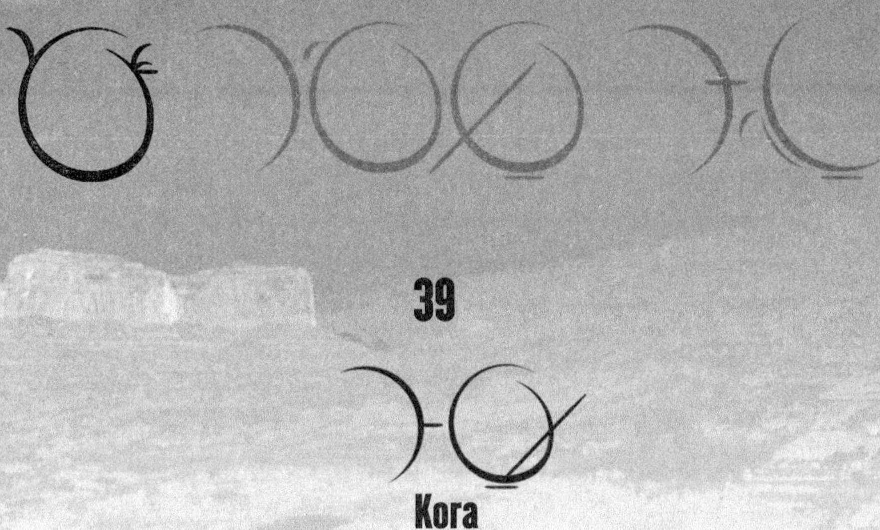

39

Kora

Unsurprisingly, rumors about my supposedly spending the night with my female assistant spread through the palace faster than sand in a windstorm. And I've allowed them to fly, because disputing anything would ruin the story I used to get Lira out of the cells, and if I'm being completely transparent, that people think I'm romantically involved with Lira doesn't bother me.

If they need something to talk about, I'd rather it be about my relationship with Lira than about Dima's escape or something negative about my capabilities as a ruler.

Thankfully, the rumors don't seem to bother Lira, either. Or at least, if they do she hasn't said so. She thanked me when I had her released and has stayed by my side ever since—whether out of duty, trust, or to give credence to the rumors, however, I don't know.

On my way down to the morning meal, Uljen stops me in the hallway. "May I speak to you for a moment?" He glances at Lira beside me, then back to me again. "Privately, if possible."

So this is about Lira, then. And the rumors. I suppose I should have expected that. I lift a shoulder. "Will it take long?"

"*Naï*, it shouldn't."

I nod and look at Lira. "You can go ahead to the meal hall. We'll join you shortly."

Lira nods and goes as Uljen and I step into an empty side room. When the doors close behind us, I look at him expectantly.

Uljen hesitates. "I'm . . . sure you've heard the rumors about you and Lira."

"Given that I started them, *sha*, you could say that."

Uljen laughs weakly and runs his hand through his hair. "Right. Well, I understand you said that to protect her so she wouldn't be implicated in the escape, but . . ."

I wait, but he doesn't finish the sentence. "But?" I prompt.

He hesitates. "I probably shouldn't be asking, and if the question makes you uncomfortable you don't have to answer, I just . . . is it true?"

I blink. "Uljen, you know what I was doing that night."

"*Naï, naï*, I know that. I just meant your relationship with her. Is it truly what everyone seems to believe it is?"

I tilt my head. "Would it bother you if it was?"

"Not at all. I'd actually be . . . relieved, I think."

It takes me a moment to process that. He'd be relieved if I were not-so-secretly in a relationship with another person? "You . . . would?"

He takes a deep breath. "Obviously, I am looking much farther ahead than I should be at the moment, but it's just . . . occurred to me that if our relationship ever became serious . . . I don't want to be *Avra-ko*, Kora."

I stare at him. "You don't want to be *Avra-ko*."

"That's what I said."

I laugh. Uljen grimaces and I shake my head. "If you don't want to help rule, then what was that nonsense when you first introduced yourself in which you said you wanted to be *Avra* in my stead?"

Uljen's grimace deepens. "I didn't say *I* wanted to be *Avra*. I said the *people* wanted me to be *Avra*. Which was true. I had to propose it to show I was listening, even if I sincerely hoped you'd refuse. Which I thought was a safe bet."

"Uh-huh. So what is it, exactly, that you're trying to say?"

Uljen pauses. "I don't want an . . . official relationship with you. I like what we're doing and I greatly enjoy spending time with you, but I don't want to marry you and take on the responsibility of a nation. I understand that means you'll eventually have to marry someone else, and that's okay. I'd like to keep our relationship . . . open. To see other people as we see fit, while still enjoying each other casually."

While it's not a suggestion I ever expected to come from him, in a way, it's a relief. As much as I like Uljen, I'm not ready to commit to anyone right now, nor is it something I really feel is important to focus on. Keeping things casual between us is the best I could have hoped for.

"That's fine," I say. "I'm happy to hear it, actually. But you are aware being *Avra-ko* isn't remarkably different from your current position as my top advisor."

"But it is," Uljen says. "The advising part itself may be similar, but I can stand off to the side now. I'm not the center of attention. And I think we both know whoever you marry is going to have endure everyone's attention with you, far more than I'd ever be comfortable with. And *Kala* forbid anything happened to you . . ." He shakes his head. "I'm certain I couldn't handle it."

I nod. "Well enough. Thank you for being honest with me."

Uljen smiles and nods. And we walk to the dining hall together–without expectation.

40

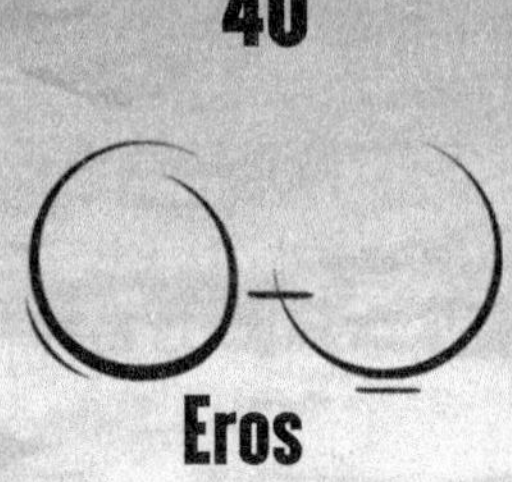

Eros

Another half-blood? How can that be—but I thought—

"I want to talk to them," I say at the same time Deimos pauses the message with a tap and says, "They could be lying."

We look at each other. "Why would they lie about being a half-blood? Admitting as much can get you killed."

"Ordinarily, *shae*, but telling *you* significantly lowers that risk, don't you think? You're obviously not going to punish them for being a half-blood when you yourself are one."

"Fine, but that still doesn't answer why they'd lie about it."

"To make you like them," Mal pipes up around a mouthful of bread.

"Precisely. Just look at how you've already reacted, Eros—first thing you said is you wanted to speak to them. How many non-royals are given the opportunity to have an audience with *ken Sira*?"

"Not enough," I answer flatly. "Which was the point of People Speak."

Deimos pauses. "That's true. But you understand what I'm saying, *shae*? People are going to try to manipulate you to gain your favor."

"If you thought they were trying to manipulate me, then why even show me?"

Deimos hesitates. Glances at the glass, then back at me. "Because . . . I acknowledge they might not be."

I look at Ven more carefully. Their markings are clearer than mine—easier to see on their darker skin—and their hair covers their ears, so really the only indication they might not be fully Sepharon is the single-colored eyes I noticed earlier. Which, given how dark their eyes are, could easily be overlooked.

"I want to talk to them through the glass," I finally say. "Can you arrange that?"

"I imagine so, but it'll depend on how responsive they are. That said, all things considered, I imagine they'll be responsive."

Deimos imagines right. Three segs later we're in a private room in the library, facing a giant wall-glass as the connection establishes. The room is small, windowless, with a floating stone table long enough for maybe three people. When Lijdo and Fejn tried to stand in here with Deimos and me, we were a little crowded, so now they're standing just outside the room. But I like the privacy of this small space. Plus it feels more official than my other private option, my bedroom.

And then Ven is bowing their head on the wall-glass, and when they look up, they're smiling. "*El Sira*, truly, it's an honor to have your ear. I can't thank you enough for taking the time to speak with me."

Maybe the polite—the properly royal—thing to do would be to buffer this conversation with polite formalities or whatever, but I jump right to the question that's been steadily growing louder in my head since seeing their message this morning.

"You're a half-blood."

Ven nods. "I don't really like that term . . . but *sha*. I am."

"Excuse me for asking," Deimos says, "but do you have any way to prove it?"

Ven tilts their head. "Well, my eyes are my biggest physical tell . . . except for this." Ven moves their hair aside, revealing their ear. Not quite notched like the Sepharon, not flat like humans. Instead they have the same kinduv raised ripple I do.

It's proof enough for me.

"Stars," I mutter. "There are other half-bloods."

Deimos nods slowly. "You said you don't like the term *half-blood*. What term would you prefer?"

Ven shrugs. "We don't really have one we've all agreed on or anything. I just tell people I'm biracial and let them assume I mean my parents come from different territories." Ven smirks but I catch on part of their sentence.

"Wait. *All* agreed? You mean there's . . . more of us?"

Ven smiles. "*Shae*, we're out there. Hidden, all of us, obviously. Those of us who can pass for Sepharon or human generally do and keep the truth to themselves but . . ." Ven gestures to me. "Some, like you, can't really get away with that, so they just keep under the feed best they can."

I play their words again and again in my head. It's more than just Ven—there are other half-bloods. I'm not the only one.

There are others out there just like me.

"Are you going to be okay?" Deimos asks me. "You look a bit faint."

"*Shae*, I'm . . . just . . ." Feeling like the world just opened up under me. Like the walls are falling over. Like the suns have collided and the moons aren't really moons, after all.

"It's a lot to take in, I know." Ven laughs lightly. "I only learned the truth a couple cycles ago and I felt like my world had turned over."

Wow.

"How many more of us are there?" I ask.

Ven runs a hand through their hair. "I don't have exact numbers–and there are probably more than any one of us are aware of . . . but I know of twenty-six. Including you."

"Of all ages?" Deimos asks.

Ven nods. "The oldest is an eighty-seven-cycle-old woman. The youngest is three."

"And how did you survive?" I ask. "You said you stay under the feed but . . . what does that mean?"

"I can't answer for everyone, but the one thing we usually have in common is our mothers didn't go to medical centers to have us if they were Sepharon, because they knew what would happen. Those of us with human mothers never really had the option to go a center anyway, obviously." Ven shrugs. "My parents were friends–my mother is a Sepharon shopkeeper in Kel'al and my father is human–from the same territory. They eventually developed what my mother called a casual relationship, though it was never really casual for my father. And the pregnancy was unintentional.

"I was lucky, though. As you can probably tell, I generally pass for Sepharon. I didn't even know I was a half-blood until I was fourteen; because I was such a friendly kid, my mom was afraid I might tell someone."

"But didn't you know because of your dad?" I ask.

"I never met my father. He died of some human illness before I was born."

"Oh. Sorry to hear that."

Ven shrugs. "I would have liked to have met him but . . . I suppose in the end it was for the best that I didn't. My mother was right not to tell me–I probably *would* have told someone. I was terrible with secrets as a child."

Deimos smiles thinly and nods. "We certainly appreciate you reaching out with this information. But is . . . that the only reason you wanted to contact *ken Sira*?"

Ven's smile fades. "I wish, but it's not the only reason, *naï*." They look right at me, their face more serious, sober. "I want to know why you haven't done anything to help us yet."

I blink. "I . . . didn't even know there were others to help until you just told me."

"*Naï*, I get that, but even then, there are laws still in place that are literally killing us. The law that demands the execution of half-blood babies, for example, or the law that makes inter-racial relationships illegal. I know you've had a lot to handle but those laws aren't even that controversial to revoke in this age. But you haven't done anything, and we're still dying. *Kafra*, it's still illegal for either of us to be on this planet, alive, breathing, and that law may not be enforced in the palace complex there in Asheron, but there are still people around the globe in hiding and dying every set because of it."

My stomach twists as the room heats around me. But they have a point. And yeah, I've been overwhelmed with everything, and if I'm being honest, changing things for half-bloods hadn't even crossed my mind since taking the throne. But it should have. I can change things for people.

"I'm sorry," I say. "You're completely right. I've been trying to do too many things at once and . . . I didn't think of it. But I appreciate you reminding me, seriously. I needed it, and I promise I'm going to do everything I can to remove the anti-half-blood laws as soon as we fix this whole . . . nanite-virus thing." I pause. "And since there are more half-bloods around than I thought, I'm happy to add them to the pool of humans eligible to go to Earth, if any want to go. I'll have to talk to Earthers about it, but they mentioned they have other species living there, too, so I don't think it should be a problem."

Deimos grimaces next to me. I'm not really sure why–he can't seriously object to my getting rid of those terrible laws and including half-bloods in my thinking, can he? But he doesn't say anything, so I ignore it for now and turn back to Ven.

"I want to invite you to stay here as a guest after Asheron is plague-free. I'd love to get to know you and hear more about–about people like us."

Ven smiles. "I'd be honored to tell you more."

I grin. I still kinduv can't get over this–there are other half-bloods! Alive, living away from the eye of the government like I had most of my life. And it makes sense others had survived and lead quiet lives like mine used to be. But with the laws the way they are and the daily reminder of how dangerous it was for someone like me to see another sunrise, I'd always assumed there just weren't any others.

But I have never been happier to be wrong about something so huge.

"Perfect." I turn to Deimos. "Do you think we could set that up?"

Deimos hesitates and glances at Ven. "Probably . . ." But he's got this uneasy look, like something's wrong, something he's not saying. Before I can ask what's burning at him, the windowless room goes completely and utterly black.

41

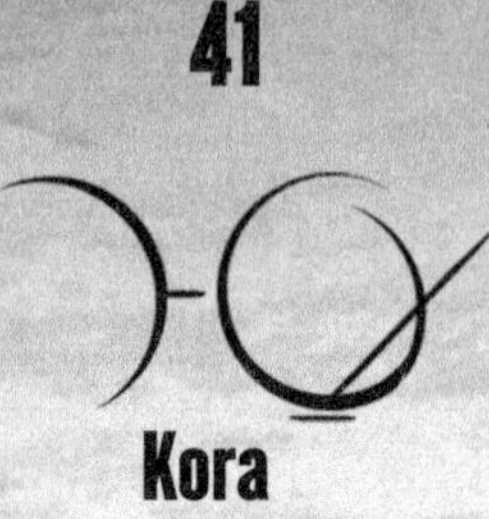

Kora

“Have you seen the feed this morning?” Uljen waltzes into the dining hall with an urgent pace that makes my stomach swoop. Nearly every set there’s some new huge information that throws everything else into a whirlwind. I’d checked the feed before walking to the dining hall with Lira for our morning meal and I’d been relieved not to see any new terrible information but perhaps that relief wasn’t meant to last.

I sip my moonflower tea and sigh. “I did, *sha*, but judging by your expression, I’d guess there’s been an update since then.”

Uljen drops onto a cushion across the table and slides his glass to me. It’s just a black screen. I glance up at him. “What am I supposed to be looking at?”

“You’re looking at Asheron’s feed right now. According to the reports it only just happened.”

I frown and tap the screen, as if that would do something. “The feed just . . . shut off?”

“Abruptly, *sha*. No one knows why yet, and it seems no one’s been able to contact anyone inside the city, either. It’s only been a few moments but people are getting nervous.”

Unease nips at the edges of my lungs as I look at the glass. I'm not entirely sure what the feed turning off could signify—the feed *never* turns off, not for anything. Could it be some sort of malfunction? Maybe, but given the way the Remnant hacked the world feed less than a term ago, it seems a rather enormous coincidence for this to happen like this.

"But before the feed turned off, nothing seemed unusual?"

"There wasn't an attack or any messages, as far as I know, *naï*," Uljen says. "It was a fairly uneventful morning."

I bite my lip and slip my fingers over my earring. I don't want to overreact and panic when it might be something harmless, something easily explained and forgotten. But what if it isn't? What if Eros and the people of Asheron are in trouble? What if the Remnant are acting out once more?

"What do you want to do?" Lira asks me.

I choose my words carefully. "I don't want anyone to be alarmed unnecessarily. Let's take a cautious approach and monitor the situation for the next few segments. If nothing has changed by noon, I want to send some men over there to investigate and make sure it isn't something serious."

Uljen nods. "I'll relay the message to the guard."

"Thank you." I lean back on my hands, no longer hungry. It's too soon to say what this is, too soon to know if I should worry.

But that doesn't stop me from imagining all the horrible things that might be happening, and all the ways I can do absolutely nothing to help.

42

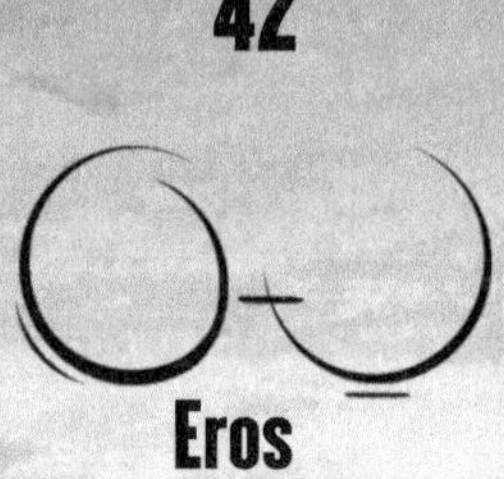

Eros

It takes all of half a mo for the door to open and the room to fill with sounds of boots and guards to enter with torches. Actual torches. With fire, like the ancient ages.

"What's going on?" I ask as Lijdo and Fejn near. "Why did the lights turn off?"

"It seems we've lost power," Lijdo says. "But not just the lights and central power–none of the portable units are working either. No glasses or solar-powered torches and I'd wager those aren't the only things not working."

"Is this the Remnant?" Deimos asks.

"Probably," I mutter the same time Lijdo says, "We don't know yet."

Which is about the mo it hits me all the guards are eying the glass, which is now off.

"It seems rather suspicious, don't you think?" Fejn says. "This stranger demands to speak to you, does so, and suddenly the palace complex loses power?"

Deimos grimaces.

"What?" I shake my head. "I don't think Ven had anything

to do with this, especially given we still have Shaw and Rani *did* tell us she'd retaliate."

"But it *is* odd," Deimos says. "It'd be a rather grand coincidence."

"Until someone comes up with proof what's happening here is remotely related to Ven contacting me, no one is going to bother them," I say firmly. "In fact, I've just invited Ven to stay as a guest at the complex for after Asheron is plague-free. We may have lost connection, but I intend to keep that promise if they'd like to visit."

Lijdo frowns. "Are you sure–"

"*Sha*. I'm positive." I look at some of the other guards who aren't specifically assigned to Deimos and me. "But more importantly right now, I want extra security posted around Shaw's cell immediately."

The guards nod and leave.

I sigh and rub my thumb over the markings on my hand. "Let's get out of this windowless room. I feel like I'm standing in a tomb."

"You know you can't trust Ven just because they're a half-blood, right?" Deimos says. "I'm glad you've found someone you can relate to, Eros, truly, I do. But don't be fooled into thinking they're safe just because they aren't human or Sepharon."

"Are we seriously back to this again?" I ask. "They proved they're a half-blood. And it's not like Ven asked for anything unreasonable."

"Maybe not, but you *did* just offer them clearance to visit the palace–"

"They couldn't have known I was going to do that–"

"Perhaps, and perhaps not, but they *could* know you'd immediately want to trust them simply because they claim to be a half-blood, like you. You have to think, Eros. You're the most powerful person on the planet. You can't just take people at their word, not anymore."

I scowl. He's right, I know that–I shouldn't trust anyone so easily, not anymore. But something about Ven felt genuine. I really don't think they were lying to me.

But then again, that could be exactly what they want. And if they're any good at–at manipulating, then I suppose I wouldn't suspect anything anyway.

I sigh. "Okay, you're right. Look, we can keep talking about this later and I'm going to keep thinking about it. But for now, we really need to focus on figuring out what's blazing going on, *shae*? And I also want to check on Mal. He was sleeping when we left for the morning meal, right?"

Deimos's shoulders relax a little and he nods. "I'm sure Mal is still in his room, but we can check first." He glances at Fejn. "I take it your communications aren't working, either?"

Fejn grimaces. "Unfortunately not."

"Okay," I say. "Let's go check on Mal and talk to the techies before people start to panic."

They nod and we start walking, but Deimos grabs my wrist and stops me. "Hold on," he says quietly. "I just want to thank you. For listening to me."

I smile weakly. "Even if you weren't my advisor, I trust you more than anyone. I'll always listen to you, okay?"

Deimos smiles and gives me a quick kiss. And as he laces his fingers in mine, we walk into the darkness together.

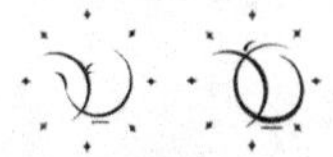

Mal and Varo aren't in his bedroom, but before worrying, we figure he might be down in the lab, which is where we're going anyway, seeing how he seems to like to hang out with the techies there. I don't really get the appeal of hanging out leagues underground when you don't have to, but whatever makes him happy, I guess.

Of course, getting down to the lab when there isn't any power to, say, run the lift thing means taking a painfully long trip down the stairs.

"Climbing back up is going to be a workout," Deimos says with a sigh. "My incredible legs don't really need more toning but I suppose I won't complain."

I roll my eyes but yeah, I'm smiling as Deimos grins at me.

The once well-lit warehouse of a room looks like a cavern without the lights. Everyone's got torches down here, which feels weird next to all the high-tech stuff floating around, though it's all off. Kinduv got to wonder if they had the torches ready as a backup or if someone had to bring them down for them.

"*El Sira!* It's good to see you." Dara comes over, holding a torch and smiling in the warm orange light. "Before you ask, Mal is down here with Varo and they're both fine."

"I was hoping you'd say that," I answer. "Thank you."

She nods. "Your nephew is very intelligent. I'd be happy to apprentice him when he comes of age."

While I'm not surprised to hear she thinks Mal is smart, that second part does catch me off. "You would?"

"He means 'thank you.'" Deimos smirks.

She laughs lightly. "You don't have to thank me. He'd be a great addition to the team. If he's interested, we'd be more than happy to take him."

"I'll talk to him about it," I say. "Mal's not the only reason we came over, though."

"*Naï*, I'd imagine not. This power loss is serious. If you'd come with me, we have made some early determinations." She brings us over to a cluster of people sitting on the floor around a flat surface I'm pretty sure was a floating table before the power outage. Which isn't surprising—we saw a lot of broken shattered glasses on our way out of the complex. Come to think of it, our beds are probably on the floor now, too.

Mal is sitting at the edge of the group with Varo next to him. Mal's darkening glasses—which he carries everywhere—are propped on top of his head, seeing how he obviously doesn't need them right now, and his stick is next to him on the floor. I'm not sure if he's noticed me yet—in the dim light, he probably can't see a damn thing—plus he's talking quietly to Varo, so I don't interrupt them. But it's good to see him. Like Dara said, he seems totally fine, and as long as Varo is keeping an eye on him, I'm not worried.

On the floored table is what I'm pretty sure is a map of Asheron. They've written notes on it in red that I can't read.

"We've sent a team out and our early assessment is the outage seems to be affecting much, if not all of the city. It could possibly go beyond Asheron—we're not sure yet, but it's going to be difficult to determine as our transports aren't working either. And as I'm sure you've guessed by our set-up here, our backup generators are also not functioning. Whatever knocked out our power seems to be affecting *all* tech that relies on power of any kind–not just those connected to our main solar grid."

"Any guesses what's causing this?" I ask. "Or how to fix it?"

"Given we haven't been able to recharge any of our portable devices–which, remember, are solar-powered and thus should be easy to recharge–it seems to be something that's actively disrupting the tech's ability to access a power source. We think it's some kind of pulse device, possibly solarmagnetic, that's blocking our access to power. If that's the case, the device would need to be turned off for us to be able to restore the power." She gestures to the map. "Unfortunately we have no way of tracking down the source with all of our tech powered down."

"The timing is terrible, too," a guy from the group around the table adds. "We were just testing the first batch of restored nanites in the medical wing. The results were promising before the outage killed them again."

I arch an eyebrow. "Nanites in the medical wing? You mean . . ."

"Given the spread of the disease, we focused the first batch on a cure." Dara smiles. "We didn't want to alert you until we finished our testing, but as my colleague said, the signs were positive until the power went out. Once we get the power back, we'll be able to finish our testing and hopefully release the nanites and end this plague nightmare."

Thank the fucken stars. "Good. That's really good news."

She nods. "We're rather helpless without power, though."

"If it's a device causing the outage, do you think it'd be in the city?" Deimos asks.

Dara hesitates. "If this outage is localized to Asheron, then *sha*. If it goes beyond Asheron . . . it may be harder to say. So first I would send someone outside the city with a glass or communication unit–something small–and see if they can recharge it outside the city, and if so, how far outside the city they need to go before they can access power again. Assuming it's localized here–and my guess is that it is, because this isn't an easy feat for a city the size of Asheron, and the resources it would take to knock out an entire territory or more would be immense–then *sha*, I'd say more likely than not, the device is somewhere in the city."

"We'll talk to the military about sending some guys out to investigate," I say. "Wherever the device is, we'll find it."

"I'm sure you will. In the meantime, we'll do everything we can to prepare to act quickly once the power is restored."

"Thank you." I look at Mal, who by now I'm assuming has recognized my voice because he's facing us and seems to be listening. "Mal, do you want to stay here or come with us?"

"I'm good here," he says.

"I'll bring him back to the palace when he's ready," Varo adds.

I nod and we turn back to the leagues of stairs waiting for us to get back to the surface. Deimos stretches his arms over his head and smacks his lips together. "Ready to make your legs look even more amazing?"

I snort. "Whatever you say."

Deimos winks at me, and we start the climb.

43

Kora

I wake, gasping, with a hand on my shoulder and a shadow standing over me. My heart races as I jerk up, reaching for the knife under my–

"I'm sorry!" Lira squeaks. "I didn't mean to startle you."

Oh. I slide my hand away from my pillow and take a deep breath. I glance at Uljen, still somehow fast asleep beside me. Evidently, he sleeps more deeply than I anticipate.

I turn back to Lira. "It's . . . fine. I'm just a bit–forget it. What's wrong? Is it Eros? Are the people of Asheron all right?"

As my eyes adjust to the darkness, Lira's guilty smile becomes easier to make out in the light of the moons. "Nothing's wrong–I don't have any news on *ken Sira* or Asheron. I just thought . . . maybe this was a bad idea. I apologize."

I rub the sleep from my eyes. "You've already woken me, so you might as well tell me what you had in mind."

Lira bites her lip. "I want to show you something. But it requires getting dressed because it's in the city, outside the complex."

"Outside the complex? What is it?"

"It's . . . a surprise."

A surprise? At this time of set? I grimace through the darkness. "What time is it?"

"Nearly night's center . . . like I said, maybe this was a bad idea. I'm sorry for waking you." She starts to turn away, but I reach out and gently grab her wrist.

"It's okay. I'll get dressed."

Lira blinks and smiles a little. "*Sha*?"

"*Sha*." I smirk. "Not like I'd be able to sleep now that you have me curious, anyway."

Lira laughs lightly as I slide out of bed. Fifteen or so moments later, we're walking over the white pathways, petal-soft sand sliding into our sandals, two guards trailing several paces behind us. The night is warm, but nowhere near the oppressive heat of the set at the time of the cycle. And to think we haven't even reached the hottest set of the cycle yet.

"The nights are always so much more pleasant," Lira says. "I've always preferred them to the sets."

"Really? That's interesting. I was never really permitted to go out at night on my own–though Dima and I did so anyway as we got a little older, especially during the festivals. It worried our parents ill but . . . some of my fondest memories are of those nights." I smile softly, but it feels–wrong, almost, to speak so airily when I don't know if Eros is in danger. When it's inevitable Asheron going dark for an extended period like this will have repercussions globally–after all, how is the rest of the world supposed to have confidence in our world leader if the capitol appears endangered? And if there hasn't been any news yet, that means the men I sent to investigate the situation still haven't returned, which means . . . what, exactly?

Whatever it is, it can't be good.

But Lira is oblivious to my concern, because she just nods with a smile. "I worked most of my life during the sets, so the nights were when my friends and I could claim segments for ourselves. Plus the weather is just always better at night anyway."

"*Sha*, that's true." I pause. "What of your friends now? Do you get to see them much?"

"Mmm . . . my ex-girlfriend took most of my friends with our separation." She rolls her eyes. "Oh well. I suppose she did me a favor–I can see now they weren't really my friends anyway."

"Ah . . . sorry to hear that."

"I'm not. I'm making better friends now." She smiles at me.

I nod at the guards as we reach the gates of the complex. They open them for us and we continue on into greater Vejla.

The streets are nearly empty at this time of night. Come to think of it, it's . . . probably somewhat dangerous for us to be walking around by ourselves. Not that Vejla is particularly dangerous–and especially not now, with the heavy guard presence on the streets, even at this time of night. But we *are* rather alone, and if Lira wanted to kill me, this would be the way to do it. The guards behind us are distant enough that she could probably get away with it if she moved quickly.

Granted, she could have easily just killed me in my sleep, given how she snuck up on me like that.

Okay. This is paranoid thinking brought on by too many betrayals and near-death experiences and worry for Eros. I need to stop. This is ridiculous.

I take a deep, steadying breath and Lira glances at me. "Are you all right?"

"*Sha*," I say. "Just . . . have a lot in my thoughts at the moment."

Lira nods. "It must be hard, being *Avra*, especially now. I mean, I'm sure it's always a difficult position to hold, but with everything especially out of sorts, I can only imagine what you must be feeling."

"Tired, mostly," I answer. "Ready for things not to be so incredibly difficult all the time."

"But do you enjoy it? Being *Avra*?"

No one's ever asked me that before–and to be true, I can't say I've ever really asked myself, either. I suppose it never really mattered if I enjoyed my position–I never elected to become *Avra*; it was a responsibility handed to me at birth.

But do I enjoy being *Avra*? Would I rather be anything else?

"At times," I finally say. "I've enjoyed it more, as of late, seeing positive results of decisions I've made. I'm at my happiest when my people are happy. It's . . . disconcerting, to say the least, to be *Avra* of a nation that hates you."

Lira grimaces. "That does sound less than ideal."

I laugh. "That's a diplomatic way of saying it."

Lira smiles then nods down the street. The shops and stalls are all closed, but we're nearing the main square in the heart of Vejla. And I have to say, the streets look so much better already than they did when I walked these streets with Eros. They're clean–and still cracked and need replacing in areas, but we can walk them without worrying about stepping on broken glass or a metal shard. Granted, many of the buildings are still crumbling and need renovation, but there are small, noticeable improvements. We're moving in the right direction.

We walk through the square and to the main temple. The last time I was here was with Eros, when I wanted to see Vejla for myself, when the streets were trash-strewn and the people eyed me with disdain.

When Eros and I found people burning the book I'd chosen to represent me in an act of protest.

When they wanted me dead.

Tonight, the space in front of the temple is empty, quiet, and clean. There aren't any fires or angry signs or shouting crowds. It almost seems like an entirely different temple, bathed in shadow and cloaked in silence.

"What are we doing here?"

"Come."

We walk up to the display case that once held my–wait. I frown. The last time I was here, the display case was shattered and my icon was burning. But now, tonight, the case is intact and my icon–the book–is sitting inside, undisturbed. They've replaced it.

But there's more. They haven't just replaced it; there are items scattered along the base of the display. Flowers, handmade dolls, even a small painting of my name.

"I don't understand," I say. "What is this?"

"The gifts are for you." Lira smiles. "This is what it looks like when the people are happy with their *Avra*. I guessed you probably hadn't seen it for yourself yet, but it's important you know when the people are happy with you."

My eyes sting even as I smile. "You're right," I say softly. "I had no idea. Thank you."

Lira smiles and nudges my shoulder with hers. "You're doing a wonderful job. Definitely an improvement over your first attempt."

"I would hope so. My first attempt was a miserable failure."

Lira laughs. "*Sha*, well . . . onto better times."

I nod. "Onto better times."

As we wander the mostly empty streets back to the palace, my steps are lighter. I hold my head up a little higher. I hadn't realized the weight of worrying the people may want to depose me at any time–now I can breathe a little more easily knowing the people are, for the most part, happier with me than they've ever been.

But as we nearly exit the city, writing on the side of an old building stops me in my tracks.

NO DEATH FOR DIMA; NO JUSTICE.

44

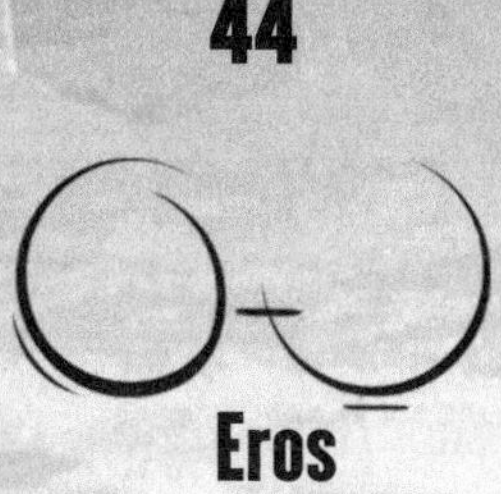

Eros

After what feels like my longest set yet, Mal goes to sleep and Deimos and I crash in my bedroom. And I wish I could say I could just relax for the rest of the night, but it's been segments since I talked to the techies and guards about sweeping the city for that fucken device knocking out the power, so the first thing I do is check my copy of the map hung outside my room, which is what the army is using to record their progress. The map has the whole city zoned out into forty-eight sections, and as they finish sweeping a section, they mark it green.

Right now, there are two green sections. And they aren't even close to the largest zones on the map. So either no one has updated this yet, or, more likely, they've barely just started.

I groan and march into my room and toss myself onto my bed. "This is going to take fucken forever."

"Probably." Deimos places his rings on the bedside table—which, now that it doesn't float, is just a stone saucer on the floor—then stretches out on his stomach next to me on the bed. "I realize it's frustrating to have to wait, but it's likely going to take them many sets to comb through the entire city without any power. They need to check every floor of every building, every alley, every crevice in Asheron. It's not a simple thing. And we're not even sure what this device would look like, or how big it is. Or even whether it's mobile, for that matter . . ."

"Has to be pretty powerful, whatever it is, to disable an entire city."

"*Shae*, but it does have its limits."

I nod, remember our last update. The power outage only extends to a league and a half outside of city limits–beyond there, all devices work again. Which isn't really helpful for us in the city, but at least it's an isolated thing.

I sigh. "Still. What if they go through the whole city and don't find anything?"

Deimos shrugs. "Then we move on to another plan. But for now there's nothing either of us can do"–he slides his hand into mine–"so let's just relax, *shae*? It's been an exhausting set."

"*Shae*," I mumble. "It has."

Deimos closes his eyes and smiles softly, his thumb gently tracing the mark on the back of my hand. He seems instantly relaxed–nothing like the moody whatever-that-was earlier. I could let it go since he seems okay now, but if I don't know what was bothering him earlier, I can't do anything to try to make sure it doesn't happen again.

"Can I ask you something?"

"*Sha*, every inch of my incredibly attractive body is real and unaltered, thank you for asking. I'm quite proud of it, too." Deimos's lips quirk into a smirk.

I laugh. "*Shae*, right, you caught me. That's exactly what I was going to ask."

Deimos opens his eyes and grins. "You know, *your* body is irresistibly attractive as well. It's very distracting, if I'm being honest. It's a miracle I get any work done at all when I'm near you."

My face is a prickling mess of sparks, and I'd like to be annoyed at how easily I blush but it's just really, really good to see Deimos smile. Plus . . . I definitely never considered myself *distracting* so that's kinduv nice.

"Glad you think so," I say.

Deimos smiles again, then slips his hand out of mine and sits up. "So what did you actually want to ask me?"

I hesitate. "It's not . . . I mean, you seem fine now, but . . ." I sigh and start over. "I was just wondering what was bothering you earlier. You seemed kinduv upset."

Deimos's smile fades. "Ah. That."

"You don't have to tell me if you don't want to, but I can't do anything to avoid upsetting you again if I don't know what it was you didn't like in the first place."

Deimos blinks. "Eros, *naï*, I'm sorry—*you* didn't upset me. It was nothing you did, truly."

"Then?"

Deimos looks away. He bites his lip quietly for a moment, but I wait in the silence. Finally, when the quiet feels thick and suffocating, he looks at me again and says, "I know I can't connect to you the same way Ven can. I suppose the reminder that someone else can understand you in a way I never truly can just . . . didn't sit well with me."

I frown. "Wait, you were jealous?"

Deimos smiles weakly and lifts a shoulder. "Is that so bad? I knew my sullenness wasn't really justified, but I couldn't help feeling inadequate. Like an outsider. And—and I realize that momentary discomfort for me is only a fraction of what you've experienced your entire life but—"

"Deimos." I smile and take his face in my hands. "I literally never have cared about someone the way I care about you. Sure, Ven and I could relate because we're both half-bloods, and it was cool to find out I'm not the only one, but that doesn't take *anything* away from how I feel about you."

"I know . . ."

"I don't think you do." I take a deep breath, my heart pounding hard against my chest. I'm going to say it. Now. "Deimos, I'm . . . I've fallen in love with you."

Deimos blinks several times before a slow grin takes over his face like quickly shifting sand. "You . . . really?"

I smile. "Really."

Then I swear I blink and Deimos is on top of me, kissing me like we've never kissed before, like we'll never be able to kiss again. My laugh dissolves in our mouths as he presses my wrists into the bed and kisses my lips, my cheek, my jaw, my ear, my lips.

Then he pulls back and laughs and I swear I've never seen him so delighted. His happiness lights up his whole face, and fuck, he's beautiful. "I'm in love with you too."

And now I'm pretty sure I'm mirroring his face-splitting grin. Because I never thought I'd hear those words; I never imagined I'd be lucky enough to have someone who could look past my skin, my ears, my not-one-but-not-the-other, my in-between-ness because no one else ever seemed interested in trying to.

But now I've got the most attractive, magnetic, overall *nicest* guy I've ever met and he's in love with me.

Me.

Kissing Deimos feels like breathing stardust. It feels like waking up one cell at a time, in a slow, warm rush. And I love everything about the way Deimos kisses me, about his soft lips and the way his tongue moves over mine, about his stubble prickling against my jaw and his hands scattering embers over my chest.

And you know, though it was awkward when Deimos caught me watching those videos, I'm glad I saw them. Because as he pulls our shirts off, slides his hands over me and shifts, skin-to-skin, I'm a little less lost, a little less terrified of where this might go. And this time, I know where to touch, kiss, how to move, too.

I roll Deimos under me and his eyes widen for just a mo, but then he grins. "Go right on ahead, handsome."

So I do.

I kiss the stubble on his jaw, smile at the light burn of rubbing my lips against him. I taste the dip just above the bump in his throat. I trace a path with my mouth over the rigid lines on the left side of his chest while sliding my hands down his sides. I'm getting stiff sampling his salty skin like this, touching him like this, listening to his breath catch and heart pound, but so is he, so I must be doing okay. So I keep moving, keep kissing, until my mouth is on his muscled stomach and my thumb runs down the line of hair running from his navel and into his pants.

My heart is racing when I hook my fingers under the waistband of his pants and look up at him. Deimos pushes up onto his elbows, face flushed even as he smiles gently at me and says, "You don't have to."

I wet my lips. "I know. I want to."

The bump in his throat bobs as he nods. And so with my pulse drumming in my ears and the room like a furnace, I take off his pants.

I've seen Deimos naked before–in glances. Out of the corner of my eye, or through the shadows as he climbed into bed with me. We've gotten dressed–and undressed–in front of each other, so it's not like I've never seen him before, but this . . .

This is different. Intentional. Up close and impossible to glance over. This is real, and now, and when I take him into my mouth there's no denying we're crossing a line I don't want to uncross.

But even with videos, I don't really know what I'm doing–I mean, all the explaining in the world isn't going to completely prepare you for actually doing this. But as I move my tongue and shift my lips, I try to watch him best I can to see what he seems to like. And judging by the way he's gripping the sheets and moving his hips, and judging by the quiet gasps and noises, I guess I must not be doing terribly. Which is a relief.

This would be blazing awkward and embarrassing if it wasn't working for him.

I keep going for a bit, and a little thrill zips down my spine every time his breath catches or he makes a noise. But as he starts breathing heavily, I pull back.

Deimos shudders and opens his eyes. "I'm sorry. Too much?"

I shake my head and force the words out even as my face flames with what I'm about to ask. "Do you have, um . . . stuff?"

He blinks a couple times and pushes up onto his elbows again. "Stuff?"

Fuck, please don't make me say it. "I want to do this with you–like, all of it. But I know we need stuff and I . . . didn't know where to get any." Plus there wasn't a chance in the Void I was going to ask Kosim or Lijdo to take me to a sex shop.

Deimos's eyes widen. "Oh."

I laugh a little. "Oh."

"I–*shae*, of course. I have some in my room. I'll get it." He stumbles out of bed, throws on his pants, then pauses and looks up at me. "You're sure you want to, *shae*? I don't want you to feel pressured into anything–"

"Go get the stuff."

Deimos laughs breathily. "Going." He rushes out of the room like a *kazim* is chasing him. It'd almost be funny if my stomach wasn't a bundle of raw wires.

I lie back on the bed and take a deep, slow breath. I'm going to have sex. With Deimos. And I mean, it literally hurts how bad I want to, so that's not throwing me off, and I shouldn't worry because he knows it'll be my first time with a guy–actually, wait. Does he? Come to think of it, I'm not sure we've really . . . talked about it.

Fuck. What if he's expecting me to have experience?

He caught me watching those videos but people probably watch sex videos to get off all the time. Though I was pretty sure he knew I didn't really know what I was doing before, and he's always been so nice about everything I figured he knew, but what if he doesn't?

My bedroom doors slide open and Deimos locks them behind him this time before sitting next to me and putting down a small jar and a flat packet.

"So," Deimos says casually. "You look terrified."

I laugh and cover my burning face. "*Kafra*."

Deimos pulls my hands away from my face and smiles at me. "We really don't have to tonight if you're not ready. I won't be disappointed—it's already been an incredible night. I was perfectly elated from the moment you said you loved me."

I smile, despite myself. "I know, and I don't feel pressured or anything, I want to do this with you. I've wanted to do this with you. But I . . ." Deimos waits patiently so I guess I'm just gonna have to say it. So I blurt it out quickly. "I've only had sex once, and it was with a woman, and we were both blazing drunk so I don't even remember it all that well and it was probably terrible for both of us. So."

Deimos arches an eyebrow. "Oh. Huh."

I cringe.

"Well . . . I'd guessed you weren't the most experienced with men, though I definitely hadn't thought you'd only slept with one person."

"*Shae*, well. Not too many people wanted to fuck the half-blood."

Deimos frowns. "You *do* know you're incredibly attractive, *shae*?"

My face warms. "Glad you think so," I mumble.

"I'm sure I'm not the only one who thinks so, but that's too bad, because you're mine." He winks at me. And I don't think he realizes how good it feels to hear someone say that. To want me like that. To be his.

Deimos lies next to me and kisses me lightly. "Well, if you want to tonight, I'd be more than happy to walk you through it. After all, the only way to get better at something is to practice." He nips my lip with a smirk. "And I love practicing."

I'm pretty fucken sure my face physically could not be redder right now—because it feels about ready to melt off my skull. "Okay," I croak. "I want to."

"I hoped you'd say that," he says right before he kisses me.

And it's not an immediate thing; we kiss and touch and move until my whole body buzzes with want, until the slightest touch sends me gasping and we're both sweating like we've run leagues under the suns. Until the nerves that hummed between my lungs melt away into something that knows nothing but need.

So when we get there and Deimos asks me if I'm sure, again, and I tell him I'm literally painfully sure, I'm not freaking out about doing this right or disappointing him anymore. I just want him closer and I want him now.

And then I have him
and he has me
and we're two suns colliding
and merging into one.
We're supernovas,
planets burning up,
ever-expanding galaxies.

We're holding each other at the end of one world and the start of something new and I never want to let go.

And I won't.

45

Kora

I'm sitting up in bed, reading my glass when Uljen wakes beside me in the morning. Uljen grimaces as he stretches and I smirk. *"Ora'denja."*

"Is the morning truly that good?" He mumbles into his palms.

"I suppose that depends on who you ask. The news today is . . ." I glance at the report on my glass again and bite my lip.

He sits up with a sigh and rubs his eyes. "How bad is it?"

"Well firstly, the report is in from the men we sent out yesterday to see what's going on in Asheron." Relief had washed over me like a cool rain when I'd seen the report upon awakening–after we hadn't heard back last night, I'd been concerned maybe something had happened to them.

"Then they're okay?" he asks.

"They're fine, thank *Kala*. But the report is interesting." I tilt the glass to him so we can both read together.

20 Jol, 800
1:43
Enno, Havan, Mir, Jura

We arrived in Asheron at 16:00, on 19 Jol, as expected. But as soon as we crossed within a quarter league of the city, our transport, communications, glasses, and so on all ceased functioning. For the first segment we tried everything to fix our technology, and it wasn't until Jura wandered back some ways that his glass began working again. Once he came over to tell us, however, it stopped working again.

We investigated within the city together–though naturally it took us much longer to actually get within the city, as we had to walk. It appears no technology whatsoever is working in the city. The guards at the quarantined city's entrance told us they had no explanation for what had happened. We couldn't take any pictures (as our tech wasn't working), but there were ports and orb guides abandoned on the streets, and many of the stores were closed–though whether that's because of the loss of technology or the disease quarantine is hard to say.

After decontaminating manually at the quarantine center, we left on foot. We ended up having to push the port through the sand for a good quarter league before we could get it working again, which delayed us quite a bit. We arrived back in Vejla at 1:00 on 20 Jol, exhausted, but unharmed.

"It's concerning." I frown. "No technology whatsoever working within the city limits explains the sudden silence, but I haven't the faintest idea what can cause that."

"Me neither, but it seems unlikely it'd be accidental. Especially as it's so localized and continues to affect new tech introduced to the area."

"Hmm . . . you're probably right. Do you think the Remnant is behind this, then?"

"Maybe." Uljen turns off the glass and sets it on the bedside table. "Either way, it's not really for us to handle."

I'd like to argue against it *not being for us to handle*—because while what happens in Asheron isn't our responsibility, it *does* affect us, particularly when the Remnant are probably hiding in Elja. But I let it go for now.

Not long after, when I've emerged from the wash room, freshly bathed, Uljen is dressed and frowning at his glass. "Did you see this update on your brother?"

My stomach swoops. Dima? Oh no. Has he been found? Were they arrested? Are they back here already? Oh, *Kala*, I can't stomach the thought of watching him die.

"*Naï*, I haven't," I say as carefully and evenly as I can muster. "What is it?"

"Dima and Jarek have received asylum in Invino. We just got the contact from *Avra* Arik d'Invino."

It takes every ounce of self-control not to say *thank Kala* aloud. Dima and Jarek are in Invino. Invino doesn't believe in the death penalty—they've never had it once in their history. Which means, as far as I'm concerned, they couldn't be in a better territory.

"I see."

Uljen smirks. "Try to contain your enthusiasm."

"I thought I was containing it quite well."

Uljen sighs and shakes his head. "You'll have to at least attempt to look strict and demand Invino return Dima and

Jarek to Elja. If the people think you approve of Dima trying to get around his sentence–"

"I know," I say. "I know. I have to act angry about this, particularly if Invino refuses."

"Which they may or may not. It really could go either way."

I take a shaky breath and nod. Right now, I can only hope Invino will refuse to return them out of their distaste for the death penalty–because then, and only then, they'll be safe. But if I play my part too well and they agree, it'll be the end of my brother. And probably the end of Jarek, too.

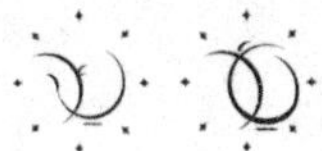

I know little about *Avra* Arik d'Invino, but what I do know is he isn't easily maneuvered. After all, Arik went through possibly the most any ruler has gone through besides Eros to take his place on the throne; he only became *Avra* after his elder brother killed his father, other brother, and attempted to kill Arik in an attempt to take the throne that led to his own disqualification and exile from Invino.

But even then, they didn't execute him. Though there are rumors the brother killed himself after his failed coup.

Still, I can't say I've ever had a conversation with Arik, so I'm not entirely sure what to expect as the technical aides set up the guides for me to speak to him–particularly as I publicly support Eros, and Arik has threatened secession. But a part of me hopes he'll be just as impossible to move on this matter as I'd like to imagine he might be. After all, if he didn't order the execution of his brother after he murdered his family and attempted to kill him . . .

Well. It's clear where he stands.

"*Avra* Kora, what a pleasure it is to speak with you." Arik's voice is warm, but his face is stony on the large glass floating against the wall, which is an odd combination.

"Likewise," I say. "I'm sure you're aware why I've asked for this meeting."

"I have a decently good idea, *sha*."

I nod. "While I'm glad to hear you've found my brother and Jarek, I'm afraid I must insist you return them to Elja. Dima was tried for very serious crimes and has run from his sentence."

"*Sha*, a sentence of execution, if I'm not mistaken. Is that correct?"

My stomach twists at the reminder, but I keep my face even. "It is, *sha*. He was tried before the Eight and that was the sentence they determined was most appropriate, given the severity of his crimes."

"I see." Arik's voice is flat, distant. It's near impossible to read the man at all—his expression is as still as stone.

I suppose my guess he'd be impossible to move may not be far from reality, after all.

"I imagine you are well aware of Invino's stance on execution," Arik says.

I nod. "I am, *sha*, but this is an Eljan matter, and thus Dima's sentence is up to Elja's court, not Invino's."

"Hmm."

That's it. That's all he says. Hmm.

I shift in my seat. I have to push. I have to appear as though this isn't just what I want, but this is what I'm demanding. I have to act the way I would if they were any other criminals, not my brother and his boyfriend. "So when can I expect Invino will return Dima and Jarek to Elja? I imagine it shouldn't take more than a set."

Arik shakes his head. "We won't be returning them to Elja. As Dima and Jarek are running from a sentence Invino considers barbaric, they are refugees here in Invino."

The news is exactly what I was hoping for, but I still have to play the part. I still have to act outraged. I scowl and raise my voice. "*Refugees*? With all due respect, they're far from–"

"I do understand Dima is a criminal, and I understand the severity of his crimes, as well," Arik says. "Therefore, as a compromise, I'd like to offer Dima carry out the equivalent sentence for such serious infractions–imprisonment for five cycles and rehabilitation through community service for life after that. He will serve his sentence in prison where he will reflect on his wrongs, then spend the rest of his life serving the community and humbling himself."

I can breathe deeply. Dima isn't going to die–and he isn't going to run from his crimes, either. The sentence is fair; he'll still be imprisoned, and he'll spend the rest of his life atoning for what he did. But he'll live.

It's exactly what I wanted–better than I dared to hope for. But if I agree too quickly, I risk angering the people and appearing weak. I need to convince them this is a fair compromise.

And better–we must get something in return for compromising.

I drum my fingers on my desk. "If we were to agree, then we must receive something in return. My people very firmly believe Dima's sentencing was just. I can't agree to these terms without any sort of recompense."

Arik's eyes narrow. "Recompense . . . such as what?"

I smile. "You'll vow to keep Invino as part of the Union of Territories and swear off any possibility of secession in the future."

Arik frowns. "That's no small thing you ask of us."

"What you ask of Elja, in refusing to return Dima and Jarek, is no small thing either."

For a long pause, neither of us speaks as Arik mulls over my terms. I force myself not to appear uncomfortable in the waiting, meeting Arik's gaze as he watches me.

Finally, he sighs and says, "I accept your terms. I'll make the public announcement regarding our decision not to secede before the end of the set."

Something like lightness dances over my stomach, but I keep my face passive and nod. "And I will speak to my people before the suns rest as well."

"So it is done." Arik nods and the feed dies.

I glance at Uljen, standing against the nearby wall, his arms crossed over his chest. "Well, I must admit that was fairly brilliant. You got what you wanted *and* secured a victory for Eros," he says. "Well performed outrage, by the way. I almost believed you."

I sigh and run my hand through my hair. "I got what I wanted, but I have no idea how to present this to the people in a way that won't enrage them. We both know the Eljans won't care about Invino agreeing not to secede. I can't have them think I'm allowing Arik to overrule my authority or Dima to get away with what he did."

Uljen lifts a shoulder. "They're likely going to think that regardless of how you present it. After all, it's exactly what you're doing–you just don't want to see it because you're biased toward your brother."

"He'll still serve a punishment–for the rest of his life, no less. I wouldn't call that *getting away* with what he did."

But Uljen pushes off the wall and shakes his head. "You know full well it's not the Eljan way. The people will know it as well. If you protect him, they won't forget it."

46

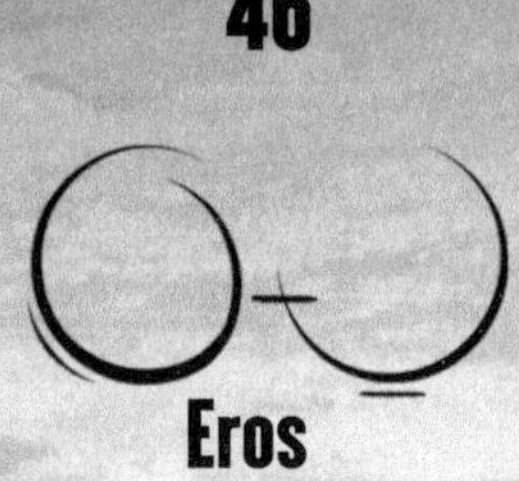

Eros

It's been a set.

Ven left this morning, after Deimos and I got back from our morning run, saying they were thankful I heard them out but they should go back home. I'm not sure if it's their discomfort with being in the palace or the lack of power or the whole quarantine situation that makes them want to leave, but I can't exactly blame them for not wanting to hang around. Things are a fucken mess here.

After saying bye to Ven and getting food, Deimos and I checked in with Kosim to see how he's doing. He's hung on there way longer than most–twenty-two sets so far, which is a relief–but his eyes are dark and he paces incessantly. Zarana says she's doing all she can to try to keep his fever down.

She doesn't know how long he has before he loses himself entirely if it turns out he can't fight it. But she promises as soon as they get power back, Kosim will be one of the first to get the trial cure they have nearly ready.

After that depressing meeting, we find Kantos to get the status on the whole searching the city thing. We didn't really receive any new information we couldn't have read on the map outside my room, though–it's slow going, and there's still a ton of the city left to search. Though he did say they were closing in on some possible leads, but not to get our hopes up since most of those end up being false alarms and dead ends.

Which leaves me with nothing much to do because we're cut off from the rest of the world. I can't check the feed, or expect any progress from the techies or medics, or monitor any damn thing because nothing works.

Stars, we're useless without tech.

"Take a walk with me." Deimos slips his hand in mine and smiles. Something in my chest squeezes a little at that smile, that easy happiness.

"Sure. Is Mal going to hang out with the techies again?"

"*Shae*." Deimos laughs a little. "I don't know why he likes it so much down there. It makes me feel buried."

"Oh, good, it's not just me."

"It's not just you. But if it keeps him entertained . . ." Deimos shrugs.

"What are they even doing down there without tech?"

"*Kala* knows. Playing games? Sleeping?" He smirks. "If we're being honest, probably preparing something or another for when we get tech back."

Lejdo and Fejn follow us out of the shade of the palace and under the twin suns. I'm finally used to the otherness of the sand here, and while I still don't love how gritty and not-soft it is, I have to admit the coolness is nice in the powerful heat. We all get filter masks at the edge of the palace complex and they give us immune boosters–again–but I guess I won't complain since *Kala* knows I really don't want to get sick. Or see Deimos sick–or Lejdo and Fejn, for that matter. Kosim in quarantine is bad enough as it is.

By the time we get into the actual city, I'm already kinduv sweaty and sticky. But so is Deimos, although he somehow manages to look regal even as sweat drips off the end of his nose.

"So," I say. "Where are we going?"

Deimos lifts a shoulder. "Nowhere in particular. I just thought it'd be good to get out of the complex for a bit. You were clearly in danger of losing your composure to boredom in there."

I laugh a little. "It's a little embarrassing how useless we are without tech. Almost reminds me of camp—except we got around fine low-tech."

"I wouldn't say we're *useless*—you're still overseeing plenty at the palace. The conversation with Kantos this morning was important."

"I know, but even then, everyone is already doing what they need to be, so not like they really . . . need me checking on them."

"They don't *need* you checking on them, but it's good that you do. It shows you're invested and you care about the work they're doing. So it's still important." Deimos smiles. "Ruling isn't always making impossible decisions and trying to take down destructive rebellious initiatives. Sometimes it's telling the people who work for you that they're doing a good job and taking a stroll with your boyfriend in the city."

The smile that bursts on my face is instant. It feels ridiculously good hearing him say that word: *boyfriend*. My boyfriend. I lightly squeeze his hand and he grins at me—the filter covers his mouth, but his smile goes all the way up to his eyes. "You look absolutely adorable right now. Filter mask and all."

"Don't ruin it."

Deimos laughs. "My apologies. I won't ruin it. Though I'll have to figure out other ways to get you to grin like that because I love that joy in your eyes."

Out of everything that's happened over the last few terms, this is the part I would've found most unbelievable a year ago. That I'd ever have this–with anyone at all, but especially with a guy, and a *Sepharon* guy, no less.

I'd stopped believing anyone would ever love me like that a long time ago. But Deimos is scrubbing away that disbelief a little more every day.

It takes some effort, but I've finally started believing this is real. I've started believing I'm not going to wake up one morning and find out it was all some dream. Deimos isn't going anywhere, and neither am I.

Asheron is quieter without tech and emptier with the quarantine, but when we pass the occasional person, we nod at them–since they can't exactly see us smile through the filter masks. It's a little eerie though–there are abandoned ports all over the streets, which combined with the sparseness of people kinduv makes it look like Asheron is abandoned. There isn't music, or food cooking on street stands, or vendors selling their wares. I'm not sure how long the city can survive like this, but we'll probably need to start considering some sortuv food distribution system if people can't get back to work soon. I'll have to talk to the Council about it when we get back.

We probably look serious as the Void with our security detail and face masks, but then Deimos swings our clasped hands a little between us, and suddenly it's like we're two snickering kids having a fun day in the city.

Which, honestly, isn't that far from the truth.

"What's your favorite spot in the city?" I ask Deimos.

He doesn't miss a mo. "Wherever you are." My face warms and I nudge him with my elbow even as the smile pricks my lips again. "What, too much?" Deimos laughs. "It's the truth, though."

"Well . . . that doesn't really answer my question, but thanks."

"Mmhmm. If you must know, without bringing you into the equation, there's a restaurant on the riverside that has the most incredible everything I've ever had."

I smirk. "Incredible everything, huh?"

"There isn't a single item on that menu that isn't orgasmic." I groan and Deimos laughs. "It's true, though! Well, not *literally* true, that would be strange and unsanitary, but the food is truly incredible. I'll take you there sometime when we have the tech back."

"It's a date, then."

"It will be, *shae*." Deimos's eyes light up. "*Ej*, do you think–"

A roar swallows his words a breath before something slams into my back, smashing me into him. The air becomes sand, the darkness rises up, and I fall, and fall, and–

47

Kora

My bones rattle in my chest as I prepare to face the people and tell them Dima and Jarek's escape to Invino is for the best. Or at least, not retaliating is. As I toe the line between appearing impartial and the truth.

What if they see through me? It's no secret that I wasn't elated over Dima's trial, nor the result. It wouldn't be a stretch to imagine I might not want Dima to be forced to return—and there's nothing I can do to hide that reality. But it's not a lie to say that pushing the issue isn't in Elja's best interests—especially considering Invino is one of the nations providing us with food to offset the famine.

I just need the people to see that.

The crowd in Vejla's center is so large I can't see the end of it from my place before them. It seems every time I come out here, more people arrive to see my addresses. Which is a positive sign, I imagine, given they aren't out here screaming. But still, it feels as though the swollen crowd is sitting on my chest, on my back, their pressure threatening to break me.

I can do this. I must.

"*Ora'denja*," I greet, my voice amplified over the crowd. "Thank you all for starting your set with me. Many of you have been wondering about the fate of the criminals Dima and Jarek, and what would become of them after Dima ran from his sentence. I understand many of you were concerned Dima would get away without atoning for his many crimes, and I want to assure you that is not the case."

I take a deep breath. And now to the part no one is going to like. "I've recently received word Dima and Jarek turned themselves in to the authorities in Invino. As you well know, Invino has outlawed executions as a sentence, which is likely precisely why Dima and Jarek chose to run there. I've demanded Invino return the men to us, as they are Eljans . . . but *Avra* Arik d'Invino has refused."

A low murmur washes through the crowd as people glance at each other. I keep speaking before anyone begins shouting. "I've spoken to our military leaders and they agree beginning a war with a nation, that at this very moment is providing vital food we need to make up for the nanite-induced famine, would be incredibly harmful both to Eljans at home and to the warriors we would lose trying to fight a war far from home."

The murmuring grows louder and I raise my voice to match them. "*However*, Dima and Jarek will not go unpunished, as I promised you at the beginning of this address. *Avra* Arik has offered a compromise to keep our nations at peace, keep Eljans fed, and still punish Dima. Rather than execution, *Avra* Arik has offered to enact their equivalent sentence: five cycles imprisonment and a lifetime of community service. If accepted, Dima would spend the rest of his life humbling himself and serving the people. And for my part, I will strip him of all titles and resources. He and Jarek will never be permitted to step foot in Elja again." That last part scrapes its way out of my mouth. It was Uljen's idea, because I have to do something to show I'm still in charge, and Dima will still suffer in a way related to *Elja*, given it was largely Eljans he wronged.

I will likely never see my brother again. But it's not the first time I've had to accept that as reality, and in the end, if it keeps him alive, I'll do it without question.

Better exiled than dead.

To my relief, the murmurs settle some. They aren't rioting over this possible reality, at least. "I'm going to accept *Avra* Arik's proposal with the added conditions I've stated. I truly believe this is best for Elja—we can't afford a war, especially not now, and especially not with Invino. It's not what we originally imagined would be Dima's atonement, but he will atone nevertheless, every set for the rest of his life, however long *Kala* wills it to be."

The people nearest me stand stiffly, their arms crossed over their chests and their lips pursed. But no one is protesting. They may not like this, but it seems most can agree war really wouldn't be a good option for us.

Maybe this will be okay after all. Maybe I worried over nothing.

"Kora."

I startle at Uljen next to me. I didn't hear him approach—and it's not exactly customary for someone to approach me in the middle of an address. I frown at him, but I can't speak without amplifying everything I say to thousands of people, so my frown is going to have to convey enough.

"I apologize," Uljen whispers. "This can't wait. There's been an attack in Asheron—a bomb, we think. You need to be briefed immediately."

My heart drops into my stomach. A bomb? In Asheron?

Is Eros okay? Are Mal and Deimos okay?

Kala, how many people were injured? How serious is this?

I turn back to the people, fighting to keep my voice even. "I apologize for the interruption. Unfortunately, I've just been informed there's a serious situation I must attend to immediately, so I have to end this address abruptly. Thank you for listening. All further updates will be released through the feed."

The crowd's whispers thunder in my ears as I follow Uljen out of the city square and back to the palace complex with my regimen of guards. And with every slam of my heart of in my chest, every panicked beat of my pulse in my ears, I can only repeat a fleeting, desperate prayer: Kala, *please let Eros be okay.*

Please.

48

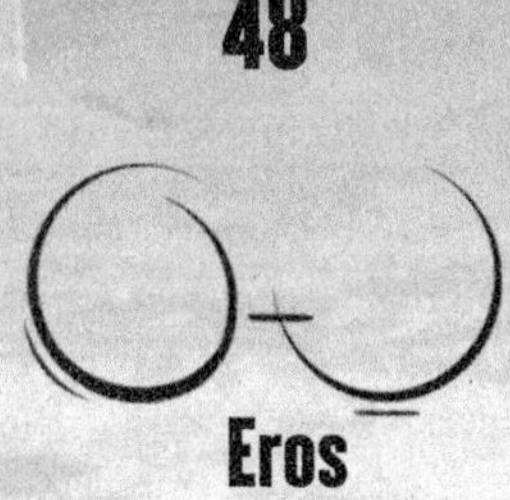

Eros

My ears are ringing and hot. Smoke bites my eyes and simmers in my lungs. My back stings and the pop and crackle of flame is too familiar–I dream about it with Day, and Nol, and Esta, and the blood, and the screaming and–

"*Kafra*," Deimos groans under me.

Oh, shit.

I roll off him, cringing as shards of stars-know-what stabs my back. Sit up, head pounding, squinting through the settling sand and thick gray smoke. Where are we? Not at camp–I know that, these sands are white, and gritty, and cool and not red, not–not like camp. I'm here. I have to stay here right now. I can't lose myself again, not now.

"Are you okay?" I ask Deimos.

He grimaces as he sits up. "I think my back is torn up, but *shae*, I'm fine. Let's get out of this smoke, *sha*?" He grabs my hand and we sortuv pull each other up. My eyes burn and I shudder with the urge to cough as we try to stumble out of the smoke, but the haze is everywhere.

"*Sira* Eros!" The call comes from Lejdo, though it takes me a mo of stumbling in a circle before I catch his silhouette through the thick air.

"We're here!" Deimos calls with a cough. Lejdo and Fejn move quickly toward us as flames crackle around us and the world becomes a gray, watery blur.

"Let's go," Fejn says as Lejdo gently nudges my shoulder. "It's not safe for you two here."

We're about halfway back to the palace when Lejdo abruptly stops and touches his ear.

"What is it?" I ask, but if Lejdo hears me, he doesn't show it. Instead, he looks at Fejn.

"Do you hear that?"

"The comms are coming back online." Fejn grins at us. "We must be getting tech back."

"Thank *Kala*," Deimos says with a sigh. "Do you think the explosion had something to do with it?"

"Maybe . . ." Lejdo squints ahead of us, shielding his eyes from the suns with his hand. "Someone's approaching." He and Fejn shift in front of us, shoulders stiff as they stand prepared to intercept whoever is coming. The low hum of bikes fills the air moments before Lejdo and Fejn relax. As the bikes pull up, I get why; Kantos steps off the lead bike and bows to me.

"I'm relieved you two are unharmed," he says. "Let's get you back to the complex. We have much to discuss."

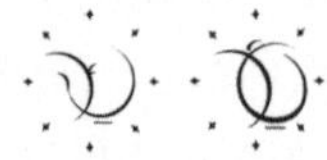

The conference room is about as packed as I've ever seen it; not only are all of my Council members there, but a bunch of different people from the guard are there, too, all with different positions. And unlike most of the rooms in the palace, this one isn't really all that big, so the room actually feels kinduv crowded. Which, weirdly, I like. It reminds me of camp, where ten to twenty people would cram into one tent, leaving barely enough room to move.

Of course, that's about the only similarity.

"The explosion was our team finding the pulse device," Kantos says. "Unfortunately, it was rigged so when the team entered the room with the device, it exploded. Three men were killed, four others injured. The survivors are in medical now–I'm not yet sure what their prognosis will be as we don't have nanites for accelerated healing, but we do have tech so . . . all we can do is pray."

"I'm sorry for your loss," I say, and half the room looks at me weird. What? Do they not say that here? As Kantos squints at me like he's trying to figure out what to say, Deimos clears his throat next to me.

"Do we know what will happen with the cure now? Zarana told us they had just about figured something out when the tech went."

"I'll check in with them and send word," Tol says. "I imagine they should be able to test then distribute something soon, though."

"Good," I say. "I also want to know how someone was able to get this thing hidden in Asheron. Did they bring it in from somewhere? Build it here? I want to make sure they can't just do this again."

"My men will certainly be investigating that," Kantos says. "We'll make sure we bring those behind this into custody."

I hesitate. "Just make sure you don't assume someone is involved just because they're human. I don't want anyone brought in unless you're sure they were involved."

Kantos's eyes widen. "I would never–"

"Just–cut the shit, will you?" I shake my head. "I'm not putting you down for whatever biases you have–let's be honest, *everyone* in this room, myself included, has some kind of biases we have to work through. I just want to make sure innocent humans aren't targeted over this."

Kantos purses his lips, but nods.

"Thank you." And then another thought hits me. "What's the status with Shaw?"

"We'll be speaking to him first, naturally," Kantos says. "He hasn't given us any information so far but breaking him is clearly our best chance at getting the information we need."

I try not to think about that–breaking Shaw. About how I've been there, trapped in a dungeon, tortured for information. About how blazed up it is–and now people are doing it someone else under *my* rule and I shouldn't be allowing that, it's so fucken wrong, but at the same time, if we're not using Shaw to our advantage then why am I wasting resources keeping him, especially when Rani clearly isn't open to negotiating?

"That's not actually what I meant," I say. "Have you heard from the men guarding him recently? If we're assuming this whole thing was the Remnant's attempt to get Shaw back–and that's what I'm assuming–then it doesn't make sense for them to go through all of this and *not* try to free him. Unless there's been an attempt I don't know about?"

"I–*naï*, *el Sira*, there hasn't been an attempt, but my men guarding him checked in less than a segment ago."

I nod, but Deimos frowns. "Are you sure?"

Kantos's brow furrows. "How would I not be certain?"

"How did they check in?"

"Via the comm, as expected now that we have power again."

"So you haven't actually seen them face-to-face."

A long pause. Kantos glances at me, then back to Deimos. "*Naï* . . . but protocol is to check in every segment through the comm. We see them during changeovers or when someone goes down there."

Deimos looks at Tol. "Can you bring up the monitoring feed on the glass, just to make sure?"

"This is a waste of time we don't have," Kantos says. "My men checked in with me in Sephari–even *if* he somehow managed to escape his cell, which is incredibly unlikely, a human wouldn't have been able to replicate that."

"You can't seriously believe that," I interrupt. "Military-trained humans speak fluent Sephari."

Kantos falters, just for a breath. "I-I would have heard his accent nevertheless."

"Really? Does my accent sound strange to you?" Kantos pauses and stares at me, like he isn't sure if it's a trick question. "Go ahead," I say. "Answer honestly."

"Your accent sounds . . . slightly southern. Eljan, naturally."

"And how about now?" I ask, clipping my vowels and enunciating like they do. "Does my accent still sound strange to you?" The panicked widening of his eyes is all the answer I need. "*Shae*, that's what I thought."

"*El Sira*?" Tol's voice sounds small in the room. When I look at them, hands shaking as they hold their glass, everything else stutters to a stop.

I know that look.

"Show us."

Tol clears their throat. "I, um, had to send a new guide down there because I couldn't access the ones ordinarily patrolling the area." Tol transfers the feed to every glass in the room. And the silence sucks the heat from my bones.

Open cell door. Six guards, throats and chests sliced open. Purple blood drenching their uniforms, shining on the smooth metal floors. Staring endlessly up at the guide chirping, "You require medical assistance. Help is on its way," over and over.

"*Kafra*," Deimos curses and not a breath later the feed disappears, replaced with a blue screen and an eerie, prolonged, beep.

"Is . . . this the tech rebooting?" I ask.

Tol frowns and shakes their head. "I don't think so. Unfortunately." They stand. "I need to get to the tech team."

And then Rani's face appears on every screen and it all makes sense. We're getting fucken hacked. Again.

"Congratulations," she says. "You've tracked down the device and restored power to Asheron–I'm sure you're very proud of yourselves. Now we're done playing games. Humans have been denied representation again and again for generations. It's time for that to end–now–and sending humans away is not the answer. We will speak to your *Sira*, Eros, and he will grant us representation in the government, as was promised us. If you refuse, that surprise we left with the device is a taste of what will come.

"You have two sets before we make our next move. Think quickly."

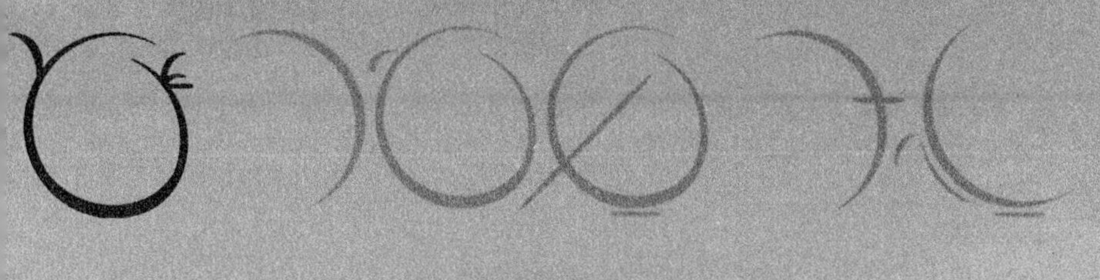

49

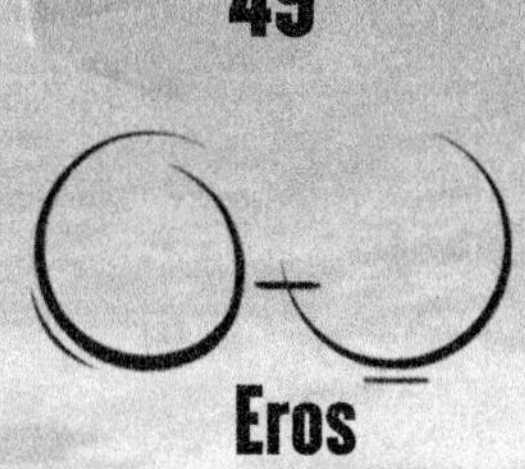

Eros

Everyone talks at once. The military leaders, Council members, even Deimos all reacting over each other in a chorus of overlapping voices that becomes a blanket of *noise*. The edges of a brainblaze licks behind my eyes and I rub my temples. I haven't had a serious brainblaze since I started taking that sleep stuff, but with Rani's words echoing in my skull and everyone trying to get their perspective in—

"Eros, are you all right?" Deimos touches my shoulder and frowns.

"Fine," I mutter. "Can you help me get everyone's attention?"

Deimos nods, takes a deep breath, and his voice booms across the room. "*El Sira* would like to speak."

The chatter slips into silence. My pulse drums in my ears as I clear my throat. "Thank you. Now if everyone could speak one at a time so we can actually understand each other, we might get something done."

"We need to track down this Remnant and annihilate them," Kantos says. "They've been killing our people and ripping our city apart for too long. Something must be done."

That word—*annihilate*—hits me like a kick to the ribs. "*Naï*," I say immediately. "We're not—*naï*."

"Kantos is right, Eros." Deimos touches my hand and frowns at me. "They unleashed *biological warfare* on the city. People have died–and now this explosion and threat of more? And we've lost our leverage with Shaw. This needs to end."

I shake my head. "I agree we need to stop them, but *annihilation* is never the answer. I won't approve of wiping any group of people out, not even the Remnant."

Kantos scowls. "And I suppose you have a better plan?"

"I want to talk to them and try to come to a peaceful compromise. There's no reason to start an all-out war right now–things are unstable enough without adding a battle to the mix."

"We're already at war," Deimos says. "You said so yourself when you spoke to Rani–they declared war on us when they unleashed a virus in the city, and when they knocked out our power, and when they *blew up* our soldiers."

"That's right," Kantos says. "We've been at war the entire time–the only difference is thus far, except when your nephew was abducted, we've only sat back and taken the abuse while the other side went unpunished."

"I'm *not* sending a military unit to go into the desert and *slaughter* a bunch of humans. I want to end this just as badly as everyone else, but I'm not going to order any bloodshed unless I absolutely have to."

Deimos purses his lips and Kantos looks like he wants to reach across the table and strangle me, but too fucken bad. I'm *Sira*. They take orders from me.

I turn to Tol. "Do you think you could get a message back to the Remnant?"

Tol considers that for a moment then nods. "I'm sure I could get a team together to trace back the hack and send a message that way."

"Good." I stand. "I'm going to try negotiating with them again. And if that doesn't work . . ." I look at Tol and take a deep breath. "Then we'll talk."

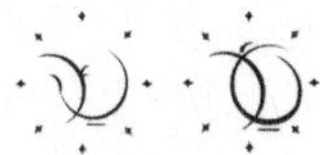

Nol once told me a story about the first ones who came to Asheron and how they tried to bury their dead. He said there were so many killed that at first they tried to build a large room underground to put them in and leave them to . . . rot, I guess. Nol said it was called a tomb.

Sitting in the techie's giant underground room again kinduv feels the way I imagine it'd feel to sit in a tomb. Except with more tech, obviously. But with the pressure of a city's worth of sand above us and surrounding us on all sides, it's only forced focus on anything and everything else that keeps me from flipping sand.

"We're in," one of the techies setting up the hack says. "Are you ready to go on feed, *el Sira*?"

I look at the guide hovering in front of my face. Roll my shoulders back, smother the buzz in my chest, and nod. "I'm ready."

The orb guide spins in the air, stabilizes, then chirps, "Recording," just as the glasses set up in front of me fill with the view of a familiar room. An underground bunker like this one, except a lot smaller, with slightly older tech, and full of humans.

Humans staring at me with wide eyes and gaping mouths. I resist the urge to smirk. We finally caught them off guard.

"My name is Eros, as I'm sure you know," I say. "I need to talk to Rani."

For a mo, nothing happens—they stare at me, I guess shocked we managed to hack them back, and processing, I guess, that I'm interrupting whatever they were doing before the feed hack started. Then, finally, a few people get up and rush out of the room, hopefully to go get Rani.

It takes a few awkward mos of us staring at each other while we wait, but finally Rani waltzes into the room with a frown. "Eros," she says stiffly. "What a surprise."

"Is it, though? You threatened me first. And it sounded like you wanted me to respond—unless you just wanted an excuse to attack us again."

Rani purses her lips and crosses her arms over her chest. "This is good—I'm glad you're reaching out. So let's talk. What's on your mind?"

"Let's end this," I say. "There's been way too much death. Come to Asheron so we can negotiate and finally move forward."

Rani laughs. "Come to Asheron? Do you think I'm dense? You'll arrest me the moment I enter the capital. Come on, Eros, surely you didn't think I'd fall for that."

I resist the urge to roll my eyes. "There's nothing to fall for, but if you'd prefer, we can meet at a neutral location instead. The important part is that we meet and talk this out. There's no reason for more people to get hurt."

Rani's eyes narrow, but she's not immediately saying no, at least. "You say that as if I've enjoyed hurting people."

"I don't care what your motivation was or whether or not you enjoyed it—the fact is, people have died, and I want it to stop. It's in everyone's best interest for this to be over."

"I don't know about that—"

"Let's meet and negotiate. Your end goal is to get representation for humans, so let's meet and talk about that."

Rani stands in stony silence for a long, uncomfortable mo. After what feels like an impossibly long stare down, she finally nods. "Okay, we'll meet. There's a town called Jel-Ta on the Eljan-Onan border. I can meet you just outside the town borders there in two sets, mid-set."

I glance at Deimos. He nods, so I turn back to the orb guide. "Deal."

"Good. Oh, and Eros?" She steps closer and tilts her head. "Try anything, my son, and I will destroy you."

She's smiling when the feed shuts off.

And I'm not sure if this is the best idea I've had since becoming *Sira*, or if it's the decision that's going to get me killed.

50

Kora

I give Eros the better part of the set to respond to the situation in Asheron before acting on the start of an idea. An idea skirting around the edges of the Remnant, who we know are stationed in Enjos, and Eros and I handling this situation together. Because Uljen is right–I've tied my fate to Eros's, and whatever he decides, I need to aid him however I can. It's in my best interest for him to succeed, and that means ending this disaster with the Remnant as soon as possible.

And because despite how things ended between us, Eros is still my friend. And after fighting for his current position for so long, I want him to do well.

So as the suns begin to set and the moons awaken in the evening sky, I sit against the wall in my bedroom, balance a glass in the air in front of me, and try to open a line with Eros. Animated sound waves jump across the screen as I wait, tap my fingers against my knee, and touch my earring. This may very well be a waste of time–I likely should have checked with Eros or Deimos to see if he'd have time to talk tonight before attempting to call. I certainly have no guarantee they even have their glasses anywhere near them.

Maybe this is a bad idea. Maybe Eros not answering is a sign. Maybe–

"How do I get this to start?" Eros's face appears on the glass as he looks over to his side, where Deimos is undoubtedly sitting.

"It's going," Deimos's voice says. "You're connected. *Ej*, Kora."

I wave with a small smile. "Good to see you both."

"Oh." Eros looks at the glass and laughs slightly. "There you are. Sorry, I'm still getting used to this tech . . . though I guess I don't really have much excuse anymore seeing how long it's been, huh?"

"It's not a problem. I'm glad to see the two of you uninjured."

"Everyone keeps saying that," Deimos says. "But our scraped and bruised backs tell quite another story."

Eros rolls his eyes. "We're fine."

"We'll see how fine you feel when you try to lay down tonight."

"I really hope you're not making innuendos in front of Kora."

"I'll make all the innuendos I please in front of whoever I'd like."

I smirk. "I'm going to have to agree with Eros's assessment, Deimos–you're clearly not seriously harmed."

"So are you just calling to say hi?" Eros says. "I'm guessing not but that'd be fine too . . ."

"Ah, *naï*, sorry." I force a small smile. "Though I probably should–I just keep imagining you're likely overwhelmed with your work and don't want any unnecessary interruptions."

Eros lifts a shoulder. "I mean, I am but I wouldn't mind anyway."

"I'll keep that in mind." I run a hand through my hair and tug a couple strands out of my loosening hair tie. If Eros is going to bring Dima up, and how my brother is now sentenced under Invino law–all of which he must surely know–now would be the time, in this pause. This quiet. And I'm prepared for the reprimand, or a comment about how he's not surprised I allowed Dima to walk away with his life, or *something*, but nothing comes.

Instead, he looks at me, allowing me to lead. And I'm not sure why he's letting this go when I defied him, when Eros rightfully despises my brother, but *Kala* knows I'm so grateful he is.

So I say, "Well firstly, you may or may not have heard I manipulated Invino into agreeing not to secede, so you're welcome."

Eros blinks and Deimos grins. "That was you?"

I'll admit I sound a bit smug when I answer, "It was."

"Wow. Well, thanks," Eros says. "How did you manage that?"

I hesitate. Would bringing up Dima break our unspoken agreement to let things pass? I suppose it's a risk I'll have to take. He asked. "It . . . was part of the terms I set when they wanted to keep Dima and Jarek."

Eros snorts. "You set terms to them doing exactly what you wanted?"

I smile, but only for a moment. "*Sha*, well, the true reason I'm calling is about the Remnant."

Eros's face darkens. "We're getting that handled."

"I'm sure, and I'm not calling to question whatever strategy you've decided to take. I just have a . . . secondary suggestion."

Eros frowns. "Secondary suggestion?"

I nod. "In case your initial plan doesn't work as well as you might hope."

"A backup plan. Right, okay."

"Sure." I hesitate. "Do you mind me asking what your plan is first?"

Deimos leans over so his face appears on the screen. "He wants to meet with their leader to *negotiate.*" He widens his eyes and arches his eyebrows, pretty effectively indicating what he thinks about that plan. Eros narrows his eyes at him, but he doesn't dispute Deimos's claim. Or how he said it.

"Okay . . ." I say slowly. Negotiate sounds . . . well. It sounds like Eros. "That's fine. So I'm sure you obviously remember you've been to the Remnant base in Enjos."

"Obviously."

"Well, as the base is in Elja, if necessary, I was thinking maybe I could help you infiltrate. I certainly remember how to get there, and I would go myself. With some technological help on your end, I'm sure we could get in and out without being seen."

Eros frowns. "And do . . . what, exactly?"

I shrug. "That's up to you. But I imagine you don't want to have to send a military unit over here, so I'm offering whatever you need. We have much easier access to the Remnant than you do."

"I think that's a great idea," Deimos says quickly. "As a—a backup plan, did you call it? But it'd certainly be preferable to you than sending Kantos and a unit of his men, *shae*?"

Eros hesitates. "It would . . ."

"And it'd only be if your plan doesn't work first," I say. "So you have a plan no matter what happens."

Eros bites his lip, then, slowly, nods. "Okay. But don't do anything unless I contact you."

I smile. "Of course not, *el Sira*."

Eros groans. "Don't call me that."

I laugh, and for a moment, even with hundreds of leagues between us, it's almost the way things were before we complicated everything with that kiss.

Almost.

"I need to talk to you."

Lira catches me in the hall, on the way to discussing the conversation I just had with Eros with the Council. I frown at her. "Can it wait? The Council is waiting for me."

"It's—really important," she says haltingly, glancing down the hall. "It'd be better if we spoke before you addressed the Council."

I haven't the faintest idea what this is about, but Lira seems . . . fidgety. She's humming with anxious energy, and now that she's approached me, I likely wouldn't be able to fully focus at the Council meeting anyway because I'd be wondering what this is about. So I nod to a nearby room and we step inside and wait for the doors to close behind us.

The room is small, with pillows and seats and glasses on the wall. A relaxation room, I suppose. It's also empty, which is the most important part.

I turn to Lira. "Go on, then. What is it?"

Lira takes a deep, shivering breath. "First . . . let me finish before you react, please. You're—you're going to be angry, and that's fine, but let me finish first."

I arch an eyebrow. "You haven't even begun and it's already sounding less than promising."

"I know. I'm sorry. Please."

I nod. "Okay. I'll refrain from . . . reacting."

"Thank you." Lira takes another deep breath, rubs her palms on her skirts, then winces a little. "I . . . I work for the Remnant."

My eyes widen. She–what? Oh, *Kala*. And she heard my meeting with Eros–where are my guards?

"I always have–I was born in the base and sent here as a . . . an informant, and to help direct other servants to them. But since I've started working with you, the information I've given them has been superficial, I swear. You've . . . you've been different, Kora, and I don't want to sabotage you in any way."

I can barely believe this. My heart is thrumming and my blood is buzzing and have I really fallen for this *again*? Another betrayal? Is my judge of character truly that incredibly poor?

Kala alejha, that night she caught me allowing my brother to escape she was probably coming back from meeting with those *kafran* rebels.

"You're a *spy*?" My voice comes out louder–angrier–than I intended, but then again, why am I attempting to temper my voice? Is she here to kill me? Did she aid the assassins into entering the palace all those nights ago?

"I know it sounds bad–"

"*Sounds* bad? Lira, this doesn't just *sound* bad–you've been working against me this entire time! How long have you been on staff here?"

Lira winces. "A few cycles."

"So you were working for them when they tried to kill me." I grip my hair. This is unbelievable. I literally can't trust anyone. Is Uljen working against me too? Does *anyone* truly support me? I turn to her again, my face burning and neck prickling. "Did you help the assassin get into the palace?"

Lira bites her lip, but the guilt in her eyes says it all. I shake my head and Lira steps toward me. "You were–you were different then, Kora, you must know that. You were benefitting from the enslavement of people and it didn't seem likely at the time you'd do anything about it. I'm glad the assassin failed, I am, but you must see I was doing what was best for my people."

The truth is, Lira is right. At the time, I hadn't given a second thought to the way I was profiting off of people's lives. I may not have established the system and I may not have particularly liked it, but I was silent. I was complicit. And if I'm being true, I'm not sure I ever would have made a move to end the practice if I hadn't met Eros, hadn't lost my position, hadn't been forced to see what life was like when you've lost the things you once took for granted.

I can't erase the way I overlooked other people's pain. The way I actively participated in it and spread it to others. Nothing can change or excuse that.

But Lira has been working for the redblood rebels all this time. How am I supposed to trust her now?

"Why are you telling me this?" I finally ask. "Why come to me and admit you work for them, unprompted?"

"Because I want to help you." Lira takes a deep breath and pulls her shoulders back. "I know how to get into the base in Enjos without prompting any alarms. I can disguise you as a freed human servant and bring you to them like I've done with others. Then you can get in and . . . do whatever you have to."

I narrow my eyes. "Why would you help me sabotage the cause you've apparently been a part of your entire life?"

"Because you're not the only one who's changed." Lira sighs and threads her fingers through her hair. "Of course I'm a proponent of human rights and representation but . . . I think what they're doing in Asheron is wrong. Eros is our best chance at real, lasting change. Trying to force him to overthrow the governmental system entirely?" Lira shakes her head. "I trust Eros to help us but he needs a chance to do it first. And it's not going to happen as long as the Remnant makes themselves an enemy."

"Or," I say, "you're luring me to the Remnant base where they can kill me once and for all. Or attempt to use me as some kind of leverage over Eros."

"I swear to you, that's not what this is."

"But how can I trust you?" The words explode out of me, a little louder than I intended. "You've been lying to me this whole time, Lira! You've been spying on me and relaying my secrets to my enemy, so how can you ever expect me to trust you again?"

Lira looks me in the eye and her voice is steady when she says, "Because I told you. I've admitted the truth to you, and I didn't have to do that. I didn't have to say anything to you—you certainly hadn't suspected me of anything. And I definitely didn't have to offer to help you infiltrate their base. I could have continued in silence without consequence, but instead I'm here, risking my neck admitting to a crime that I know you could have me executed for." She pauses. "But I'm trusting you with my life, just as I'm asking you to trust me in return. Besides, if I wanted to kill you, I wouldn't have warned you by telling you I work for the Remnant, first. And it's not like I haven't had plenty of opportunities that I allowed to pass me by–because I *don't* want to hurt you, Kora. I want to see you succeed as badly as I do Eros."

It's a convincing argument and I want more than anything to believe her. I want to believe I can trust her. I can overlook her past betrayal just as she's moved on from my past, terrible decisions. I want it to be easy to silence every whisper insisting she can't be trusted.

And the more I think about it, the more I know I don't have a choice. The truth is I don't have a good way to get into the Remnant base without raising alarms. And I don't want to send anyone else–who could I trust with such an important task? No one. I can only trust myself.

What Lira is suggesting is exactly the kind of quiet sabotage we might need–the kind we might actually get away with. I have to trust her–not completely, but enough to go with her–if I'm going to get this done.

"Fine," I say at last. "But if you try anything, I swear to *Kala*, Lira–"

"I won't," Lira says quickly. "I swear to you, Kora, I'm on your side. I want Eros and you to succeed. I want us to work together, humans and Sepharon, worldwide. And I think trusting Eros is the best way to get there."

"So be it," I say, but even as Lira sighs a breath of relief and wraps me in a hug, I can't help but wonder if I'm going to live to regret this.

PART IV

51

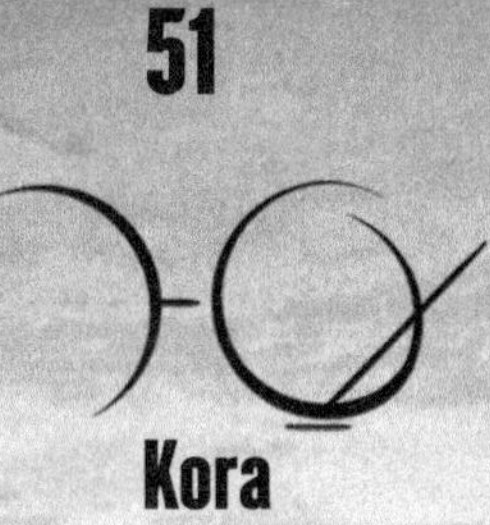

Kora

It took the better part of a segment for Lira to mix the face paint to the perfect shade of brown to match my skin. She bit her lip as she worked, furrowing her brow and muttering under her breath as she added in darker browns, then lighter, then darker, then lighter, holding up the small tub of paint to my face before shaking her head and going back to work.

I tap my fingers idly against my leg. I imagine Eros is likely as anxious about his meeting as I am about doing this. When I mentioned to him I'd found someone who could get me into the Remnant base undetected, he didn't ask, which is just as well. He'd likely think this was a bad idea.

"Okay, it's ready." Lira dips her fingers into the paint. "Just sit still and close your eyes."

I do as instructed, my heart pounding as her soft fingers slip over my skin. After two sets of planning and fretting, we're mere segments away from moonrise, from the time we'll go out into the desert, just the two of us, and walk into the Remnant base. Right through the front door. Or their equivalent of a front door, anyway.

But first we need to cover up my markings, and that means the paint. I sit in just a chest wrap and skirt as Lira's paint-cooled fingers slide over my cheeks, my nose, my forehead and eyelids and temples and jaw. She moves down my neck with both of her hands now, then over my collarbones, my shoulders, tucking her fingers just under my wrap so the paint covers all exposed skin.

I shiver. "Won't this dry and crack?"

Lira shakes her head as she works her way down my right arm. "*Naï*, it's mixed with the same substance you used to paint the servants white. When it dries it becomes powdery and soft–and it's waterproof and will likely take a couple washes to come off."

"You seem to be very knowledgable about this."

She hesitates and glances at me with a weak smile. "We . . . used it to cover our tattoos and paint markings on ourselves. So we could go into the city, you know? It worked well enough."

"Ah." I pause. "Well. I suppose it's a good thing you know how."

"Tonight it certainly is, *sha*." She pauses and glances at my scarred arm. "I'm going to cover this arm now, okay?"

It was nice of her to ask. Though I suppose that means she's noticed I don't especially like having my scars touched. I nod and she continues spreading the smooth liquid over my skin, erasing the pink, the gnarled, melted markings of my injured arm.

"I used to think *Kala*'s mark looked so odd on the Sepharon," Lira says. "But looking at them up close . . . they're actually quite beautiful. Sometimes, anyway."

I smile. "Thank you."

"Is the design genetic? I know it varies person to person, but does a particular . . . *style* get passed down parent to child?"

"It can, *sha*. Though it's not always parent to child. Sometimes it skips a generation or two. And sometimes the markings seem a little more spontaneous."

Lira nods. "Stand, please."

I do and she kneels in front of me, coating her hands in the paint before gripping my ankle and slowly running her hands up my calf. Her touch is gentle–almost intimate. She's so careful to cover every bit of my skin, to touch everywhere that might be visible, to make sure I'm completely covered. And it's bizarre, in a way, watching the paint spread over my leg and erase away the markings I've always had. But Lira did an excellent job–the shade she created matches my skin perfectly. As the shine of the wet paint dries to matte powder-smooth skin, I almost feel naked without *Kala*'s mark tracing a maze over me.

Then she reaches my thigh and glances up at me. "I'll have to go under your skirt a little, in case it gets kicked up. I won't go too high."

"I'm not worried."

Once she's thoroughly covered a decent way up my thigh, she moves on to the next leg. She works quietly, carefully, concentrating. She looks at me like an architect at a building, worrying her lip as she runs her slick hands over me again and again until my skin is covered. Until my legs, my stomach, my back and shoulders and arms and neck and face are all covered.

"What about my ears and eyes?" I ask when she's done.

"Well the eyes are easy." Lira digs into a small pack she brought and pulls out a tiny glass container with two little pools of liquid. Floating in each are clear circles with a ring of brown.

I glance at her. "What is that?"

"They're eye colors," she says. "You put them in your eyes and they cover up the color of your irises."

My stomach twists as I stare at her. "They . . . are masks for your *eyes*?"

Lira laughs. "Don't look so affronted. It doesn't hurt a bit, I promise. Just look up and try not to blink until I tell you."

"Naturally," I say as if it's a simple thing to just look away and not blink while someone sticks their fingers in your eyes. Eventually, though, she gets them in and the uncomfortable feeling of something *not right* in my eyes fades a little more with every blink.

"Perfect." Lira smiles. "Now your eyes are as brown as mine."

"And my ears?"

"Ah, right." Lira pulls out two squishy gray half-circles from her pack. "I just have to paint these real quick, then we'll fit and blend them over your ears. It'll cover the notches. Hopefully."

"Hopefully?"

Lira smiles weakly. "Well it's not like I've had to disguise a Sepharon as a human before. But I think this should work. We had opposite versions to make our ears looked notched so . . . it's similar enough."

And so it is. Half a segment later, my ears are adjusted and my body is painted and my eyes are a single color and I have to say–looking in the mirror, I can almost believe it. The illusion holds well.

"Wow," I say. "This is . . . there's no way I would have been able to disguise myself like this. Thank you."

"You're welcome." She pauses and looks me over. "There's just one thing left. Give me your left arm."

I do as she says and she picks up a small brush and dips it into a jar of black. She carefully paints on my upper arm and it only takes a moment to figure out what she's doing–the marking I would have if I were truly a freed servant.

"There," she says when she's finished. "Congratulations, Kora. You're now a human. Sort of."

"Hopefully I'll be human enough for the Remnant."

"Hopefully," Lira agrees.

Neither of us speak of what will happen if I'm not. We don't have to.

If this goes wrong, it may very well be the last mistake I ever make.

52

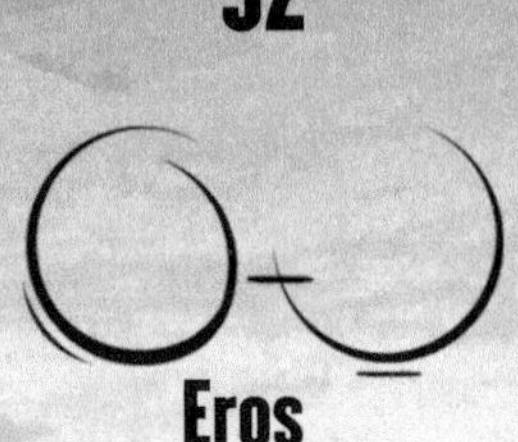

Eros

It seems unnecessary, but we take a flying port to the meet point. I spend the whole time staring out the window, watching the sands shift from white to pink, swallowing my stomach as Deimos holds my hand.

All I can think is this whole thing is probably a huge mistake.

All I can think is I never should have agreed to send Kora to the Remnant base as a backup, not even with her insider contact, whoever she is. There's too much that could go wrong—they could be found out, and then what? What if she's hurt—or killed? What if I made these decisions without thinking them through—at least not enough? This could all go to the Void.

It's stifling in the port cabin. The air is thick and heavy. Suffocating. The low hum of the engines is an endless roar in my ears. I clench and unclench the hand Deimos isn't holding and tap my fingers on my knee and try to breathe, try not to focus on how this is probably all going to go really, really wrong because if I focus on that, I might—

"You aren't hearing a word I'm saying, are you?"

Deimos's voice cuts through the roar in my head. I look away from the window. Look at him. Try to focus. He's talking to me.

"Sorry," I say. "I do now."

"You're panicking," Deimos answers. It's not a question.

"I'm . . ." Deimos arches an eyebrow at me, daring me to deny it. I cave. "Okay, fine. A little."

Deimos snorts. "You can't panic *a little*. That isn't panic then, that's just anxiety."

"What if I fuck this up?" I ask. "What if the whole Kora thing fucks this up? What if–"

"Eros." Deimos takes my face in his hands and looks me in the eye. "We don't know what's going to happen, of course we don't. But whatever does, good or bad, we'll handle it. Just take it a step at a time, *shae*? Worrying about what *might* happen next isn't going to help you."

He's right, but it's not as easy as just . . . not thinking about it. If I could just not think about it I wouldn't think about it. "I can't just . . . turn it off."

Deimos smiles weakly. "I know. But I'm here with you, *shae*? Whatever happens, we'll face it together. So do your best to focus on that."

I take a deep breath. Force myself to look at him and smile a little. "Fine."

"*Sha*, you are." Deimos winks at me and takes my hand again.

And somehow, he actually has me laughing again.

53

Kora

"Where are you going?"

The squeak that escapes my mouth is only half as embarrassing as the jolt that races through me and makes me take half a step back into Lira as Uljen emerges from the shadows of the hallway. "*Kala* above, Uljen, you nearly gave me a heart attack. What are you doing sneaking through the halls at this time of set?"

"What am *I* doing?" Uljen squints at me. "What happened to your . . . did you cut your hair off?"

"It's a wig," Lira says proudly. "Convincing, isn't it? Bought it a couple sets ago—I picked it out myself."

Uljen stares at me and slowly shakes his head. "This . . . Kora, please tell me you're not about to do something . . . ill-advised."

I press my lips together. Uljen will definitely think this venture is *ill-advised*, to say the least. It's why I didn't involve him; he wouldn't understand why it's necessary, why I have to do this to help Eros, and myself in the process.

But I'm not going to lie to him. I'm participating in far too much deception already as it is.

"Lira and I are going to Enjos to infiltrate the Remnant, as a backup plan in case Eros's negotiations don't go well."

Uljen's eyes widen. "You–what?"

"I know you won't approve," I say quickly, "but to be honest, Uljen, I don't need your approval. I've already made this decision and told Eros I would–"

"How could Eros ask you to do such a thing?" Uljen exclaims. He steps forward and grips my shoulders. "Kora, surely you must know how dangerous this is. Not only to you and Lira, but to Eros as well–if you're found out–"

"We won't be found out," Lira says. "We have a good plan. We're going to end this together."

Uljen ignores Lira and keeps looking into my eyes. The terror in his face, in the tremble of his grip–heat snakes into my chest and curls in my stomach. He's genuinely scared for me. "Please don't go," he begs. "I-I understand you feel as though you have to help Eros, and I understand supporting him is vital, but he can't ask you to risk your life for him. This is too much Kora, please–"

"He didn't ask me." The words come out so softly I barely hear them roll off my lips. "I volunteered. He's hinging everything on a negotiation, Uljen. He didn't have another plan, and if it fails–"

"And what if it *succeeds*? You haven't even given him a chance, Kora–"

"Which is why this is merely a contingency plan." I point to my ear. "I'm wearing a comm and Deimos is, as well. He'll keep me updated, and if all goes well, Lira and I will leave without doing a thing. But we must be in place in case it *doesn't* go well and Eros needs us to do something."

"Do something like what? Kill someone?"

"I don't know."

Uljen releases my shoulders and runs his palms over his face. "This is madness. You should send someone in your stead, not risk yourself."

I shake my head. "This is too important. I don't expect you to understand, but I can't trust anyone else with this."

"Then I'm going with you."

My words catch, stutter, and die in my throat as I process what Uljen just said. "You–what?"

"I'm not letting you go in there alone. I'm going with you."

Lira snorts. "She won't be alone; I'll be there with her the entire time."

Uljen scowls at Lira so darkly it's a little–frightening. "She needs someone she can *trust*."

Lira's eyes narrow and she steps toward Uljen. "I have served Kora faithfully, not that I need to justify myself to you. But unlike you, Kora doesn't base who she can trust and who she can't dependent on whether they're Sepharon or human."

"I'm not–"

"Okay," I interrupt. "That's enough. Uljen, I'm sorry, but you can't come with us. I need you here in case anything happens–and not to mention you'd ruin our cover story. I understand you're worried and I appreciate your concern, but I'm going to be fine. Everything will be fine. You'll see."

Even in the shadows, Uljen seems paler. "Please," he croaks. "Kora, I don't want to lose you."

Something twists–hot and sharp–in my chest. Uljen's fear, his feelings, are genuine. And I hate that I'm hurting him, I hate that this decision is affecting him so profoundly.

But I also hate that he doesn't trust me to make my own decisions. That he thinks I need his guidance on every little thing.

"I'm sorry, Uljen," I say at last. "But you don't want to be *Avra-ko*. You can't lose what you never had to begin with."

And then I walk past him, swallowing bile and smothering the image imprinted in my mind: the hurt on Uljen's face as I stepped on his heart and walked away.

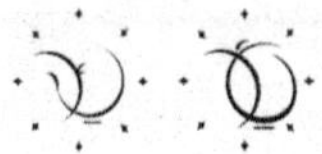

The closer we get to Enjos, the more sure I am this was a terrible idea. When the city's remains rise on the horizon, my stomach churns painfully and the heat of the early morning sticks to my skin. As Lira maneuvers the bike over the smooth red sands, and the first buildings drift past us, my heart beats in my throat like a fist.

And when we stop in front of the abandoned temple where I kissed Eros, where I came with Deimos to rescue him, where the Remnant has their base hidden deep beneath the sand, I can barely force my lungs to take in air.

Breathe. Just breathe.

Worse still, I can't stop seeing Uljen's face as I walked past him. As I reminded him he didn't want a serious relationship. As I told him to stay behind.

Why do I push everyone away? Why do I sabotage my relationships again and again?

But am I really this time? Uljen doesn't want the responsibility of having a serious relationship with someone in power. Someone like me. He wants to keep our relationship open. He doesn't want to commit.

So why did it feel like a betrayal when I reminded him of his own wishes? Why does it feel like I've done irreparable damage to a relationship I thought was going well? Why must good things end?

"You . . . don't look well." Lira smiles weakly and takes my hand. "Everything is going to be fine—they'll be more than happy to welcome you to the base, don't worry."

I suppose we can't speak openly, not here. The Remnant are watching and listening. Even before I've seen anyone, even before we've entered the temple, our deception has already begun.

Then Lira hugs me and brings her lips close to my ear. "Are you sure about this?" she whispers hot against my skin.

I'm not sure. I'm nowhere near remotely sure. I'm a breath away from outright panic, from getting back on the bike and driving away and never returning to this *Kala* forsaken place.

But if I'm being truly honest, if I'm thinking rationally, the chance to back out was several sets ago. Right now, Eros is counting on me to provide him a way out if he needs it. I've already told him I'll be there. He's already planning on having this contingency plan ready.

It's too late to back out now.

So even though I'm nowhere remotely near sure, even though I'm wishing more than anything I could turn back time and never suggest this to begin with, even though I'm starting to doubt the wisdom of this plan, I nod and answer back in a whisper of my own.

"I'm sure."

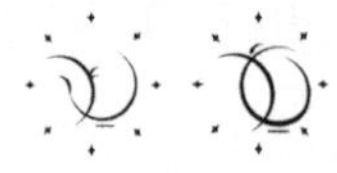

We uncover a door buried in the sand not unlike the one hidden in the temple sand garden in Vejla, climb into cold, complete darkness, and walk in the eerie, silent black for what feels like much too long. We have only a small light that Lira brought to reveal our steps. Finally, Lira taps my shoulder and motions to a thick, black, circular door at the end of the impossibly long tunnel.

"Not so bad, right?" Lira says lightly.

My heart thrums endlessly in my ears.

Lira turns to the door and speaks. "Hey, everyone, this is the girl I was telling you about. Her name is Enna. Let us in, please."

A moment later, a deep thunk echoes through the hall, followed by a noise like thunder as the door rolls into the wall, clearing the way for us to enter. We step over the lip of the doorframe sticking out of the sandstone ground and enter.

"Lira," a pale woman says, and then that's about all I understand because the rest is in redblood. I wipe my sweaty palms on the sides of my thighs and try to keep my breathing even. The two speak to each other for a couple moments while Lira gestures to me and I try not to feel so out of place—though I suppose feeling out of place would be natural even if I were a redblood.

"So you only speak Sephari?"

I start at the words I can actually understand. The woman is speaking to me. "*Sha*," I say. "I was raised with a . . . a Sepharon family before I began at the palace complex."

The woman nods. "That's not a problem—we'll teach you English. You're not the first in need of language lessons and I'm sure you won't be the last." She smiles kindly. She seems genuine. And she isn't looking at me too closely, so I suppose maybe this disguise is actually working. I imagine the dim lighting down here helps as well.

"Thank you," I say. "I . . . appreciate your hospitality."

"And we're happy to welcome you to our family, Enna." She smiles and nods down the hall. "Lira will take you to your new room. Most everyone isn't awake yet, but once they are, we'll have you registered."

"Thank you." I smile softly at Lira, who smiles back. Her eyes say everything she isn't speaking: that I had nothing to worry about, that everything is going fine, that maybe this wasn't such a terrible idea after all. Maybe Eros actually won't need us, and we'll be able to go back home without incident.

But as I walk down the quiet hall with Lira, I can't help but suspect that daring to hope for so much is dangerous.

54

Eros

Rani is already there when we arrive. I'm not sure if that's a good or bad thing—on one hand, we don't have to wait, but on the other it would have been good to get the place checked out before we started talking.

The meeting spot outside of Jel-Ta is a quiet, barren area. The sand is pink—a weird mix of the gritty white sand and soft red powders from home, and it feels harder, somehow, as we walk on it. Almost packed. And warmer than the white sands I'd gotten used to in Asheron.

Rani is standing next to a prickle plant bush, arms crossed, two bearded men with long hair, who as far as I can tell are identical, on her either side. There's something about them that keeps drawing my gaze back; they're tall and built like—

Wait. They have markings. They're Sepharon. And I think I know them.

"Since when do Sepharon work for the Remnant?" I whisper to Deimos.

Deimos lifts an eyebrow and shrugs. "I didn't know any did, if I'm being perfectly honest."

"I know them. They're the guys who nearly executed me in Jol's Arena."

Deimos's eyes widen and he looks at the men again, then back to me. "Are you sure?"

I glance at them again, meet their steely gazes. I didn't get a really good look at them that set, if I'm being honest, but I remember them. And maybe–if they were working for the Remnant all along . . . were they how I got uncuffed? Did they help plant the bombs that destroyed the arena and let me escape?

"Good to see you, Eros." Rani looks me over like you might an opponent. Which I guess I am to her, now.

"Sure." I take a deep breath and roll my shoulders back. "I don't want to fight anymore. I've never wanted to fight with you or the Remnant. Let's end this; no one else has to die."

"I agree. And if we work together, no one else has to get hurt. All we've wanted from the beginning is your cooperation."

I grimace. "The thing is, what I said to you way back in Enjos hasn't changed. I still need time to stabilize everything before I can move on to making major changes. I want to help you, and the Remnant, and humans worldwide, but I need your patience."

Rani snorts. "You spent our patience a while ago."

"Of course I did." I run my hand through my hair and take a deep breath. "Look, we *both* need to make some compromises for this to work. I can't dismantle the monarchy system that's kept the peace for generations and I'm not going to. But we want the same thing: for humans and Sepharon to be treated equally here, and I think we can get there if we work together."

"And how do you expect us to trust you enough to work with you if you've broken the only promise you made to us?"

I shake my head. "I haven't broken my promise; I swore to work with you and that's what I'm trying to do. But you can't expect me to fix everything all at once–and you've only made it harder because you've given me *more* to try to fix before I can even think about changing laws for the better."

Rani scowls. "Then your priorities are fucked. Equality for humans should be on the top of your list–"

"They *are*," I answer. "Along with fixing the nanites before people around the globe starve, and learning how to fucken govern so I don't make mistakes that will leave people dead, and trying to keep the territories peacefully together, and eradicating the disease *you* unleashed, and–"

"Okay," Rani says quickly. "Enough, I get it."

"I don't think you do." I step toward her, scowling. "You have to run a faction, so you know what it's like to be in charge of people. But you have *no* idea what it's like to have an entire fucken planet counting on you, everyone with their own opinions about how to rule and what to prioritize. You don't get it, and you have no idea how much harder you've made my job."

"If you're trying to make me feel bad for you–"

"I'm trying to make you understand I haven't been ignoring you and I haven't broken any promises, I just haven't had a chance to even *think* about changing major laws to help humans because I've had too much to deal with at once."

Rani crosses her arms over her chest and looks about a breath away from snapping my head off, but she stays quiet.

I sigh. "I've heard you, and I've heard the Remnant. I know things have been hard, and you're tired of hiding, and I don't want you–any of you–to have to hide anymore. I think we're getting there, but you have to give me the time to do the work."

"How long?"

It's the first time she's shown even a consideration to the whole time thing. Does that mean she might actually cave? *Don't hold your breath yet.* "Five cycles," I say. "I know it seems like a lot, and I'm not saying I won't get anything done before then, but humans are already free now to start with. I want to prioritize making half-bloods legal and end our targeted executions. I want to give people a chance to live without worrying every set might be the set they're found out and killed."

"But in the meantime, you won't be doing anything on the government level," Rani says flatly. "We want representation, Eros, not empty promises."

"I know," I answer. "I do, really. So I want to add a human representative to my Council."

Rani's eyebrows shoot up. "You . . . do?"

I nod. "I don't know who yet, but I was thinking I'd announce it and let the people choose some–"

"Take Shaw." I blink as Rani steps closer. "I'll agree to your terms–five years with the promise of working together, if you take Shaw as your representative."

Shaw is pretty literally the last human I would want to work with every damn set. He's obnoxious, too biased toward Rani, and honestly, way too used to giving out orders.

But I have to make some compromises if I want this to work.

I sigh and extend my arm. "Fine. Agree and deal done."

Rani takes my arm and shakes it, once. "Done deal."

55

Kora

The Remnant underground base is a maze. A dingy maze, with flickering lights hanging on string-like wires against the sandy walls, and deep shadows painting every corner. We take more turns than I can ever hope to remember, pass door after identical door of black metal, and nod at the occasional person who passes us by.

I'm grateful Lira is here—how would I have ever hoped to navigate this labyrinth without her help? The truth is I likely wouldn't have been able to, and stumbling around down here not only without any direction but without a disguise half as good as what Lira put together would have guaranteed our failure.

"I don't know how you manage to remember how to get anywhere down here," I whisper.

Lira laughs lightly. "You get used to it. Though I'll be the first to admit it can be confusing—I still take a wrong turn every once and so."

"That doesn't surprise me." To be true, I think it'd surprise me more if she *didn't* make any mistakes down here. Are there multiple floors? That'd be even more confusing, if there were layers to this maze. But before I can ask, Lira stops at her bedroom door, which looks like every other black, circular door.

"So we'll wait in your room until we hear?" I whisper.

Lira hesitates, then nods and rests her palm on the door. It rolls aside with a grinding sound, then we enter the room and the door closes behind me.

It takes me a moment to parse what I expected—a small room with a bed, some kind of storage for clothes, maybe a mirror, nothing lavish—to what is in front of me: a large room with rows of desks and seating and glasses, and large glasses hung on the walls at the end of the room, full of people who all turn to look at us.

This is—not a bedroom.

A man with skin like Jarek's and a shaved head walks down the center aisle with a smirk, clapping slowly. "I have to say, I'm impressed," he says in Sephari.

Lira answers him in English and they have a conversation I don't understand as the man glances at me and Lira gestures at me and the room is eerily silent otherwise. My skin prickles with stares. With a cold trickle crawling down my spine. With my heart pounding just a little harder, just a little faster.

Something isn't right. Lira said we were going to her room, and this is clearly not her room. Did she change her mind? But if she changed her mind, why didn't she tell me?

Unless she didn't change her mind.

Unless this—bringing me here—was her plan all along.

I cross my arms over my stomach and touch the knives stored under my shirt, at my sides. The weapons I didn't tell Lira about because I didn't think it necessary. Because even though I wanted to, I suppose I didn't trust her completely. Because maybe *Kala*, or fate, or something else whispered in my ear something wasn't right.

Because right now, something isn't right.

After several moments of tense conversation I can't understand and the stares nipping my skin and my heart thrumming with every breath, the man turns to me and smiles.

"It's good to finally meet you in person, Kora. Lira's told us lots about you–and you were dating Eros for a while, right?"

I don't answer. He seems to know the answer anyway, so there's little point, and I'm not sure I want to grace anyone with a response right now, not when I'm relatively sure there isn't a soul in this room not plotting against me.

I look at Lira. She bites her lip and–incredibly, almost looks apologetic. "Everything will be fine," she says. "I promise."

As if I could believe a word that comes out of her mouth after this.

So I suppose Uljen was right. I've walked right into a trap. And Lira led me there with a smile, and promises, and *Kala* I trusted her. After everything I finally brought myself to trust someone and she betrayed me. Although I suppose, as I felt a need to bring my knives, I didn't really trust her completely. Not that that lessens the blow any.

I really can't trust anyone.

"Oh, how rude of me, I haven't introduced myself. Name's Shaw." The man grins a predatory smile. I don't move. "So with that out of the way, tell me, cuz I'm real curious–what was your plan? You come down here with Lira, who you're actually thick enough to believe would *betray* us, all covered in paint and shit to pass as human and . . . then what? You kill me? Was that the plan? Did Eros send you?"

"I don't know why you don't ask Lira," I answer. "Seeing how she came up with half the plan herself."

Shaw laughs. "Of course she did." He grins at Lira but she just looks away, arms crossed over her chest.

"To be true," I say, "I was hoping I wouldn't have to do anything."

"What, so you came down just to visit? Somehow I find that hard to believe."

"It was a backup plan," Lira says softly. She doesn't look at me, which is probably a wise move on her part because I'm sure the glare I'm giving her is less than pleasant. "For if things don't go well with Rani and Eros's meeting."

Shaw laughs. "Well, looks like we were on the same page, then, seeing how you're *our* backup plan, too."

"Killing me won't solve anything," I say evenly even as my breath shakes.

"Maybe not," Shaw says. "But threatening to kill you will make Eros hesitate, and actually killing you will sure feel nice after all the shit you've pulled."

Lira's eyes widen. "What? You said it'd be a bluff! We aren't *killing* her!"

"Did I?" Shaw shrugs. "I don't remember saying that."

Lira glares at him. "You fucken liar–"

"Oh, c'mon, Lira." Shaw rolls his eyes and looks at her. "You didn't *really* think we'd just let her walk out of here, did you? After everything she's done, you can't possibly think she doesn't deserve to get hers."

"She's gotten better! She's been making changes–"

"Fucken suns in the sky, Lira, you're unbelievable–"

"I'm leaving," I say loudly. Lira and Shaw both look at me, Lira looking like she's just been slapped and Shaw like I just told a great joke. He even snickers.

"That's cute that you think that, but you're not going anywhere." He nods to someone behind me and I lower my hands to my sides, pulse drumming in my ears as I wait.

My back prickles with the knowledge of someone approaching. Deep breaths. I'll stay calm. I'll focus on one step at a time. I won't let anyone take me.

Someone grips my shoulder–I spin around and ram the heel of my palm into his nose. It crunches as he screams and drops to his knees, hands over his face as blood pours between his fingers. Two more men approach me from either side, one with a baton that crackles lightly–energized–and the other with a phaser.

I breathe deeply as the man points the phaser at me. "Put your hands above your head where I can see them."

I bring my hands up by my ears, watching him as he steps closer, as the crackle of the baton behind me grows louder. Then I scream, fake a lunge toward him, and duck. He shoots–the shot flies above my head and hits the man behind me. The dropped baton rolls beside my foot and I grab it and swing it at the man with the phaser, up and between his legs. It connects with a buzz–the man makes a high-pitched strangled scream and crumples in a ball on the ground.

"Stop it!" Lira is screaming. "Leave her alone–Shaw, no!"

A glint of silver to my left–a knife–I swing the humming baton high and connect with a skull so hard the impact reverberates into my shoulder.

Shaw's eyes roll to the back of his head before he drops like a rock.

And the room goes very quiet and very still.

"Oh god," Lira says. "Oh god, oh god, oh god–" She drops to her knees beside Shaw and checks for a pulse.

"Kora?" says a voice in my ear, and with a start I remember the comm. It's Deimos. I completely forget we were connected. "Kora, Eros and Rani have made a deal. Go home and do *not* engage the Remnant, understand? Everything is okay." He laughs quietly, full of air and disbelief as I watch Lira desperately check for signs of life. "*Kala*, I can't believe it," Deimos says softly in my ear. "We actually did it."

But as Lira looks up at me, she doesn't have to say it. The truth is evident enough.

Shaw is dead.

56

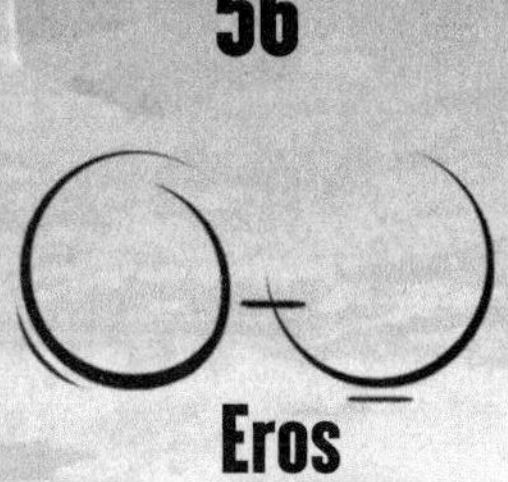

Eros

As Deimos and I cross the sandy distance between where I'd stood talking to Rani and our port, I can barely believe the lightness in my chest. I'd been too afraid to dare to believe we could negotiate successfully, that we could solve this nightmare with a conversation. I hadn't wanted to be disappointed when it invariably went wrong, when I had to make decisions I didn't want to because I'd been backed into a corner with no other way out but through.

But it didn't happen. I didn't need Kora's backup—Deimos is calling her off right now. I didn't need a second plan because for fucken once the primary plan actually worked. And stars, it feels so blazing good.

Deimos stops walking and I glance back at him, my smile still glued to my mouth.

But Deimos's smile melts off his face. He touches his ear and looks at me, wide-eyed. "What did you just say?" he hisses to the comm.

My stomach twists. I step toward Deimos as he pales a shade and shakes his head slightly, and I don't know what that means, I don't know what's going on, but this–this obviously isn't good.

"What is it?" I whisper. "Is Kora okay?"

If Kora got hurt trying to help us–

"Oh, Eros," Deimos says softly, just as someone screams. Rani, crossing the sands toward us with murder in her eyes and storms on her shoulders.

"What happened?" I say quickly. "Tell me now."

"I-I don't know," Deimos stutters. "Kora says they attacked her and in the process of defending herself–Shaw is dead."

My blood goes cold. Kosim and Fejn reach for their phasers, but I lift my hand. "*Naï*, let me handle this. Don't hurt her. She's . . . her brother just died."

Kosim and Fejn grimace, but they don't pull out their phasers and they stay behind as I step toward Rani, my hands up in surrender. "Rani, I'm so sorry. I didn't–"

Her fist juts out so quickly I've barely registered something coming toward me before pain explodes across my jaw. I stagger back, hands raised, dodging her second and third swings as tears stream down her face.

"You fucken traitor!" she screams. "I made a deal with you and you *killed* him!"

The next time she swings I catch her fist, then her other fist as she tries again. "Listen to me. I'm so sorry for your loss, but I didn't order *anyone*'s death, I swear to you–"

Her knee jolts up and I move in time to not get hit where she was aiming, but a knee to the stomach hurts nearly as bad. I double over and drop her fists, dodging another strike as I stagger out of the way. "I don't want to hurt you!" I force myself upright even as the pain echoes in my stomach. "Rani, please, we have a deal–"

"Fuck you and your deal!" she screams. "Deal is *off*! I will never work with you, you fucken mutt!"

That word hurts worse than any punch to the stomach or jaw. And I shouldn't care, it shouldn't matter that it came from her, because she may have given birth to me but she's not my mother, she's never been my mother–but it aches, deep, to hear it. From anyone, but especially from her.

Then she pulls out a knife and lunges toward me with a scream. I dodge to the side as she swipes and catch a glimpse of–

My heart drops to my stomach.

Lejdo is aiming a phaser at her.

"*Nai!*" I lunge in front of Rani as the burst rips through the air and a force like a kick with a metal boot rams into my chest.

The suns are rising orange and red but for a mo they almost look gold. A gold rising over me as sands warm my back and every breath licks my lungs with flames. As screams fill my ears and for once they're not mine because I can't get enough breath to make a noise that loud, that agonized, that terrified, and then Deimos is crouched over me and brushing my hair back and he's saying *stay with me, please Eros, don't go* and we've been here before except then I was waking up to his tear-streaked face and this time his hand is in mine and I'm fading.

The world goes a little gray. A little dark.

"Stay with me. Eros, please, I'm begging you. I need you. I love you. Eros, please . . ."

57

Kora

"What did you *do*?" Lira screams, though she's just an arm's length in front of me.

I don't know how to answer. I was defending myself. They were attacking me, and I fought back, and he had a *knife*, what was I supposed to do? Let him stab me?

But I can't bring myself to say the words, to defend myself, because a man is dead and the baton that killed him is still buzzing in my tight grip.

I wasn't trying to kill anyone. I just wanted them to let me go. I needed them not to touch me. And they had weapons, and outnumbered me, and . . .

Someone grabs my arm and yanks it hard behind my back, twisting my wrist and forcing me to drop the baton. I wince at the pain but don't fight it.

"What do we do with her?" the person who grabbed me asks. His grip is strong but his voice is soft.

"I-I don't know." Lira furiously wipes at her face, but it doesn't do much good because she bursts into another sob a moment later as she runs her hand over Shaw's head, cradling his corpse in her lap.

"We should kill her," a woman says, glaring at me from across the room. "Life for a life."

Lira shakes her head and says a fluid string in English. As the conversation explodes in the room, as these grieving strangers decide what to do with me, all I catch are names: Rani, Eros, Kora.

Shaw.

My stomach churns. If they decide they want to execute me right here, I won't be able to fight my way out. There's too many of them, and I don't even know how to escape if I tried. There are too many turns, too many identical doors and dingy mirror-like hallways. If they decide the way to respond to this is to kill me, I'll die here, leagues under the sand, far from home.

Uljen was right. I never should have come here.

Finally, Lira stands. Her fists shake at her sides as she glowers at me. "We're going to keep you until Rani gets here and decides what to do with you."

"So that's it?" I say flatly. "You'll just let them kill me if they decide that's what they want to do."

Lira wipes her nose with the back of her hand. "You killed one of ours, Kora."

"He had a knife," I hiss. "He was going to kill *me*. Was I supposed to let him?"

"He wasn't going to kill you," Lira says softly. "Just incapacitate you."

I shake my head, but there's little use in arguing. Lira's already made it clear she's not a friend of mine.

The man holding me tugs me back. I let him turn me around and lead me to the door, past the glares and stares and dirty looks from redbloods all around me. Never mind that they lured me down here. Never mind that they wanted me here so they could use me as leverage, just as Eros wanted me here so he could use me as backup. And I'm not angry at Eros, I'm not–it was *my* idea to begin with–but I can't help but wonder what these redbloods expected when they decided to bring me here. Did they think I'd be demure? Go quietly? Cry when I realized I'd been betrayed? Did they really not expect I would fight for my life?

"Wait." A woman steps forward, touching her ear. Listening to a comm, I would guess. "It's Commander Jakande. She . . ." She frowns and says something in English, then purses her lips, shakes her head, and looks around and asks something I don't understand. Others are shaking their heads, many touching their ear. I suppose many of them are wearing comms and heard what she just did.

Then the man behind me releases my arm as the woman looks at me, disdain barely concealed in her face. "Commander Jakande says you're free to go. We'll show you out."

58

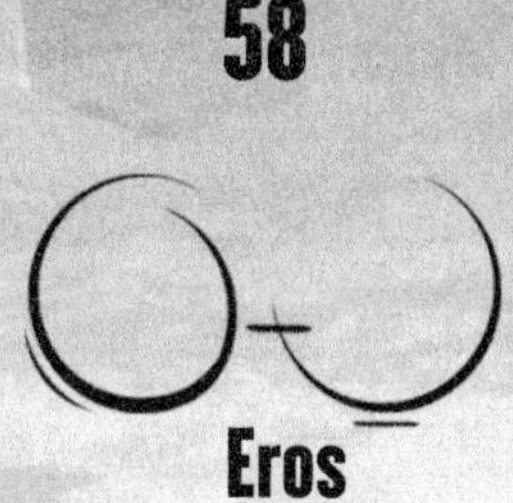

Eros

Everything hurts. Breathing hurts. Shifting in bed and shoving the blanket–it's too fucken hot for that shit–off me hurts.

"Oh, thank *Kala*." Deimos sighs, squeezing my hand lightly. "How do you feel?"

I peer through bleary eyes and wait for the room to focus. The room is–not really a room, more like a curtained-off closet. Footsteps and murmurs of voices beyond the curtain filter through the air. The hot air. Stifling air. Deimos is at my bedside and–

I squint. "Rani?"

Deimos glances back to where Rani is standing, her arms crossed over her chest. "Glad you're not dead," she says flatly.

"*Shae*, well." Deimos grimaces and looks at me. "Staying here to see you through is the least she could do after you saved her life for reasons I can't fathom."

And he's right. I did. I saved her. After she called me a mutt, after she beat me, after she kidnapped my nephew, and made my sets as *Sira* an endless nightmare, and kept Mal and I captive all those sets ago, and the beginning–at the very start–abandoned me for personal gain. For power.

I couldn't save Day, or Nol, or Esta, or Aren. I couldn't save the people I cared about most. But I saved Rani.

Stars, I'm so tired. I close my eyes and mutter, "No more killing."

Deimos kisses my knuckles, calls for Lejdo and asks him to let the feed know I'm stable. I let the room drift away for a bit, holding Deimos's hand as I give in to exhaustion.

When I wake again, sometime later, Rani and Deimos are still there, and everything doesn't hurt as bad. I guess they gave me something while I was sleeping. At least I can breathe without wincing.

Deimos helps me sit up and I drink a full bottle of water without pause. Then I look at Rani.

I'm not going to have a relationship with her–I'd accepted that, and honestly, after everything, I don't want one. I'll be happiest never having to deal with her again.

But it doesn't matter that we don't get along and will never have a relationship. She didn't deserve to die. And whether I like it or not, she's the best chance of peace we have.

"I'm tired of fighting," I say.

Rani bites her lip. "So am I."

"I'm sorry about Shaw, but I want to keep most of our deal. We have a real chance to work together and I'm happy to introduce a human representative."

"I don't want that job," Rani says, thank the fucken suns.

"What if . . ." Deimos hesitates. "Let me finish before you react. What if instead of you choosing a representative, Rani, *all* the humans choose representatives to serve on a human Council that will work in Asheron with Eros. Maybe a larger scale version of what Kora did in Elja to choose Uljen. Humans from every territory could pick someone in a . . . vote. Then those eight would form the human Council. Chosen directly by the people, *shae*?"

"I like that idea." I glance at Rani, and she nods.

"It's . . . a good idea."

"Well of course it is." Deimos grins. "I thought of it."

I shove him lightly and he laughs.

"Where am I, by the way?" I ask. "This doesn't look like the palace infirmary."

"It isn't. We're in Jel-Ta. You needed immediate medical attention–internal bleeding and burns and not to mention the broken ribs . . . but they've taken good care of you here."

I nod. "That's fine. Are there any guides around? I need to make a broadcast."

Deimos arches an eyebrow. "Now? From your hospital bed."

"Now. I don't want the set to pass without getting this over with."

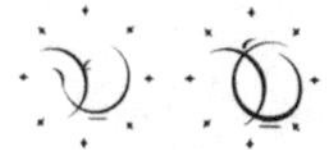

In the end, it's Fejn who finds an orb guide for me to use. It's an overexcitable guide that zips around my head at least four times and bounces in the air, chirping while Deimos helps me look–not like I just took a phaser burst to the chest earlier this morning.

Finally, I'm as prepped as I'm going to be, the guide hovers still in front of me, and it broadcasts me to every glass on the planet. Which isn't at all terrifying to think about.

I take a deep breath, and thank the stars for drugs because it doesn't hurt. "People of Safara, it's been . . . a hard term for all of us. Between famine, disease, attacks, and uncertainty,

I know the adjustment period to having a *Sira* like me hasn't been easy. But enough is enough.

"I can't stop territories from seceding and I'm not going to try to force anyone to stay. I'm also not going to stop humans from leaving on the ship we're preparing for those who want to leave, those who want to try their chances on Earth, galaxies away. But if I'm being honest, I don't think splitting us up is going to make us stronger as a people, and I don't think our differences are so impossible to overcome that our society needs to fracture to move forward. I truly believe we can work together and become a united front: Sepharon, humans, and people a mix of the two, like me."

Deep breath in. Deep breath out.

"I'm going to work with humans to get them equal treatment, and I've agreed to work with eight human representatives, one from each territory, to do that–humans around the globe will choose their territory's representative through a vote. If some Sepharon don't like that idea . . ." I shake my head. "Honestly? Too bad. Safara is just as much home to the humans, home to people like me, as it is to the Sepharon. We've all lived here for generations, we don't know any other home, and we're generations late to getting over that reality and moving on. The only way to move forward peacefully is to accept Safara is home for everyone, and to make it a place where we're all welcome, regardless of the color of our blood or the markings on our skin.

"This is the way forward I'm taking. Now it's up to you to decide whether or not you're with me."

I nod at the guide and it turns off the feed and zips away. And just like that, I've done it. I've laid out a plan without a Council, without people telling me what's best, without ignoring what I've known all along.

I just hope the way forward doesn't end up being the way to the end of my rule and my life.

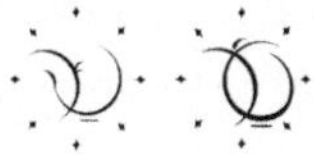

We get back to the palace in Asheron by suns fall after the Jel-Ta medic lectures me about taking it easy and drinking lots of fluid and insisting to Deimos that he make sure I sleep because somehow the medic knew I couldn't be trusted with that, which Deimos found hilarious.

Inside, out of the heat of the desert night, Tol is waiting for us with a huge grin.

"You look happy," I say, as if that weren't obvious.

"I am." Tol's grin widens. "Notice anything different, *el Sira*?"

"Uh . . ." I glance at Deimos, shivering slightly at the cool air making my skin bumpy. Wait. Cool air?

"Oh!" Deimos says, "The air! Sorry–I know I'm not *ken Sira*, thank *Kala* . . ."

"Does that mean . . ." I'm almost too nervous to say it. To hope it. "The nanites?" I ask.

"The first batch has been released as a successful cure for the disease in the city, and the second batch is being tested right now in the complex." Tol extends their arms, gesturing around them. "That's gone largely well, so once the team addresses a few glitches they'll begin releasing those to the larger populace. Granted, it'll take several terms before we reach full coverage again, and there will be issues along the way, but it's better than their original estimation of a few cycles, *sha*?"

The relief is like jumping into a cool bath on a hot day. Or maybe that's just the air coolant. Either way. "That's amazing news," I say. "Thank you. Do you know where Mal is?"

Tol's smile fades slightly and my stomach lurches. If something is wrong with Mal– "I believe he's waiting for you both in your room. He . . . wanted to discuss something with you, if I'm not mistaken."

"Thank you," I say quickly.

Mal is sprawled out on my bed, and for a mo I think he's asleep but then he sits up abruptly, hair sticking out at all angles as he groans and says, "*Finally.* That took fucken *forever*."

I smile and sit next to him. "Sorry. There were some . . . complications we weren't expecting."

"*Shae*, whatever." Mal waves his hand, then fiddles with his darkening glasses. "It gave me time to practice this conversation and I want you guys to listen before you say *naï*."

Deimos sits on Mal's other side. "So sure we're going to say *naï*."

"Well, I'm sure Uncle Eros is going to want to say *naï*, but I'm hoping you'll convince him."

I grimace. "This sounds promising already."

"Like I said, listen first." Mal hops off the bed and faces us, arms pulled behind his back, stick leaning against the bed. He takes a deep breath, then says, "Okay. So I've been thinking about this a lot. And I-I know it's a lot, but I'm sure it's what I want to do."

I glance at Deimos. He shrugs. "Um," I say. "What is it . . . exactly, that you want to do?"

Mal presses his lips together, then pulls his shoulders back. "I . . . want to go on the ship with the humans to Earth."

It takes a mo–two–for those words to sink in. And Mal was right about what my reaction would be, because there's no fucken way I'm going to let my thirteen-year-old nephew *leave the fucken planet*. "*Naï*," I say.

"Let him finish." Deimos puts his hand on my knee and looks at Mal. "Go ahead. Explain why you want this."

Mal nods. "It's just . . . I've lost everything here. I don't have my home anymore, I don't have my family–besides you, Uncle Eros, and you're great but–but staying here reminds me of . . . everything. And I think it's really good what you're doing and trying to get everyone to have equal rights and everything, but the Sepharon aren't going to just . . . stop hating us." He shrugs. "Being here at the palace has been nice and people are okay to me and everything, but I don't like being the only human here. And I know that might change and that's good, but I'll still always be an outsider here, and it's still always going to be dangerous for humans to just . . . live."

I hate that he's right. I hate that I can't fix this and make everyone be more decent overnight. I hate that I can't protect him from the hate, and the anger, and I hate that I know exactly what he means about never really being fully accepted, not really, not here.

But he's so young. And this isn't a reversible decision. He can't just decide to come back if he doesn't like it on Earth. And he'll be alone.

"You realize things won't be perfect on Earth either, right?" I say. "You'll probably be discriminated against there too–for being Safara-born. You can't get away from assholes by switching planets–they're everywhere."

"I know," Mal says. "And I'm not expecting it to be perfect, but . . . that's where we came from, you know?"

"And who's going to take care of you? You're thirteen, Mal, you need some kinduv adult–"

"You really think I'm going to be the only underage orphan on that ship?" Mal sighs heavily, like he can't believe he actually has to explain this. "The travel time will be four cycles anyway, so by the time I get there, I'll be almost eighteen and old enough to take care of myself. And I'll be treated like a refugee–they're setting up centers to help us get started. So I'll be fine. I mean, I practically take care of myself here anyway–the only difference is I won't have a bodyguard following me around."

My heart thuds heavily in my chest. Maybe this is my fault. I haven't been able to pay as much attention to him as I wanted but with everything going to shit–what was I supposed to do?

Shit. Did I do this?

"I know you don't want to agree," Mal says. "And I get it but . . . I'm not going to have another chance like this. I want to go. And if you don't let me, I seriously won't forgive you. I won't be happy here, and I'll always remember you refused me my only chance to go back to my roots and start fresh somewhere else."

"Great," I mumble. "No pressure."

"I think we should let him go," Deimos says softly. "He seems to be confident about this decision."

"I am," Mal says. "I've been thinking about it for a long time. Pretty much since I suggested the ship, really."

"I just–I thought you liked the techies and the tech stuff. They even said they'd be happy to apprentice you once you're of age and welcome you to the team–"

"I do. They're nice, and if I was going to stay, I probably would. And, I dunno, maybe I'll still go into tech, but I don't want to do it here. I have too many bad memories here. Safara has never been a home to me."

I'm not sure if it will hurt him more, in the long run, to let him go or make him stay. But the truth is, I was never supposed to be his dad. I was never equipped to take care of him while also trying to hold the planet together. And even if things finally calm down, Mal's right—nothing is going to change overnight. And I can't blame him for not wanting to stick around for the ugly in-between phase.

"Please," Mal says. "Please let me go."

And it hurts to say it. It hurts to agree. It hurts to know he's going to leave and I'm never going to see him again in person. I'll be able to talk to him via glass, sure, but it's not the same. And it hurts to acknowledge I'll have lost literally every one of my family members in just under three full terms.

"You know," Deimos says quietly. "The fortune speaker did warn you about this."

I glance at him—I'd totally forgotten about her, but he's right. *You must let them go when the time comes*, she'd said. *No matter how much you love them, you can't tie them down.*

Holding on to him because I don't want it to be final, to be real, would be selfish.

So if I'm going to be fair to Mal, if I'm going to let him decide his own destiny and not force him into a system that will make him bitter and angry—then I don't really have a choice.

I have to let him go.

59

Kora

When I returned to the palace complex alone, and alive, and mostly uninjured two terms ago, after nearly dying underground and killing a man in my own defense, after nearly ruining Eros's plan for peace with an ill-advised plan of my own, Uljen pulled me into his arms and held me tightly. He closed his eyes and we breathed together, in silence, as I shivered against him and gripped him tightly.

"You were right," I said after some silence. "I never should have gone. It was a terrible idea."

Uljen had grimaced. "I don't care about right or wrong, I'm just so *kafran* relieved you're okay."

I pulled away from him and offered a small smile. "Next time I have a terrible idea like that, talk me out of it."

He laughed. "I'll do my best."

Now I sit in my garden, watching the suns rise as the feed reports on the ship preparing to take off in Asheron as Uljen sleeps in my bedroom behind me. Our first venture off the planet in generations, with an automated system, Sepharon technical and medical crew who will make the trip there and back, and redbloods ready to say good-bye forever.

Eros allowed Mal to use his glass to call me and say farewell. And though I hadn't seen him in person since the wedding, and our friendship was brief, I'll certainly still miss him.

I don't know what this world will look like in a cycle, in five, in ten. Inara vowed not to secede after all shortly after Invino did, and Sekka'l . . . well. If any territory was going to have to leave, I can't say I'll be all that sorry to see them go. I just hope if they decide to leave, it won't catalyze a fracturing we won't be able to do undo.

But for now, at least, things have finally cooled. I can focus on building Elja's economy and infrastructure, as well as strengthening programs for the impoverished to try to narrow the gap between classes. I have forms to fill out and meetings to attend and advisors to listen to and all the menial work of ruling, but for the first time in too long, I'm not afraid. Not for myself, not for Eros—I can breathe, truly freely, for possibly the first time in my life.

Naï, I don't know what the cycles will bring us.

But for the first time in too long, I truly believe the world will only better from here.

60

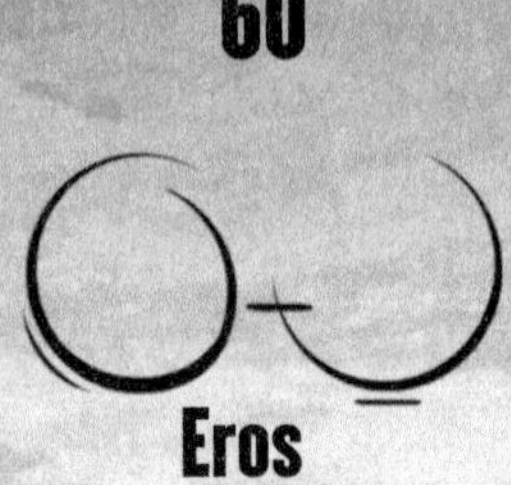

Eros

Mal hugs me so tightly I think my ribs might break, but it's not tight enough. I don't want to let him go. I don't want to let him go. But it doesn't matter. It's his life, and I have to let him have this. I can't get in his way. I won't.

"The ship staff will take good care of you," Deimos says. "They're good people, and I think you know many of them from the tech team, *shae*?"

Mal slowly lets me go, takes a deep breath, and nods. "*Shae*, I do. It'll be okay. They know what they're doing."

"We should be able to talk any time," I say. "You remember how to use the glass to call me right?"

Mal rolls his eyes. "*Shae*, Uncle Eros, you only showed me like, ten times."

Deimos snickers and puts his arm over my shoulder. "He'll be all right, Eros."

He will. I trust that. I believe that. But that doesn't make it any easier to ignore my aching throat or the spot in my chest that hurts every time I remember this good-bye is forever. But maybe it's not the kinduv permanent good-bye I've had to say before—Mal isn't dying; he's going to live a better life somewhere else. Somewhere where he can be happy and hopefully more accepted than he is here. He's going to grow up and live a long life, and yeah, that long life will be somewhere I can't follow, somewhere I can't see him, but maybe just knowing he's happy will be enough.

I hope.

"Okay. I'm going now," Mal says.

Deimos nods. "We should be headed outside to oversee the launch anyway." He ruffles Mal's hair. "Don't forget about us, okay?"

Mal smiles softly. "I won't."

He steps forward and gives me one more hug, and I don't care if he thinks it's embarrassing—I kiss his head and hold him tight. "I just . . . want you to know, I'll be with you wherever the stars reach."

Mal takes a shaky breath and nods. "I know."

And then I let him go. And as Mal joins the other humans lining up to get registered and assigned and allowed entry, Deimos tugs my side and pulls me away. So I walk. One step after another, forcing myself not to look back, not to check to see if he's okay, not to baby him.

"He'll be okay," Deimos says again.

I close my eyes. Breathe deep. Grip Aren's bracelet. Force myself to believe it.

Mal will be okay.

And so will I.

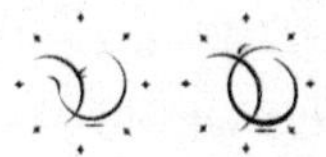

Deimos holds my hand as we stand at the front of the crowd, at the barricades in front of the launch pad. The shuttle to the ship is sleek, and silver, and glass, repainted with refreshed English lettering and upgraded to make it faster, stronger, safer than it was when it arrived here ages ago.

The suns rise in the horizon behind the shuttle, painting the lightening sky gold. The engines roar like a thousand ports starting up at once, like a thunderstorm, like the rush of my heart every time Deimos's eyes crinkle at the corners when he smiles. He twines his fingers with mine as the hot air blown out from the shuttle's launch hits our faces, kicking up sand and the cheer of the crowd.

In the end, with the nanites working again, Kosim was the first to try the cure—and started getting better in a matter of segments. After testing on a few other patients, the distribution started quickly. All the while humans gathered in Asheron to leave. When all was said and done, just over 10,000 humans decided to leave along with twenty or so half-bloods. And to be honest, I don't know if I'm going to regret making this happen, I don't know if this is going to turn out to be a terrible idea, I don't know if that ship is going to make it to Earth, and I don't know how well they'll be treated there if—when—they do arrive.

But this wasn't something the Council wanted, or the Sepharon wanted, or even my father wanted. This is something, with Mal's prompting, I did on my own. This is something I did: giving humans a chance to rebuild and start new worlds away from our own.

The shuttle lifts into the air, reflecting the golden sky so perfectly it looks like the whole shuttle is molten gold. And as the rising gold climbs higher and higher above us, Deimos squeezes my hand.

"I want you to know I'm with you," he says. "No matter what happens. Good or bad, I'm yours."

My heart skips a beat as I glance at him with a smile. "You know, that almost sounded like a proposal."

"That's fortunate," Deimos says. "Because ill-timed as it may or may not be, I'm relatively certain it was."

"Relatively certain?"

"You could just say, *sha, of course I'll marry you, handsome love of my life. Prince with a body like no other. Boy so clever and wonderful I just can't keep my–*"

"You're so good at saying *sha* for me I'm not sure you even need me." Deimos laughs and I smile and nudge him with my shoulder. "You know I'm yours. And if you want to be *officially* mine, you won't get any complaints from me."

"Excellent. Our wedding party will be *excellent*."

I groan. "Please don't make me regret agreeing to this."

"Never." Deimos smiles and nods at the gold-tinted shuttle high above us, sliding into the clouds. And so we watch together, hand-in-hand, as one cycle of our lives closes and a new one begins.

One where we're together, whatever that means, and even the stars aren't out of reach.

And it's good.

It's good.

THE END

Minor Recurring Characters List

IN ELJA:

Uljen (OOL-yen): Kora's advisor

Dima (DEE-ma): Kora's twin brother

Jarek (YA-rek): formerly Dima's second-in-command; currently Dima's boyfriend

Lira (LEE-ruh): Kora's new personal assistant

Roek (RO-ek): the oldest of Elja's Council members

Torven (TOR-ven): Eljan Council member; once her father's closest friend but has always been kind to Kora.

Izra (EEZ-rah): Eljan Council member

Barra (BAHR-ra): Eljan Council member

IN ASHERON:

Mija (MEE-yah): Eros's stylist

Arodin (AH-roh-deen): High Priest

Rion (REE-ohn): Asheron Council member

Kenna (KEN-nah): Asheron Council member

Tol: Asheron Council member and Scientific Advisor

Menos (MEH-nos): oldest of Asheron's Council members

Roma (RO-mah): former *Sira* and Eros's uncle; currently (and permanently) comatose

Kosim (KO-seem): Eros's personal bodyguard

Fejn (FEYN): Deimos's personal bodyguard

Varo (VA-roh): Mal's personal bodyguard

Lijdo (LEE-doh): also Eros's personal bodyguard

Zarana (za-RAH-nah): the head palace medic

Glossary/Pronunciation Guide

Note: /r/ is rolled (similar to a Spanish /r/) and /j/ is closer to an English /y/.

Sepharon (SEH-fah-rohn, as pronounced by Sepharon; SEH-fur-on, as pronounced by nomads): the native species of Safara.

Safara (SAH-fah-rah): the planet the Sepharon and nomads live on; in a separate solar system from Earth.

Sephari (SEH-fah-ree, as pronounced by Sepharon; SEH-fur-ee, as pronounced by nomads): the language all Sepharon speak.

el/ol Avra (el/ohl AH-vrah): my/your majesty; Avrae are rulers of the eight territories.

el/ol Sira (el/ohl SEE-rah): my/your high majesty; the Sira is the high ruler who all Avrae must submit to.

Avrae/Sirae (AH-vray/SEE-ray): plural forms of Avra and Sira

ko (koh): a ruler's spouse; ranks directly under the ruler.

kaï (KAH-ee): prince

saï (SAH-ee): princess

kjo/sjo (kyoh/syoh): plural forms of kaï and saï

Kala (kah-lah): God

ve (veh): sir

ken (kehn): the, as part of a title

sha (shah): yes

naï (NAH-ee): no

kazim (KAH-zeem): wildcat

[City] ora'jeve: (oh-RAH-yeh-veh): [City] greets you (all)–the equivalent to "Welcome to [city]."

or'jiva (ohr-YEE-vah): greetings (to one person)

ljuma (LYOO-mah): a tangy fruit.

azuka (AH-zoo-kah): a powerful drink, somewhat equivalent to alcohol.

zeïli (zeh-EE-lee): a leaf that's dried and smoked for a relaxing and mood-boosting effect.

lijara/lijarae (lee-YAH-rah/lee-YAH-ray): umbrella term equivalent to queer people (lijarae is the plural form)

ulae (OO-lay): a traditional uniform worn by Ona's military men since before the Great War.

kata (kah-tah): a flat food wrap, similar to a tortilla

ko (koh): used to refer to spouses of Avrae and Sirae (often as Avra-ko or Sira-ko)

balaika (bah-LIE-kah): a modern—and very popular—A'Sharan style dance

mana eran (mah-nah EH-ran): my brother

shae (SHAY): A'Sharan variation of "sha"; equivalent to "yeah"

ora'denja (OH-rah den-YAH): good morning (to you)

denna (dennah): literally "a morning"; response to ora'denja

kafra (KAH-fra): a swear word, similar in intensity to "fuck"

Kala alehja (KAH-lah ah-LAY-ha): God above; phrase used to express exasperation

kelo (keh-low): a cold, sweet dessert

sko/skoi (sko/skoy): a swear word used to describe someone who is a jerk (skoi is plural)

ej (ey): kind of like "hey"

ljnte (LEEN-teh): hot, white, sweet and spicy energy drink

Jorva (YOR-vah): Sepharon holy book

ufrike (oo-FREE-keh): an intoxicating drink

ora'jeve (oh-RAH-yeh-veh): welcome, to many people

or'jiva (ohr-YEE-vah): welcome/greetings (to one person)

sennak (sen-NAHK): a light blue rock webbed with white and silver; popular in Daïvi

General terms:

breath: (in terms of time) second

(sun)sets: equivalent to a day.

term: month (50 sets)

cycle: year (8 terms)

mo: moment: minute

Nomad slang:

brainblaze: migraine

blazing: somewhat equivalent British English "bloody."

blazed: angry/ticked off

throwing sand: freaking out

Acknowledgments

When I first began writing with the intention to publish something like thirteen years ago, my goal was to publish a trilogy. And here, at long last, I'm so proud and thrilled to say I've done just that—but I didn't do so alone.

Endless thanks to the team that helped me bring this book into being, including:

My Creator. Working at this dream and watching it unfold has been an absolute delight. I can't wait to see where my words take me next.

My fantastic agent and professional cheerleader, Louise Fury, thank you so much for being in my corner and believing in my stories and in me. These words never would have made it onto actual pages in actual books without your enthusiasm and confidence.

The Skyhorse team who translated this story from a document to pages to an actual book. My incredible editor, Nicole Frail, thank you for pushing me to make this last leg of Eros and Kora's journey the best part yet. Kate Gartner, thank you for gifting me with yet another jaw-dropping cover, and Joshua Barnaby, so many thanks for making each of these books as beautiful inside as they are on the out.

My genius CPs, Laura and Caitlin, thank you once again for your incredible suggestions and ever-increasing support. And to Mark and Charlotte, thank you so much for your insight, guidance, and encouragement.

A big group hug to my lovely Simmons peers and professors: the Core Four, Writing I and II classes, and more—getting to know you all has been a highlight of my new life here, and I can't thank you enough for your absolutely fantastic support.

And last, but not least, my lovely Twitter friends and Community of Awesome, to you, reading this book right now–thank you for joining me on this truly epic adventure of making my dreams come true one at a time.